This is a test. Take notes. This will count as ¾ of your final grade. Hints: remember, in chess, kings cancel each other out and cannot occupy adjacent squares, are therefore all-powerful and totally powerless, cannot affect one another, produce stalemate. Hinduism is a polytheistic religion; the sect of Atman worships the divine spark of life within Man; in effect saying, "Thou art God." Provisos of equal time are not served by one viewpoint having media access to two hundred million people in prime time while opposing viewpoints are provided with a soapbox on the corner. Not everyone tells the truth. Operational note: these sections may be taken out of numerical sequence: rearrange to suit yourself for optimum clarity. Turn over your test papers and begin.

—From "The Deathbird"

# COLLIER NUCLEUS FANTASY
# & SCIENCE FICTION

Consulting Editor, James Frenkel

## Books by Harlan Ellison

Web of the City (1958)
The Deadly Streets (1958)
The Sound of a Scythe (1960)
A Touch of Infinity (1960)
Children of the Streets (1961)
Gentleman Junkie and other stories of the hung-up
    generation (1961)
Memos from Purgatory (1961)
Spider Kiss (1961)
Ellison Wonderland (1962)
Paingod and other delusions (1965)
I Have No Mouth & I Must Scream (1967)
Doomsman (1967)
Dangerous Visions (Editor) (1967)
From the Land of Fear (1967)
Nightshade & Damnations: the finest stories of
    Gerald Kersh [Editor] (1968)
Love Ain't Nothing But Sex Misspelled (1968)
The Beast That Shouted Love at the Heart of the World
    (1969)
The Glass Teat essays of opinion on television (1970)
Over the Edge (1970)
Partners in Wonder sf collaborations with 14 other wild
    talents (1971)
Alone Against Tomorrow (1971)
Again, Dangerous Visions [Editor] (1972)
All the Sounds of Fear [British publication only] (1973)
The Time of the Eye [British publication only] (1974)
Approaching Oblivion (1974)
The Starlost #1: Phoenix Without Ashes
    [with Edward Bryant] (1975)
Deathbird Stories (1975)
The Other Glass Teat further essays of opinion on
    television (1975)
No Doors, No Windows (1975)
Strange Wine (1978)
The Book of Ellison [Edited by Andrew Porter] (1978)
The Illustrated Harlan Ellison [Edited by Byron Preiss]
    (1978)

The Fantasies of Harlan Ellison (1979)
All the Lies That Are My Life (1980)
Shatterday (1980)
Stalking the Nightmare (1982)
Sleepless Nights in the Proscrustean Bed: Essays [Edited by Marty Clark] (1984)
Medea: Harlan's World [Editor] (1985)
An Edge in My Voice (1985)
Demon with a Glass Hand [Graphic Adaptation with Marshall Rogers] (1986)
The Essential Ellison [Edited by Terry Dowling with Richard Delap & Gil Lamont] (1987)
Night and the Enemy [Graphic Adaptation with Ken Steacy] (1987)
Angry Candy (1988)
Harlan Ellison's Watching (1989)
The Harlan Ellison Hornbook (1990)

# Deathbird
# Stories

---

Harlan
Ellison

**Collier Books**
**Macmillan Publishing Company**
**New York**

Copyright © 1975, 1976, 1980 by Harlan Ellison
Copyright © 1983 by The Kilimanjaro Corporation

Previously published by Bluejay Books

Collier Books
Macmillan Publishing Company
866 Third Avenue, New York, NY 10022
Collier Macmillan Canada, Inc.

Library of Congress Cataloging-in-Publication Data
Ellison, Harlan.
      Deathbird stories/Harlan Ellison.—1st Collier books ed.
         p.   cm.
      ISBN 0-02-028361-X
      1. Fantastic fiction, American.    2. Science fiction,
American.
   I. Title.
   PS3555.L62D4   1990
   813'.54—dc20            89-28239         CIP

First Collier Books Edition

10   9   8   7   6   5   4   3   2

Printed in the United States of America

*At last, through the labyrinth.*
*And not a moment too soon.*
*This book, finally, for*
**The Electric Baby**

# Contents

**TO COUNT LEO TOLSTOY**
14 February 1910

*"To me God does not yet exist; but there is a creative force constantly struggling to evolve an executive organ of godlike knowledge and power: that is, to achieve omnipotence and omniscience; and every man and woman born is a fresh attempt to achieve this object. . . .*

*"The current theory that God already exists in perfection involves the belief that God deliberately created something lower than Himself when He might just as easily have created something equally perfect. That is a horrible belief. . . .*

*"You said that my manner in [Man and Superman] was not serious enough—that I made people laugh in my most earnest moments. But why should I not? Why should humor and laughter be excommunicated? Suppose the world were only one of God's jokes, would you work any the less to make it a good joke instead of a bad one?"*

—GEORGE BERNARD SHAW

"If God did not exist, it would be necessary to invent him."

—VOLTAIRE: *Epître à M. Saurin, 10 Novembre 1770*

"It is expedient there should be gods, and, since it is expedient, let us believe that gods exist."

—OVID: *Ars Amatoria I*

"Men rarely (if ever) manage to dream up a god superior to themselves. Most gods have the manners and morals of a spoiled child."

—ROBERT A. HEINLEIN, 1973

**CAVEAT LECTOR**

It is suggested that the reader not attempt to read this book at one sitting. The emotional content of these stories, taken without break, may be extremely upsetting. This note is intended *most* sincerely, and not as hyperbole.

H.E.

# Introduction:
# Oblations at Alien Altars

Gods can do anything. They fear nothing: they are gods. But there is one rule, one Seal of Solomon that can confound a god, and to which *all* gods pay service, to the letter:

When belief in a god dies, the god dies.

When the last acolyte renounces his faith and turns to another deity, the god ceases to be.

They know the terrible simplicity of that truth, the mightiest and the mingiest of gods. They have seen their fellow gods go down to obscurity and banishment for lack of believers. They saw Achelöus wither when the *cornucopia* was ripped from his head by Heracles; they saw the twelve Aesir and their Asgardian heaven-home turned to mist when the Vikings took up the cross; they saw Ahriman dwindle and die when the ancient Persian empire was overrun; they saw Alaghom Naom, the "Mother of Mind," lost to men when the Conquistadores brutalized the Mayan religion; they saw Ama-Terasu, the Japanese sun goddess, go up in a nova of light brighter than the sun from which she took her name, on a special day in Hiroshima; and Amen-Ra, and Anaïtis, and Anath, and Anshar (and Kishar), and Anu, and Anubis, and Apollo . . . all of them shimmered and became insubstantial as their temples were reduced to rubble.

Volume after volume of sacred books of gods.

And that's only into the "A's."

As the time passes for men and women, so does it pass for gods, for they are made viable and substantial only through the massed beliefs of masses of men and women. And when puny mortals no longer worship at their altars, the gods die.

To be replaced by newer, more relevant gods.

Perhaps one day soon the time will pass for Jehovah and Buddha and Zoroaster and Brahma. Then the Earth will know other gods. Already we begin to worship these other, newer gods. Already the Church fights to hold its own. The young grow away from the old religions, the world seems to swing between the old and the new; more and more each day interest in the occult, in the magical, in the phantasmagorical surges to the fore—leaving priests and rabbis and ministers concerned where their next god will come from.

This group of stories deals with the new gods, with the new devils, with the modern incarnations of the little people and the wood sprites and the demons. The grimoires and *Necronomicons* of the gods of the freeway, of the ghetto blacks, of the coaxial cable; the paingod and the rock god and the god of neon; the god of legal tender, the god of business-as-usual and the gods that live in city streets and slot machines. The God of Smog and the God of Freudian Guilt. The Machine God.

They are a strange, unpredictable lot, these new, vital, muscular gods. How we will come to worship them, what boons they may bestow, their moods and their limitations—these are the subjects of these stories.

A New Testament of deities for the computerized age of confrontation and relevance. A grimoire and a guide. A pantheon of the holiest of holies for modern man.

Know them now . . . they rule the nights through which we move.

Kitty Genovese met one of them, as did the students of Kent State University. Black men have known them far longer than white men, but have been ill served by them.

So know them now, in these stories. Offerings can be made at their altars in new-car showrooms and gambling casinos and in crash-pads and penthouses.

Worship in the temple of your soul, but know the names of those who control your destiny. For, as the God of Time so aptly put it, "It's later than you think."

HARLAN ELLISON
1 November 1973

# Deathbird
# Stories

*When the new god comes to the Big
Apple, its Kyrie Eleison turns out to be
a prayer Kitty Genovese simply couldn't
sing. But thirty-eight others knew the tune.*

# The Whimper of Whipped Dogs

On the night after the day she had stained the louvered window shutters of her new apartment on East 52nd Street, Beth saw a woman slowly and hideously knifed to death in the courtyard of her building. She was one of twenty-six witnesses to the ghoulish scene, and, like them, she did nothing to stop it.

She saw it all, every moment of it, without break and with no impediment to her view. Quite madly, the thought crossed her mind as she watched in horrified fascination, that she had the sort of marvelous line of observation Napoleon had sought when he caused to have constructed at the *Comédie-Française* theaters, a curtained box at the rear, so he could watch the audience as well as the stage. The night was clear, the moon was full, she had just turned off the 11:30 movie on channel 2 after the second commercial break, realizing she had already seen Robert Taylor in *Westward the Women*, and had disliked it the first time; and the apartment was quite dark.

She went to the window, to raise it six inches for the night's sleep, and she saw the woman stumble into the courtyard. She was sliding along the wall, clutching her left arm with her right hand. Con Ed had installed mercury-vapor lamps on the poles; there had been sixteen assaults in seven months; the courtyard was illuminated with a chill purple glow that made the blood streaming down the woman's left arm look black and shiny. Beth saw every detail with utter clarity, as though magnified a thousand power under a microscope, solarized as if it had been a television commercial.

The woman threw back her head, as if she were trying to scream, but there was no sound. Only the traffic on First Avenue, late cabs foraging for singles paired for the night at Maxwell's Plum and Friday's and Adam's Apple. But that was over there, beyond. Where *she* was, down there seven floors below, in the courtyard, everything seemed silently suspended in an invisible force-field.

Beth stood in the darkness of her apartment, and realized she had raised the window completely. A tiny balcony lay just over the low sill; now not even glass separated her from the sight; just the wrought-iron balcony railing and seven floors to the courtyard below.

The woman staggered away from the wall, her head still thrown back, and Beth could see she was in her mid-thirties, with dark hair cut in a shag; it was impossible to tell if she was pretty: terror had contorted her features and her mouth was a twisted black slash, opened but emitting no sound. Cords stood out in her neck. She had lost one shoe, and her steps were uneven, threatening to dump her to the pavement.

The man came around the corner of the building, into the courtyard. The knife he held was enormous—or perhaps it only seemed so: Beth remembered a bone-handled fish knife her father had used one summer at the lake in Maine: it folded back on itself and locked, revealing eight inches of serrated blade. The knife in the hand of the dark man in the courtyard seemed to be similar.

The woman saw him and tried to run, but he leaped across the distance between them and grabbed her by the hair and pulled her head back as though he would slash her throat in the next reaper-motion.

*Then* the woman screamed.

The sound skirled up into the courtyard like bats trapped in an echo chamber, unable to find a way out, driven mad. It went on and on. . . .

The man struggled with her and she drove her elbows into his sides and he tried to protect himself, spinning her around by her hair, the terrible scream going up and up and never stopping. She came loose and he was left with a fistful of hair torn out by the roots. As she spun out, he slashed straight across and opened her up just below the breasts. Blood sprayed through her clothing and the man was soaked; it seemed to drive him even more berserk. He went at her again, as she tried to hold herself together, the blood pouring down over her arms.

She tried to run, teetered against the wall, slid sidewise, and the man struck the brick surface. She was away, stumbling over a flower bed, falling, getting to her knees as he threw himself on her again. The knife came up in a flashing arc that illuminated the blade strangely with purple light. And still she screamed.

Lights came on in dozens of apartments and people appeared at windows.

He drove the knife to the hilt into her back, high on the right shoulder. He used both hands.

Beth caught it all in jagged flashes—the man, the woman, the knife, the blood, the expressions on the faces of those watching from the windows. Then lights clicked off in the windows, but they still stood there, watching.

She wanted to yell, to scream, "What are you doing to that woman?" But her throat was frozen, two iron hands that had been immersed in dry ice for ten thousand years clamped around her neck. She could feel the blade sliding into her own body.

Somehow—it seemed impossible but there it was down there, happening somehow—the woman struggled erect and *pulled* herself off the knife. Three steps, she took three steps and fell into the flower bed again. The man was howling now, like a great beast, the sounds inarticulate, bubbling up from his stomach. He fell on her and the knife went up and came down, then again, and again, and finally it was all a blur of motion, and her scream of lunatic bats went on till it faded off and was gone.

Beth stood in the darkness, trembling and crying, the sight filling her eyes with horror. And when she could no longer bear to look at what he was doing down there to the unmoving piece of meat over which he worked, she looked up and around at the windows of darkness where the others still stood—even as she had stood—and somehow she could see their faces, bruise-purple with the dim light from the mercury lamps, and there was a universal sameness to their expressions. The women stood with their nails biting into the upper arms of their men, their tongues edging from the corners of their mouths; the men were wild-eyed and smiling. They all looked as though they were at cock fights. Breathing deeply. Drawing some sustenance from the grisly scene below. An exhalation of sound, deep, deep, as though from caverns beneath the earth. Flesh pale and moist.

And it was then that she realized the courtyard had grown foggy, as though mist off the East River had rolled up 52nd Street in a veil that would obscure the details of what the knife and the man were still doing . . . endlessly doing it . . . long after there was any joy in it . . . still doing it . . . again and again . . .

But the fog was unnatural, thick and gray and filled with tiny scintillas of light. She stared at it, rising up in the empty space of the courtyard. Bach in the cathedral, stardust in a vacuum chamber.

Beth saw eyes.

There, up there, at the ninth floor and higher, two great eyes, as surely as night and the moon, there were *eyes*. And—a face? Was that a face, could she be sure, was she imagining it . . . a face? In the roiling vapors of chill fog something lived, something brooding and patient and utterly malevolent had been summoned up to witness what was happening down there in the flower bed. Beth tried to look away, but could not. The eyes, those primal burning eyes, filled with an abysmal antiquity yet frighteningly bright and anxious like the eyes of a child; eyes filled with tomb depths, ancient and new, chasm-filled, burning, gigantic and deep as an abyss, holding her, compelling her. The shadowy play was being staged not only for the tenants in their windows, watching and drinking of the scene, but for some *other*. Not on frigid tundra or waste moors, not in subterranean caverns or on some faraway world circling a dying sun, but here, in the city, here the eyes of that *other* watched.

Shaking with the effort, Beth wrenched her eyes from those burning depths up there beyond the ninth floor, only to see again the horror that had brought that *other*. And she was struck for the first time by the awfulness of what she was witnessing, she was released from the immobility that had held her like a coelacanth in shale, she was filled with the blood thunder pounding against the membranes of her mind: she had *stood* there! She had done nothing, nothing! A woman had been butchered and she had said nothing, done nothing. Tears had been useless, tremblings had been pointless, she *had done nothing!*

Then she heard hysterical sounds midway between laughter and giggling, and as she stared up into that great face rising in the fog and chimneysmoke of the night, she heard *herself* making those deranged gibbon noises and from the man below a pathetic, trapped sound, like the whimper of whipped dogs.

She was staring up into that face again. She hadn't wanted to see it again—ever. But she was locked with those smoldering eyes, overcome with the feeling that they were childlike, though she *knew* they were incalculably ancient.

Then the butcher below did an unspeakable thing and Beth reeled with dizziness and caught the edge of the window before she could tumble out onto the balcony; she steadied herself and fought for breath.

She felt herself being looked at, and for a long moment of frozen terror she feared she might have caught the attention of that face up there in the fog. She clung to the window, feeling everything growing faraway and dim, and stared straight across the court. She *was* being watched. Intently. By the young man in the seventh-floor window across from her own apartment. Steadily, he was looking at her. Through the strange fog with its burning eyes feasting on the sight below, he was staring at her.

As she felt herself blacking out, in the moment before unconsciousness, the thought flickered and fled that there was something terribly familiar about his face.

It rained the next day. East 52nd Street was slick and shining with the oil rainbows. The rain washed the dog turds into the gutters and nudged them down and down to the catch-basin openings. People bent against the slanting rain, hidden beneath umbrellas, looking like enormous, scurrying black mushrooms. Beth went out to get the newspapers after the police had come and gone.

The news reports dwelled with loving emphasis on the twenty-six tenants of the building who had watched in cold interest as Leona Ciarelli, 37, of 455 Fort Washington Avenue, Manhattan, had been systematically stabbed to death by Burton H. Wells, 41, an unemployed electrician, who had been subsequently shot to death by two off-duty police officers when he burst into Michael's Pub on 55th Street, covered with blood and brandishing a knife that authorities later identified as the murder weapon.

She had thrown up twice that day. Her stomach seemed incapable of retaining anything solid, and the taste of bile lay along the back of her tongue. She could not blot the scenes of the night before from her mind; she re-ran them again and again, every movement of that reaper arm playing over and over as though on a short loop of memory. The woman's head thrown back for silent screams. The blood. Those eyes in the fog.

She was drawn again and again to the window, to stare down into the courtyard and the street. She tried to superimpose over the bleak Manhattan concrete the view from her window in Swann House at Bennington: the little yard and another white, frame dormitory; the fantastic apple trees; and from the other window the rolling hills and gorgeous Vermont countryside; her memory skittered through the change of seasons. But there was always concrete and the rain-slick streets; the rain on the pavement was black and shiny as blood.

She tried to work, rolling up the tambour closure of the old rolltop desk she had bought on Lexington Avenue and hunching over the graph sheets of choreographer's charts. But Labanotation was merely a Jackson Pollock jumble of arcane hieroglyphics to her today, instead of the careful representation of eurhythmics she had studied four years to perfect. And before that, Farmington.

The phone rang. It was the secretary from the Taylor Dance Company, asking when she would be free. She had to beg off. She looked at her hand, lying on the graph sheets of figures Laban had devised, and she saw her fingers trembling. She had to beg off. Then she called Guzman at the Downtown Ballet Company, to tell him she would be late with the charts.

"My God, lady, I have ten dancers sitting around in a rehearsal hall getting their leotards sweaty! What do you expect me to do?"

She explained what had happened the night before. And as she told him, she realized the newspapers had been justified in holding that tone against the twenty-six witnesses to the death of Leona Ciarelli. Paschal Guzman listened, and when he spoke again, his voice was several octaves lower, and he spoke more slowly. He said he understood and she could take a little longer to prepare the charts. But there was a distance in his voice, and he hung up while she was thanking him.

She dressed in an argyle sweater vest in shades of dark purple, and a pair of fitted khaki gabardine trousers. She had to go out, to walk around. To do what? To think about other things. As she pulled on the Fred Braun chunky heels, she idly wondered if that heavy silver bracelet was still in the window of Georg Jensen's. In the elevator, the young man from the window across the courtyard stared at her. Beth felt her body begin to tremble again. She went deep into the corner of the box when he entered behind her.

Between the fifth and fourth floors, he hit the *off* switch and the elevator jerked to a halt.

Beth stared at him and he smiled innocently.

"Hi. My name's Gleeson, Ray Gleeson, I'm in 714."

She wanted to demand he turn the elevator back on, by what right did he pre*sume* to do such a thing, what did he mean by this, turn it on at once or suffer the consequences. That was what she *wanted* to do. Instead, from the same place she had heard the gibbering laughter the night before, she heard her voice, much smaller and much less possessed than she had trained it to be, saying, "Beth O'Neill, I live in 701."

The thing about it, was that *the elevator was stopped.* And she was frightened. But he leaned against the paneled wall, very well dressed, shoes polished, hair combed and probably blown dry with a hand dryer, and he *talked* to her as if they were across a table at L'Argenteuil. "You just moved in, huh?"

"About two months ago."

"Where did you go to school? Bennington or Sarah Lawrence?"

"Bennington. How did you know?"

He laughed, and it was a nice laugh. "I'm an editor at a religious book publisher; every year we get half a dozen Bennington, Sarah Lawrence, Smith girls. They come hopping in like grasshoppers, ready to revolutionize the publishing industry."

"What's wrong with that? You sound like you don't care for them."

"Oh, I *love* them, they're marvelous. They think they know how to write better than the authors we publish. Had one darlin' little item who was given galleys of three books to proof, and she rewrote all three. I think she's working as a table-swabber in a Horn & Hardart's now."

She didn't reply to that. She would have pegged him as an anti-feminist, ordinarily, if it had been anyone else speaking. But the eyes. There was something terribly familiar about his face. She was enjoying the conversation; she rather liked him.

"What's the nearest big city to Bennington?"

"Albany, New York. About sixty miles."

"How long does it take to drive there?"

"From Bennington? About an hour and a half."

"Must be a nice drive, that Vermont country, really pretty. They went coed, I understand. How's that working out?"

"I don't know, really."

"You don't know?"

"It happened around the time I was graduating."

"What did you major in?"

"I was a dance major, specializing in Labanotation. That's the way you write choreography."

"It's all electives, I gather. You don't have to take anything required, like sciences, for example." He didn't change tone as he said, "That was a terrible thing last night. I saw you watching. I guess a lot of us were watching. It was a really terrible thing."

She nodded dumbly. Fear came back.

"I understand the cops got him. Some nut, they don't even know why he killed her, or why he went charging into that bar. It was really an awful thing. I'd very much like to have dinner with you one night soon, if you're not attached."

"That would be all right."

"Maybe Wednesday. There's an Argentinian place I know. You might like it."

"That would be all right."

"Why don't you turn on the elevator, and we can go," he said, and smiled again. She did it, wondering why she had stopped the elevator in the first place.

On her third date with him, they had their first fight. It was at a party thrown by a director of television commercials. He lived on the ninth floor of their building. He had just done a series of spots for *Sesame Street* (the letters "U" for Underpass, "T" for Tunnel, lower-case "b" for boats, "c" for cars; the numbers 1 to 6 and the numbers 1 to 20; the words *light* and *dark*) and was celebrating his move from the arena of commercial tawdriness (and its attendant $75,000 a year) to the sweet fields of educational programming (and its accompanying descent into low-pay respectability). There was a logic in his joy Beth could not quite understand, and when she talked with him about it, in a far corner of the kitchen, his arguments didn't seem to parse. But he seemed happy, and his girlfriend, a long-legged ex-model from Philadelphia, continued to drift to him and away from him, like some exquisite undersea plant, touching his hair and kissing his neck, murmuring words of pride and barely submerged sexuality. Beth found it bewildering, though the celebrants were all bright and lively.

In the living room, Ray was sitting on the arm of the sofa,

hustling a stewardess named Luanne. Beth could tell he was hustling; he was trying to look casual. When he *wasn't* hustling, he was always intense, about everything. She decided to ignore it, and wandered around the apartment, sipping at a Tanqueray and tonic.

There were framed prints of abstract shapes clipped from a calendar printed in Germany. They were in metal Bonniers frames.

In the dining room a huge door from a demolished building somewhere in the city had been handsomely stripped, teaked and refinished. It was now the dinner table.

A Lightolier fixture attached to the wall over the bed swung out, levered up and down, tipped, and its burnished globe-head revolved a full three hundred and sixty degrees.

She was standing in the bedroom, looking out the window, when she realized *this* had been one of the rooms in which light had gone on, gone off; one of the rooms that had contained a silent watcher at the death of Leona Ciarelli.

When she returned to the living room, she looked around more carefully. With only three or four exceptions—the stewardess, a young married couple from the second floor, a stockbroker from Hemphill, Noyes—*everyone* at the party had been a witness to the slaying.

"I'd like to go," she told him.

"Why, aren't you having a good time?" asked the stewardess, a mocking smile crossing her perfect little face.

"Like all Bennington ladies," Ray said, answering for Beth, "she is enjoying herself most by not enjoying herself at all. It's a trait of the anal retentive. Being here in someone else's apartment, she can't empty ashtrays or rewind the toilet paper roll so it doesn't hang a tongue, and being tightassed, her nature demands we go.

"All right, Beth, let's say our goodbyes and take off. The Phantom Rectum strikes again."

She slapped him and the stewardess's eyes widened. But the smile remained frozen where it had appeared.

He grabbed her wrist before she could do it again. "Garbanzo beans, baby," he said, holding her wrist tighter than necessary.

They went back to her apartment, and after sparring silently with kitchen cabinet doors slammed and the television being tuned too loud, they got to her bed, and he tried to perpetuate the metaphor by fucking her in the ass. He had her on elbows and knees before she realized what he was doing; she struggled to turn over and he rode her bucking and tossing without a sound. And when it was clear to him that she would never permit it, he grabbed her breast from underneath and squeezed so hard she howled in pain. He dumped her on her back, rubbed himself between her legs a dozen times, and came on her stomach.

Beth lay with her eyes closed and an arm thrown across her face. She wanted to cry, but found she could not. Ray lay on her and said nothing. She wanted to rush to the bathroom and shower, but he did not move, till long after his semen had dried on their bodies.

"Who did you date at college?" he asked.

"I didn't date anyone very much." Sullen.

"No heavy makeouts with wealthy lads from Williams and Dartmouth . . . no Amherst intellectuals begging you to save them from creeping faggotry by permitting them to stick their carrots in your sticky little slit?"

"Stop it!"

"Come on, baby, it couldn't all have been knee socks and little round circle-pins. You don't expect me to believe you didn't get a little mouthful of cock from time to time. It's only, what? about fifteen miles to Williamstown? I'm sure the Williams werewolves were down burning the highway to your cunt on weekends; you can level with old Uncle Ray. . . ."

"*Why are you like this?!*" She started to move, to get away from him, and he grabbed her by the shoulder, forced her to lie down again. Then he rose up over her and said, "I'm like this because I'm a New Yorker, baby. Because I live in this fucking city every day. Because I have to play patty-cake with the ministers and other sanctified holy-joe assholes who want their goodness and lightness tracts published by the Blessed Sacrament Publishing and Storm Window Company of 277 Park Avenue, when what I *really* want to do is toss the stupid psalm-suckers out the thirty-seventh-floor window and listen to them quote chapter-and-worse all the way down. Because I've lived in this great big snapping dog of a city all my life and I'm mad as a mudfly, for chrissakes!"

She lay unable to move, breathing shallowly, filled with a sudden pity and affection for him. His face was white and strained, and she knew he was saying things to her that only a bit too much Almadén and exact timing would have let him say.

"What do you expect from me," he said, his voice softer now, but no less intense, "do you expect kindness and gentility and understanding and a hand on *your* hand when the smog burns your eyes? I can't do it, I haven't got it. No one has it in this cesspool of a city. Look around you; what do you think is happening here? They take rats and they put them in boxes and when there are too many of them, some of the little fuckers go out of their minds and start gnawing the rest to death. *It ain't no different here, baby!* It's rat time for everybody in this madhouse. You can't expect to jam as many people into this stone thing as we do, with buses and taxis and dogs shitting themselves scrawny and noise night and day and no money and not enough places to live and no place to go to have a decent think . . . you can't do it without making the time right for some godforsaken other kind of thing to be born! You can't hate everyone around you, and kick every beggar and nigger and *mestizo* shithead, you can't have cabbies stealing from you and taking tips they don't deserve, and then cursing you, you can't walk in the soot till your collar turns black, and your body stinks with the smell of flaking brick and decaying brains, you can't do it without calling up some kind of awful—"

He stopped.

His face bore the expression of a man who has just received brutal word of the death of a loved one. He suddenly lay down, rolled over, and turned off.

She lay beside him, trembling, trying desperately to remember where she had seen his face before.

He didn't call her again, after the night of the party. And when they met in the hall, he pointedly turned away, as though he had given her some obscure chance and she had refused to take it. Beth thought she understood: though Ray Gleeson had not been her first affair, he had been the first to reject her so completely. The first to put her not only out of his bed and his life, but even out of his world. It was as though she were invisible, not even beneath contempt, simply not there.

She busied herself with other things.

She took on three new charting jobs for Guzman and a new group that had formed on Staten Island, of all places. She worked furiously and they gave her new assignments; they even paid her.

She tried to decorate the apartment with a less precise touch.

Huge poster blowups of Merce Cunningham and Martha Graham replaced the Brueghel prints that had reminded her of the view looking down the hill toward Williams. The tiny balcony outside her window, the balcony she had steadfastly refused to stand upon since the night of the slaughter, the night of the fog with eyes, that balcony she swept and set about with little flower boxes in which she planted geraniums, petunias, dwarf zinnias, and other hardy perennials. Then, closing the window, she went to give herself, to involve herself in this city to which she had brought her ordered life.

And the city responded to her overtures:

Seeing off an old friend from Bennington, at Kennedy International, she stopped at the terminal coffee shop to have a sandwich. The counter—like a moat—surrounded a center service island that had huge advertising cubes rising above it on burnished poles. The cubes proclaimed the delights of Fun City. *New York Is a Summer Festival,* they said, and *Joseph Papp Presents Shakespeare in Central Park* and *Visit the Bronx Zoo* and *You'll Adore Our Contentious but Lovable Cabbies.* The food emerged from a window far down the service area and moved slowly on a conveyor belt through the hordes of screaming waitresses who slathered the counter with redolent washcloths. The lunchroom had all the charm and dignity of a steel-rolling mill, and approximately the same noise level. Beth ordered a cheeseburger that cost a dollar and a quarter, and a glass of milk.

When it came, it was cold, the cheese unmelted, and the patty of meat resembling nothing so much as a dirty scouring pad. The bun was cold and untoasted. There was no lettuce under the patty.

Beth managed to catch the waitress's eye. The girl approached with an annoyed look. "Please toast the bun and may I have a piece of lettuce?" Beth said.

"We dun' do that," the waitress said, turned half away as though she would walk in a moment.

"You don't do what?"

"We dun' toass the bun here."

"Yes, but I *want* the bun toasted," Beth said firmly.

"An' you got to pay for extra lettuce."

"If I was asking for *extra* lettuce," Beth said, getting annoyed, "I would pay for it, but since there's *no* lettuce here, I don't think I should be charged extra for the first piece."

"We dun' do that."

The waitress started to walk away. "Hold it," Beth said, raising her voice just enough so the assembly-line eaters on either side stared at her. "You mean to tell me I have to pay a dollar and a quarter and I can't get a piece of lettuce or even get the bun toasted?"

"Ef you dun' like it . . ."

"Take it back."

"You gotta pay for it, you order it."

"I said take it back, I don't want the fucking thing!"

The waitress scratched it off the check. The milk cost 27¢ and tasted going-sour. It was the first time in her life that Beth had said *that* word aloud.

At the cashier's stand, Beth said to the sweating man with the felt-tip pens in his shirt pocket, "Just out of curiosity, are you interested in complaints?"

"No!" he said, snarling, quite literally snarling. He did not look up as he punched out 73¢ and it came rolling down the chute.

The city responded to her overtures:

It was raining again. She was trying to cross Second Avenue, with the light. She stepped off the curb and a car came sliding through the red and splashed her. "Hey!" she yelled.

"Eat shit, sister!" the driver yelled back, turning the corner.

Her boots, her legs and her overcoat were splattered with mud. She stood trembling on the curb.

The city responded to her overtures:

She emerged from the building at One Astor Place with her big briefcase full of Laban charts; she was adjusting her rain scarf about her head. A well-dressed man with an attaché case thrust the handle of his umbrella up between her legs from the rear. She gasped and dropped her case.

The city responded and responded and responded.

Her overtures altered quickly.

The old drunk with the stippled cheeks extended his hand and mumbled words. She cursed him and walked on up Broadway past the beaver film houses.

She crossed against the lights on Park Avenue, making hackies slam their brakes to avoid hitting her; she used *that* word frequently now.

When she found herself having a drink with a man who had

elbowed up beside her in the singles' bar, she felt faint and knew she should go home.

But Vermont was so far away.

Nights later. She had come home from the Lincoln Center ballet, and gone straight to bed. Lying half-asleep in her bedroom, she heard an alien sound. One room away, in the living room, in the dark, there was a sound. She slipped out of bed and went to the door between the rooms. She fumbled silently for the switch on the lamp just inside the living room, and found it, and clicked it on. A black man in a leather car coat was trying to get *out* of the apartment. In that first flash of light filling the room she noticed the television set beside him on the floor as he struggled with the door, she noticed the police lock and bar had been broken in a new and clever manner *New York* magazine had not yet reported in a feature article on apartment ripoffs, she noticed that he had gotten his foot tangled in the telephone cord that she had requested be extra-long so she could carry the instrument into the bathroom, I don't want to miss any business calls when the shower is running; she noticed all things in perspective and one thing with sharpest clarity: the expression on the burglar's face.

There was something familiar in that expression.

He almost had the door open, but now he closed it, and slipped the police lock. He took a step toward her.

Beth went back, into the darkened bedroom.

The city responded to her overtures.

She backed against the wall at the head of the bed. Her hand fumbled in the shadows for the telephone. His shape filled the doorway, light, all light behind him.

In silhouette it should not have been possible to tell, but somehow she knew he was wearing gloves and the only marks he would leave would be deep bruises, very blue, almost black, with the tinge under them of blood that had been stopped in its course.

He came for her, arms hanging casually at his sides. She tried to climb over the bed, and he grabbed her from behind, ripping her nightgown. Then he had a hand around her neck and he pulled her backward. She fell off the bed, landed at his feet and his hold was broken. She scuttled across the floor and for a moment she had the respite to feel terror. She was going to die, and she was frightened.

He trapped her in the corner between the closet and the bureau and kicked her. His foot caught her in the thigh as she folded tighter, smaller, drawing her legs up. She was cold.

Then he reached down with both hands and pulled her erect by her hair. He slammed her head against the wall. Everything slid up in her sight as though running off the edge of the world. He slammed her head against the wall again, and she felt something go soft over her right ear.

When he tried to slam her a third time she reached out blindly for his face and ripped down with her nails. He howled in pain and she hurled herself forward, arms wrapping themselves around his waist. He stumbled backward and in a tangle of thrashing arms and legs they fell out onto the little balcony.

Beth landed on the bottom, feeling the window boxes jammed up against her spine and legs. She fought to get to her feet, and her nails hooked into his shirt under the open jacket, ripping. Then she was on her feet again and they struggled silently.

He whirled her around, bent her backward across the wrought-iron railing. Her face was turned outward.

*They were standing in their windows, watching.*

Through the fog she could see them watching. Through the fog she recognized their expressions. Through the fog she heard them breathing in unison, bellows breathing of expectation and wonder. Through the fog.

And the black man punched her in the throat. She gagged and started to black out and could not draw air into her lungs. Back, back, he bent her farther back and she was looking up, straight up, toward the ninth floor and higher. . . .

*Up there: eyes.*

The words Ray Gleeson had said in a moment filled with what he had become, with the utter hopelessness and finality of the choice the city had forced on him, the words came back. *You can't live in this city and survive unless you have protection . . . you can't live this way, like rats driven mad, without making the time right for some god-forsaken other kind of thing to be born . . . you can't do it without calling up some kind of awful . . .*

God! A new God, an ancient God come again with the eyes and hunger of a child, a deranged blood God of fog and street violence.

A God who needed worshipers and offered the choices of death as a victim or life as an eternal witness to the deaths of *other* chosen victims. A God to fit the times, a God of streets and people.

She tried to shriek, to appeal to Ray, to the director in the bedroom window of his ninth-floor apartment with his long-legged Philadelphia model beside him and his fingers inside her as they worshiped in their holiest of ways, to the others who had been at the party that had been Ray's offer of a chance to join their congregation. She wanted to be saved from having to make that choice.

But the black man had punched her in the throat, and now his hands were on her, one on her chest, the other in her face, the smell of leather filling her where the nausea could not. And she understood Ray had *cared,* had wanted her to take the chance offered; but she had come from a world of little white dormitories and Vermont countryside; it was not a real world. *This* was the real world and up there was the God who ruled this world, and she had rejected him, had said no to one of his priests and servitors. *Save me! Don't make me do it!*

She knew she had to call out, to make appeal, to try and win the approbation of that God. *I can't . . . save me!*

She struggled and made terrible little mewling sounds trying to summon the words to cry out, and suddenly she crossed a line, and screamed up into the echoing courtyard with a voice Leona Ciarelli had never known enough to use.

"Him! Take him! Not me! I'm yours, I love you, I'm yours! Take him, not me, please not me, take him, take him, I'm yours!"

And the black man was suddenly lifted away, wrenched off her, and off the balcony, whirled straight up into the fog-thick air in the courtyard, as Beth sank to her knees on the ruined flower boxes.

She was half-conscious, and could not be sure she saw it just that way, but up he went, end over end, whirling and spinning like a charred leaf.

And the form took firmer shape. Enormous paws with claws and shapes that no animal she had ever seen had ever possessed, and the burglar, black, poor, terrified, whimpering like a whipped dog, was stripped of his flesh. His body was opened with a thin incision, and there was a rush as all the blood poured from him like a sudden cloudburst, and yet he was still alive, twitching with the involuntary horror of a frog's leg shocked with an electric current. Twitched, and twitched again as he was torn piece by piece to shreds. Pieces of flesh and bone and half a face with an eye blinking furiously, cascaded down past Beth, and hit the cement below with sodden thuds. And still he was alive, as his organs were squeezed and musculature and bile and shit and skin were rubbed, sandpapered together and let fall. It went on and on, as the death of Leona Ciarelli had gone on and on, and she understood with the blood-knowledge of survivors *at any cost* that the reason the witnesses to the death of Leona Ciarelli had done nothing was not that they had been frozen with horror, that they didn't want to get involved, or that they were inured to death by years of television slaughter.

They were worshippers at a black mass the city had demanded be staged; not once, but a thousand times a day in this insane asylum of steel and stone.

Now she was on her feet, standing half-naked in her ripped nightgown, her hands tightening on the wrought-iron railing, begging to see more, to drink deeper.

Now she was one of them, as the pieces of the night's sacrifice fell past her, bleeding and screaming.

Tomorrow the police would come again, and they would question her, and she would say how terrible it had been, that burglar, and how she had fought, afraid he would rape her and kill her, and how he had fallen, and she had no idea how he had been so hideously mangled and ripped apart, but a seven-story fall, after all . . .

Tomorrow she would not have to worry about walking in the streets, because no harm could come to her. Tomorrow she could even remove the police lock. Nothing in the city could do her any further evil, because she had made the only choice. She was now a dweller in the city, now wholly and richly a part of it. Now she was taken to the bosom of her God.

She felt Ray beside her, standing beside her, holding her, protecting her, his hand on her naked backside, and she watched the fog swirl up and fill the courtyard, fill the city, fill her eyes and her soul and her heart with its power. As Ray's naked body pressed tightly inside her, she drank deeply of the night, knowing whatever voices she heard from this moment forward would be the voices not of whipped dogs, but those of strong, meat-eating beasts.

At last she was unafraid, and it was so good, so very good *not* to be afraid.

> "When inward life dries up, when feeling decreases and apathy increases, when one cannot affect or even genuinely touch another person, violence flares up as a daimonic necessity for contact, a mad drive forcing touch in the most direct way possible."

—Rollo May, *Love and Will*

*God, in the latest, chrome-plated,
dual-carb, chopped & channeled,
eight-hundred-horsepowered incarnation.
God's unspoken name is Vroooom!*

# Along the Scenic Route

The blood-red Mercury with the twin-mounted 7.6 mm Spandaus cut George off as he was shifting lanes. The Merc cut out sharply, three cars behind George, and the driver decked it. The boom of his gas-turbine engine got through George's baffling system without difficulty, like a fist in the ear. The Merc sprayed JP-4 gook and water in a wide fan from its jet nozzle and cut back in, a matter of inches in front of George's Chevy Piranha.

George slapped the selector control on the dash, lighting YOU STUPID BASTARD, WHAT DO YOU THINK YOU'RE DOING and I HOPE YOU CRASH & BURN, YOU SON OF A BITCH. Jessica moaned softly with uncontrolled fear, but George could not hear her: he was screaming obscenities.

George kicked it into Overplunge and depressed the selector button extending the rotating buzzsaws. Dallas razors, they were called, in the repair shoppes. But the crimson Merc pulled away doing an easy 115.

"I'll get you, you beaver-sucker!" he howled.

The Piranha jumped, surged forward. But the Merc was already two dozen car-lengths down the Freeway. Adrenaline pumped through George's system. Beside him, Jessica put a hand on his arm. "Oh, forget it, George; it's just some young snot," she said. Always conciliatory.

"My masculinity's threatened," he murmured, and hunched over the wheel. Jessica looked toward heaven, wishing a bolt of lightning had come from that location many months past, striking Dr. Yasimir directly in his Freud, long before George could have picked up psychiatric justifications for his awful temper.

"Get me Collision Control!" George snarled at her.

Jessica shrugged, as if to say *here we go again,* and dialed CC on the peek. The smiling face of the Freeway Sector Control Operator blurred green and yellow, then came into sharp focus. "Your request, sir?"

"Clearance for duel, Highway 101, northbound."

"Your license number, sir?"

"XUPD 88321," George said. He was scanning the Freeway, keeping the blood-red Mercury in sight, obstinately refusing to stud on the tracking sights.

"Your proposed opponent, sir?"

"Red Mercury GT. '88 model."

"License, sir."

"Just a second." George pressed the stud for the instant replay and the last ten miles rolled back on the movieola. He ran it forward again till he caught the instant the Merc had passed him, stopped the film, and got the number. "MFCS 90909."

"One moment, sir."

George fretted behind the wheel. "*Now* what the hell's holding her up? Whenever you want service, they've got problems. But boy, when it comes tax time—"

The Operator came back and smiled. "I've checked our master Sector grid, sir, and I find authorization may be permitted, but I am required by law to inform you that your proposed opponent is more heavily armed than yourself."

George licked his lips. "What's he running?"

"Our records indicate 7.6 mm Spandau equipment, bulletproof screens and coded optionals."

George sat silently. His speed dropped. The tachometer fluttered, settled.

"Let him go, George," Jessica said. "You know he'd take you."

Two blotches of anger spread on George's cheeks. "Oh, yeah!?!" He howled at the Operator, "Get me a confirm on that Mercury, Operator!"

She blurred off, and George decked the Piranha; it leaped forward. Jessica sighed with resignation and pulled the drawer out from beneath her bucket. She unfolded the g-suit and began stretching into it. She said nothing, but continued to shake her head.

"We'll *see!*" George said.

"Oh, George, when will you ever grow up?"

He did not answer, but his nostrils flared with barely restrained anger.

The Operator smeared back and said, "Opponent confirms, sir. Freeway Underwriters have already cross-filed you as mutual beneficiaries. Please observe standard traffic regulations, and good luck, sir."

She vanished, and George set the Piranha on sleepwalker as he donned his own g-suit. He overrode the sleeper and was back on manual in moments.

"Now, you stuffer, *now* let's see!" 100, 110, 120.

He was gaining rapidly on the Merc now. As the Chevy hit 120, the mastercomp flashed red and suggested crossover. George punched the selector and the telescoping arms of the buzzsaws retracted into the axles, even as the buzzsaws stopped whirling. In a moment they had been drawn back in, now merely fancy decorations in the hubcaps. The wheels retracted into the underbody of the Chevy and the air-cushion took over. Now the Chevy skimmed along, two inches above the roadbed of the Freeway.

Ahead, George could see the Merc also crossing over to air-cushion. 120. 135. 150.

"George, this is crazy!" Jessica said, her face in that characteristic shrike expression. "You're no hot-rodder, George. You're a family man, and this is the family car!"

George chuckled nastily. "I've had it with these fuzzfaces. Last year . . . you remember last year? . . . you remember when that punk stuffer ran us into the abutment? I swore I'd never put up with that kind of thing again. Why'd'you think I had all the optionals installed?"

Jessica opened the tambour doors of the glove compartment and slid out the service tray. She unplugged the jar of anti-flash salve and began spreading it on her face and hands. "I *knew* I shouldn't have let you put that laser thing in this car!" George chuckled again. Fuzzfaces, punks, rodders!

George felt the Piranha surge forward, the big reliable stirling engine recycling the hot air for more and more efficient thrust. Unlike the Merc's inefficient kerosene system, there was no exhaust emission from the nuclear power plant, the external combustion engine almost noiseless, the big radiator tailfin in the rear dissipating the tremendous heat, stabilizing the car as it swooshed along, two inches off the roadbed.

George knew he would catch the blood-red Mercury. Then one

smartass punk was going to learn he couldn't flout law and order by running decent citizens off the freeways!

"Get me my gun," George said.

Jessica shook her head with exasperation, reached under George's bucket, pulled out his drawer and handed him the bulky .45 automatic in its breakaway upside-down shoulder rig. George studded in the sleeper, worked his arms into the rig, tested the oiled leather of the holster, and when he was satisfied, returned the Piranha to manual.

"Oh, God," Jessica said, "John Dillinger rides again."

"Listen!" George shouted, getting more furious with each stupidity she offered. "If you can't be of some help to me, just shut your damned mouth. I'd put you out and come back for you, but I'm in a duel . . . can you understand that? I'm in a duel!" She murmured a yes, George, and fell silent.

There was a transmission queep from the transceiver. George studded it on. No picture. Just vocal. It had to be the driver of the Mercury, up ahead of them. Beaming directly at one another's antennae, using a tightbeam directional, they could keep in touch: it was a standard trick used by rods to rattle their opponents.

"Hey, Boze, you not really gonna custer me, are you? Back'm, Boze. No bad trips, true. The kid'll drop back, hang a couple of biggies on ya, just to teach ya little lesson, letcha swimaway." The voice of the driver was hard, mirthless, the ugly sound of a driver used to being challenged.

"Listen, you young snot," George said, grating his words, trying to sound more menacing than he felt, "I'm going to teach *you* the lesson!"

The Merc's driver laughed raucously.

"Boze, you *de*-mote me, true!"

"And stop calling me a bozo, you lousy little degenerate!"

"Ooooo-weeee, got me a thrasher this time out. Okay, Boze, you be custer an' I'll play arrow. Good shells, baby Boze!"

The finalizing queep sounded, and George gripped the wheel with hands that went knuckle-white. The Merc suddenly shot away from him. He had been steadily gaining, but now as though it had been springloaded, the Mercury burst forward, spraying gook and water on both sides of the forty-foot lanes they were using. "Cut in his afterburner," George snarled. The driver of the Mercury had injected water into the exhaust for added thrust through the jet nozzle. The boom of the Merc's big, noisy engine hit him, and George studded in the rear-mounted propellers to give him more speed. 175. 185. 195.

He was crawling up the line toward the Merc. Gaining, gaining. Jessica pulled out her drawer and unfolded her crash-suit. It went on over the g-suit, and she let George know what she thought of his turning their Sunday Drive into a kamikaze duel.

He told her to stuff, and did a sleeper, donned his own crash-suit, applied flash salve, and lowered the bangup helmet onto his head.

Back on manual he crawled, crawled, till he was only fifty yards behind the Mercury, the gas-turbine vehicle sharp in his tinted windshield. "Put on your goggles . . . I'm going to show that punk who's a bozo. . . ."

He pressed the stud to open the laser louvers. The needle-nosed glass tube peered out from its bay in the Chevy's hood. George read the power drain on his dash. The MHD power generator used to drive the laser was charging. He remembered what the salesman at Chick Williams Chevrolet had told him, pridefully, about the laser gun, when George had inquired about the optional.

*Dynamite feature, Mr. Jackson. Absolutely sensational. Works off a magneto hydro dynamic power generator. Latest thing in defense armament. You know, to achieve sufficient potency from a $CO_2$ laser, you'd need a glass tube a mile long. Well, sir, we both know that's impractical, to say the least, so the project engineers at Chevy's big Bombay plant developed the "stack" method. Glass rods baffled with mirrors—360 feet of stack, the length of a football field . . . plus end-zones. Use it three ways. Punch a hole right through their tires at any speed under a hundred and twenty. If they're running a GT, you can put that hole right into the kerosene fuel tank, blow them off the road. Or, if they're running a stirling, just heat the radiator. When the radiator gets hotter than the engine, the whole works shuts down. Dynamite. Also . . . and this is with proper CC authorization, you can go straight for the old jugular. Use the beam on the driver. Makes a neat hole. Dynamite!*

"I'll take it," George murmured.

"What did you say?" Jessica asked.

"Nothing."

"George, you're a family man, not a rodder!"

"Stuff it!"

Then he was sorry he'd said it. She meant well. It was simply that . . . well, a man had to work hard to keep his balls. He looked sidewise at her. Wearing the Armadillo crash-suit, with its overlapping discs of ceramic material, she looked like a ferryflight pilot. The bangup hat hid her face. He wanted to apologize, but the moment had arrived. He locked the laser on the Merc, depressed the fire stud, and a beam of blinding light flashed from the hood of the Piranha. With the Merc on air-cushion, he had gone straight for the fuel tank.

But the Merc suddenly wasn't in front of him. Even as he had fired, the driver had sheered left into the next forty-foot-wide lane, and cut speed drastically. The Merc dropped back past them as the Piranha swooshed ahead.

"He's on my back!" George shouted.

The next moment Spandau slugs tore at the hide of the Chevy. George slapped the studs, and the bulletproof screens went up. But not before pingholes had appeared in the beryllium hide of the Chevy, exposing the boron fiber filaments that gave the car its lightweight maneuverability. "Stuffer!" George breathed, terribly frightened. The driver was on his back, could ride him into the ground.

He swerved, dropping flaps and skimming the Piranha back and forth in wide arcs, across the two lanes. The Merc hung on. The Spandaus chattered heavily. The screens would hold, but what else was the driver running? What were the "coded optionals" the CC Operator had mentioned?

"Now see what you've gotten us into!"

"Jess, shut up, shut up!"

The transceiver queeped. He studded it on, still swerving. This time the driver of the Merc was sending via microwave video. The face blurred in.

He was a young boy. In his teens. Acne.

"Punk! Stinking punk!" George screamed, trying to swerve, drop back, accelerate. Nothing. The blood-red Merc hung on his tailfin, pounding at him. If one of those bullets struck the radiator tailfin, ricocheted, pierced to the engine, got through the lead shielding around the reactor. Jessica was crying, huddled inside her Armadillo.

He was silently glad she was in the g-suit. He would try something illegal in a moment.

"Hey, Boze. What's your slit look like? If she's creamy'n'nice I might letcha drop her at the next getty, and come back for her later. With your insurance, baby, and my pickle, I can keep her creamy'n'-nice."

"Fuzzfaced punk! I'll see you dead first!"

"You're a real thrasher, old dad. Wish you well, but it's soon over. Say bye-bye to the nice rodder. You gonna die, old dad!"

George was shrieking inarticulately.

The boy laughed wildly. He was up on something. Ferro-coke, perhaps. Or D4. Or merryloo. His eyes glistened blue and young and deadly as a snake.

"Just wanted you to know the name of your piledriver, old dad. *You* can call me Billy. . . ."

And he was gone. The Merc slipped forward, closer, and George had only a moment to realize that this Billy could not possibly have the money to equip his car with a laser, and that was a godsend. But the Spandaus were hacking away at the bulletproof screens. They weren't meant for extended punishment like this. Damn that Detroit iron!

He had to make the illegal move *now*.

Thank God for the g-suits. A tight turn, across the lanes, in direct contravention of the authorization. And in a tight turn, without the g-suits, doing—he checked the speedometer and tach—250 mph, the blood slams up against one side of the body. The g-suits would squeeze the side of the body where the blood tried to pool up. They would live. If . . .

He spun the wheel hard, slamming down on the accelerator. The Merc slewed sidewise and caught the turn. He never had a chance. He pulled out of the illegal turn, and their positions were the same. But the Merc had dropped back several car-lengths. Then from the transceiver there was a queep and he did not even stud-in as the Police Copter overhead tightbeamed him in an authoritative voice:

"XUPD 88321. Warning! You will be in contravention of your dueling authorization if you try another maneuver of that sort! You are warned to keep to your lanes and the standard rules of road courtesy!"

Then it queeped, and George felt the universe settling like silt over him. He was being killed by the system.

He'd have to eject. The seats would save him and Jessica. He tried to tell her, but she had fainted.

*How did I get into this?* he pleaded with himself. *Dear God, I swear if you get me out of this alive I'll never never never go mad like this again. Please God.*

Then the Merc was up on him again, pulling up *alongside!*

The window went down on the passenger side of the Mercury, and George whipped a glance across to see Billy with his lips skinned back from his teeth under the windblast and acceleration, aiming a .45 at him. Barely thinking, George studded the bumpers.

The super-conducting magnetic bumpers took hold, sucked Billy into his magnetic field, and they collided with a crash that shook the .45 out of the rodder's hand. In the instant of collision, George realized he had made his chance, and dropped back. In a moment he was riding the Merc's tail again.

Naked barbarism took hold. He wanted to kill now. Not crash the other, not wound the other, not stop the other—*kill the other!* Messages to God were forgotten.

He locked-in the laser and aimed for the windshield bubble. His sights caught the rear of the bubble, fastened to the outline of Billy's head, and George fired.

As the bolt of light struck the bubble, a black spot appeared, and remained for the seconds the laser touched. When the light cut off, the black spot vanished. George cursed, screamed, cried, in fear and helplessness.

The Merc was equipped with a frequency-sensitive laserproof windshield. Chemicals in the windshield would "go black," opaque at certain frequencies, momentarily, anywhere a laser light touched them. He should have known. A duelist like this Billy, trained in weaponry, equipped for whatever might chance down a Freeway. Another coded optional. George found he was crying, piteously, within the cavern of his bangup hat.

Then the Merc was swerving again, executing a roll and dip that George could not understand, could not predict. Then the Merc dropped speed suddenly, and George found himself almost running up the jet nozzle of the blood-red vehicle.

He spun out and around, and Billy was behind him once more,

closing in for the kill. He sent the propellers to full spin and reached for eternity. 270. 280. 290.

Then he heard the sizzling, and jerked his head around to see the back wall of the car rippling. *Oh my God,* he thought, in terror, *he can't afford a laser, but he's got an inductor beam!*

The beam was setting up strong local eddy currents in the beryllium hide of the Chevy. He'd rip a hole in the skin, the air would whip through, the car would go out of control.

George knew he was dead.

And Jessica.

And all because of this punk, this rodder fuzzface!

The Merc closed in confidently.

George thought wildly. There was no time for anything but the blind plunging panic of random thought. The speedometer and the tach agreed. They were doing 300 mph.

Riding on air-cushions.

The thought slipped through his panic.

It was the only possibility. He ripped off his bangup hat, and fumbled Jessica's loose. He hugged them in his lap with his free hand, and managed to stud down the window on the driver's side. Instantly, a blast of wind and accelerated air skinned back his lips, plastered his cheeks hollowly, made a death's head of Jessica's features. He fought to keep the Chevy stable, gyro'd.

Then, holding the bangup hats by their straps, he forced them around the edge of the window where the force of his speed jammed them against the side of the Chevy. Then he let go. And studded up the window. And braked sharply.

The bulky bangup hats dropped away, hit the roadbed, rolled directly into the path of the Merc. They disappeared underneath the blood-red car, and instantly the vehicle hit the Freeway. George swerved out of the way, dropping speed quickly.

The Merc hit with a crash, bounced, hit again, bounced and hit, bounced and hit. As it went past the Piranha, George saw Billy caroming off the insides of the car.

He watched the vehicle skid, wheelless, for a quarter of a mile down the Freeway before it caught the inner breakwall of the lane-divider, shot high in the air, and came down turning over. It landed on the bubble, which burst, and exploded in a flash of fire and smoke that rocked the Chevy.

At three hundred miles per hour, two inches above the Freeway, riding on air, anything that broke up the air bubble would be a lethal weapon. He had won the duel. That Billy was dead.

George pulled in at the next getty, and sat in the lot. Jessica came around finally. He was slumped over the wheel, shaking, unable to speak.

She looked over at him, then reached out a trembling hand to touch his shoulder. He jumped at the infinitesimal pressure, felt through the g- and crash-suits. She started to speak, but the peek queeped, and she studded it on.

"Sector Control, sir." The Operator smiled.

He did not look up.

"Congratulations, sir. Despite one possible infraction, your duel has been logged as legal and binding. You'll be pleased to know that the occupant of the car you challenged was rated number one in the entire Central and Eastern Freeway circuit. Now that Mr. Bonney has been finalized, we are entering your name on the dueling records. Underwriters have asked us to inform you that a check will be in the mails to you within twenty-four hours.

"Again, sir, congratulations."

The peek went dead, and George tried to focus on the parking lot of the neon and silver getty. It had been a terrible experience. He never wanted to use a car that way again. It had been some other George, certainly not him.

"I'm a family man," he repeated Jessica's words. "And this is just a family car . . . I . . ."

She was smiling gently at him. Then they were in each other's arms, and he was crying, and she was saying that's all right, George, you had to do it, it's all right.

And the peek queeped.

She studded it on and the face of the Operator smiled back at her. "Congratulations, sir, you'll be pleased to know that Sector Control already has fifteen duel challenges for you.

"Mr. Ronnie Lee Hauptman of Dallas has asked for first challenge, and is, at this moment, speeding toward you with an ETA of 6:15 this evening. In the event Mr. Hauptman does not survive, you have waiting challenges from Mr. Fred Bull of Chatsworth, California . . . Mr. Leo Fowler of Philadelphia . . . Mr. Emil Zalenko of . . ."

George did not hear the list. He was trying desperately, with clubbed fingers, to extricate himself from the strangling folds of the g- and crash-suits. But he knew it was no good. He would have to fight.

In the world of the Freeway, there was no place for a walking man.

*The Author wishes to thank Mr. Ben Bova, formerly of Avco Everett Research Laboratory (Everett, Massachusetts), for his assistance in preparing the extrapolative technical background of this story.*

*Posing the question: does the god of love
use underarm deodorant, vaginal spray
and fluoride toothpaste?*

# On the Downhill Side

*"In love, there is always one who kisses and one who offers the cheek."*

—French proverb

I knew she was a virgin because she was able to ruffle the silken mane of my unicorn. Named Lizette, she was a Grecian temple in which no sacrifice had ever been made. Vestal virgin of New Orleans, found walking without shadow in the thankgod coolness of cockroach-crawling Louisiana night. My unicorn whinnied, inclined his head, and she stroked the ivory spiral of his horn.

Much of this took place in what is called the Irish Channel, a strip of street in old New Orleans where the lace curtain micks had settled decades before; now the Irish were gone and the Cubans had taken over the Channel. Now the Cubans were sleeping, recovering from the muggy today that held within its hours the *déjà vu* of muggy yesterday, the *déjà rêvé* of intolerable tomorrow. Now the crippled bricks of side streets off Magazine had given up their nightly ghosts, and one such phantom had come to me, calling my unicorn to her—thus, clearly, a virgin—and I stood waiting.

Had it been Sutton Place, had it been a Manhattan evening, and had we met, she would have kneeled to pet my dog. And I would have waited. Had it been Puerto Vallarta, had it been 20° 36' N, 105° 13' W, and had we met, she would have crouched to run her fingertips over the oil-slick hide of my iguana. And I would have waited. Meeting in streets requires ritual. One must wait and not breathe too loud, if one is to enjoy the congress of the nightly ghosts.

She looked across the fine head of my unicorn and smiled at me. Her eyes were a shade of gray between onyx and miscalculation. "Is it a bit chilly for you?" I asked.

"When I was thirteen," she said, linking my arm, taking a tentative two steps that led me with her, up the street, "or perhaps I was twelve, well no matter, when I was that approximate age, I had a marvelous shawl of Belgian lace. I could look through it and see the mysteries of the sun and the other stars unriddled. I'm sure someone important and very nice has purchased that shawl from an antique dealer, and paid handsomely for it."

It seemed not a terribly responsive reply to a simple question.

"A queen of the Mardi Gras Ball doesn't get chilly," she added, unasked. I walked along beside her, the cool evasiveness of her arm binding us, my mind a welter of answer choices, none satisfactory.

Behind us, my unicorn followed silently. Well, not entirely silently. His platinum hoofs clattered on the bricks. I'm afraid I felt a straight pin of jealousy. Perfection does that to me.

"When were you queen of the Ball?"

The date she gave me was one hundred and thirteen years before.

It must have been brutally cold down there in the stones.

There is a little book they sell, a guide to manners and dining in New Orleans: I've looked: nowhere in the book do they indicate the proper responses to a ghost. But then, it says nothing about the wonderful cemeteries of New Orleans' West Bank, or Metairie. Or the gourmet dining at such locations. One seeks, in vain, through the mutable, mercurial universe, for the compleat guide. To everything. And, failing in the search, one makes do the best one can. And suffers the frustration, suffers the ennui.

Perfection does that to me.

We walked for some time, and grew to know each other, as best we'd allow. These are some of the high points. They lack continuity. I don't apologize, I merely pointed it out, adding with some truth, I feel, that *most* liaisons lack continuity. We find ourselves in odd places at various times, and for a brief span we link our lives to others—even as Lizette had linked her arm with mine—and then, our time elapsed, we move apart. Through a haze of pain occasionally; usually through a veil of memory that clings, then passes; sometimes as though we have never touched.

"My name is Paul Ordahl," I told her. "And the most awful thing that ever happened to me was my first wife, Bernice. I don't know how else to put it—even if it sounds melodramatic, it's simply what happened—she went insane, and I divorced her, and her mother had her committed to a private mental home."

"When I was eighteen," Lizette said, "my family gave me my coming-out party. We were living in the Garden District, on Prytania Street. The house was a lovely white Plantation—they call them antebellum now—with Grecian pillars. We had a persimmon-green gazebo in the rear gardens, directly beside a weeping willow. It was six-sided. Octagonal. Or is that hexagonal? It was the loveliest party. And while it was going on, I sneaked away with a boy . . . I don't remember his name . . . and we went into the gazebo, and I let him touch my breasts. I don't remember his name."

We were on Decatur Street, walking toward the French Quarter; the Mississippi was on our right, dark but making its presence known.

"Her mother was the one had her committed, you see. I only heard from them twice after the divorce. It had been four stinking years and I really didn't want any more of it. Once, after I'd started making some money, the mother called and said Bernice had to be put in the state asylum. There wasn't enough money to pay for the private home any more. I sent a little; not much. I suppose I could have sent more, but I was remarried, there was a child from her previous marriage. I didn't want to send any more. I told the mother not to call me again. There was only once after that . . . it was the most terrible thing that ever happened to me."

We walked around Jackson Square, looking in at the very black grass, reading the plaques bolted to the spear-topped fence, plaques telling how New Orleans had once belonged to the French. We sat on one of the benches in the street. The street had been closed to traffic, and we sat on one of the benches.

"Our name was Charbonnet. Can you say that?"

I said it, with a good accent.

"I married a very wealthy man. He was in real estate. At one time he owned the entire block where the *Vieux Carré* now stands, on Bourbon Street. He admired me greatly. He came and sought my hand, and my *maman* had to strike the bargain because my father was too weak to do it; he drank. I can admit that now. But it didn't matter, I'd already found out how my suitor was set financially. He wasn't common, but he wasn't quality, either. But he was wealthy and I married him. He gave me presents. I did what I had to do. But I refused to let him make love to me after he became friends with that awful Jew who built the Metairie Cemetery over the race track because they wouldn't let him race his Jew horses. My husband's name was Dunbar. Claude Dunbar, you may have heard the name? Our parties were *de rigueur.*"

"Would you like some coffee and *beignets* at Du Monde?"

She stared at me for a moment, as though she wanted me to say something more, then she nodded and smiled.

We walked around the Square. My unicorn was waiting at the curb. I scratched his rainbow flank and he struck a spark off the cobblestones with his right front hoof. "I know," I said to him, "we'll soon start the downhill side. But not just yet. Be patient. I won't forget you."

Lizette and I went inside the Café Du Monde and I ordered two coffees with warm milk and two orders of *beignets* from a waiter who was originally from New Jersey but had lived most of his life only a few miles from College Station, Texas.

There was a coolness coming off the levee.

"I was in New York," I said. "I was receiving an award at an architects' convention—did I mention I was an architect—yes, that's what I was at the time, an architect—and I did a television interview. The mother saw me on the program, and checked the newspapers to find out what hotel we were using for the convention, and she got my room number and called me. I had been out quite late after the banquet where I'd gotten my award, quite late. I was sitting on the side of the bed, taking off my shoes, my tuxedo tie hanging from my unbuttoned collar, getting ready just to throw clothes on the floor and sink away, when the phone rang. It was the mother. She was a terrible person, one of the worst I ever knew, a shrike, a terrible, just a terrible person. She started telling me about Bernice in the asylum. How they had her in this little room and how she stared out the window most of the time. She'd reverted to childhood, and most of the time she couldn't even recognize the mother; but when she did, she'd say something like, 'Don't let them hurt me, Mommy, don't let them hurt me.' So I asked her what she wanted me to do, did she want money for Bernice or what . . . Did she want me to go see her since I was in New York . . . and she said God no. And then she did an awful thing to me. She said the last time she'd been to see Bernice, my ex-wife had turned around and put her finger to her lips and said, 'Shhh, we have to be very quiet. Paul is working.' And I swear, a snake uncoiled in my stomach. It was the most terrible thing I'd ever heard. No matter how secure you are that you honest to God had *not* sent someone to a madhouse, there's always that little core of doubt, and saying what she'd said just burned out my head. I couldn't even think about it, couldn't even really *hear* it, or it would have collapsed me. So down came these iron walls and I just kept on talking, and after a while she hung up.

"It wasn't till two years later that I allowed myself to think about it, and then I cried; it had been a long time since I'd cried. Oh, not because I believed that nonsense about a man isn't supposed to cry, but just because I guess there hadn't been anything that important to cry *about*. But when I let myself hear what she'd said, I started crying, and just went on and on till I finally went in and looked into the bathroom mirror and I asked myself, face-to-face, if I'd done that, if I'd ever made her be quiet so I could work on blueprints or drawings. . . .

"And after a while I saw myself shaking my head no, and it was easier. That was perhaps three years before I died."

She licked the powdered sugar from the *beignets* off her fingers, and launched into a long story about a lover she had taken. She didn't remember his name.

It was sometime after midnight. I'd thought midnight would signal the start of the downhill side, but the hour had passed, and we were still together, and she didn't seem ready to vanish. We left the Café Du Monde and walked into the Quarter.

I despise Bourbon Street. The strip joints, with the pasties over nipples, the smell of need, the dwarfed souls of men attuned only to flesh. The noise.

We walked through it like art connoisseurs at a showing of motel room paintings. She continued to talk about her life, about the men she had known, about the way they had loved her, the ways in which she had spurned them, and about the trivia of her past existence. I continued to talk about my loves, about all the women I had held dear in my heart for however long each had been linked with me. We talked across each other, our conversation at right angles, only meeting in the intersections of silence at story's end.

She wanted a julep and I took her to the Royal Orleans Hotel and we sat in silence as she drank. I watched her, studying that phantom face, seeking for even the smallest flicker of light off the ice in her eyes, hoping for an indication that glacial melting could be forthcoming. But there was nothing, and I burned to say correct words that might cause heat. She drank and reminisced about evenings with young men in similar hotels, a hundred years before.

We went to a night club where a Flamenco dancer and his two-woman troupe performed on a stage of unpolished woods, their star-shining black shoes setting up resonances in me that I chose to ignore.

Then I realized there were only three couples in the club, and that the extremely pretty Flamenco dancer was playing to Lizette. He gripped the lapels of his bolero jacket and clattered his heels against the stage like a man driving nails. She watched him, and her tongue made a wholly obvious flirtatious trip around the rim of her liquor glass. There was a two-drink minimum, and as I have never liked the taste of alcohol, she was more than willing to prevent waste by drinking mine as well as her own. Whether she was getting drunk or simply indulging herself, I do not know. It didn't matter. I became blind with jealousy, and dragons took possession of my eyes.

When the dancer was finished, when his half hour show was concluded, he came to our table. His suit was skin tight and the color of Arctic lakes. His hair was curly and moist from his exertions, and his prettiness infuriated me. There was a scene. He asked her name, I interposed a comment, he tried to be polite, sensing my ugly mood, she overrode my comment, he tried again in Castilian, *th*-ing his *esses,* she answered, I rose and shoved him, there was a scuffle. We were asked to leave.

Once outside, she walked away from me.

My unicorn was at the curb, eating from a porcelain *Sèvres* soup plate filled with *flan.* I watched her walk unsteadily up the street toward Jackson Square. I scratched my unicorn's neck and he stopped eating the egg custard. He looked at me for a long moment. Ice crystals were sparkling in his mane.

We were on the downhill side.

"Soon, old friend," I said.

He dipped his elegant head toward the plate. "I see you've been to the Las Americas. When you return the plate, give my best to *Señor Pena.*"

I followed her up the street. She was walking rapidly toward the Square. I called to her, but she wouldn't stop. She began dragging her left hand along the steel bars of the fence enclosing the Square. Her fingertips thudded softly from bar to bar, and once I heard the chitinous *clak* of a manicured nail.

"Lizette!"

She walked faster, dragging her hand across the dark metal bars.

"Lizette! Damn it!"

I was reluctant to run after her; it was somehow terribly demeaning. But she was getting farther and farther away. There were bums in the Square, sitting slouched on the benches, their arms out along the backs. Itinerants, kids with beards and knapsacks. I was suddenly frightened for her. Impossible. She had been dead for a hundred years. There was no reason for it . . . I was afraid for her!

I started running, the sound of my footsteps echoing up and around the Square. I caught her at the corner and dragged her around. She tried to slap me, and I caught her hand. She kept trying to hit me, to scratch my face with the manicured nails. I held her and swung her away from me, swung her around, and around, dizzyingly, trying to keep her off-balance. She swung wildly, crying out and saying things inarticulately. Finally, she stumbled and I pulled her in to me and held her tight against my body.

"Stop it! Stop, Lizette! I . . . *Stop it!*" She went limp against me and I felt her crying against my chest. I took her into the shadows and my unicorn came down Decatur Street and stood under a streetlamp, waiting.

The chimera winds rose. I heard them, and knew we were well on the downhill side, that time was growing short. I held her close and smelled the woodsmoke scent of her hair. "Listen to me," I said, softly, close to her. "Listen to me, Lizette. Our time's almost gone. This is our last chance. You've lived in stone for a hundred years; I've heard you cry. I've come there, to that place, night after night, and I've heard you cry. You've paid enough, God knows. So have I. We can *do* it. We've got one more chance, and we can make it, if you'll try. That's all I ask. Try."

She pushed away from me, tossing her head so the auburn hair swirled away from her face. Her eyes were dry. Ghosts can do that. Cry without making tears. Tears are denied us. Other things; I won't talk of them here.

"I lied to you," she said.

I touched the side of her face. The high cheekbone just at the hairline. "I know. My unicorn would never have let you touch him if you weren't pure. I'm not, but he has no choice with me. He was assigned to me. He's my familiar and he puts up with me. We're friends."

"No. Other lies. My life was a lie. I've told them all to you. We can't make it. You have to let me go."

I didn't know exactly where, but I knew how it would happen. I argued with her, trying to convince her there was a way for us. But she couldn't believe it, hadn't the strength or the will or the faith. Finally, I let her go.

She put her arms around my neck and drew my face down to hers, and she held me that way for a few moments. Then the winds rose, and there were sounds in the night, the sounds of calling, and she left me there, in the shadows.

I sat down on the curb and thought about the years since I'd died. Years without much music. Light leached out. Wandering. Nothing to pace me but memories and the unicorn. How sad I was for *him;* assigned to me till I got my chance. And now it had come and I'd taken my best go, and failed.

Lizette and I were the two sides of the same coin; devalued and impossible to spend. Legal tender of nations long since vanished, no longer even names on the cracked papyrus of cartographers' maps. We had been snatched away from final rest, had been set adrift to roam for our crimes, and only once between death and eternity would we receive a chance. This night . . . this nothing special night . . . this was our chance.

My unicorn came to me, then, and brushed his muzzle against my shoulder. I reached up and scratched around the base of his spiral horn, his favorite place. He gave a long, silvery sigh, and in that sound I heard the sentence I was serving on him, as well as myself. We had been linked, too. Assigned to one another by the one who had ordained this night's chance. But if I lost out, so did my unicorn; he who had wandered with me through all the soundless, lightless years.

I stood up. I was by no means ready to do battle, but at least I could stay in for the full ride . . . all the way on the downhill side. "Do you know where they are?"

My unicorn started off down the street.

I followed, hopelessness warring with frustration. Dusk to dawn is the full ride, the final chance. After midnight is the downhill side.

Time was short, and when time ran out there would be nothing for Lizette or me or my unicorn *but* time. Forever.

When we passed the Royal Orleans Hotel I knew where we were going. The sound of the Quarter had already faded. It was getting on toward dawn. The human lice had finally crawled into their flesh-mounds to sleep off the night of revelry. Though I had never experienced directly the New Orleans in which Lizette had grown up, I longed for the power to blot out the cancerous blight that Bourbon Street and the Quarter had become, with its tourist filth and screaming neon, to restore it to the colorful yet healthy state in which it had thrived a hundred years before. But I was only a ghost, not one of the gods with such powers, and at that moment I was almost at the end of the line held by one of those gods.

My unicorn turned down dark streets, heading always in the same general direction, and when I saw the first black shapes of the tombstones against the night sky, the *lightening* night sky, I knew I'd been correct in my assumption of destination.

The Saint Louis Cemetery.

Oh, how I sorrow for anyone who has never seen the world-famous Saint Louis Cemetery in New Orleans. It is the perfect grave-yard, the complete graveyard, the finest graveyard in the universe. (There is a perfection in some designs that informs the function to-tally. There are Danish chairs that could be nothing *but* chairs, are so totally and completely *chair* that if the world as we know it ended, and a billion years from now the New Orleans horsy cockroaches became the dominant species, and they dug down through the alluvial layers, and found one of those chairs, even if they themselves did not use chairs, were not constructed physically for the use of chairs, had never seen a chair, *still* they would know it for what it had been made to be: a chair. Because it would be the essence of *chairness*. And from it, they could reconstruct the human race in replica. *That* is the kind of graveyard one means when one refers to the world-famous Saint Louis Cemetery.)

The Saint Louis Cemetery is ancient. It sighs with shadows and the comfortable bones and their afterimages of deaths that became great merely because those who died went to be interred in the Saint Louis Cemetery. The water table lies just eighteen inches below New Orleans—there are no graves in the earth for that reason. Bodies are entombed aboveground in crypts, in sepulchers, vaults, mausoleums. The gravestones are all different, no two alike, each one a testament to the stonecutter's art. Only secondarily testaments to those who lie beneath the markers.

We had reached the moment of final nightness. That ultimate moment before day began. Dawn had yet to fill the eastern sky, yet there was a warming of tone to the night; it was the last of the downhill side of my chance. Of Lizette's chance.

We approached the cemetery, my unicorn and I. From deep in the center of the skyline of stones beyond the fence I could see the ice-chill glow of a pulsing blue light. The light one finds in a refrigerator, cold and flat and brittle.

I mounted my unicorn, leaned close along his neck, clinging to his mane with both hands, knees tight to his silken sides, now rippling with light and color, and I gave a little hiss of approval, a little sound of go.

My unicorn sailed over the fence, into the world-famous Saint Louis Cemetery.

I dismounted and thanked him. We began threading our way between the tombstones, the sepulchers, the crypts.

The blue glow grew more distinct. And now I could hear the chimera winds rising, whirling, coming in off alien seas. The pulsing of the light, the wail of the winds, the night dying. My unicorn stayed close. Even we of the spirit world know when to be afraid.

After all, I was only operating off a chance; I was under no god's protection. Naked, even in death.

There is no fog in New Orleans.

Mist began to form around us.

Except sometimes in the winter, there is no fog in New Orleans.

I remembered the daybreak of the night I'd died. There had been mist. I had been a suicide.

My third wife had left me. She had gone away during the night, while I'd been at a business meeting with a client; I had been engaged to design a church in Baton Rouge. All that day I'd steamed the old wallpaper off the apartment we'd rented. It was to have been our first home together, paid for by the commission. I'd done the steaming myself, with a tall ladder and a steam condenser and two flat pans with steam holes. Up near the ceiling the heat had been so awful I'd almost fainted. She'd brought me lemonade, freshly squeezed. Then I'd showered and changed and gone to my meeting. When I'd returned, she was gone. No note.

Lizette and I were two sides of the same coin, cast off after death for the opposite extremes of the same crime. She had never loved. I had loved too much. Overindulgence in something as delicate as love is to be found monstrously offensive in the eyes of the God of Love. And some of us—who have never understood the salvation in the Golden Mean—some of us are cast adrift with but one chance. It can happen.

Mist formed around us, and my unicorn crept close to me, somehow smaller, almost timid. We were moving into realms he did not understand, where his limited magics were useless. These were realms of potency so utterly beyond even the limbo creatures—such as my unicorn—so completely alien to even the intermediary zone wanderers—Lizette and myself—that we were as helpless and without understanding as those who live. We had only one advantage over living, breathing, as yet undead humans: we *knew* for certain that the realms on the other side existed.

Above, beyond, deeper: where the gods live. Where the one who had given me my chance, had given Lizette *her* chance, where He lived. Undoubtedly watching.

The mist swirled up around us, as chill and final as the dust of pharaohs' tombs.

We moved through it, toward the pulsing heart of blue light. And as we came into the penultimate circle, we stopped. We were in the outer ring of potency, and we saw the claiming things that had come for Lizette. She lay out on an altar of crystal, naked and trembling. They stood around her, enormously tall and transparent. Man shapes without faces. Within their transparent forms a strange, silvery fog swirled, like smoke from holy censers. Where eyes should have been on a man or a ghost, there were only dull flickering firefly glowings, inside, hanging in the smoke, moving, changing shape and position. No eyes at all. And tall, very tall, towering over Lizette and the altar.

For me, overcommitted to love, when dawn came without salvation, there was only an eternity of wandering, with my unicorn as sole companion. Ghost forevermore. Incense chimera viewed as dust-devil on the horizon, chilling as I passed in city streets, forever gone, invisible, lost, empty, helpless, wandering.

But for her, empty vessel, the fate was something else entirely. The God of Love had allowed her the time of wandering, trapped by day in stones, freed at night to wander. He had allowed her the final chance. And having failed to take it, her fate was with these claiming creatures, gods themselves . . . of another order . . . higher or lower I had no idea. But terrible.

"*Lagniappe!*" I screamed the word. The old Creole word they used in New Orleans when they want a little extra; a bonus of *croissants*, a few additional carrots dumped into the shopping bag, a baker's dozen, a larger portion of clams or crabs or shrimp. "*Lagniappe!* Lizette, take a little more! Try for the extra! Try . . . demand it . . . there's time . . . you have it coming to you . . . you've paid . . . I've paid . . . it's ours . . . *try!*"

She sat up, her naked body lit by lambent fires of chill blue cold from the other side. She sat up and looked across the inner circle to me, and I stood there with my arms out, trying desperately to break through the outer circle to her. But it was solid and I could not pass. Only virgins could pass.

And they would not let her go. They had been promised a feed, and they were there to claim. I began to cry, as I had cried when I finally heard what the mother had said, when I finally came home to the empty apartment and knew I had spent my life loving too much, demanding too much, myself a feeder at a board that *could* be depleted and emptied and serve up no more. She wanted to come to me, I could *see* she wanted to come to me. But they would have their meal.

Then I felt the muzzle of my unicorn at my neck, and in a step he had moved through the barrier that was impenetrable to me, and he moved across the circle and stood waiting. Lizette leaped from the altar and ran to me.

It all happened at the same time. I felt Lizette's body anchor in to mine, and *we* saw my unicorn standing over there on the other side, and for a moment *we* could not summon up the necessary reactions, the correct sounds. We knew for the first time in either our lives or our deaths what it was to be paralyzed. Then reactions began washing over me, we, us in wave after wave: cascading joy that Lizette had come to . . . us; utter love for this Paul ghost creature; realization that instinctively part of us was falling into the same pattern again; fear that that part would love too much at this mystic juncture; resolve to temper our love; and then anguish at the sight of our unicorn standing there, waiting to be claimed. . . .

We called to him . . . using his secret name, one we had never spoken aloud. We could barely speak. Weight pulled at his throat, our throats. "Old friend . . ." We took a step toward him but could not pass the barrier. Lizette clung to me, Paul held me tight as I trembled with terror and the cold of that inner circle still frosting my flesh.

The great transparent claimers stood silently, watching, waiting, as if content to allow us our moments of final decision. But their impatience could be felt in the air, a soft purring, like the death rattle always in the throat of a cat. "Come back! Not for me . . . don't do it for me . . . it's not fair!"

Paul's unicorn turned his head and looked at us.

My friend of starless nights, when we had gone sailing together through the darkness. My friend who had walked with me on endless tours of empty places. My friend of gentle nature and constant companionship. Until Lizette, my friend, my only friend, my familiar assigned to an onerous task, who had come to love me and to whom I had belonged, even as he had belonged to me.

I could not bear the hurt that grew in my chest, in my stomach; my head was on fire, my eyes burned with tears first for Paul, and now for the sweetest creature a god had ever sent to temper a man's anguish . . . and for myself. I could not bear the thought of never knowing—as Paul had known it—the silent company of that gentle, magical beast.

But he turned back, and moved to them, and they took that as final decision, and the great transparent claimers moved in around him, and their quickglass hands reached down to touch him, and for an instant they seemed to hesitate, and I called out, "Don't be afraid . . ." and my unicorn turned his head to look across the mist of potency for the last time, and I saw he *was* afraid, but not as much as he would have been if I had not been there.

Then the first of them touched his smooth, silvery flank and he gave a trembling sigh of pain. A ripple ran down his side. Not the quick flesh movement of ridding himself of a fly, but a completely alien, unnatural tremor, containing in its swiftness all the agony and loss of eternities. A sigh went out from Paul's unicorn, though he had not uttered it.

We could feel the pain, the loneliness. My unicorn with no time left to him. Ending. All was now a final ending; he had stayed with me, walked with me, and had grown to care for me, until that time when he would be released from his duty by that special God; but now freedom was to be denied him; an ending.

The great transparent claimers all touched him, their ice fingers caressing his warm hide as we watched, helpless, Lizette's face buried in Paul's chest. Colors surged across my unicorn's body, as if by becoming more intense the chill touch of the claimers could be beaten off. Pulsing waves of rainbow color that lived in his hide for moments, then dimmed, brightened again and were bled off. Then the colors leaked away one by one, chroma weakening: purple-blue, manganese violet, discord, cobalt blue, doubt, affection, chrome green, chrome yellow, raw sienna, contemplation, alizarin crimson, irony, silver, severity, compassion, cadmium red, white.

They emptied him . . . he did not fight them . . . going colder and colder . . . flickers of yellow, a whisper of blue, pale as white . . . the tremors blending into one constant shudder . . . the wonderful golden eyes rolled in torment, went flat, brightness dulled, flat metal . . . the platinum hoofs caked with rust . . . and he stood, did not try to escape, gave himself for us . . . and he was emptied. Of everything. Then, like the claimers, we could see through him. Vapors swirled within the transparent husk, a fogged glass, shimmering . . . then nothing. And then they absorbed even the husk.

The chill blue light faded, and the claimers grew indistinct in our sight. The smoke within them seemed thicker, moved more slowly, horribly, as though they had fed and were sluggish and would go away, back across the line to that dark place where they waited, always waited, till their hunger was aroused again. And my unicorn was gone. I was alone with Lizette. I was alone with Paul. The mist died away, and the claimers were gone, and once more it was merely a cemetery as the first rays of the morning sun came easing through the tumble and disarray of headstones.

We stood together as one, her naked body white and virginal in my weary arms; and as the light of the sun struck us we began to fade, to merge, to mingle our bodies and our wandering spirits one into the other, forming one spirit that would neither love too much, nor too little, having taken our chance on the downhill side.

We faded and were lifted invisibly on the scented breath of that good God who had owned us, and were taken away from there. To be born again as one spirit, in some other human form, man or woman we did not know which. Nor would we remember. Nor did it matter.

This time, love would not destroy us. This time out, we would have luck.

The luck of silken mane and rainbow colors, platinum hoofs and spiral horn.

*Where the old gods go, and why it's unwise to seek admittance.*

# O Ye of Little Faith

Niven felt for the rock wall behind him. His fingertips grazed the crumbling rocks. The wall curved. He prayed that it curved. It *had* to curve, to go around the bowl in which he was trapped, or he was dead. That simply: he was dead. The minotaur advanced another few feet, pawing the red-dust earth with hooves of gold now dulled by a faint dusty crimson patina. The minotaur advanced another few feet, raking at the red-dust earth with his trident, sending a thin, stinging spray into Niven's face. Niven blinked back tears from the dirt.

The creature's gimlet eyes were as red as the ground it stomped. Head of a bull, gigantic body of an Atlas, something out of a child's fable, it stepped carefully toward him, prodding the air with the blood-encrusted trident.

The minotaur bellowed, a sound of rage almost human but ending as a beast's groan. The eyes. The malevolent little red eyes. Red and vengeful; not merely with volcanic hatred, but with something else . . . something incredibly ancient, primeval, a rage born of loss and frustration from a time before men had walked the Earth. A time when the minotaurs and their fellow-myths had ruled the world. A world where they no longer belonged, a world that did not believe they had *ever* existed.

And now, somehow, in some inexplicable fashion, Niven—a man with no particular talents—had been thrown crosswise and slantwise through universes into a place, a time, a continuum (an Earth?) where the minotaur still roamed. Where the minotaur could at last have his full revenge on the creatures that had replaced him. It was the day of reckoning for *Homo sapiens.*

Niven backed around the bowl, feeling the dirt of the wall crumbling in his fingers as he felt behind him; in his other hand he brandished the rough-wood club he had found underfoot as he ran from the beast. He let it droop in his hand a moment, the weight of it difficult to keep at the ready for very long. The minotaur's face of frenzy glowed with heat. It leaped. Niven swung the club with a bunching of muscles that sent him whirling half-around. The minotaur dug the trident deep in the dirt and ground to a snorting halt, two feet in front of the flat arc swing of the club. Niven spun around completely, and the club struck the wall and shattered to splinters.

The minotaur's half-growl, half-snort bore traces of triumphant amusement as it exploded behind the dark-haired man, and Niven felt sweat come to his back. The impact of the blow against the wall had sent a tremor through his entire body; his left arm was quite numb. Yet it had saved him. There was an opening in the wall, an opening in the rock-wall of the deep valley bowl, an opening he would not have seen backing around the wall. Now there was a scant hope of staying alive.

As the minotaur gathered itself for a leap that would send its gigantic body plunging into Niven, the man slipped sidewise, and was inside the mountain.

He turned then, and ran. Behind him the light from that weird place—vaguely blue and light-mote laden—faded and was abruptly lost as he caromed around a sharp turn in the passage. It was dark now, pitch absolute dark, and all Niven could see was the scintillance of tiny sparks behind his eyes. Suddenly he found himself longing to see even that light behind him, that snippet of blue and cadaverous gray in a sky that had never been roof of any world *he* had known.

And then he was falling. . . .

Suddenly, and without any sense of having moved, between one step and the next, he plunged over a lip of stone, and was falling. Down and down, tumbling over and over, and the walls of moist slippery stone reeled around him, unseen but cold, as he tried to grab some small hold.

His fingertips skinned away from friction, and the pain was excruciating . . . for a long moment . . . but was lost in the next instant as a gasp that became a shriek was torn from him. He plunged sickeningly, impacting painfully against an unseen out-cropping with his shoulders and the back of his neck . . . he felt his spine crack . . . and continued falling, and suddenly was submerged in water . . . black and viscous . . . bottomless . . . closing over him, filling his mouth with foulness, blind, dragged into the grave-chill body of a moist lover terrible in her possessiveness, jealousy and need.

Vapors of night. Echoes of never. Niven thrashed in a whirlpool vortex of total unawareness. Memories—released from their crypt beneath his conscious mind—escaped, gibbering, rushed in a horde into his skull. He was back in the old soothsayer's shop. Had it been just a few minutes before finding himself trapped by the minotaur? Merely a few minutes when he had stood in the prognosticator's shop in a Tijuana back alley, a tourist with a girl on one arm and a wisecrack on his lips? Had it been only that long ago, a matter of seconds, or a sometime *long ago*, when darkness had parted and swallowed him—as he was now being swallowed by these Stygian waters?

*Huaraches,* the sign had said, and *Serapes.*

Berta stared at him across her Tom Collins. He could not look at her. He toyed with the straw in his Cuba Libre. He whistled soundlessly, then bit the inside of his lip absently. He looked off across the Avenida Revolución. Tijuana throbbed with an undercurrent of immorality and availability. Anything you might want. A ten-year-old virgin—male or female. Authentic French perfume minus the tariff. Weed. Smack. Peyote caps. Bongo drums, hand-carved Don Quixotes, sandals, bullfights, jai alai, horse races, toteboard betting or off-track betting, your photograph wearing a sombrero sitting astride a weary jackass. Jackass on jackass, a study in dung. Strip shows where the nitty-gritty consists of the pudenda flat-out on the bar-top for convenient dining. Private shows with big dogs and tiny gentlemen and women with breasts as big as casaba melons. Divorces, marriages, tuck-and-roll auto seat covers. Or a quick abortion.

It had been lunacy for them to come down here. But they'd had to. Berta had needed the D&C, and now it was over, and she was feeling just fine thank you, just fine. So they had stopped for a drink. She should be resting in a motel halfway between San Diego and Los Angeles, but he knew she wanted to talk. There was so much to talk *about.* So now they sat in the street café and he could not talk to her. He could not even look at her. He could not explain that he was a man trapped within himself. He knew she was aware of it, but like all women she needed him to come only far enough outside himself to let her share his fear. Just far enough that he could not make it. She needed him to verbalize it, to ask for it—if not help then—companionship through his country of mental terrors. But he could not give her what she wanted. He could not give her himself.

Their affair had been subject to the traditional rules. A lotta laughs, a lotta passion, and then she had gotten pregnant.

And in their mutual concern, something deeper had passed between them. There was a chance, for the first time in Niven's life, that he might cleave to someone and find not disillusionment, derangement and disaster, but reality and a little peace.

She had arranged the abortion, he had paid for it, and now they were together here, as she waited for him to speak. Voiceless, imprisoned in his past and his sense of the reality of the world in which he had been *forced* to live, Niven knew he was letting her slip away.

But could not help himself.

"Jerry." He wanted to pretend she had not spoken, knowing she was trying to help him get started. But he found himself looking up. She wasn't beautiful, but he liked the face very much. It was a face he could live with. She smiled. "Where are we going, Jerry?"

He knew what he had to answer to please her, to win her, but he said, "I don't know what that means."

"It means: there's nothing artificial or unwanted holding us together any more. *Or* holding us apart. What do we do now?"

He knew what he had to answer to please her, to win her, but he said, "We do whatever we want to do. Don't push on me too hard."

Her eyes flashed for an instant. "I'm not *pushing*, Jerry, I'm inquiring. I'm thirty-five and I'm unattached and it's getting frightening going to bed alone without a future. Does that seem rational to you?"

"Rational, but unnecessary. You've got a few good weeks left in you."

"It isn't funny time for me, Jerry. I have to know. Have you got room in your world for me?"

He knew what he had to answer to please her, to win her, but he said, "There's barely room enough in my world for *me*, baby. And if you knew what my world was like, you wouldn't want to come into it. You see before you the last of the cynics, the last of the misogynists, the last of the bitter men. I look out on a landscape littered with the refuse of a misspent youth. All my gods and goddesses had feet of shit, and there they lie, like Etruscan statuary, the noses bashed off. Believe me, Berta, you don't want into my world."

Her face was lined in resignation now. "Unraveling the charming syntax, what you're telling me is: we had a good time and we made a small mistake, but it's corrected now, so get lost."

"No, I'm saying—"

But she was up from the curbside table and stalking across the street. He threw a bill down on the tablecloth and went after her.

She managed to keep ahead of him. Mostly because he wanted to give her time to cool off. As they passed a narrow side alley he pulled abreast of her, taking her arm gently, and she allowed him to draw her into its shadowed coolness. "All it takes is believing, Jerry! Is that so much to ask?"

"Believe," he snapped, the instant fury that always lay beneath the surface of his charm boiling up. "Believe. The same stupid mealy-mouth crap they tell the rednecks in the boondocks. Believe in this, and believe in that, and have faith, and holy holy you'll get your ass saved. Well, I *don't* believe."

"Then how can any woman believe in *you?*"

It was more than anger that forced the words from him. It was a helplessness that translated itself into cynical ruthlessness. "I'd say that was *her* problem."

She pulled her arm free and, turning without really seeing where she was going, she plunged down the alley. Down a flight of dim steps, and on again, a lower level of the same alley. "Berta!" he called after her.

*Huaraches,* the sign had said, and *Serapes.*

A shop in a dingy back alley in a seedy border town more noted for street-corner whores than for wrinkled and leathery tellers-of-the-future who sold *Huaraches* and *Serapes* in their spare time. But he had quickly followed her, trying to find a way out of his own inarticulateness, to settle the senseless quarrel they were having and salvage this one good thing from a past filled with broken glass. He wanted to tell her his need was not a temporary thing, not a matter of good times only, of transitory bodies reaching and never quite finding one another. He wanted to tell her that he had lost all belief in his world, a world that seemed incapable of bringing to him any richness, any meaning, any vitality. But his words—if they came at all—he knew would come with ill-restrained fury, with anger and sharpness, insulting her, forcing her to walk away as she now walked away.

He had followed her, down the alley.

And the old, wizened, papyrus-tough Mexican had limped out of his shop, bent almost double with age, like a blue-belly lizard, all alertness and cunning, and had offered to tell them of the future.

"No thanks," Niven had said, catching up to her at that moment.

But she had tossed her head, defiance, and had entered the shop, leaving him standing in the alley. Niven had followed her, hoping she would turn in an instant, and come out again, and he would find the words. But she had gone deeper into the musky dimness of the shop, and the old prognosticator had begun casting the runes, had begun mixing the herbs and bits of offal and vileness he averred were necessary for truth and brightness in the visions. A bit of wild dog hair. A strip of flesh from the instep of a drowned child. Three drops of menstrual blood from a whore. The circular sucker from the underside of a polyp's tentacle. Other things. Unspeakable, nameless, foul-smelling, terrible.

And then, strangely, he had said he would not tell the future of Berta . . . but of Niven.

There in the fetid closeness of a shop whose dimensions were lost in dusk, the old Mexican said Niven was a man without belief, without faith, without trust, and so was damned; a man doomed and forsaken. He said all the dark and tongueless things Niven had never been able to say of himself. And Niven, in fury, in frenzy brought on by a hurricane of truth, smashed the old man, swung across the little round table with all the strength in his big body, clubbed the old man, and in the same movement swept the strange mixed ingredients from the filthy table, as Berta screamed—from somewhere far away.

And in that instant, a silent explosion. A force and impact that had hurled him out of himself. In that timeless, breathless instant Niven had been there/not-there. He had somehow inexplicably been moved *elsewhere*. In a bowl, in a valley, in a land, in a time or place or somewhere facing a minotaur. A creature of mythology, a creature from the past of man's fables.

*Huaraches*, the sign had said, and *Serapes*.

Facing a live minotaur just a moment ago. Facing the creature that had left the world before there had been a name to fit the men that Niven had become. A god without worshippers, this minotaur. In a world that did not believe, facing a man who did not believe.

And in that instant—like the previous instant of truth—Niven was *all* the men who had forsaken their gods. Who had allowed the world to tell them they were alone; and believed it. Now he had to face one of the lost gods. A god who now sought revenge on the race of Men who had devised machines that would banish them from the real world.

Down and down and down into the waters of nowhere Niven plunged, all thoughts simply one thought, all memories crashing and jarring, all merged and melded and impinging upon a dense tapestry of seaweed images.

His breath seemed to clog in his throat. His stomach bulged with the amount of water he had swallowed, with the pressure on his temples, with the blackness that deluged him behind his eyes. Niven felt memory depart and consciousness at once returning—and leaving. He was coming back from the past to awareness, only to let it slip away finally as he drowned.

He made feeble swimming motions, overhand movements of arms that had sensation only by recall, not by his own volition. He moved erratically in the water, as thick as gelatin, and his movement toward the bottomless bottom was arrested. He moved upward through the water now, and saw a dim light, far ahead and above him.

An eternity. There. Toward it he struggled, and when he thought it was ended, he reached a ledge. He pulled himself toward it, and the dark water seeped through him till he was limp and dying. Then his head broke water. He was in an underground cavern. He spewed out mouthfuls of warm, evil-tasting water.

For a very long time he lay half on the ledge, half in the water, till someone came and pulled him up. Niven lay there on his stomach, learning to live again, while the one who had saved him stood silently waiting. Niven tried to get to his feet, and he was helped. He could not see who the man was, though he could feel a long robe in the dimness, and there was a light, a sort of corona that seemed to come dimly from the man. Then together, with the man supporting him, Niven went away from there, and they climbed for a long while between walls of stone, to the world that was outside.

He stood in the light, and was tired and sad and blinded by things he did not believe. Then the man left him, and as he walked slowly away, Niven recognized the beard and the infinitely sad eyes and the way he was dressed, and even the light.

And Jesus left him, with a sad smile, and Niven stood alone, for another time that was long, and empty.

Once, late that night, he thought he heard the bull-ram horn of Odin, ringing across this dim, shadowed land, but he could not be sure. And once he heard a sound of something passing, and when he opened his eyes to look it was a cat-headed woman, and he thought *Bast,* and she slipped smoothly away into the darkness without saying a word to him. And toward morning there was a light in the sky that seemed to be a burning chariot, Phaëthon the charioteer, Helios's burning chariot, but that was probably the effects of the drowning, the hunger, the sorrow. He could not be certain.

So he wandered. And time passed without ever moving. In the land without a name; and *his* name was Niven; but it was no more important a name than Apollo or Vishnu or Baal, for it was not a name men believed in. It was only the name of a man who had not believed. And if gods cannot be called back, when their names have been known, then how can a man whose name was *never* known be called back?

For him, his god had been Berta, but he had not given her an opportunity to believe in him. He had prevented her from having faith in him, and so there were no believers for a man named Niven, as there were no true believers for Serapis or Perseus or Mummu.

Very late the next night, Niven realized he would always, *always* live in this terrible Coventry where old gods went to die; gods who would never speak to him; and with no hope of return.

For as he had believed in no god . . .

No god believed in him.

*Kurt Weill and Maxwell Anderson
wrote, "Maybe God's gone away,
forgetting His promise He made that day:
and we're lost out here in the stars." And
maybe He/She's just waiting for the right
signal to come back, whaddaya think?*

# Neon

Truly concerned whether or not he would live, the surgeons labored for many hours over Roger Charna. They cryogenically removed the pain areas in his anterior hypothalamic nucleus, and froze parts of him to be worked on later. Finally, it seemed they would be successful, and he would live. They bestowed on him three special gifts to this end: a collapsible metal finger, the little finger of the left hand; a vortex spiral of neon tubing in his chest, it glowed bright red when activated; and a right eye that came equipped with sensors that fed informational load from both the infrared and ultraviolet ends of the spectrum.

He was discharged from the hospital and tried to reestablish the life-pattern he'd known before the accident, but it was useless. Ruth's family had sent her abroad, and he had the feeling she had been more than anxious to go. She could not have helped seeing the Sunday supplement piece on the operation. His employers at the apartment house had been pleasant, but they made good sense when they said as a doorman he was useless to them. They gave him a month's termination wages.

He had no difficulty getting another job, happily enough. The proprietors of a bookstore on Times Square felt he was a marvelous publicity item, and they hired him on the spot. He worked the seven o'clock to three A.M. shift, selling paperbacks and souvenirs to tourists and the theater crowd.

The first message he had from her was in the lightflesh of the *Newsweek* sign on the other side of 46th Street. He was sweeping out the front of the bookstore when he looked up and saw ROGER! UP HERE! ROGER! spelled out in the rapidly changing lights. It spasmed and changed and became an advertisement for timely news. He blinked and shook his head. Then he saw the crimson spiral shining through his shirt, flickering on and off. There was a soft cotton candy feeling in his stomach. He swept the cigarette butts and dustballs furiously . . . out onto the sidewalk and across the sidewalk and into the gutter. He walked back to the bookstore, looking up and over his shoulder only as he stepped through the doorway. The sign was as he had always seen it before. Nothing strange there.

At his dinner break, he walked to the papaya stand near the corner of 42nd and Broadway and stood at the counter chatting with Caruso (which was not his name, but because he wanted to become an opera singer and went into the basement of the juice stand and sang arias from *Il Trovatore* and *I Pagliacci*, that was the name by which he was known).

"How do you feel?" Caruso asked him.

"Oh, I'm okay. I'm a little tired."

"You been to the doctor?"

"No. They said I didn't need to come around unless I hurt or something seemed wrong."

"You got to take care of yourself. You can't fool around with your health, yeah?" He was genuinely concerned.

"How're *you?*" Roger Charna asked. Caruso wrapped the semi-transparent square of serrated-edged paper around the hot dog and handed the bunned frank to him. Charna reached for the plastic squeeze-bottle of mustard.

"Couldn't be better," Caruso said. He drew off a large papaya juice and slid it across the counter. "I'm into Gilbert & Sullivan. *Pirates of Penzance.* I hear there's a big Gilbert & Sullivan revival coming on."

Roger Charna ate without making a reply. He felt very sorry for Caruso. When he had first met him, the boy was not quite twenty, working at the stand, high hopes for a singing career. Now he was going to fat, his hair was thinning prematurely, and the dreams were only warm-bed whispers to impress the girls Caruso hustled off Times Square. It would come to nothing. Ten years from now, should Roger come back, he knew Caruso would still be there, singing in the basement, pulling 35¢ slices of pizza (that would probably cost $1.25) from the big Grimaldi oven, filling the sugar jars, carrying cases of Coke syrup downstairs to be stored, the dreams losing their color, gravity pulling it all down.

Then he realized *he* might still be on Times Square, ten years from now. The pity backed up in its channel and washed over him.

The 7-Up sign winked once and began pulsing. His chest spiral picked up the beat. Pain hit him. Roger looked up and the sign was flickering on and off. His chest spiral had changed color, now pulsed deep blue in sync with the 7-Up sign, right through his shirt. The girl on the sign moved smoothly and directly to stare down at him. Her mouth began moving. Roger Charna could not read lips.

"Caruso." The counterman turned from reloading the hot dog broiler and smiled. "Huh?" Roger pointed across the street, up at the 7-Up sign. "Take a look over there and tell me what you see." Caruso moved to the end of the counter and stared up. "What?" Roger pointed to the sign. "The sign, the 7-Up sign." Caruso looked again. "What am I supposed to see?" Roger sighed and finished his hot dog. "I think I'll go see the doctor tomorrow morning."

"You got to take care of yourself. You been a very sick guy, yeah?"

Roger nodded and laid out the coins in payment for the dog and papaya. Caruso pushed them back with the heel of his hand. "Iss onna house." Roger found himself still nodding.

The coins back in his pants pocket, he walked up Broadway to the bookstore, wishing the *New York Times* still had its neon newsservice on the island at 42nd Street.

It might all come clear if whoever was trying to reach him had free access to unlimited language.

By this time Roger knew either someone was trying to talk to him, or he was going insane. Odds were bad.

He was invited to a party. He went because they asked him. He paid a dollar at the door: a woman who had had her left breast removed for what he found out later were non-carcinogenic reasons, took the money. She was topless; she smiled a great deal. He also discovered, later in the evening, that these people had answered an advertisement in an underground newspaper. It had been headed with a photograph from Tod Browning's *Freaks*—pinhead twins joined at the rump. Roger did not feel at ease with them.

In the group was a man who sought carnal knowledge of blimps. He had been arrested three times for trying to fuck the Goodyear dirigible. Even among his own kind he was looked on with distaste; unable to find the species of sex partners his pathology demanded, he had grown steadily more perverted and had taken to attacking helicopters; the mere mention of an autogyro gave him a noticeable erection.

He was offered a sloe gin fizz in a pink frosted glass by a young woman who removed her glass eye and sucked on it while discussing the moral imperatives of the sponge boycott in Brooksville, Florida. She rolled the eye around on her tongue and Roger walked away quickly.

"The dollar was for the spaghetti," explained a man with a prosthetic arm and a leather cone where his nose should have been. "My wife would have told you about that when she invited you, because you're a celebrity and we certainly don't want to charge *you*, but if we made an exception, well, *every*one would want the dollar back. But you can have as much spaghetti as you want." He pulled the cone forward on its elastic band and scratched at the raw, red scar-tissue beneath. "Actually, I'll tell you what: come on in the bathroom for a couple of minutes and I can slip the buck back to you, they'll never know." Roger slipped sidewise around a bookcase and left the man scratching.

The room was rather nice, large and airy, filled with kinetic sculptures and found object constructs that covered the walls and dominated the floor space. There were half a hundred light paintings of bent neon tubing and fluorescent designs. They looked expensive. Roger wondered why his dollar was necessary.

Seven people were seated at the feet of a moon-faced woman perched on a three-legged aluminum stool. The entire left side of her face was blotched with a huge strawberry birthmark. She had a coatimundi on her shoulder; it was nibbling leaves of lettuce she had safety-pinned to her dress like epaulets.

A man who bore a startling resemblance to a plucked carrion bird snagged Roger's arm as he moved toward the front door. He stammered hideously. "Uh . . . uh . . . uh . . ." he babbled, till something snapped in his right cheek and he launched into a convoluted diatribe that began with a confession of his having been defrocked as a molecular biologist, veered insanely through a recitation of the man's affection for Bermuda shorts, and reached a far horizon at which he said, with eyes rolling: "Now everybody doesn't know this," and he pulled Roger closer, "but the universe, the entire frigging universe is going to collapse around everyone's ears in just seventy-two billion years. I smoke a lot."

Roger skinned loose, and turning, thumped against a dwarf who had been surreptitiously trying to look up the skirt of a young woman with a harelip. "Excuse me," Roger said, assisting the dwarf to his feet. He brushed him off and started to move, but the dwarf had thrown both arms around Roger's leg. "They remaindered me," the dwarf said, rather pathetically. "Before, I swear *before* the damned book had a chance, they remaindered me. Can you perceive the pain, the ex*quis*ite pain of being carried into Marboro's on Third and seeing a stack, a virtual, a veritable, I mean motherGod a phallic Annapurna *moun*tain of copies of the finest, what I mean the sin*cer*est study of the anopheles mosquito ever written. That book was a work of love, excuse me for using the word but I mean to say *ardor;* and those butchers at Doubleday, those mau-maus, my *God,* they're vivi*sec*tionists, for Pete's sake . . . if he were alive today, Ferdinand de Lesseps would absolutely *whirl* in his grave."

"I have to go to the bathroom," Roger said, trying to pry his leg loose. The dwarf unwound and sat there looking frayed. Roger smiled self-consciously and moved away. He started back for the door.

Everything dropped into the ultraviolet.

The little finger of his left hand began to resonate with the tinny voice of Times Square Caruso hashing out "I'm Called Little Buttercup" as the neon spiral in his chest gave him a shock and began flickering in gradually bloodier shades of crimson. Caruso seguéd into Kurt Weill's "Pirate Jenny," a tune Roger was certain the papaya juice stand attendant had never heard.

The ultraviolet smelled purple; it sounded like the nine-pound hammers of Chinese laborers striking the rails of the Union Pacific Railroad; it sprang out as auras and halos and nimbuses around everyone in the room; Roger clutched his chest.

His eyes rolled up in his head and the images burned there like the braziers of Torquemada's dungeons. He blinked and his eyes rolled down again bringing with them images as burning bright as the crosses of Ku Klux Klansmen in Selma, Alabama: it was all in his right eye. He feared what lay ahead in the infrared. But that never happened; it was all in the ultraviolet.

The room burned around the edges, deep purple and a kind of red that he realized—with some embarrassment—matched up only with the red just inside the slit in the head of his penis during his recurring bouts with prostatitis. Every neon sculpture and fluorescent painting in the room was jangling at him. A half a hundred roadsigns from someone who was trying to talk to him. *I believe I'm a closet psychotic,* he thought, but nothing stopped.

The neon tubes on the walls writhed with the burning edges of the soft-boiled sun as it bubbled down into the black horizon. They re-formed and slopped color words of pink and vermilion across the airy walls.

ROGER, YOU'RE MAKING IT MURDER TO GET THROUGH TO YOU.

He tried running, but all the movement was inside his skin; none of it got to the outside.

I CAN'T BELIEVE YOU PREFER THE COMPANY OF THESE DIS-GUSTING PERVERTS. LOOK, I LOVE YOU, THAT'S THE LONG, THE SHORT AND THE COLOR OF IT, ROGER. WHAT SAY?

His metal little finger was singing the bell song from *Lakmé* and he hated it. His chest spiral was bubbling and he had the immediate fear his shirt would catch fire. All the women in the room were frozen in place, their hair vibrating like cilia, each strand standing up and away individually, emitting purple sparks like St. Elmo's fire. The men looked like X-rays of rickets cases.

"Who are you?" Roger said in a choked voice.

I THOUGHT YOU'D NEVER ASK. I'M THE RIGHT WOMAN FOR YOU. GOD KNOWS YOU'VE HAD A CRUMMY TIME OF IT, AND I'M SENT TO MAKE IT EASIER FOR YOU. IT'S THE REAL LOVE YOU'VE BEEN WAITING FOR, ROGER.

"Where are you?"

RIGHT HERE. IN THE LIGHTS.

"I'm going to be sick."

RIGHT HERE, COME ON, ROGER, JUST FIRM UP NOW!

"Haven't I suffered enough already?"

ROGER, SELF-PITY JUST WON'T GET IT. IT'S TRUE YOU'VE SUF-FERED, AND THAT'S WHY YOU WIN THE LOTTERY OF LOVE WITH ME, BUT YOU'VE GOT TO STOP BEING MAUDLIN ABOUT IT.

"Not only am I a put-together thing, a righteous freak, but now I'm going completely insane."

ROGER, WILL YOU HAVE A LITTLE TRUST, FOR GOD'S SAKE? I'M PART OF THE REPAYMENT FOR WHAT'S HAPPENED TO YOU. ALL IT TAKES IS BELIEF AND A COUPLE OF STEPS.

He felt his right hand groping in the empty air around his right side—while his left hand sang "Pace, Pace, Mio Dio," from *La Forza del Destino*—and he came up with an aquamarine Italian marble egg.

"Listen, I think you're terrific," Roger said, playing for time.

YOU'RE PLAYING FOR TIME.

*She's on to me,* Roger thought desperately. He flung the Italian marble egg at the neon wall sculptures, it struck, geysers of sparks erupted, a curtain caught fire, a woman's dress went up in a puff of Gucci, people began shrieking, the ultraviolet dissipated in an instant, everything returned to normal, Roger was scared out of his mind . . . and he ran out of there as fast as he could.

His finger had grown hoarse, and finally shut up.

Roger called in sick and begged off work for a few days. They were understanding, but the big Labor Day weekend was coming up, they'd laid in a large stock of Sicilian switchblades and copies of the steamier works of Akbar del Piombo and Anonymous in the *Travelers' Companion* series, and they expected him—neon coil, weird eye and metal finger included—on the ready line when the marks, kadodies and reubens fresh from Michigan's Ionia State Fair descended on sinful Times Square. Roger mumbled various okays and went for extended walks along the night-hot Hudson River Drive.

The big Spry sign blinking across the Hudson from Jersey caught his eye.

YOU ARE THE DAMNEDEST, MOST OBSTINATE HUMAN BEING I HAVE EVER ENCOUNTERED, said the Spry sign, forming words it was clearly incapable of forming.

Roger began running . . . blindly along the breakwater. The sign gave him no peace. It continued jabbering at him. ROGER! FOR CRINE OUT LOUD, ROGER, WILL YOU STOP JUST A MOMENT AND LISTEN TO ME!

He ran up West 114th Street, stumbling over a gentleman of the evening who was lying half in, half out of the doorway of an apartment building. Roger excused himself and would have waited for a response to make sure he had not damaged the fellow, but the man had somehow gotten his tongue stuck deep inside the neck of an empty Boone's Farm Apple Wine bottle, and speech was beyond him.

Roger grabbed an IRT express downtown, and sitting in the

clattering hell of the subway car he tried to ignore the overhead fluorescents that babbled I'M TRYING TO SAVE YOUR SOUL, YOU CLOWN. I'M IN LOVE WITH YOU. ARE YOU BEING ASSAULTED BY LOVE EVERY DAY SO MUCH YOU CAN TURN DOWN A TERRIFIC OFFER LIKE THIS?

Roger closed his eyes. It didn't help. His chest coil was obviously activated and it was pulsing in time with the overheads. He opened his eyes and with a sudden weariness that had swept over him like a sea of sand he opened his mouth and gave a primal scream. No one in the subway car noticed.

He got out on Times Square and, of course, she was everywhere. In the signs of the sea food restaurant on the other side of 42nd Street, in the marquees of the skin flick theaters, in the neon of the pornobook shops, in every flashing, bubbling, flickering, hallucinating light that made up the visual pollution by which Times Square proclaimed its wares and snagged its victims.

"Okay!" he howled, standing in the middle of the sidewalk as the mobs split around him. "Okay! I quit! I've had enough! I give up! Name it, just name it, I'll do it! I've had the course! I'm only human and I've had it!"

TERRIFIC! AT LONG LAST! said the neon come-ons. THERE'S A LADDER OVER THERE BY THAT MOVIE, SEE IT?

Roger looked and, yes, there was a twenty-foot ladder up under the marquee of a movie house playing a double bill comprising *Leather Lovers* and *Rebecca of Sinnybrook Farm.* "Now what?" Roger said, softly.

I CAN'T HEAR YOU, the neon replied.

"I said: What the hell now, you goddam pain in the ass!" he screamed, at the highest decibel count he had ever achieved, his throat going raw. People shied away.

CLIMB UP THE LADDER, YOU SWEET THING.

"Oh, God," Roger mumbled, "this is just terrible; just terrible. I hate this a lot."

But he climbed the ladder, just as the assistant manager of the theater—a zit-laden young man in a soiled tuxedo and argyle socks—emerged from the lobby carrying the heavy boxes of marquee letters to change the bill. "Hey! Hey, you! Weirdo, what the gahdam flop hell you think you're doin'? Get offa there you freako-pervo-devo!"

Roger went up and up, and when he was standing at the top he was on a level with the neon theater name. It said, very suddenly, TAKE ME! TAKE ME NOW!

And for no particular reason Roger could name, he reached out with both hands, swung himself onto the marquee, and—ripping open his shirt so his coil was exposed—he slammed himself against the love-message.

There was a blinding flash of light that pulsed and continued flashing like endless novae, over and over and over resembling—said a narcotics squad cop who had worked on the ski patrol at Stowe, Vermont—who happened to be emerging from the theater handcuffed to two Queens junkies he'd caught scoring in the highest row of the balcony—resembling nothing so much as the sunlight glassflashing off the thin crust of ice-over-powder at the summit of a snow-covered mountain.

Someone else said it was the exact color of tuna fish salad.

But when the light faded, Roger Charna was gone, all save the little finger of his left hand, lying on the sidewalk humming a medley of tunes from *The Student Prince, Blossom Time* and *The Desert Song,* a very peculiar eyeball that seemed to have developed a terrible case of glaucoma, and a dollar and thirty-five cents in change.

Someone else said it was the exact color of the cardboard they used to reinforce his shirts when they came from the Chinese hand laundry.

And one thing more.

Every neon sign in Times Square had a new color added to its spectrum. It seemed to reside somewhere between silver and orange, bled off into the ultraviolet and the infrared at one and the same time, had tinges of vermilion at the top and jade at the bottom, and resembled no other color ever seen by human eyes. The color sounded like a Louisville Slugger connecting solidly with a hardball in that special certain way that produces a line drive high into the right center bleachers. It smelled like a forest of silver pines just after the rain, with scents of camomile, juniper, melissa and mountain gentian thrown in. It felt like the flesh of a three-week-old baby's instep. It tasted like lithograph ink, but there are people who *like* the taste of lithograph ink.

Someone said it was the exact color of caring.

* * *

On another plane of existence, where things were vastly different from those in the world that had given Roger Charna his neon chest spiral, observations were made and the new color was seen.

"There it is," they said.

"Yep, there it is," they said.

"Took them long enough," they said.

"Well, now that they're ready we can go and show them how to do it," they said.

"They're going to like this," they said.

"A lot," they said.

And they set out immediately, and it took no time at all to get there, and when they arrived they changed everything and everyone enjoyed it a lot.

And everyone said the angels were the exact color of charna, which wasn't a bad name for it at all.

*Have you ever noticed: the most vocal superpatriots are the old men who send young men off to die? Well, it might just be that the heaviest reverential act when worshipping the god of war is to be the biggest mutherin traitor of them all. Check Spiro, I think he's having a seizure.*

# Basilisk

*What though the Moor the basilisk has slain*
*And pinned him lifeless to the sandy plain,*
*Up through the spear the subtle venom flies,*
*The hand imbibes it, and the victor dies.*

                    —Lucan: *Pharsalia*
                (Marcus Annaeus Lucanus,
                        A.D. 39–65)

Returning from a night patrol beyond the perimeter of the firebase, Lance Corporal Vernon Lestig fell into a trail trap set by hostiles. He was bringing up the rear, covering the patrol's withdrawal from recently overrun sector eight, when he fell too far behind and lost the bush track. Though he had no way of knowing he was paralleling the patrol's trail, thirty yards off their left flank, he kept moving forward hoping to intersect them. He did not see the pungi stakes set at cruel angles, frosted with poison, tilted for top-point efficiency, sharpened to infinity.

Two set close together penetrated the barricade of his boot; the first piercing the arch and his weight driving it up and out to emerge just below the anklebone, still inside the boot; the other ripping through the sole and splintering against the fibula above the heel, without breaking the skin.

Every circuit shorted out, every light bulb blew, every vacuum imploded, snakes shed their skins, wagon wheels creaked, plate-glass windows shattered, dentist drills ratcheted across nerve ends, vomit burned tracks up through throats, hymens were torn, fingernails bent double dragged down blackboards, water came to a boil; lava. Nova pain. Lestig's heart stopped, lubbed, began again, stuttered; his brain went dead refusing to accept the load; all senses came to full stop; he staggered sidewise with his untouched left foot, pulling one of the pungi stakes out of the ground, and was unconscious even during the single movement; and fainted, simply directly fainted with the pain.

This was happening: great black gap-mawed beast padding through outer darkness toward him. On a horizonless journey through myth, coming toward the moment *before* the piercing of flesh. Lizard dragon beast with eyes of oil-slick pools, ultraviolet death colors smoking in their depths. Corded silk-flowing muscles sliding beneath the black hairless hide, trained sprinter from a lost land, smoothest movements of choreographed power. The never-sleeping guardian of the faith, now gentlestepping down through mists of potent barriers erected to separate men from their masters.

In that moment before boot touched the bamboo spike, the basilisk passed through the final veils of confounding time and space and dimension and thought, to assume palpable shape in the forest world of Vernon Lestig. And in the translation was changed, altered wonderfully. The black, thick and oily hide of the death-breath dragon beast shimmered, heat lightning across flat prairie land, golden flashes seen spattering beyond mountain peaks, and the great creature was a thousand colored. Green diamonds burned up from the skin of the basilisk, the deadly million eyes of a nameless god. Rubies gorged with the water-thin blood of insects sealed in amber from the dawn of time pulsed there. Golden jewels changing from instant to instant, shape and scent and hue . . . they were there in the tapestry mosaic of the skin picture. A delicate, subtle, gaudy flashmaze kaleidoscope of flesh, taut over massive muscled threats.

The basilisk was in the world.

And Lestig had yet to experience his pain.

The creature lifted a satin-padded paw and laid it against the points of the pungi stakes. Slowly, the basilisk relaxed and the stakes pierced the rough sensitive blackmoon shapes of the pads. Dark, steaming serum flowed down over the stakes, mingling with the Oriental poison. The basilisk withdrew its paw and the twin wounds healed in an instant, closed over and were gone.

Were gone. Bunching of muscles, a leap into air, a caldron roiling of dark air, and the basilisk sprang up into nothing and was gone. Was gone.

As the moment came to an exhalation of end, and Vernon Lestig walked onto the pungi stakes.

It is a well-known fact that one whose blood slakes the thirst of the *vrykolakas*, the vampire, himself becomes one of the drinkers of darkness, becomes a celebrant of the master deity, becomes himself possessed of the powers of the disciples of that deity.

The basilisk had not come from the vampires, nor were his powers those of the blood drinkers. It was not by chance that the basilisk's master had sent him to recruit Lance Corporal Vernon Lestig. There is an order to the darkside universe.

He fought consciousness, as if on some cellular level he knew what pain awaited him with the return of his senses. But the red tide washed higher, swallowed more and more of his deliquescent body, and finally the pain thundered in from the blood-sea, broke in a long, curling comber and coenesthesia was upon him totally. He screamed and the scream went on and on for a long time, till they came back to him and gave him an injection of something that thinned the pain, and he lost contact with the chaos that had been his right foot.

When he came back again, it was dark and at first he thought it was night; but when he opened his eyes it was still dark. His right foot itched mercilessly. He went back to sleep, no coma, sleep.

When he came back again, it was still night and he opened his eyes and he realized he was blind. He felt straw under his left hand and knew he was on a pallet and knew he had been captured; and then he started to cry because he knew, without even reaching down to find out, that they had amputated his foot. Perhaps his entire leg. He cried about not being able to run down in the car for a pint of half-and-half just before dinner; he cried about not being able to go out to a movie without people trying not to see what had happened to him; he cried about Teresa and what she would have to decide now; he cried about the way clothes would look on him; he cried about the things he would have to say every time; he cried about shoes; and so many other things. He cursed his parents and his patrol and the hostiles and the men who had sent him here and he wanted, wished, prayed desperately that any one of them could change places with him. And when he was long finished crying, and simply wanted to die, they came for him, and took him to a hooch where they began questioning him. In the night. The night he carried with him.

They were an ancient people, with a heritage of enslavement, and so for them anguish had less meaning than the thinnest whisper of crimson cloud high above a desert planet of the farthest star in the sky. But they knew the uses to which anguish could be put, and for them there was no evil in doing so: for a people with a heritage of enslavement, evil is a concept of those who forged the shackles, not those who wore them. In the name of freedom, no monstrousness is too great.

So they tortured Lestig, and he told them what they wanted to know. Every scrap of information he knew. Locations and movements and plans and defenses and the troop strength and the sophistication of armaments and the nature of his mission and rumors he'd picked up and his name and his rank and every serial number he could think of, and the street address of his home in Kansas, and the sequence of his driver's license, and his gas credit card number and the telephone number of Teresa. He told them everything.

As if it were a reward for having held nothing back, a gummed gold star placed beside his chalked name on a blackboard in a kindergarten schoolroom, his eyesight began to come back slightly. Flickering, through a haze of gray; just enough light permitted through to show him shapes, the change from daylight to darkness; and it grew stronger, till he could actually *see* for whole minutes at a time . . . then blindness again. His sight came and went, and when they realized he could see them, they resumed the interrogations on a more strenuous level. But he had nothing left to tell; he had emptied himself.

But they kept at him. They threatened to hammer bamboo slivers into his damaged eyeballs. They hung him up on a shoulder-high wooden wall, his arms behind him, circulation cut off, weight pulling the arms from their shoulder sockets, and they beat him across the belly with lengths of bamboo, with bojitsu sticks. He could not even cry any more. They had given him no food and no water and he could not manufacture tears. But his breath came in deep, husking spasms from his chest, and one of the interrogators made the mistake of stepping forward to grab Lestig's head by the hair, yanking it up, leaning in close to ask another question, and Lestig—falling falling—exhaled deeply, struggling to live; and there was that breath, and a terrible thing happened.

When the reconnaissance patrol from the firebase actualized control of the hostile command position, when the Huey choppers dropped into the clearing, they advised Supermart HQ that every hostile but one in the immediate area was dead, that a Marine Lance

Corporal named Lestig, Vernon C. 526-90-5416, had been found lying unconscious on the dirt floor of a hooch containing the bodies of nine enemy officers who had died horribly, most peculiarly, sickeningly, you've gotta see what this place looks like, HQ, jesus you ain't gonna believe what it smells like in here, you gotta see what these slopes look like, it musta been some terrible disease that could of done this kinda thing to 'em, the new Lieutenant got really sick an' puked and what do you want us to do with the one guy that crawled off into the bushes before *it* got him, his face is melting, and the troops're scared shitless and . . .

And they pulled the recon group out immediately and sent in the Intelligence section, who sealed the area with Top Security, and they found out from the one with the rotting face—just before he died—that Lestig had talked, and they medivacked Lestig back to a field hospital and then to Saigon and then to Tokyo and then to San Diego and they decided to court-martial him for treason and conspiring with the enemy, and the case made the papers big, and the court-martial was held behind closed doors and after a long time Lestig emerged with an honorable and they paid him off for the loss of his foot and the blindness and he went back to the hospital for eleven months and in a way regained his sight, though he had to wear smoked glasses.

And then he went home to Kansas.

Between Syracuse and Garden City, sitting close to the coach window, staring out through the film of roadbed filth, Lestig watched the ghost image of the train he rode superimposed over flatland Kansas slipping past outside. The mud-swollen Arkansas River was a thick, brown underline to the horizon.

"Hey, you Corporal Lestig?"

Vernon Lestig refocused his eyes and saw the wraith in the window. He turned and the sandwich butcher with his tray of candy bars, soft drinks, ham&cheese on white or rye, newspapers and *Reader's Digests,* suspended from his chest by a strap around the neck, was looking at him.

"No thanks," Lestig said, refusing the merchandise.

"No, hey, really, aren't you that Corporal Lestig—" He uncurled a newspaper from the roll in the tray and opened it quickly. "Yeah, sure, here you are. See?"

Lestig had seen most of the newspaper coverage, but this was local, Wichita. He fumbled for change. "How much?"

"Ten cents." There was a surprised look on the butcher's face, but it washed down into a smile as he said, understanding it, "You been out of touch in the service, didn't even remember what a paper cost, huh?"

Lestig gave him two nickels and turned abruptly to the window, folding the paper back. He read the article. It was a stone. There was a note referring to an editorial, and he turned to that page and read it. People were outraged, it said. Enough secret trials, it said. We must face up to our war crimes, it said. The effrontery of the military and the government, it said. Coddling, even ennobling traitors and killers, it said. He let the newspaper slide out of his hands. It clung to his lap for a moment then fell apart to the floor.

"I didn't say it before, but they should of shot you, you want *my* opinion!" The butcher said it, going fast, fast through the aisle, coming back the other way, gaining the end of the car and gone. Lestig did not turn around. Even wearing the smoked glasses to protect his damaged eyes, he could see too clearly. He thought about the months of blindness, and wondered again what had happened in that hooch, and considered how much better off he might be if he were *still* blind.

The Rock Island Line was a mighty good road, the Rock Island Line was the way to go. To go home. The land outside dimmed for him, as things frequently dimmed, as though the repairwork to his eyes was only temporary, a reserve generator cut in from time to time to sustain the power-feed to his vision, and dimming as the drain drank too deep. Then light seeped back in and he could see again. But there was a mist over his eyes, over the land.

Somewhere else, through another mist, a great beast sat haunch-back, dripping chromatic fire from jeweled hide, nibbling at something soft in its paw, talons extended from around blackmoon pads. Watching, breathing, waiting for Lestig's vision to clear.

He had rented the car in Wichita, and driven back the sixty-five miles to Grafton. The Rock Island Line no longer stopped there. Passenger trains were almost a thing of the past in Kansas.

Lestig drove silently. No radio sounds accompanied him. He did not hum, he did not cough, he drove with his eyes straight ahead, not seeing the hills and valleys through which he passed, features of the land that gave the lie to the myth of totally flat Kansas. He drove like a man who, had he the power of images, thought of himself as a turtle drawn straight to the salt sea.

He paralleled the belt of sand hills on the south side of the Arkansas, turned off Route 96 at Elmer, below Hutchinson, due south onto 17. He had not driven these roads in three years, but then, neither had he swum or ridden a bicycle in all that time. Once learned, there was no forgetting.

Or Teresa.

Or home. No forgetting.

Or the hooch.

Or the smell of it. No forgetting.

He crossed the North Fork at the western tip of Cheney Reservoir and turned west off 17 above Pretty Prairie. He pulled into Grafton just before dusk, the immense running sore of the sun draining itself off behind the hills. The deserted buildings of the zinc mine—closed now for twelve years—stood against the sky like black fingers of a giant hand opened and raised behind the nearest hill.

He drove once around the town mall, the Soldiers and Sailors Monument and the crumbling band shell its only ornaments. There was an American flag flying at half-mast from the City Hall. And another from the Post Office.

It was getting dark. He turned on his headlights. The mist over his eyes was strangely reassuring, as if it separated him from a land at once familiar and alien.

The stores on Fitch Street were closed, but the Utopia Theater's marquee was flashing and a small crowd was gathered waiting for the ticket booth to open. He slowed to see if he recognized anyone, and people stared back at him. A teenaged boy he didn't know pointed and then turned to his friends. In the rearview mirror Lestig saw two of them leave the queue and head for the candy shop beside the movie house. He drove through the business section and headed for his home.

He stepped on the headlight brightener but it did little to dissipate the dimness through which he marked his progress. Had he been a man of images, he might have fantasized that he now saw the world through the eyes of some special beast. But he was not a man of images.

The house in which his family had lived for sixteen years was empty.

There was a realtor's FOR SALE sign on the unmowed front lawn. Gramas and buffalo grass were taking over. Someone had taken a chain saw to the oak tree that had grown in the front yard. When it had fallen, the top branches had torn away part of the side porch of the house.

He forced an entrance through the coal chute at the rear of the house, and through the sooty remains of his vision he searched every room, both upstairs and down. It was slow work: he walked with an aluminum crutch.

They had left hurriedly, mother and father and Neola. Coat hangers clumped together in the closets like frightened creatures huddling for comfort. Empty cartons from a market littered the kitchen floor and in one of them a tea cup without a handle lay upside-down. The fireplace flue had been left open and rain had reduced the ashes in the grate to a black paste. Mold grew in an open jar of blackberry preserves left on a kitchen cabinet shelf. There was dust.

He was touching the ripped shade hanging in a living room window when he saw the headlights of the cars turning into the driveway. Three of them pulled in, bumper to bumper. Two more slewed in at the curb, their headlights flooding the living room with a dim glow. Doors slammed.

Lestig crutched back and to the side.

Hard-lined shapes moved in front of the headlights, seemed to be grouping, talking. One of them moved away from the pack and an arm came up, and something shone for a moment in the light, then a Stillson wrench came crashing through the front window in an explosion of glass.

"Lestig, you motherfuckin' bastard, come on out of there!"

He moved awkwardly but silently through the living room, into the kitchen and down the basement stairs. He was careful opening the coal chute window from the bin, and through the narrow slit he saw someone moving out there. They were all around the house. Coal shifted under his foot.

He let the window fall back smoothly and turned to go back upstairs. He didn't want to be trapped in the basement. From upstairs he heard the sounds of windows being smashed.

He took the stairs clumsily, clinging to the banister, his crutch useless, but moved quickly through the house and climbed the stairs to the upper floor. The top porch doorway was in what had been his parents room; he unlocked and opened it. The screen door was hanging off at an angle, leaning against the outer wall by one hinge. He stepped out onto the porch, careful to avoid any places where the falling tree had weakened the structure. He looked down, back flat to the wall, but could see no one. He crutched to the railing, dropped the aluminum prop into the darkness, climbed over and began shinnying down one of the porch posts, clinging tightly with his thighs, as he had when he'd been a small boy, sneaking out to play after he'd been sent to bed.

It happened so quickly, he had no idea, even later, what had actually transpired. Before his foot touched the ground, someone grabbed him from behind. He fought to stay on the post, like a monkey on a stick, and even tried to kick out with his good foot; but he was pulled loose from the post and thrown down violently. He tried to roll, but he came up against a mulberry bush. Then he tried to dummyup, fold into a bundle, but a foot caught him in the side and he fell over onto his back. His smoked glasses fell off, and through the sooty fog he could just make out someone dropping down to sit on his chest, something thick and long being raised above the head of the shape . . . he strained to see . . . strained . . .

And then the shape screamed, and the weapon fell out of the hand and both hands clawed at the head, and the someone staggered to its feet and stumbled away, crashing through the mulberry bushes, still screaming.

Lestig fumbled around and found his glasses, pushed them onto his face. He was lying on the aluminum crutch. He got to his foot with the aid of the prop, like a skier righting himself after a spill.

He limped away behind the house next door, circled and came up on the empty cars still headed-in at the curb, their headlights splashing the house with dirty light. He slid in behind the wheel, saw it was a stick shift and knew with one foot he could not manage it. He slid out, moved to the second car, saw it was an automatic, and quietly opened the door. He slid behind the wheel and turned the key hard. The car thrummed to life and a mass of shapes erupted from the side of the house.

But he was gone before they reached the street.

He sat in the darkness, he sat in the sooty fog that obscured his sight, he sat in the stolen car. Outside Teresa's home. Not the house in which she'd lived when he'd left three years ago, but in the house of the man she'd married six months before, when Lestig's name had been first splashed across newspaper front pages.

He had driven to her parents' home, but it had been dark. He could not—or would not—break in to wait, but there had been a note taped to the mailbox advising the mailman to forward all letters to Teresa McCausland to this house.

He drummed the steering wheel with his fingers. His right leg ached from the fall. His shirtsleeve had been ripped and his left forearm bore a long, shallow gash from the mulberry bush. But it had stopped bleeding.

Finally, he crawled out of the car, dropped his shoulder into the crutch's padded curve, and rolled like a man with sea legs, up to the front door.

The white plastic button in the baroque backing was lit by a tiny nameplate bearing the word HOWARD. He pressed the button and a chime sounded somewhere on the other side of the door.

She answered the door wearing blue denim shorts and a man's white shirt, buttondown and frayed; a husband's castoff.

"Vern . . ." Her voice cut off the sentence before she could say *oh* or *what are you* or *they said* or *no!*

"Can I come in?"

"Go away, Vern. My husband's—"

A voice from inside called, "Who is it, Terry?"

"Please go away," she whispered.

"I want to know where Mom and Dad and Neola went."

"Terry?"

"I can't talk to you . . . go away!"

"What the hell's going on around here, I *have* to know."

"Terry? Someone there?"

"Goodbye, Vern. I'm . . ." She slammed the door and did not say the word *sorry.*

He turned to go. Somewhere great corded muscles flexed, a serpentine throat lifted, talons flashed against the stars. His vision fogged, cleared for a moment, and in that moment rage sluiced through him. He turned back to the door, and leaned against the wall and banged on the frame with the crutch.

There was the sound of movement from inside, he heard Teresa arguing, pleading, trying to stop someone from going to answer the noise, but a second later the door flew open and Gary Howard stood in the doorway, older and thicker across the shoulders and angrier than Lestig had remembered him from senior year in high school, the last time they'd seen each other. The annoyance look of expecting Bible salesman, heart fund solicitor, girl scout cookie dealer, evening doorbell prankster changed into a smirk.

Howard leaned against the jamb, folded his arms across his chest so the off-tackle pectorals bunched against his Sherwood green tank top.

"Evening, Vern. When'd you get back?"

Lestig straightened, crutch jammed back into armpit. "I want to talk to Terry."

"Didn't know just when you'd come rolling in, Vern, but we knew you'd show. How was the war, old buddy?"

"You going to let me talk to her?"

"Nothing's stopping her, old buddy. My wife is a free agent when it comes to talking to ex-boyfriends. My *wife,* that is. You get the word . . . old buddy?"

"*Terry?*" He leaned forward and yelled past Howard.

Gary Howard smiled a ladies' choice dance smile and put one hand flat against Lestig's chest. "Don't make a nuisance of yourself, Vern."

"I'm talking to her, Howard. Right now, even if I have to go through you."

Howard straightened, hand still flat against Lestig's chest. "You miserable cowardly sonofabitch," he said, very gently, and shoved. Lestig flailed backward, the crutch going out from under him, and he tumbled off the front step.

Howard looked down at him, and the president of the senior class smile vanished. "Don't come back, Vern. The next time I'll punch out your fucking heart."

The door slammed and there were voices inside. High voices, and then the sound of Howard slapping her.

Lestig crawled to the crutch, and using the wall stood up. He thought of breaking in through the door, but he was Lestig, track . . . once . . . and Howard had been football. Still was. Would be, on Sunday afternoons with the children he'd made on cool Saturday nights in a bed with Teresa.

He went back to the car and sat in the darkness. He didn't know he'd been sitting there for some time, till the shadow moved up to the window and his head came around sharply.

"Vern . . . ?"

"You'd better go back in. I don't want to cause you any more trouble."

"He's upstairs doing some sales reports. He got a very nice job as a salesman for Shoop Motors when he got out of the Air Force. We live nice, Vern. He's really very good to me. . . . Oh, Vern . . . why? Why'd you *do* it?"

"You'd better go back in."

"I waited, God you *know* I waited, Vern. But then all that terrible thing happened. . . . Vern, why did you *do* it?"

"Come on, Terry. I'm tired, leave me alone."

"The whole town, Vern. They were so ashamed. There were reporters and TV people, they came in and talked to *every*one. Your mother and father, Neola, they couldn't stay here any more."

"Where are they, Terry?"

"They moved away, Vern. Kansas City, I think."

"Oh, Jesus."

"Neola's living closer."

"Where?"

"She doesn't want you to know, Vern. I think she got married. I know she changed her name. . . . Lestig isn't such a good name around here any more."

"I've got to talk to her, Terry. Please. You've got to tell me where she is."

"I can't, Vern. I promised."

"Then call her. Do you have her number? Can you get in touch with her?"

"Yes, I think so. Oh, Vern . . ."

"Call her. Tell her I'll stay here in town till I can talk to her. Tonight. Please, Terry!"

She stood silently. Then said, "All right, Vern. Do you want her to meet you at your house?"

He thought of the hard-lined shapes in the glare of headlamps, and of the thing that had run screaming as he lay beside the mulberry bush. "No. Tell her I'll meet her in the church."

"St. Matthew's?"

"No. The Harvest Baptist."

"But it's closed, it has been for years."

"I know. It closed down before I left. I know a way in. She'll remember. Tell her I'll be waiting."

Light erupted through the front door, and Teresa Howard's face came up as she stared across the roof of the stolen car. She didn't even say goodbye, but her hand touched his face, cool and quick; and she ran back.

Knowing it was time once again to travel, the dragon-breath deathbeast eased sinuously to its feet and began treading down carefully through the fogs of limitless forevers. A soft, expectant purring came from its throat, and its terrible eyes burned with joy.

He was lying full out in one of the pews when the loose boards in the vestry wall creaked, and Lestig knew she had come. He sat up, wiping sleep from his fogged eyes, and replaced the smoked glasses. Somehow, they helped.

She came through the darkness in the aisle in front of the altar, and stopped. "Vernon?"

"I'm here, Sis."

She came toward the pew, but stopped three rows away. "Why did you come back?"

His mouth was dry. He would have liked a beer. "Where else should I have gone?"

"Haven't you made enough trouble for Mom and Dad and me?"

He wanted to say things about his right foot and his eyesight, left somewhere in Southeast Asia. But even the light smear of skin he could see in the darkness told him her face was older, wearier, changed, and he could not do that to her.

"It was terrible, Vernon. Terrible. They came and talked to us and they wouldn't let us alone. And they set up television cameras and made movies of the house and we couldn't even go out. And when they went away the people from town came, and they were even worse, oh God, Vern, you can't believe what they did. One night they came to break things, and they cut down the tree and Dad tried to stop them and they beat him up so bad, Vern. You should have seen him. It would have made you cry, Vern."

And he thought of his foot.

"We went away, Vern. We had to. We hoped—" She stopped.

"You hoped I'd be convicted and shot or sent away."

She said nothing.

He thought of the hooch and the smell.

"Okay, Sis. I understand."

"I'm sorry, Vernon. I'm really sorry, dear. But why did you do this to us? Why?"

He didn't answer for a long time, and finally she came to him, and put her arms around him and kissed his neck, and then she slipped away in the darkness and the wall boards creaked, and he was alone.

He sat there in the pew, thinking nothing. He stared at the shadows till his eyes played him tricks and he thought he saw little speckles of light dancing. Then the light glimmers changed and coalesced and turned red and he seemed to be staring first into a mirror, and then into the eyes of some monstrous creature, and his head hurt and his eyes burned. . . .

And the church changed, melted, swam before his eyes and he fought for breath, and pulled at his throat, and the church re-formed and he was in the hooch again; they were questioning him.

He was crawling.

Crawling across a dirt floor, pulling himself forward with his fingers leaving flesh-furrows in the earth, trying to crawl away from them.

"Crawl! Crawl and perhaps we will let you live!"

He crawled and their legs were at his eye level, and he tried to reach up to touch one of them, and they hit him. Again and again. But the pain was not the worst of it. The monkey cage where they kept him boxed for endless days and nights. Too small to stand, too narrow to lie down, open to the rain, open to the insects that came and nested in the raw stump of his leg, and laid their eggs, and the itching that sent lilliputian arrows up into his side, and the light that hung from jerry-rigged wires through the trees, the light that never went out, day or night, and no sleep, and the questions, the endless questions . . . and he crawled . . . God how he crawled . . . if he could have crawled around the world on both bloody hands and one foot, scouring away the knees of his pants, he would have crawled, just to sleep, just to stop the arrows of pain . . . he would have crawled to the center of the earth and drunk the menstrual blood of the planet . . . for only a time of quiet, a straightening of his legs, a little sleep. . . .

*Why did you do this to us, why?*

Because I'm a human being and I'm weak and no one should be expected to be able to take it. Because I'm a man and not a book of rules that says I have to take it. Because I was in a place without sleep and I didn't want to be there and there was no one to save me. Because I wanted to live.

He heard boards creaking.

He blinked his eyes and sat silently and listened, and there was movement in the church. He reached for his smoked glasses, but they were out of reach, and he reached farther and the crutch slid away from the pew seat and dropped with a crash. Then they were on him.

Whether it was the same bunch he never knew.

They came for him and vaulted the pews and smashed into him before he could use whatever it was he'd used on the kid at the house, the kid who lay on a table in the City Hall, covered with a sheet through which green stains and odd rotting smells oozed.

They jumped him and beat him, and he flailed up through the mass of bodies and was staring directly into a wild-eyed mandrill face, and he *looked* at him.

*Looked* at him. As the deathbeast struck.

The man screamed, clawed at his face, and his face came away in handfuls, the rotting flesh dripping off his fingers. He fell back, carrying two others with him, and Lestig suddenly remembered what had happened in the hooch, remembered breathing and looking and here in this house of a God gone away he spun on them, one by one, and he breathed deeply and exhaled in their faces and stared at them across the evil night wasteland of another universe, and they shrieked and died and he was all alone once more. The others, coming through the vestry wall, having followed Neola, having been telephoned by Gary Howard, who had beaten the information from his wife, the others stopped and turned and ran. . . .

So that only Lestig, brother to the basilisk, who was itself the servant of a nameless dark one far away, only Lestig was left standing amid the twisted body shapes of things that had been men.

Stood alone, felt the power and the fury pulsing in him, felt his eyes glowing, felt the death that lay on his tongue, deep in his throat, the wind death in his lungs. And knew night had finally fallen.

They had roadblocked the only two roads out of town. Then they took eight-cell battery flashlights and Coleman lanterns and cave-crawling lamps, and some of them who had worked the zinc mine years before, they donned their miner's helmets with the lights on them, and they even wound rags around clubs and dipped them in kerosene and lit them, and they went out searching for the filthy traitor who had killed their sons and husbands and brothers, and not one of them laughed at the scene of crowd lights moving through the town, like something from an old film. A film of hunting the monster. They did not draw the parallel, for had they drawn the parallel, they would still never have laughed.

And they searched through the night, but did not find him. And when the dawn came up and they doused their lamps, and the parking lights replaced headlights on the caravans of cars that ringed the town, they still had not found him. And finally they gathered in the mall, to decide what to do.

And he was there.

He stood on the Soldiers and Sailors Monument high above them, where he had huddled all through the night, at the feet of a World War I doughboy with his arm upraised and a Springfield in his fist. He was there, and the symbolism did not escape them.

"Pull him down!" someone shouted. And they surged toward the marble-and-bronze monument.

Vernon Lestig stood watching them come toward him, and seemed unconcerned at the rifles and clubs and war-souvenir Lugers coming toward him.

The first man to scale the plinth was Gary Howard, with the broken-field cheers of the crowd smile on his face. Lestig's eyes widened behind the smoked glasses, and very casually he removed them, and he *looked* at the big, many-toothed car salesman.

The crowd screamed in one voice and the forward rush was halted as the still-smoking body of Teresa's husband fell back on them, arms flung out wide, torso twisted.

In the rear, they tried to run. He cut them down. The crowd stopped. One man tried to raise a revolver to kill him, but he dropped, his face burned away, smoking pustules of ruined flesh where his eyes had been.

They stopped. Frozen in a world of muscles that trembled, of running energy with no place to go.

"I'll show you!" he yelled. "I'll show you what it's like! You want to know, so I'll show you!"

Then he breathed, and men died. Then he looked and others fell. Then he said, very quietly, so they would hear him: "It's easy, till it happens. You never know, patriots! You live all the time and you say one thing or another, all your rules about what it takes to be brave, but you never *know*, till that one time when you find out. *I* found out, it's not so easy. Now *you'll* find out."

He pointed to the ground.

"Get down on your knees and crawl, patriots! Crawl to me and maybe I'll let you live. Get down like animals and crawl on your bellies to me."

There was a shout from the crowd; and the man died.

*"Crawl, I said!* Crawl to me!"

Here and there in the crowd people dropped from sight. At the rear a woman tried to run away and he burned her out and the husk fell, and all around her, within sight of the wisps of smoke from her face, people fell to their knees. Then entire groups dropped; then one whole side of the mob went down. Then they were all on their knees.

"Crawl! Crawl, brave ones, crawl nice my people! Crawl and learn it's better to *live,* any way at all, to stay alive, because you're human! Crawl and you'll understand your slogans are shit, your rules are for others! Crawl for your goddamned lives and you'll understand! *Crawl!"*

And they crawled. They crept forward on hands and knees, across the grass, across cement and mud and the branches of small bushes, across the dirt. They crawled toward him.

And far away, through mists of darkness, the Helmet-Headed

One sat on his throne, high above all, with the basilisk at his feet, and he smiled.

"Crawl, God damn you!"

But he did not know the name of the God he served.

"Crawl!"

And in the middle of the mob, a woman who had hung a gold star in her front window, crawled across a .32 Police Positive, and her hand touched it, and she folded her fingers around it, and suddenly she raised up and screamed, "For Kennyyyyy . . . !" and she fired.

The bullet smashed Lestig's collarbone and he spun sidewise, up against the Yank's puttees, and he tried to regain his stance but the crutch had fallen, and now the crowd was on its feet and firing . . . and firing . . .

They buried the body in an unmarked grave, and no one talked of it. And far away, on a high throne, tickling the sleek hide of the basilisk that reclined at his feet like a faithful mastiff, even the Armed One did not speak of it. There was no need to speak of it. Lestig was gone, but that was to have been expected.

The weapon had been deactivated, but Mars, the Eternal One, the God Who Never Dies, the Lord of Futures, Warden of the Dark Places, Ever-Potent Scion of Conflict, Master of Men, Mars sat content.

The recruiting had gone well. Power to the people.

*The god of the slot machine: new*
*religions, new souls, new limbos.*

# Pretty Maggie Moneyeyes

With an eight hole-card and a queen showing, with the dealer showing a four up, Kostner decided to let the house do the work. So he stood, and the dealer turned up. Six.

The dealer looked like something out of a 1935 George Raft film: Arctic diamond-chip eyes, manicured fingers long as a brain surgeon's, straight black hair slicked flat away from the pale forehead. He did not look up as he peeled them off. A three. Another three. Bam. A five. Bam. Twenty-one, and Kostner saw his last thirty dollars—six five-dollar chips—scraped on the edge of the cards, into the dealer's chip racks. Busted. Flat. Down and out in Las Vegas, Nevada. Playground of the Western World.

He slid off the comfortable stool-chair and turned his back on the blackjack table. The action was already starting again, like waves closing over a drowned man. He had been there, was gone, and no one had noticed. No one had seen a man blow the last tie with salvation. Kostner now had his choice: he could bum his way into Los Angeles and try to find something that resembled a new life . . . or he could go blow his brains out through the back of his head.

Neither choice showed much light or sense.

He thrust his hands deep into the pockets of his worn and dirty chinos, and started away down the line of slot machines clanging and rattling on the other side of the aisle between blackjack tables.

He stopped. He felt something in his pocket. Beside him, but all-engrossed, a fiftyish matron in electric lavender capris, high heels and Ship 'n' Shore blouse was working two slots, loading and pulling one while waiting for the other to clock down. She was dumping quarters in a seemingly inexhaustible supply from a Dixie cup held in her left hand. There was a surrealistic presence to the woman. She was almost automated, not a flicker of expression on her face, the eyes fixed and unwavering. Only when the gong rang, someone down the line had pulled a jackpot, did she look up. And at that moment Kostner knew what was wrong and immoral and deadly about Vegas, about legalized gambling, about setting the traps all baited and open in front of the average human. The woman's face was gray with hatred, envy, lust and dedication to the game—in that timeless instant when she heard another drugged soul down the line winning a minuscule jackpot. A jackpot that would only lull the player with words like *luck* and *ahead of the game.* The jackpot lure: the sparkling, bobbling many-colored wiggler in a sea of poor fish.

The thing in Kostner's pocket was a silver dollar.

He brought it out and looked at it.

The eagle was hysterical.

But Kostner pulled to an abrupt halt, only one half-footstep from the sign indicating the limits of Tap City. He was still with it. What the high-rollers called the edge, the *vigerish,* the fine hole-card. One buck. One cartwheel. Pulled out of the pocket not half as deep as the pit into which Kostner had just been about to plunge.

*What the hell,* he thought, and turned to the row of slot machines.

He had thought they'd all been pulled out of service, the silver dollar slots. A shortage of coinage, said the United States Mint. But right there, side by side with the nickel and quarter bandits, was one cartwheel machine. Two thousand dollar jackpot. Kostner grinned foolishly. If you're gonna go out, go out like a champ.

He thumbed the silver dollar into the coin slot and grabbed the heavy, oiled handle. Shining cast aluminum and pressed steel. Big black plastic ball, angled for arm ease, pull it all day and you won't get weary.

Without a prayer in the universe, Kostner pulled the handle.

*She had been born in Tucson, mother full-blooded Cherokee, father a bindlestiff on his way through. Mother had been working a truckers' stop, father had popped for spencer steak and sides. Mother had just gotten over a bad scene, indeterminate origins, unsatisfactory culminations. Mother had popped for bed. And sides. Margaret Annie Jessie had come nine months later; black of hair, fair of face, and born* into a life of poverty. Twenty-three years later, a determined product of Miss Clairol and Berlitz, a dream-image formed by Vogue and intimate association with the rat race, Margaret Annie Jessie had become a contraction.

Maggie.

Long legs, trim and coltish; hips a trifle large, the kind that promote that specific thought in men, about getting their hands around it; belly flat, isometrics; waist cut to the bone, a waist that works in any style from dirndl to disco-slacks; no breasts—all nipple, but no breast, like an expensive whore (the way O'Hara pinned it)—and no padding . . . forget the cans, baby, there's other, more important action; smooth, Michelangelo-sculpted neck, a pillar, proud; and all that face.

Outthrust chin, perhaps a tot too much belligerence, but if you'd walloped as many gropers as you too, sweetheart; narrow mouth, petulant lower lip, nice to chew on, a lower lip as though filled with honey, bursting, ready for things to happen; a nose that threw the right sort of shadow, flaring nostrils, the acceptable words—aquiline, patrician, classic, allathat; cheekbones as stark and promontory as a spit of land after ten years of open ocean; cheekbones holding darkness like narrow shadows, sooty beneath the taut-fleshed bone-structure; amazing cheekbones, the whole face, really; an ancient kingdom's uptilted eyes, the touch of the Cherokee, eyes that looked out at you, as you looked in at them, like someone peering out of the keyhole as you peered in; actually, dirty eyes, they said you can get it.

Blonde hair, a great deal of it, wound and rolled and smoothed and flowing, in the old style, the pageboy thing men always admire; no tight little cap of slicked plastic; no ratted and teased Annapurna of bizarre coiffure; no ironed-flat discothèque hair like number 3 flat noodles. Hair, the way a man wants it, so he can dig his hands in at the base of the neck and pull all that face very close.

An operable woman, a working mechanism, a rigged and sudden machinery of softness and motivation.

Twenty-three, and determined as hell never to abide in that vale of poverty her mother had called purgatory for her entire life; snuffed out in a grease fire in the last trailer, somewhere in Arizona, thank God no more pleas for a little money from babygirl Maggie hustling drinks in a Los Angeles topless joint. (There ought to be some remorse in there *somewhere, for a Mommy gone where all the good grease-fire victims go. Look around, you'll find it.)*

*Maggie.*

*Genetic freak. Mommy's Cherokee uptilted eye-shape, and Polack quickscrewing Daddy WithoutaName's blue as innocence color.*

*Blue-eyed Maggie, dyed blonde, alla that face, alla that leg, fifty bucks a night can get it and it sounds like it's having a climax.*

*Irish-innocent blue-eyed-innocent French-legged-innocent Maggie. Polack. Cherokee. Irish. All-woman and going on the market for this month's rent on the stucco pad, eighty bucks' worth of groceries, a couple month's worth for a Mustang, three appointments with the specialist in Beverly Hills about that shortness of breath after a night on the hustle bump the sticky thigh the disco lurch the gotcha sweat: woman minutes. Increments under the meat; perspiration purchases, yeah it does.*

*Maggie, Maggie, Maggie, pretty Maggie Moneyeyes, who came from Tucson and trailers and rheumatic fever and a surge to live that was all kaleidoscope frenzy of clawing scrabbling no-nonsense. If it took lying on one's back and making sounds like a panther in the desert, then one did it, because nothing, but nothing was as bad as being dirt-poor, itchy-skinned, soiled-underwear, scuff-toed, hairy and ashamed lousy with the no-gots. Nothing!*

*Maggie. Hooker. Hustler. Grabber. Swinger. If there's a buck in it, there's rhythm and the onomatopoeia is Maggie Maggie Maggie.*

*She who puts out. For a price, whatever that might be.*

*Maggie was dating Nuncio. He was Sicilian. He had dark eyes and an alligator-grain wallet with slip-in pockets for credit cards. He was a spender, a sport, a high-roller. They went to Vegas.*

*Maggie and the Sicilian. Her blue eyes and his slip-in pockets. But mostly her blue eyes.*

The spinning reels behind the three long glass windows blurred, and Kostner knew there wasn't a chance. Two thousand dollar jackpot. Round and round, whirring. Three bells or two bells and a jackpot bar, get 18; three plums or two plums and a jackpot bar, get 14; three oranges or two oranges and a jac—

Ten, five, two bucks for a single cherry cluster in first position. Something . . . I'm drowning . . . something . . .

The whirring . . .

Round and round . . .

As something happened that was not considered in the pit-boss manual.

The reels whipped and snapped to a stop, clank clank clank, tight in place.

Three bars looked up at Kostner. But they did not say JACK-POT. They were three bars from which stared three blue eyes. Very blue, very immediate, very JACKPOT!!

Twenty silver dollars clattered into the payoff trough at the bottom of the machine. An orange light popped on in the casino cashier's cage, bright orange on the jackpot board. And the gong began clanging overhead.

The Slot Machine Floor Manager nodded once to the Pit Boss, who pursed his lips and started toward the seedy-looking man still standing with his hand on the slot's handle.

The token payment—twenty silver dollars—lay untouched in the payoff trough. The balance of the jackpot—one thousand nine hundred and eighty dollars—would be paid manually by the casino cashier. And Kostner stood, dumbly, as the three blue eyes stared up at him.

There was a moment of idiotic disorientation, as Kostner stared back at the three blue eyes; a moment in which the slot machine's mechanisms registered to themselves; and the gong was clanging furiously.

All through the hotel's casino people turned from their games to stare. At the roulette tables the white-on-white players from Detroit and Cleveland pulled their watery eyes away from the clattering ball and stared down the line for a second, at the ratty-looking guy in front of the slot machine. From where they sat, they could not tell it was a two grand pot, and their rheumy eyes went back into billows of cigar smoke, and that little ball.

The blackjack hustlers turned momentarily, screwing around in their seats, and smiled. They were closer to the slot-players in temperament, but they knew the slots were a dodge to keep the old ladies busy, while the players worked toward their endless twenty-ones.

And the old dealer, who could no longer cut it at the fast-action boards, who had been put out to pasture by a grateful management, standing at the Wheel of Fortune near the entrance to the casino, even he paused in his zombie-murmuring ("Annnnother winner onna Wheel of Forchun!") to no one at all, and looked toward Kostner and that incredible gong-clanging. Then, in a moment, still with no players, he called *another* nonexistent winner.

Kostner heard the gong from far away. It had to mean he had won two thousand dollars, but that was impossible. He checked the payoff chart on the face of the machine. Three bars labeled JACK-POT meant JACKPOT. Two thousand dollars.

But these three bars did not say JACKPOT. They were three gray bars, rectangular in shape, with a blue eye directly in the center of each bar.

Blue eyes?

*Somewhere, a connection was made, and electricity, a billion volts of electricity, were shot through Kostner. His hair stood on end, his fingertips bled raw, his eyes turned to jelly, and every fiber in his musculature became radioactive. Somewhere, out there, in a place that was not this place, Kostner had been inextricably bound to—to some-one. Blue eyes?*

The gong had faded out of his head, the constant noise level of the casino, chips chittering, people mumbling, dealers calling plays, it had all gone, and he was embedded in silence.

Tied to that someone else, out there somewhere, through those three blue eyes.

Then in an instant, it had passed, and he was alone again, as though released by a giant hand, the breath crushed out of him. He staggered up against the slot machine.

"You all right, fellah?"

A hand gripped him by the arm, steadied him. The gong was still clanging overhead somewhere, and he was breathless from a journey he had just taken. His eyes focused and he found himself looking at the stocky Pit Boss who had been on duty while he had been playing blackjack.

"Yeah . . . I'm okay, just a little dizzy is all."

"Sounds like you got yourself a big jackpot, fellah." The Pit Boss grinned; it was a leathery grin; something composed of stretched muscles and conditioned reflexes, totally mirthless.

"Yeah . . . great . . ." Kostner tried to grin back. But he was still shaking from that electrical absorption that had kidnapped him.

"Let me check it out," the Pit Boss was saying, edging around Kostner, and staring at the face of the slot machine. "Yeah, three jackpot bars, all right. You're a winner."

Then it dawned on Kostner! Two thousand dollars! He looked down at the slot machine and saw—

Three bars with the word JACKPOT on them. No blue eyes, just words that meant money. Kostner looked around frantically, was he losing his mind? *From somewhere, not in the casino, he heard a tinkle of rhodium-plated laughter.*

He scooped up the twenty silver dollars. The Pit Boss dropped another cartwheel into the Chief, and pulled the jackpot off. Then the Pit Boss walked him to the rear of the casino, talking to him in a muted, extremely polite tone of voice. At the cashier's window, the Pit Boss nodded to a weary-looking man at a huge Rolodex cardfile, checking credit ratings.

"Barney, jackpot on the cartwheel Chief; slot five-oh-oh-one-five." He grinned at Kostner, who tried to smile back. It was difficult. He felt stunned.

The cashier checked a payoff book for the correct amount to be drawn and leaned over the counter toward Kostner. "Check or cash, sir?"

Kostner felt buoyancy coming back to him. "Is the casino's check good?" They all three laughed at that. "A check's fine," Kostner said. The check was drawn, and the Check-Riter punched out the little bumps that said two thousand. "The twenty cartwheels are a gift," the cashier said, sliding the check through to Kostner.

He held it, looked at it, and still found it difficult to believe. Two grand, back on the golden road.

As he walked back through the casino with the Pit Boss, the stocky man asked pleasantly, "Well, what are you going to do with it?" Kostner had to think a moment. He didn't have any plans. But then the sudden realization came to him: "I'm going to play that slot machine again." The Pit Boss smiled: a congenital sucker. He would put all twenty of those silver dollars back into the Chief, and then turn to the other games. Blackjack, roulette, faro, baccarat . . . in a few hours he would have redeposited the two grand with the hotel casino. It always happened.

He walked Kostner back to the slot machine, and patted him on the shoulder. "Lotsa luck, fellah."

As he turned away, Kostner slipped a silver dollar into the machine, and pulled the handle.

The Pit Boss had taken only five steps when he heard the incredible sound of the reels clicking to a stop, the clash of twenty token silver dollars hitting the payoff trough, and that goddamned gong went out of its mind again.

*She had known that sonofabitch Nuncio was a perverted swine. A walking filth. A dungheap between his ears. Some kind of monster in nylon undershorts. There weren't many kinds of games Maggie hadn't played, but what that Sicilian de Sade wanted to do was outright vomity!*

*She nearly fainted when he suggested it. Her heart—which the Beverly Hills specialist had said she should not tax—began whumping frantically. "You pig!" she screamed. "You filthy dirty ugly pig you, Nuncio you pig!" She had bounded out of the bed and started to throw on clothes. She didn't even bother with a brassiere, pulling the poorboy sweater on over her thin breasts, still crimson with the touches and love-bites Nuncio had showered on them.*

*He sat up in the bed, a pathetic-looking little man, gray hair at the temples and no hair atall on top, and his eyes were moist. He was porcine, was indeed the swine she called him, but he was helpless before her. He was in love with his hooker, with the tart whom he was supporting. It had been the first time for the swine Nuncio, and he was helpless. Back in Detroit, had it been a floozy, a bimbo, a chippy broad, he would have gotten out of the double bed and rapped her around pretty good. But this Maggie, she tied him in knots. He had suggested . . . that, what they should do together . . . because he was so consumed with her. But she was furious with him. It wasn't that bizarre an idea!*

*"Gimme a chanct'a talk t'ya, honey . . . Maggie . . ."*

*"You filthy pig, Nuncio! Give me some money, I'm going down to the casino, and I don't want to see your filthy pig face for the rest of the day, remember that!"*

*And she had gone in his wallet and pants, and taken eight hundred and sixteen dollars, while he watched. He was helpless before her. She was something stolen from a world he knew only as "class" and she could do what she wanted with him.*

*Genetic freak Maggie, blue-eyed posing mannequin Maggie, pretty Maggie Moneyeyes, who was one-half Cherokee and one-half a buncha other things, had absorbed her lessons well. She was the very model of a "class broad."*

*"Not for the rest of the day, do you understand?" She stared at him till he nodded; then she went downstairs, furious, to fret and gamble and wonder about nothing but years of herself.*

*Men stared after her as she walked. She carried herself like a challenge, the way a squire carried a pennon, the way a prize bitch carried herself in the judge's ring. Born to the blue. The wonders of mimicry and desire.*

*Maggie had no lust for gambling, none whatever. She merely wanted to taste the fury of her relationship with the swine Sicilian, her need for solidity in a life built on the edge of the slide area, the senselessness of being here in Las Vegas when she could be back in Beverly Hills. She grew angrier and more ill at the thought of Nuncio upstairs in the room, taking another shower. She bathed three times a day. But it was different with him. He knew she resented his smell; he had the soft odor of wet fur sometimes, and she had told him about it. Now he bathed constantly, and hated it. He was a foreigner to the bath. His life had been marked by various kinds of filths, and baths for him now were more of an obscenity than dirt could ever have been. For her, bathing was different. It was a necessity. She had to keep the patina of the world off her, had to remain clean and smooth and white. A presentation, not an object of flesh and hair. A chromium instrument, something never pitted by rust and corrosion.*

*When she was touched by them, by any one of them, by the men, by all the Nuncios, they left little pitholes of bloody rust on her white, permanent flesh; cobwebs, sooty stains. She had to bathe. Often.*

*She strolled down between the tables and the slots, carrying eight hundred and sixteen dollars. Eight one hundred dollar bills and sixteen dollars in ones.*

*At the change booth she got cartwheels for the sixteen ones. The*

*Chief waited. It was her baby. She played it to infuriate the Sicilian. He had told her to play the nickel slots, the quarter or dime slots, but she always infuriated him by blowing fifty or a hundred dollars in ten minutes, one coin after another, in the big Chief.*

*She faced the machine squarely, and put in the first silver dollar. She pulled the handle that swine Nuncio. Another dollar, pulled the handle how long does this go on? The reels cycled and spun and whirled and whipped in a blurringspinning metalhumming overandover-andover as Maggie blue-eyed Maggie hated and hated and thought of hate and all the days and nights of swine behind her and ahead of her and if only she had all the money in this room in this casino in this hotel in this town right now this very instant just an instant thisinstant it would be enough to whirring and humming and spinning and over-andoverandoverandover and she would be free free free and all the world would never touch her body again the swine would never touch her white flesh again and then suddenly as dollarafterdollarafterdollar went aroundaroundaround hummmmming in reels of cherries and bells and bars and plums and oranges there was suddenly painpainpain a SHARP pain!pain!pain! in her chest, her heart, her center, a needle, a lancet, a burning, a pillar of flame that was purest pure purer PAIN!*

*Maggie, pretty Maggie Moneyeyes, who wanted all that money in that cartwheel Chief slot machine, Maggie who had come from filth and rheumatic fever, who had come all the way to three baths a day and a specialist in Very Expensive Beverly Hills, that Maggie suddenly had a seizure, a flutter, a slam of a coronary thrombosis and fell instantly dead on the floor of the casino. Dead.*

*One instant she had been holding the handle of the slot machine, willing her entire being, all that hatred for all the swine she had ever rolled with, willing every fiber of every cell of every chromosome into that machine, wanting to suck out every silver vapor within its belly, and the next instant—so close they might have been the same—her heart exploded and killed her and she slipped to the floor . . . still touching the Chief.*

*On the floor.*
*Dead.*
*Struck dead.*
*Liar. All the lies that were her life.*
*Dead on a floor.*

[A moment out of time ◼ lights whirling and spinning in a cotton candy universe ◼ down a bottomless funnel roundly sectioned like a goat's horn ◼ a cornucopia that rose up cuculiform smooth and slick as a worm belly ◼ endless nights that pealed ebony funeral bells ◼ out of fog ◼ out of weightlessness ◼ suddenly total cellular knowledge ◼ memory running backward ◼ gibbering spastic blindness ◼ a soundless owl of frenzy trapped in a cave of prisms ◼ sand endlessly draining down ◼ billows of forever ◼ edges of the world as they splintered ◼ foam rising drowning from inside ◼ the smell of rust ◼ rough green corners that burn ◼ memory the gibbering spastic blind memory ◼ seven rushing vacuums of nothing ◼ yellow ◼ pinpoints cast in amber straining and elongating running like live wax ◼ chill fevers ◼ overhead the odor of stop ◼ this is the stopover before hell or heaven ◼ this is limbo ◼ trapped and doomed alone in a mist-eaten nowhere ◼ a soundless screaming a soundless whirring a soundless spinning spinning spinning ◼ spinning ◼ spinning ◼ spinning ◼ spinning ◼ spinninggggggggggggggggg]

Maggie had wanted all the silver in the machine. She had died, willing herself into the machine. Now looking out from within, from inside the limbo that had become her own purgatory, Maggie was trapped, in the oiled and anodized interior of the silver dollar slot machine. The prison of her final desires, where she had wanted to be, completely trapped in that last instant of life between life/death. Maggie, gone inside; all soul now; trapped for eternity in the cage soul of the soulless machine. Limbo. Trapped.

"I hope you don't mind if I call over one of the slot men," the Slot Machine Floor Manager was saying, from a far distance. He was in his late fifties, a velvet-voiced man whose eyes held nothing of light and certainly nothing of kindness. He had stopped the Pit Boss as the stocky man had turned in mid-step to return to Kostner and the jackpotted machine; he had taken the walk himself. "We have to make sure, you know how it is: somebody didn't fool the slot, you know, maybe it's outta whack or something, you know."

He lifted his left hand and there was a clicker in it, the kind children use at Halloween. He clicked half a dozen times, like a rabid cricket, and there was a scurrying in the pit between the tables.

Kostner was only faintly aware of what was happening. Instead of being totally awake, feeling the surge of adrenaline through his veins, the feeling any gambler gets when he is ahead of the game, a kind of desperate urgency when he has hit it for a boodle, he was numb, partaking of the action around him only as much as a drinking glass involves itself in the alcoholic's drunken binge.

All color and sound had been leached out of him.

A tired-looking, resigned-weary man wearing a gray porter's jacket, as gray as his hair, as gray as his indoor skin, came to them, carrying a leather wrap-up of tools. The slot repairman studied the machine, turning the pressed steel body around on its stand, studying the back. He used a key on the back door and for an instant Kostner had a view of gears, springs, armatures and the clock that ran the slot mechanism. The repairman nodded silently over it, closed and relocked it, turned it around again and studied the face of the machine.

"Nobody's been spooning it," he said, and went away.

Kostner stared at the Floor Manager.

"Gaffing. That's what he meant. Spooning's another word for it. Some guys use a little piece of plastic, or a wire, shove it down through the escalator, it kicks the machine. Nobody thought that's what happened here, but you know, we have to make sure, two grand is a big payoff, and twice . . . well, you know, I'm sure you'll understand. If a guy was doing it with a boomerang—"

Kostner raised an eyebrow.

"—uh, yeah, a boomerang, it's another way to spoon the machine. But we just wanted to make a little check, and now everybody's satisfied, so if you'll just come back to the casino cashier with me—"

And they paid him off again.

So he went back to the slot machine, and stood before it for a long time, staring at it. The change girls and the dealers going off-duty; the little old ladies with their canvas work gloves worn to avoid calluses when pulling the slot handles, the men's room attendant on his way up front to get more matchbooks, the floral tourists, the idle observers, the hard drinkers, the sweepers, the busboys, the gamblers with poached-egg eyes who had been up all night, the showgirls with massive breasts and diminutive sugar daddies, all of them conjectured mentally about the beat-up walker who was staring at the silver dollar Chief. He did not move, merely stared at the machine . . . and they wondered.

The machine was staring back at Kostner.

Three blue eyes.

The electric current had sparked through him again, as the machine had clocked down and the eyes turned up a second time, as he had *won* a second time. But this time he knew there was something more than luck involved, for no one else had seen those three blue eyes.

So now he stood before the machine, waiting. It spoke to him. Inside his skull, where no one had ever lived but himself, now someone else moved and spoke to him. A girl. A beautiful girl. Her name was Maggie, and she spoke to him.

*I've been waiting for you. A long time, I've been waiting for you, Kostner. Why do you think you hit the jackpot? Because I've been waiting for you, and I want you. You'll win all the jackpots. Because I want you, I need you. Love me, I'm Maggie, I'm so alone, love me.*

Kostner had been staring at the slot machine for a very long time, and his weary brown eyes had seemed to be locked to the blue eyes on the jackpot bars. But he knew no one else could see the blue eyes, and no one else could hear the voice, and no one else knew about Maggie.

He was the universe to her. Everything to her.

He thumbed in another silver dollar, and the Pit Boss watched, the slot machine repairman watched, the Slot Machine Floor Manager watched, three change girls watched, and a pack of unidentified players watched, some from their seats.

The reels whirled, the handle snapped back, and in a second they flipped down to a halt, twenty silver dollars tokened themselves into the payoff trough and a woman at one of the crap tables belched a fragment of hysterical laughter.

And the gong went insane again.

The Floor Manager came over and said, very softly, "Mr. Kostner, it'll take us about fifteen minutes to pull this machine and check it out. I'm sure you understand." As two slot repairmen came out of the back, hauled the Chief off its stand, and took it into the repair room at the rear of the casino.

While they waited, the Floor Manager regaled Kostner with stories of spooners who had used intricate magnets inside their clothes, of boomerang men who had attached their plastic implements under their sleeves so they could be extended on spring-loaded clips, of cheaters who had come equipped with tiny electric drills in their hands and wires that slipped into the tiny drilled holes. And he kept saying he knew Kostner would understand.

But Kostner knew the Floor Manager would not understand.

When they brought the Chief back, one of the repairmen nodded assuredly. "Nothing wrong with it. Works perfectly. Nobody's been boomin' it."

But the blue eyes were gone on the jackpot bars.

Kostner knew they would return.

They paid him off again.

He returned and played again. And again. And again. They put a "spotter" on him. He won again. And again. And again. The crowd had grown to massive proportions. Word had spread like the silent communications of the telegraph vine, up and down the Strip, all the way to downtown Vegas and the sidewalk casinos where they played night and day every day of the year, and the crowd surged in a tide toward the hotel, and the casino, and the seedy-looking walker with his weary brown eyes. The crowd moved to him inexorably, drawn like lemmings by the odor of the luck that rose from him like musky electrical cracklings. And he won. Again and again. Thirty-eight thousand dollars. And the three blue eyes continued to stare up at him. Her lover was winning. Maggie and her Moneyeyes.

Finally, the casino decided to speak to Kostner. They pulled the Chief for fifteen minutes, for a supplemental check by experts from the slot machine company in downtown Vegas, and while they were checking it, they asked Kostner to come to the main office of the hotel.

The owner was there. His face seemed faintly familiar to Kostner. Had he seen it on television? The newspapers?

"Mr. Kostner, my name is Jules Hartshorn."

"I'm pleased to meet you."

"Quite a string of luck you're having out there."

"It's been a long time coming."

"You realize, this sort of luck is impossible."

"I'm compelled to believe it, Mr. Hartshorn."

"Um. As am I. It's happening to my casino. But we're thoroughly convinced of one of two possibilities, Mr. Kostner; one, either the machine is inoperable in a way we can't detect; or two, you are the cleverest spooner we've ever had in here."

"I'm not cheating."

"As you can see, Mr. Kostner, I'm smiling. The reason I'm smiling is at your naïveté in believing I would take your word for it. I'm perfectly happy to nod politely and say of course you aren't cheating. But no one can win thirty-eight thousand dollars on nineteen straight jackpots off one slot machine; it doesn't even have mathematical odds against its happening, Mr. Kostner. It's on a cosmic scale of improbability with three dark planets crashing into our sun within the next twenty minutes. It's on a par with the Pentagon, the Forbidden City and the Kremlin all three pushing the red button at the same microsecond. It's an impossibility, Mr. Kostner. An impossibility that's happening to me."

"I'm sorry."

"Not really."

"No, not really. I can use the money."

"For what, exactly, Mr. Kostner?"

"I hadn't thought about it, really."

"I see. Well, Mr. Kostner, let's look at it this way. I can't stop you from playing, and if you continue to win, I'll be required to pay off. And no stubble-chinned thugs will be waiting in an alley to jackroll you and take the money. The checks will be honored. The best I can hope for, Mr. Kostner, is the attendant publicity. Right now, every high-roller in Vegas is in that casino, waiting for you to drop cartwheels into that machine. It won't make up for what I'm losing, if you continue the way you've been; but it'll help. Every sucker in town likes to rub up next to luck. All I ask is that you cooperate a little."

"The least I can do, considering your generosity."

"An attempt at humor."

"I'm sorry. What is it you'd like me to do?"

"Get about ten hours' sleep."

"While you pull the slot and have it worked over thoroughly?"

"Yes."

"If I wanted to keep winning, that might be a pretty stupid move on my part. You might change the thingamajig inside so I couldn't win if I put back every dollar of that thirty-eight grand."

"We're licensed by the state of Nevada, Mr. Kostner."

"I come from a good family, too, and take a look at me. I'm a bum with thirty-eight thousand dollars in my pocket."

"Nothing will be done to that slot machine, Kostner."

"Then why pull it for ten hours?"

"To work it over thoroughly in the shop. If something as undetectable as metal fatigue or a worn escalator tooth or—we want to make sure this doesn't happen with other machines. And the extra time will get the word around town; we can use the crowd. Some of those tourists will stick to our fingers, and it'll help defray the expense of having you break the bank at this casino—on a slot machine."

"I have to take your word."

"This hotel will be in business long after you're gone, Kostner."

"Not if I keep winning."

Hartshorn's smile was a stricture. "A good point."

"So it isn't much of an argument."

"It's the only one I have. If you want to get back out on that floor, I can't stop you."

"No Mafia hoods ventilate me later?"

"I beg your pardon?"

"I said: no Maf—"

"You have a picturesque manner of speaking. In point of fact, I haven't the faintest idea what you're talking about."

"I'm sure you haven't."

"You've got to stop reading *The National Enquirer*. This is a legally run business. I'm merely asking a favor."

"Okay, Mr. Hartshorn, I've been three days without any sleep. Ten hours will do me a world of good."

"I'll have the desk clerk find you a quiet room on the top floor. And thank you, Mr. Kostner."

"Think nothing of it."

"I'm afraid that will be impossible."

"A lot of impossible things are happening lately."

He turned to go, as Hartshorn lit a cigarette.

"Oh, by the way, Mr. Kostner?"

Kostner stopped and half-turned. "Yes?"

His eyes were getting difficult to focus. There was a ringing in his ears. Hartshorn seemed to waver at the edge of his vision like heat lightning across a prairie. Like memories of things Kostner had come across the country to forget. Like the whimpering and pleading that kept tugging at the cells of his brain. The voice of Maggie. Still back in there, saying . . . things . . .

*They'll try to keep you from me.*

All he could think about was the ten hours of sleep he had been promised. Suddenly it was more important than the money, than forgetting, than anything. Hartshorn was talking, was saying things, but Kostner could not hear him. It was as if he had turned off the sound and saw only the silent rubbery movement of Hartshorn's lips. He shook his head trying to clear it.

There were half a dozen Hartshorns all melting into and out of one another. And the voice of Maggie.

*I'm warm here, and alone. I could be good to you, if you can come to me. Please come, please hurry.*

"Mr. Kostner?"

Hartshorn's voice came draining down through exhaustion as thick as velvet flocking. Kostner tried to focus again. His extremely weary brown eyes began to track.

"Did you know about that slot machine?" Hartshorn was saying. "A peculiar thing happened with it about six weeks ago."

"What was that?"

"A girl died playing it. She had a heart attack, a seizure while she was pulling the handle, and died right out there on the floor."

Kostner was silent for a moment. He wanted desperately to ask Hartshorn what color the dead girl's eyes had been, but he was afraid the owner would say blue.

He paused with his hand on the office door. "Seems as though you've had nothing but a streak of bad luck on that machine."

Hartshorn smiled an enigmatic smile. "It might not change for a while, either."

Kostner felt his jaw muscles tighten. "Meaning I might die, too, and wouldn't *that* be bad luck."

Hartshorn's smile became hieroglyphic, permanent, stamped on him forever. "Sleep tight, Mr. Kostner."

*In a dream, she came to him. Long, smooth thighs and soft golden down on her arms; blue eyes deep as the past, misted with a fine scintillance like lavender spiderwebs; taut body that was the only body Woman had ever had, from the very first. Maggie came to him.*

Hello, I've been traveling a long time.

"Who are you?" *Kostner asked, wonderingly. He was standing on a chilly plain, or was it a plateau? The wind curled around them both, or was it only around him? She was exquisite, and he saw her clearly, or was it through a mist? Her voice was deep and resonant, or was it light and warm as night-blooming jasmine?*

I'm Maggie. I love you. I've waited for you.

"You have blue eyes."

Yes. *With love.*

"You're very beautiful."

Thank you. *With female amusement.*

"But why me? Why let it happen to me? Are you the girl who—are you the one that was sick—the one who—?"

I'm Maggie. And you, I picked you, because you need me. You've needed someone for a long long time.

*Then it unrolled for Kostner. The past unrolled and he saw who he was. He saw himself alone. Always alone. As a child, born to kind and warm parents who hadn't the vaguest notion of who he was, what he wanted to be, where his talents lay. So he had run off, when he was in his teens, and alone always alone on the road. For years and months and days and hours, with no one. Casual friendships, based on food, or sex, or artificial similarities. But no one to whom he could cleave, and cling, and belong. It was that way till Susie, and with her he had found light. He had discovered the scents and aromas of a spring that was eternally one day away. He had laughed, really laughed, and known with her it would at last be all right. So he had poured all of himself into her, giving her everything; all his hopes, his secret thoughts, his tender dreams; and she had taken them, taken him, all of him, and he had known for the first time what it was to have a place to live, to have a home in someone's heart. It was all the silly and gentle things he laughed at in other people, but for him it was breathing deeply of wonder.*

*He had stayed with her for a long time, and had supported her, supported her son from the first marriage; the marriage Susie never talked about. And then one day, he had come back, as Susie had always known he would. He was a dark creature of ruthless habits and vicious nature, but she had been his woman, all along, and Kostner realized he had been used as a stop-gap, as a bill-payer till her wandering terror came home to nest. Then she had asked him to leave. Broke, and tapped out in all the silent inner ways a man can be drained, he had left, without even a fight, for all the fight had been leached out of him. He had left, and wandered west, and finally come to Las Vegas, where he had hit bottom. And found Maggie. In a dream, with blue eyes, he had found Maggie.*

*I want you to belong to me. I love you. Her truth was vibrant in Kostner's mind. She was his, at last someone who was special, was his.*

*"Can I trust you? I've never been able to trust anyone before. Women, never. But I need someone. I really need someone."*

*It's me, always. Forever. You can trust me.*

*And she came to him, fully. Her body was a declaration of truth and trust such as no other Kostner had ever known before. She met him on a windswept plain of thought, and he made love to her more completely than he had known any passion before. She joined with him, entered him, mingled with his blood and his thought and his frustration, and he came away clean, filled with glory.*

*"Yes, I can trust you, I want you, I'm yours," he whispered to her, when they lay side by side in a dream nowhere of mist and soundlessness. "I'm yours."*

*She smiled, a woman's smile of belief in her man; a smile of trust and deliverance. And Kostner woke up.*

The Chief was back on its stand, and the crowd had been penned back by velvet ropes. Several people had played the machine, but there had been no jackpots.

Now Kostner came into the casino, and the "spotters" got themselves ready. While Kostner had slept, they had gone through his clothes, searching for wires, for gaffs, for spoons or boomerangs. Nothing.

Now he walked straight to the Chief, and stared at it.

Hartshorn was there. "You look tired," he said gently to Kostner, studying the man's weary brown eyes.

"I am, a little." Kostner tried a smile; it didn't work. "I had a funny dream."

"Oh?"

"Yeah . . . about a girl . . ." He let it die off.

Hartshorn's smile was understanding. Pitying, empathic and understanding. "There are lots of girls in this town. You shouldn't have any trouble finding one with your winnings."

Kostner nodded, and slipped his first silver dollar into the slot. He pulled the handle. The reels spun with a ferocity Kostner had not heard before and suddenly everything went whipping slantwise as he felt a wrenching of pure flame in his stomach, as his head was snapped on its spindly neck, as the lining behind his eyes was burned out. There was a terrible shriek, of tortured metal, of an express train ripping the air with its passage, of a hundred small animals being gutted and torn to shreds, of incredible pain, of night winds that tore the tops off mountains of lava. And a keening whine of a voice that wailed and wailed and wailed as it went away from there in blinding light—

*Free! Free! Heaven or Hell it doesn't matter! Free!*

The sound of a soul released from an eternal prison, a genie freed from a dark bottle. And in that instant of damp soundless nothingness, Kostner saw the reels snap and clock down for the final time:

One, two, three. Blue eyes.

But he would never cash his checks.

The crowd screamed through one voice as he fell sidewise and lay on his face. The final loneliness . . .

*The Chief was pulled. Bad luck. Too many gamblers resented its very presence in the casino. So it was pulled. And returned to the company, with explicit instructions it was to be melted down to slag. And not till it was in the hands of the ladle foreman, who was ready to dump it into the slag furnace, did anyone remark on the final tally the Chief had clocked.*

*"Look at that, ain't that weird," said the ladle foreman to his bucket man. He pointed to the three glass windows.*

*"Never saw jackpot bars like that before," the bucket man agreed. "Three eyes. Must be an old machine."*

*"Yeah, some of these old games go way back," the foreman said, hoisting the slot machine onto the conveyor track leading to the slag furnace.*

"*Three eyes, huh. How about that. Three brown eyes.*" *And he threw the knife-switch that sent the Chief down the track, to puddle in the roaring inferno of the furnace.*

*Three brown eyes.*

*Three brown eyes that looked very very weary. That looked very very trapped. That looked very very betrayed. Some of these old games go way back.*

*It's not enough merely to worship a god.
You've got to know which one's in
charge. And Heaven help you if you
mess around on the wrong turf.*

# Corpse

Walking uptown against traffic on Lexington Avenue, I was already in the Seventies when I saw three young vandals ruthlessly stripping the hulk of a 1959 Pontiac someone had deserted beside a curb in front of a condemned church building. They had pried up the hood of the car with a crowbar; apparently it had rusted or been wired closed before being abandoned. And as I paced past on the opposite side of the street, they began using mallets and spikes to shatter the engine mounts. Their teeth were very white, and they appeared extraordinarily healthy, as they smiled while they worked. I presumed they would eventually sell the engine to a junk dealer.

I am a religious man. I have always been a religious man—and one would think that should count for something. Apparently it does not. I've learned to my dismay that worship is like the stock market. (Though God knows an assistant professor in Latin American literature makes hardly enough to dabble with any degree of verve.) There are winning issues and there are, of course, losers. Placing one's faith on a failing stock can be no less disastrous then placing one's faith on a downtrending deity.

Mona Sündberg frequently invites me to her buffet dinners. Why, I have no idea; we are under no illusions about each other. We are just barely friends. Tolerators is more like it.

She had promised, nonetheless, that I would meet Carlos D'Agostino. My excitement at the prospect can hardly be described. Not merely because he is certainly one of the half dozen finest prose stylists in the world today but also because the position as his translator was still open, and the chance of his taking me on, of living in Venice, of finally being swept out of the backwash eddy of academic ennui into the mainstream of literature, made me—quite frankly—weak in the stomach.

I had stopped at a Marboro and picked up a lovely *Orlando*

*Furioso* with Doré engravings, remaindered at only $3.89, which I intended to present to Mona as a congratulatory gift on the occasion of her divorce, her fourth.

There was a battered hubcap lying in the middle of 71st Street, halfway down the block. It had been pressed flat by the passage of trucks, and a thin pool of water had collected in the shallow center depression. It reminded me of an Incan ceremonial saucer from the burial caves at Machu Picchu, a saucer stained dark, perhaps from blood.

Franklin Xavier (I never for a moment believed that was actually his name) was a disastrous man, and it was clear to all of us that Mona had married him solely for his connections with the Academy and its social whirl. Having tired of all three, Mona had left him and flown —God only knows why—from Basle to Minneapolis, of all places, to get her divorce. I have no idea how long one must reside in a place like Minneapolis to obtain a divorce, but at last she was back and had reopened the town house.

D'Agostino never put in an appearance. However, he did call from the Brasserie tendering his apologies. I stood quite clearly in Mona's line of sight as she spoke to him but she never mentioned my name. The buffet was good, as usual. Excellent, really: Mona employs a marvelous caterer. I was, of course, monumentally disappointed. But I left the *Orlando*; there is, after all, a form to these gestures.

I spent the following Sunday correcting term papers. It was infinitely depressing. The suspicion has been growing in me of late that Columbia University is registering not human beings, but chacma baboons. And they all seem to have cars. One cannot walk the streets of New York without feeling their monoxide breath filling one's lungs. The suspicion has also been growing in me that there are more cars than people in the city. Looking out across the burnished fields of parked vehicles that clog every empty space between buildings, one can hardly think otherwise. Segal came in from Connecticut to take me to the *Midsummer Night's Dream* everyone has been raving about, and afterward we picked up his car from an indoor lot: nine floors of chrome and steel, packed fender to fender, a *building* to house automobiles. One can hardly think otherwise.

Monday, late in the afternoon, Ophelia called me into his office and closed the door very carefully and stood with his left palm pressed against it as if expecting a sudden seismic rippling to ease it open. It was an unpleasant conversation. The quality of my work is down. My interest is flagging. Questionnaires returned by my students indicate the level of my teaching is low. The Evaluation Committee is deeply concerned. The Appraisal Committee has sent through a reminder that my last publication was four years ago.

He never mentioned the word tenure, or the words lack of it. My contract is up for renewal in May.

He used the word *mediocrity* frequently.

I stared past his balding, liver-spotted head and watched cars on the street outside, going other places. I imagined myself a Toltec, suddenly appearing on this street of thousands of years hence, seeing for the first time these terrible shining creatures with the great glass eyes and the sleek, many-colored hides, their mouths holding grille fangs all symmetrical and burnished; and I felt my lungs fill with air as I saw the unfortunate men and women who had been swallowed by these creatures, being swept past at incredible speeds.

And I wondered why they did not seem distressed at having been swallowed whole.

When he let me go, with vague ominous remarks about other tomorrows and other faces, I was shaking. I went back to my apartment and sat in the dark, trying not to think, only the sounds of automobile horns drifting up from the West Side Highway impinging.

On the sere grass center divider of the Grand Central Parkway, just beyond Flushing Meadow Park, where the sumptuous skeletal remains of the World Fair lie stunned and useless, I saw an entire family—mother, father and three children—stripping an abandoned Chrysler Imperial. They had the seats out, leaning against the body of the car, and the oldest son was liberating the radio from the dashboard. As the father jacked up the rear end, the two little girls placed bricks under the frame, enabling the mother to remove the tires. I read the word *polyglas* in an advertisement. One can say that word several times without causing it to discharge its informational content.

They reminded me of grave robbers defiling corpses.

When I mentioned it to several of my students after the morning class, one of them handed me an ecological newspaper in which the following was noted: "In 1967 Chicago, New York and Philadelphia reported finding thirty thousand abandoned cars annually."

I felt a certain glee. So cars die as well. And are abandoned, and lie unburied; and the ghouls come like predatory birds and pick them to pieces. It helped get me through the day, that bit of information. I repeated it to Emil Kane and his wife at dinner that weekend, and they laughed politely. I've found myself thinking about cars a great deal lately. That is peculiar for me.

His wife—a woman whose cooking depresses me—particularly since she and Kane are two of my last remaining invitations to dine —where has everyone gone—is it my imagination or is there a mass exodus from this city—ah, his wife, she reads a great deal. Banal left-wing publications. She added to the conversation the dull information that more American lives (she phrases it in that manner) have been taken by the automobile than by all the wars the nation has fought. I questioned the statistic. She went to a wicker flower basket where magazines were stacked, and she rummaged.

She opened one and leafed through it and pounced on a heavy-line block at the top of a page, and showed it to me. It said about 1,750,000 persons have died as a result of automobile accidents since the vehicle was introduced. In the first nine years of the war in Indochina 40,000 Americans were killed in combat; during that same period 437,000 were killed in auto accidents—eleven times as many.

"How interesting," I said. If one is unable to buy Courvoisier, one should forcibly restrain oneself from serving strawberries Romanoff for dessert.

Seven million automobiles are discarded annually in the United States. How interesting.

I must confess to a certain contentiousness of nature. Over coffee I turned Kane's wife's liberal nature against her. "Consider," I said. She looked up from crumb-gathering with a tiny battery-powered silent butler, and smiled.

"Consider. We anguish over our maltreated minorities. The black people, those we used to feel guiltless in calling 'Negroes,' the Puerto Ricans, Amerinds (obviously the noblest of us all), Mexican-Americans—"

"We must call *them* 'Chicanos,' " Kane's wife said, thinking she had made a joke. I ignored the remark. Levity on such topics surges well into gaucherie.

"All the minorities," I persisted. "Yet we treat with utter contempt the largest minority in our society."

"Women," she said.

"Hardly," I replied. "Women have the best of all possible worlds today."

She wanted to discuss it. I laid a hand against the air and stopped her. "No. Let me finish, Catherine. The automobile is the largest single minority in the country today. A larger group than males, or females, or Nisei, or under-thirty youth, or Republicans, or even the poor. In point of fact, they may even be the majority. Yet we use them as beasts of burden, we drive them into one another, wounding them, we abandon them by roadsides, unburied, unloved, we sell and trade them like Roman slave masters, we give them thought only insofar as they reflect our status."

Kane was grinning. He sensed my argument was based more in a distaste for his wife than any genuine conviction on my part. "What's your point?"

I spread my hands. "Simply, that I find it not at all inappropriate that they seek revenge against us. That they have only managed to kill 1,750,000 of us since 1896 when Ford first successfully tested the internal combustion engine on a horseless carriage . . . strikes me as a certain ineptitude on their part."

Kane laughed openly, then. "Thom, *really!*"

"Yes. Really."

"You attribute to inanimate objects a sentience that is clearly not present. I've seen you rail at Walt Disney for a good deal less anthropomorphism."

Orson Welles once performed (a bit flamboyantly, I've always felt) in a film called *Black Magic.* He assumed the role of Cagliostro and mesmerized everyone with whom he came into contact. In the film, Welles had a dark, piercing stare. He looked up from under heavy brows and spoke sepulchrally. Very affecting. This was the pose I now assumed with Kane and his wife. "No anthropomorphism at all. The group mind is hardly a new concept. It occurs in insects, in certain aquatic species, even in the plant world. If—as we now believe, because of the discovery of quasars—the 'big bang' theory of the conception of the universe is correct, that it all sprang full-blown into existence—and even Hoyle has given up on the 'constantly regenerating' theory—then surely it isn't such a quantum jump in logic to assume sentience can suddenly big-bang into existence."

They just looked at me. I believe they thought I was serious.

I made my final point. "Our Neanderthal ancestors. Does not a big bang of suddenly-sparked intelligence answer the question of how we came to be sitting here? I submit the same has happened with automobiles. A mass mind, a gestalt, if you prefer. But a society within a society. The world of the wheeled."

When I was six years old my mother developed a nasty bronchial cough. It was most strongly advised by the family physician that she go to Arizona for several months. She took me with her. I missed the keystone subjects of arithmetic during that school year, as a result. To this day, and surreptitiously of course, I still have recourse to my fingers when subtracting bank balances. For this reason I have never been interested in science or the rather tedious rigors of mathematics. I have never been able to read a text on the physical or social sciences completely. What I had said to them was the sheerest gibberish, through which holes could be punched by any first-year physics major. But Kane was a Chaucerian scholar—and he was amused by it all—while his wife was merely a fraud.

I took my leave soon after, leaving them both amazed and perplexed. The conversation had stimulated me; it had been the first gloriously bizarre sequence I had played in many months.

I decided to walk home though the night was chill and my apartment quite a distance. I have always been a religious man.

Consider the similarities between the cultures of South America and the Mideast; similarities difficult to explain. The simultaneous presence in both cultures of the religious figure of the fish, the Gregorian calendar, which parallels the stone calendars of the early Americans, the pyramid, which exists in both but in no other primitive society. Is it possible there was a link, two thousand years ago, between the land of, say, Judea and the land of the Aztecs? There is a story told—a fable only—of a white god who came upon the shores of the Aztecs during a period in history that would parallel the years from ages twelve to thirty during which nothing was heard of Jesus of Nazareth. They are known as the "lost" years of Jesus. The legend goes that this white man, whose like had never before been seen, went among the people and spoke of things that seemed wondrous and magical, of a kingdom of life after death. It was he, the story says, who introduced the symbol of the fish with its religious significance. Did he, as well, bring the pyramid structure and the calendar? We will never know, though historians have speculated that Jesus may well have taken passage with Phoenician sailors and found his way to the new continent. We will never know, but the legend adds one more mystery: the white prophet promised to return. And the people waited, and beat from purest gold an infinitude of gifts for his return.

Abandoned automobiles brought to a wrecking yard are first pressed flat by a stamping press. They are then stacked for the crusher. The crusher runs them down a treadmill track to a cubicle with sliding walls. They are pressed horizontally. Then the endwalls move together and the compressed remains of the automobile are squashed into a block that weighs several tons. The blocks, the cubes, are lifted by an enormously powerful electromagnet and stacked for reuse or resale. *Requiescat in pace.*

Bernal Díaz del Castillo, conquistador with Cortés, in his personal history entitled *The Discovery and Conquest of Mexico,* 1517–1521, tells of being met on the beach by Indians who came bearing great gifts of gold, as though they had *expected* the arrival of the Spaniards. Cortés, now judged by history to have been a senseless butcher, began slaughtering the natives almost before the boats had beached. Castillo comments that they were unarmed, seemed, in fact, to be ready to *worship* the white men who had come from the sea. But when the Spanish massacre began, the terror-filled word went back through the jungle, up the line to the endless procession of natives carrying their golden oblations in litters, and they buried the gold along the trail and vanished back the way they had come. A conclusion can be drawn. The natives of Tabasco who came to meet Cortés were filled with awe and love for the strangers. They were waiting for them, to pay them homage. Only the rampaging slaughter of their kind cleared their minds of the dreams of . . . what? A white god returned as promised? We will never know.

Gold ingots and gorgeous objects of the precious metal are being found, to this day, along the jungle trails inland from the sea at Tabasco.

The cubes of squared automobiles sit in the reclamation yards through rain and Winter, through night and Resale. They do not speak. They are not expected to speak.

In May I was terminated. I took a position as a junior editor with a Latin American book publisher, far uptown on the West Side. Mona Sündberg and her paramour went off to ski in Lapland. So they said. I don't know if it is possible to ski in Lapland. Emil Kane was mugged and robbed in broad daylight on Sixth Avenue. His wife blamed niggers. Blacks, I told her, when she called to impart the news. She never called back. I have grown to understand this kind of woman.

Working quite late one evening, I found myself on Fifth Avenue, far uptown. Passing under the viaduct where the IRT Seventh Avenue subway thunders aboveground, I saw a group of black, colored, Negro children smashing the windows of abandoned cars left naked under the brick structure. They were using ball-peen hammers.

If sentience suddenly sparks, and if they do, indeed, have a group mind, then they must have a society. One can hardly think otherwise. A culture. A species. A mass belief. With gods and legends and secret dreams they dream while their motors idle.

I sought no trouble with the children. They seemed capable of anything. But as I passed a dark-blue Chevrolet with its doors gone, I saw a small plastic figure of the Blessed Virgin Mary on the dashboard. For the first time in my life, I felt I must perform an act of senseless commitment. I felt tears in my eyes. I wanted to save the figure from the depredations of the grave robbers.

I bent over so they might not see me as I made my way to the car, and I reached inside and grasped the white plastic form of Mary.

There was a thunderous sound . . . surely the subway train clattering overhead.

When I opened my eyes I looked out from the pillar wall of the viaduct. I could see very clearly through the bricks. The night was no lighter. The children were still at their work.

I could not speak, nor could I move. I was imprisoned in the stone. As I am.

Why, Emil Kane's wife might ask, why Thom, are you there forever in stone, eternally crypted in brick? To which I would reply, I've learned to my dismay, that worship is like the stock market. There are winning issues and there are, of course, losers. Placing one's faith on a failing stock can be no less disastrous than placing one's faith on a downtrending deity.

He is a young God, and a jealous one. He does not like his graves robbed, the corpses of his supplicants defiled. But the children *believe*, you see; and I did not. Hardly a crime. But 'twill serve.

I am a religious man. I have always been a religious man—and one would think that should count for something.

Apparently it does not.

*Alchemical transmogrification in lotus land.*
*Contemporary wine and wafer, if you believe.*

# Shattered Like a Glass Goblin

So it was there, eight months later, that Rudy found her; in that huge and ugly house off Western Avenue in Los Angeles; living with them, *all* of them; not just Jonah, but all of them.

It was November in Los Angeles, near sundown, and unaccountably chill even for the fall in that place always near the sun. He came down the sidewalk and stopped in front of the place. It was gothic hideous, with the grass half-cut and the rusted lawnmower sitting in the middle of an unfinished swath. Grass cut as if a placating gesture to the outraged tenants of the two lanai apartment houses that loomed over that squat structure on either side. (Yet how strange . . . the apartment buildings were taller, the old house hunched down between them, but *it* seemed to dominate *them*. How odd.)

Cardboard covered the upstairs windows.

A baby carriage was overturned on the front walk.

The front door was ornately carved.

Darkness seemed to breathe heavily.

Rudy shifted the duffel bag slightly on his shoulder. He was afraid of the house. He was breathing more heavily as he stood there, and a panic he could never have described tightened the fat muscles on either side of his shoulderblades. He looked up into the corners of the darkening sky, seeking a way out, but he could only go forward. Kristina was in there.

Another girl answered the door.

She looked at him without speaking, her long blonde hair half-obscuring her face; peering out from inside the veil of Clairol and dirt.

When he asked a second time for Kris, she wet her lips in the corners, and a tic made her cheek jump. Rudy set down the duffel bag with a whump. "Kris, please," he said urgently.

The blonde girl turned away and walked back into the dim hallways of the terrible old house. Rudy stood in the open doorway, and suddenly, as if the blonde girl had been a barrier to it, and her departure had released it, he was assaulted, like a smack in the face, by a wall of pungent scent. It was marijuana.

He reflexively inhaled, and his head reeled. He took a step back, into the last inches of sunlight coming over the lanai apartment building, and then it was gone, and he was still buzzing, and moved forward, dragging the duffel bag behind him.

He did not remember closing the front door, but when he looked, some time later, it was closed behind him.

He found Kris on the third floor, lying against the wall of a dark closet, her left hand stroking a faded pink rag rabbit, her right hand at her mouth, the little finger crooked, the thumb-ring roach holder half-obscured as she sucked up the last wonders of the joint. The closet held an infinitude of odors—dirty sweat socks as pungent as stew, fleece jackets on which the rain had dried to mildew, a mop gracious with its scent of old dust hardened to dirt, the overriding weed smell of what she had been at for no one knew how long—and it held her. As pretty as pretty could be.

"Kris?"

Slowly, her head came up, and she saw him. Much later, she tracked and focused and she began to cry. "Go away."

In the limpid silences of the whispering house, back and above him in the darkness, Rudy heard the sudden sound of leather wings beating furiously for a second, then nothing.

Rudy crouched down beside her, his heart grown twice its size in his chest. He wanted so desperately to reach her, to talk to her. "Kris . . . please . . ." She turned her head away, and with the hand that had been stroking the rabbit she slapped at him awkwardly, missing him.

For an instant, Rudy could have sworn he heard the sound of someone counting heavy gold pieces, somewhere off to his right, down a passageway of the third floor. But when he half-turned, and looked out through the closet door, and tried to focus his hearing on it, there was no sound to home in on.

Kris was trying to crawl back farther into the closet. She was trying to smile.

He turned back, on hands and knees and he moved into the closet after her.

"The rabbit," she said, languorously. "You're crushing the rabbit." He looked down, his right knee was lying on the soft matted-fur head of the pink rabbit. He pulled it out from under his knee and threw it into a corner of the closet. She looked at him with disgust. "You haven't changed, Rudy. Go away."

"I'm outta the army, Kris," Rudy said gently. "They let me out on a medical. I want you to come back, Kris, please."

She would not listen, but pulled herself away from him, deep into the closet, and closed her eyes. He moved his lips several times, as though trying to recall words he had already spoken, but there was no sound, and he lit a cigarette, and sat in the open doorway of the closet, smoking and waiting for her to come back to him. He had waited eight months for her to come back to him, since he had been inducted and she had written him telling him, *Rudy, I'm going to live with Jonah at The Hill.*

There was the sound of something very tiny, lurking in the infinitely black shadow where the top step of the stairs from the second floor met the landing. It giggled in a glass harpsichord trilling. Rudy knew it was giggling at *him,* but he could make no movement from that corner.

Kris opened her eyes and stared at him with distaste. "Why did you come here?"

"Because we're gonna be married."

"Get out of here."

"I love you, Kris. Please."

She kicked out at him. It didn't hurt, but it was meant to. He backed out of the closet slowly.

Jonah was down in the living room. The blonde girl who had answered the door was trying to get his pants off him. He kept shaking his head no, and trying to fend her off with a weak-wristed hand. The record player under the brick-and-board bookshelves was playing Simon & Garfunkel, "The Big Bright Green Pleasure Machine."

"Melting," Jonah said gently. "Melting," and he pointed toward the big, foggy mirror over the fireplace mantel. The fireplace was crammed with unburned wax milk cartons, candy bar wrappers, newspapers from the underground press, and kitty litter. The mirror was dim and chill. "*Melting!*" Jonah yelled suddenly, covering his eyes.

"Oh shit!" the blonde girl said, and threw him down, giving up at last. She came toward Rudy.

"What's wrong with him?" Rudy asked.

"He's freaking out again. Christ, what a drag he can be."

"Yeah, but what's *happening* to him?"

She shrugged. "He sees his face melting, that's what he says."

"Is he on marijuana?"

The blonde girl looked at him with sudden distrust. "Mari—? Hey, who *are* you?"

"I'm a friend of Kris's."

The blonde girl assayed him for a moment more, then by the way her shoulders dropped and her posture relaxed, she accepted him. "I thought you might've just walked in, you know, maybe the Laws. You know?"

There was a Middle Earth poster on the wall behind her, with its brightness faded in a long straight swath where the sun caught it every morning. He looked around uneasily. He didn't know what to do.

"I was supposed to marry Kris. Eight months ago," he said.

"You want to fuck?" asked the blonde girl. "When Jonah trips he turns off. I been drinking Coca-Cola all morning and all day, and I'm really horny."

Another record dropped onto the turntable and Stevie Wonder blew hard into his harmonica and started singing, "I Was Born to Love Her."

"I was engaged to Kris," Rudy said, feeling sad. "We was going to be married when I got out of basic. But she decided to come over here with Jonah, and I didn't want to push her. So I waited eight months, but I'm out of the army now."

"Well, *do* you or *don't* you?"

Under the dining room table. She put a satin pillow under her. It said: *Souvenir of Niagara Falls, New York.*

When he went back into the living room, Jonah was sitting up on the sofa, reading Hesse's *Magister Ludi.*

"Jonah?" Rudy said. Jonah looked up. It took him a while to recognize Rudy.

When he did, he patted the sofa beside him, and Rudy came and sat down.

"Hey, Rudy, where y'been?"

"I've been in the army."

"Wow."

"Yeah, it was awful."

"You out now? I mean for good?"

Rudy nodded. "Uh-huh. Medical."

"Hey, that's good."

They sat quietly for a while. Jonah started to nod, and then said to himself, "You're not very tired."

Rudy said, "Jonah, hey listen, what's the story with Kris? You know, we were supposed to get married about eight months ago."

"She's around someplace," Jonah answered.

Out of the kitchen, through the dining room where the blonde girl lay sleeping under the table, came the sound of something wild, tearing at meat. It went on for a long time, but Rudy was looking out the front window, the big bay window. There was a man in a dark gray suit standing talking to two policemen on the sidewalk at the edge of the front walk leading up to the front door. He was pointing at the big, old house.

"Jonah, can Kris come away now?"

Jonah looked angry. "Hey, listen, man, nobody's *keeping* her here. She's been grooving with all of us and she likes it. Go ask her. Christ, don't bug *me!*"

The two cops were walking up to the front door.

Rudy got up and went to answer the doorbell.

They smiled at him when they saw his uniform.

"May I help you?" Rudy asked them.

The first cop said, "Do you live here?"

"Yes," said Rudy. "My name is Rudolph Boekel. May I help you?"

"We'd like to come inside and talk to you."

"Do you have a search warrant?"

"We don't want to search, we only want to talk to you. Are you in the army?"

"Just discharged. I came home to see my family."

"Can we come in?"

"No, sir."

The second cop looked troubled, "Is this the place they call 'The Hill'?"

"Who?" Rudy asked, looking perplexed.

"Well, the neighbors said this was 'The Hill' and there were some pretty wild parties going on here."

"Do you hear any partying?"

The cops looked at each other. Rudy added, "It's always very quiet here. My mother is dying of cancer of the stomach."

They let Rudy move in, because he was able to talk to people who came to the door from the outside. Aside from Rudy, who went out to get food, and the weekly trips to the unemployment line, no one left The Hill. It was usually very quiet.

Except sometimes there was a sound of growling in the back hall leading up to what had been a maid's room; and the splashing from the basement, the sound of wet things on bricks.

It was a self-contained little universe, bordered on the north by acid and mescaline, on the south by pot and peyote, on the east by speed and redballs, on the west by downers and amphetamines. There were eleven people living in The Hill. Eleven, and Rudy.

He walked through the halls, and sometimes found Kris, who would not talk to him, save once, when she asked him if he'd ever been heavy behind *anything* except love. He didn't know what to answer her, so he only said, "Please," and she called him a square and walked off toward the stairway leading to the dormered attic.

Rudy had heard squeaking from the attic. It had sounded to him like the shrieking of mice being torn to pieces. There were cats in the house.

He did not know why he was there, except that he didn't understand why *she* wanted to stay. His head always buzzed and he sometimes felt that if he just said the right thing, the right way, Kris would come away with him. He began to dislike the light. It hurt his eyes.

No one talked to anyone else very much. There was always a struggle to keep high, to keep the *group high* as elevated as possible. In that way they cared for each other.

And Rudy became their one link with the outside. He had written to someone—his parents, a friend, a bank, someone—and now there was money coming in. Not much, but enough to keep the food stocked, and the rent paid. But he insisted Kris be nice to him.

They all made her be nice to him, and she slept with him in the little room on the second floor where Rudy had put his newspapers and his duffel bag. He lay there most of the day, when he was not out on errands for The Hill, and he read the smaller items about train wrecks and molestations in the suburbs. And Kris came to him and they made love of a sort.

One night she convinced him he should "make it, heavy behind acid" and he swallowed fifteen hundred mikes cut with Methedrine, in two big gel caps, and she was stretched out like taffy for six miles. He was a fine copper wire charged with electricity, and he pierced her flesh. She wriggled with the current that flowed through him, and became softer yet. He sank down through the softness, and carefully observed the intricate woodgrain effect her teardrops made as they rose in the mist around him. He was down-drifting slowly, turning and turning, held by a whisper of blue that came out of his body like a spiderweb. The sound of her breathing in the moist crystal pillared cavity that went down and down was the sound of the very walls themselves, and when he touched them with his warm metal fingertips she drew in breath heavily, forcing the air up around him as he sank down, twisting slowly in a veil of musky looseness.

There was an insistent pulsing growing somewhere below him, and he was afraid of it as he descended, the high-pitched whining of something threatening to shatter. He felt panic. Panic gripped him, flailed at him, his throat constricted, he tried to grasp the veil and it tore away in his hands; then he was falling, faster now, much faster, and *afraid!*

Violet explosions all around him and the shrieking of something that wanted him, that was seeking him, pulsing deeply in the throat of an animal he could not name, and he heard her shouting, heard her wail and pitch beneath him and a terrible crushing feeling in him. . . .

And then there was silence.

That lasted for a moment.

And then there was soft music that demanded nothing but inattention. So they lay there, fitted together, in the heat of the tiny room, and they slept for some hours.

After that, Rudy seldom went out into the light. He did the shopping at night, wearing shades. He emptied the garbage at night, and he swept down the front walk, and did the front lawn with scissors because the lawnmower would have annoyed the residents of the lanai apartments (who no longer complained, because there was seldom a sound from The Hill).

He began to realize he had not seen some of the eleven young people who lived in The Hill for a long time. But the sounds from above and below and around him in the house grew more frequent.

Rudy's clothes were too large for him now. He wore only underpants. His hands and feet hurt. The knuckles of his fingers were larger, from cracking them, and they were always an angry crimson.

His head always buzzed. The thin perpetual odor of pot had saturated into the wood walls and the rafters. He had an itch on the outside of his ears he could not quell. He read newspapers all the time, old newspapers whose items were imbedded in his memory. He remembered a job he had once held as a garage mechanic, but that seemed a very long time ago. When they cut off the electricity in The Hill, it didn't bother Rudy, because he preferred the dark. But he went to tell the eleven.

He could not find them.

They were all gone. Even Kris, who should have been there somewhere.

He heard the moist sounds from the basement and went down with fur and silence into the darkness. The basement had been flooded. One of the eleven was there. His name was Teddy. He was attached to the slime-coated upper wall of the basement, hanging close to the stone, pulsing softly and giving off a thin purple light, purple as a bruise. He dropped a rubbery arm into the water, and let it hang there, moving idly with the tireless tide. Then something came near it, and he made a *sharp* movement, and brought the thing up still writhing in his rubbery grip, and inched it along the wall to a dark, moist spot on his upper surface, near the veins that covered its length, and pushed the thing at the dark-blood spot, where it shrieked with a terrible sound, and went in and there was a sucking noise, then a swallowing sound.

Rudy went back upstairs. On the first floor he found the one who was the blonde girl, whose name was Adrianne. She lay out thin and white as a tablecloth on the dining room table as three of the others he had not seen in a very long while put their teeth into her, and through their hollow sharp teeth they drank up the yellow fluid from the bloated pus-pockets that had been her breasts and her buttocks. Their faces were very white and their eyes were like soot-smudges.

Climbing to the second floor, Rudy was almost knocked down by the passage of something that had been Victor, flying on heavily ribbed leather wings. It carried a cat in its jaws.

He saw the thing on the stairs that sounded as though it was counting heavy gold pieces. It was not counting heavy gold pieces. Rudy could not look at it; it made him feel sick.

He found Kris in the attic, in a corner breaking the skull and sucking out the moist brains of a thing that giggled like a harpsichord.

"Kris, we have to go away," he told her. She reached out and touched him, snapping her long, pointed, dirty fingernails against him. He rang like crystal.

In the rafters of the attic Jonah crouched, gargoyled and sleeping. There was a green stain on his jaws, and something stringy in his claws.

"Kris, please," he said urgently.

His head buzzed.

His ears itched.

Kris sucked out the last of the mellow good things in the skull of the silent little creature, and scraped idly at the flaccid body with hairy hands. She settled back on her haunches, and her long, hairy muzzle came up.

Rudy scuttled away.

He ran loping, his knuckles brushing the attic floor as he scampered for safety. Behind him, Kris was growling. He got down to the second floor and then to the first, and tried to climb up on the Morris chair to the mantel, so he could see himself in the mirror, by the light of the moon, through the fly-blown window. But Naomi was on the window, lapping up the flies with her tongue.

He climbed with desperation, wanting to see himself. And when he stood before the mirror, he saw that he was transparent, that there was nothing inside him, that his ears had grown pointed and had hair on their tips; his eyes were as huge as a tarsier's and the reflected light hurt him.

Then he heard the growling behind and below him.

The little glass goblin turned, and the werewolf rose up on its hind legs and touched him till he rang like fine crystal.

And the werewolf said with very little concern, "Have you ever grooved heavy behind *anything* except love?"

"Please!" the little glass goblin begged, just as the great hairy paw slapped him into a million coruscating rainbow fragments all expanding consciously into the tight little enclosed universe that was The Hill, all buzzing highly contacted and tingling off into a darkness that began to seep out through the silent wooden walls. . . .

*The new gods move in mysterious ways,*
*their will to make known: business as*
*usual, with miracles as loss-leaders.*
*Brings to mind the ancient Chinese*
*admonition, "Be careful what you wish*
*for . . . you might get it."*

# Delusion for a Dragon Slayer

This is true:

Chano Pozo, the incredibly talented conga drummer of the bop '40s, was inexplicably shot and killed by a beautiful Negress in the Rio Café, a Harlem bar, on December 2nd, 1948.

Dick Bong, pilot of a P-38 "Lightning" in World War Two, America's "Ace of Aces" with forty Japanese kills to his credit, who came through the hellfire of war unscratched, perished by accident when the jet engine of a Lockheed P-80 he was test-flying "flamed-out" and quit immediately after takeoff, August 7th, 1945. There was no reason for the mechanical failure, no reason for Bong to have died.

Marilyn Monroe, an extremely attractive young woman who had only recently begun to realize she possessed an acting ability far beyond that of "sex symbol" tagged on her early in her career, during the timeless early hours of August 6th, 1962, left this life as a result of accidentally swallowing too many barbiturates. Despite lurid conjecture to the contrary, the evidence that she had been trying to phone someone for help as the tragedy coursed through her system remains inescapable. It was an accident.

William Bolitho, one of the most incisive and miraculously talented commentators on society and its psychological motivations, whose "Murder for Profit" revolutionized psychiatric and penological attitudes toward the mentalities of mass murderers, died suddenly—and again, tragically—in June of 1930, in a hospital in Avignon, victim of the mistaken judgment of an obscure French physician who let a simple case of appendicitis drop into peritonitis.

True.

All of these random deaths plucked from a staggering and nearly endless compendium of "accidental tragedies" have one thing in common. With each other, and with the death of Warren Glazer Griffin. None of them should have happened. Each of them could have been avoided, yet none of them could have been avoided. For each of them was preordained. Not in the ethereal, mystic, supernatural flummery of the Kismet-believers, but in the complex rhythmic predestination of those who have been whisked out of their own world, into the mist-centuries of their dreams.

For Chano Pozo, it was a dark and smiling woman of mystery.

For Dick Bong, a winged Fury sent to find only him.

For Marilyn Monroe, a handful of white chalk pills.

For Bolitho, an inept quack forever doomed to apologies.

And for Warren Glazer Griffin, a forty-one-year-old accountant who, despite his advanced age, was still troubled by acne, and who had never ventured farther from his own world than Tenafly, New Jersey, on a visit to relatives one June in 1959, it was a singular death: ground to pulp between the triple-fanged rows of teeth in the mouth of a seventy-eight-foot dragon in a Land That Never Existed.

Wherein lies a biography, an historical footnote, a cautionary tale, and a keynote to the meaning of life.

Or, as Goethe summed it:

"Know thyself? If I knew myself, I'd run away."

The giant black "headache ball" of the wreckers struck the shell of a wall, and amid geysers of dust and powder and lath and plaster and brick and decayed wood, the third story of the condemned office building crumbled, shivered along its width and imploded, plunging in upon itself, dumping jigsaw pieces into the hollow structure. The sound was a cannonade in the early-morning eight-o'clock street.

Forty years before, an obscure billionaire named Rouse, who had maintained a penthouse love-nest in the office building, in an unfashionable section of the city even then, had caused to be installed a private gas line to the kitchen of the flat; he was a lover of money, a lover of women, and a lover of flaming desserts. A private gas line. Gas company records of this installation had been either lost, destroyed, or—as seems more likely—carefully edited to exclude mention of the line. Graft, as well as bootlegging, had aided Rouse in his climb to that penthouse. The wreckers knew nothing of the gas line, which had long since gone to disuse, and the turnoff of a small valve on the third floor, which had originally jetted the vapor to the upper floor. Having no knowledge of the line, and having cleared all safety precautions with the city gas company as to existing installations, the wreckers hurled their destructive attentions at the third story with assurance. . . .

Warren Glazer Griffin left his home at precisely seven forty-five every weekday except Thursday (on which day he left at eight o'clock, to collect billing ledgers from his firm's other office, farther downtown; an office that did not open till 8:15 weekdays). This was Thursday. He had run out of razor blades. That simple. He had had to pry a used blade out of the disposal niche in the blade container, and it had taken him ten extra minutes. He hurried and managed to leave the apartment house at 8:06 A.M. His routine was altered for the first time in seventeen years. That simple. Hurrying down the block to the Avenue, turning right and hesitating, realizing he could not make up the lost minutes by merely trotting (and without even recognizing the subliminal panic that gripped him at being off schedule), he dashed across the Avenue, and cut through the little service alley running between the shopping mart, still closed, and the condemned office building with its high board fence constructed of thick doors from now-demolished offices. . . .

> U.S. WEATHER BUREAU FORECAST: partly cloudy today with a few scattered showers. Sunny and slightly warmer tomorrow (Friday). Gusty winds. High today 62. High Friday 60, low 43. Relative humidity . . .

Forty years past, a billionaire named Rouse.
A desire for flaming desserts.
A forgotten gas main.
A struggle for a used razor blade.
A short cut through an alley.
Gusty winds . . .

The "headache ball" plunged once more into the third story, struck the bottled-up pressure valve; the entire side of the building erupted skyward on a spark struck by two bricks scratching together, ripping the massive iron sphere from its cable. The ball rose, arced and, borne on an unusually heavy wind, plummeted over the restraining board fence. It landed with a deafening crash in the alley.

Directly on the unsuspecting person of Warren Glazer Griffin, crushing him to little more than pulp, burying him five feet deep beneath cement and dirt and loam. Every building in the neighborhood shuddered at the impact.

And in several moments, cemetery silence fell once more in the chilly, eight-o-clock morning streets.

A soft, theremin humming, in little circles of sound, from all around him: the air was alive with multicolored whispers of delight.

He opened his eyes and realized he was lying on the yellow-wood, highly polished deck of a sailing vessel; to his left he could see beneath the rail a sea of purest vermilion, washing in thin lines of black and color, away behind the ship. Above him the golden silken sails billowed in the breeze, and tiny spheres of many-colored lights kept pace with the vessel, as though they were lightning bugs, sent to run convoy. He tried to stand up, and found it was not difficult: except he was now six feet three inches in height, not five feet seven.

Griffin looked down the length of his body, and for a suspended instant of eye-widening timelessness, he felt vertiginous. It was total displacement of ego. He was himself, and another himself entirely. He looked down, expecting to see the curved, pot-bellied and pimpled body he had worn for a very long time, but instead saw someone else, standing down below him, where he should have been. *Oh my God,* thought Warren Glazer Griffin, *I'm not me.*

The body that extended down to the polished deck was a handsome instrument. Composed of the finest bronzed skin tone, the most sculptured anthracite-hard musculature, proportions just the tiniest bit exaggerated; he was lovely and godlike, extremely godlike. Turning slowly, he caught his reflection in the burnished smoothness of a warrior's bronze shield, hung on a peg at the side of the forecastle. He was Nordic blond, aquiline-nosed, steely-blue-eyed. *No one can be that Aryan,* was his only thought, flushed with amazement, as he saw the new face molded to the front of his head.

He felt the hilt of the sword warm against his side.

He pulled it free of its scabbard, and stared in fascination at the face of the old, gnarled marmoset-eyed wizard whose countenance was an intaglio of pitted metal and jewels and sandblast block briar; engraved there in hard relief on the handle. The face smiled gently at him.

"What it is all about, is this," the wizard said softly, so that not even the sea birds careening over the deck would hear. "This is Heaven. But let me explain." Griffin had not considered an interruption. He was silent and struck dumb. "Heaven is what you mix all the days of your life, but you call it dreams. You have one chance to buy your Heaven with all the intents and ethics of your life. That is why everyone considers Heaven such a lovely place. Because it is dreams, special dreams, in which you exist. What you have to do is live up to them."

"I—" started Griffin, but the wizard cut him off with a blink.

"No, listen, please, because after this, all the magic stops, and you have to do it alone.

"You create your own Heaven, and you have the opportunity to live in it, but you have to do it on your own terms, the highest terms of which you are capable. So sail this ship through the straits, navigate the shoals, find the island, overcome the foam-devil that guards the girl, win her love, and you've played the game on your own terms."

Then the wizard's face settled back into immobility, and Warren Glazer Griffin sat down heavily on the planking of the forecastle, mouth agape, eyes wide, and the realization of it all fixed firmly— unbelievably, but firmly—in his head.

*Gee whiz,* thought Griffin.

The sound of rigging shrieking like terns brought him out of his middle-class stupor, and he realized the keel of the strange and wonderful wind-vessel was coming about. The steady beatbeatbeat of pole-oars against mirror waters rose to meet the descending hum of a dying breeze, and the ship moved across reflective waters toward a mile-high breaker that abruptly rose out of the sea.

Griffin realized it had not leaped from the sea bottom, as his first impression seemed to be, but had gradually grown on the horizon, some moments after the watch in the nest had hallooed its imminent appearance. Yet he had not heard any such gardyloo; he was surfeited with thoughts of this other body, the golden god with the incredibly handsome face.

"Cap'n," said one of the hands, lumbering with sea legs toward him. "We're hard on the straits. Most of the men're shackled a'ready."

Griffin nodded silently, turned to follow the seaman. They moved back toward the lazzarette, and the seaman opened the hatch, dropped through. Griffin followed close behind him, and in the small-ish compartment found the other sea-hands shackled wrist and ankle to the inner keel of the hold. He gagged for a moment with the overpowering stench of salted bully beef and fish, a sickly, bittersweet smell that made his eyes smart with its intensity.

Then he moved to the seaman, who had already fastened his own ankle-shackles and one wrist manacle. He clamped the rusting manacle still undone, and now all hands aboard the wind-vessel were locked immobile.

"Good luck, Cap'n!" The last seaman smiled. And he winked. The other men joined in, in their own ways, with a dozen different accents, some in languages Griffin could not even begin to place. But all well-wishing. Griffin once more nodded in the strong, silent manner of someone other than himself, someone to the rank born.

Then he climbed out of the lazzarette and went aft to the wheel.

Overhead, the sky had darkened to a shining blackness, a patent-leather black that would have sent back inverted reflections had there been anything soaring close enough to the sky to reflect. In the mote-dancing waters of the ocean, a ghost ship sailed along upside-down, hull-to-hull with Griffin's vessel. And above him the quaint and tittering globes of light ricocheted and multiplied, filling the sudden night with the incense of their vibrancy. Their colors began to blend, to merge, to run down the sky in washes of color that made Griffin smile, and blink and drop his mouth open with awe. It was all the fireworks of another universe, just once hurled into an onyx sky, left to burn away whatever life was possible. Yet that was merely the beginning:

The colors came. As he set his feet squarely, and the deltoids bunched furiously beneath his golden skin, the two men who were Warren Glazer Griffin began the complex water slalom that would send the vessel through the straits, past the shoals, and into the cove that lay beyond. And the colors came. The vessel tacked before the wind, which seemed to gather itself and enter in an arrowed spear-pointed direction of unity, behind the massive golden sails. The wind was with him, sending him straight for the break in the heartless stone barrier. But the colors came.

Softly at first, humming, creeping, boiling up from nowhere at the horizon line; twisting and surging like snake whirlwinds with adolescent intent; building, spiraling, climbing in vague streamers and tendrils of unconsciousness, the colors came.

In a rising, keening spiral of hysteria they came, first pulsing in primaries, then secondaries, then comminglings and off shades, and finally in colors that had no names. Colors like racing, and pungent, and far-seen shadows, and bitterness, and something that hurt, and something that pleasured. Oh, mostly the pleasures, one after another, singing, lulling, hypnotically arresting the eye as the ship sped into the heart of the maelstrom of weird, advancing, sky-eating colors. The siren colors of the straits. The colors that came from the air and the island and the world itself, which hushed and hurried across the world to here, to meet when they were needed, to stop the seamen who slid over the waves to the break in the breakwall. The colors, defense, that sent men to the bottom, their hearts bursting with songs of color and charm. The colors that top-filled a man to the brim and kept him poised there with a surface tension of joy and wonder, colors cascading like waterfalls of flowers in his head, millioncolors, blossomshades, brightnesses, joycrashing everythings that made a man hurl back and strain his throat to sing sing, sing chants of amazement and forever—

—as his ship plunged like a cannonball into the reefs and shattered into a billion wooden fragments, tiny splinters of dark wood against the boiling treacherous sea, and the rocks crushed and staved in the sides, and men's heads went to pulp as they hurtled forward and their vessel was cut out from under them, the colors the colors, the God beautiful colors!

As Griffin sang his song of triumph, the men with eyes clapped tightshut, belowdecks, saved from berserking, depending on this golden giant of a man who was their own personal this-trip God, who would bring them through the hole in the faceless evil rocks.

Griffin, singing!

Griffin, golden god from Manhattan!

Griffin, man of two skins, Chinese puzzle man within man, hands cross-locked over the wood of the wheel, tacking points this way, points that way, playing compass and swashbuckler with the deadly colors that lapped at his senses, filled his eyes with delight, clogged his nostrils with the scents of glory, all the tiny theremin hummings now merged, all the little colormotes now united, running in slippery washes down and down the sky as he hurried the vessel toward the rocks and then in one sweep as he spun spun spun the wheel two-handed across, whip whip whip, and *through* into the bubbling white water, with rock-teeth screeching old women along the hull of his vessel, and tearing gouged gashes of darker deepness along the planking, but *through!*

Griffin, who chuckled with merriment at his grandeur, his stature, his chance taking, who had risked the lives of all his men for the moment of forever to be gained on that island. And winning! Making his wager with eternity, and winning—for an instant, before the great ship struck the buried reefs that tore away the bottom of the ship; and the lazzarette filled in an instant; and his men, who trusted him not to gamble them away so cheaply, wailed till their screams became waterlogged, and were gone; and Griffin felt himself lifted, tossed, hurled, flung like a bit of suet and the thought that invaded, consumed, gnawed at him in rage and frustration: that he had defeated the siren colors, had gotten through the treacherous straits, but had lost his men, his ship, even himself, by the treachery of his own self-esteem; that he had gloated over his wondrousness, and vanity had sent him whipping farther inshore, to be dashed on reefs; and the bitterness welled in him as he struck the water with a paralyzing crash, and sank immediately beneath the boiling white-faced waves.

Out on the reefs, the wind-vessel, with its adamantine trim, with its onyx and alabaster fittings, with its silken golden sails, with its marvelous magical swiftness, sank beneath the waters without a murmur

(unless those silent insane shrieggggngggg wails were the sounds of men shackled helplessly to an open coffin)

and all that could be heard was the pounding war drums of the waves, and the gutted, emptying, shrill keen of an animal whose throat had been slashed—the sound of the colors fading back to their million lairs around the universe, till they would be called again. Then, after a while, even the water calmed.

Crickets gossiped shamelessly, close beside his head. He awoke to find his eyes open, staring up into a pale, cadaverous paper-thin cut-out that was the moon. Clouds scudding across its mottled slimness sent strange shadows washing across the night sky, the beach, the jungle, Warren Glazer Griffin.

*Well, I certainly messed* that *up,* was his first thought, and in an instant the thought was gone, and the Nordic god-man's thoughts superimposed more strenuously. Griffin felt his arms out wide on the white sand, and scraped them across the clinging grains till he was able to jack himself up, straining his back heavily. Propped on elbows, legs spread-eagled before him, he stared out to sea, to the great barrier wall that encircled the island, and scanned the dark expanse for some sign of ship or men. There was nothing. He let his mind linger for long moments on the vanity and ego that had cost so many lives.

Then he painfully climbed to his feet, and turned to look at the island. Jungle rose up in a thick tweedy tangle, as high as the consumptive moon, and the warp of dark vine tracery merged with a woof of sounds. Massed sounds, beasts, insects, night birds, unnamable sounds that chittered and rasped and howled and shrieked—even as his men had shrieked—and the scent-sound of moist meat being ripped from the carcass of an ambushed soft creature was predominant. It was a living jungle, a presence in itself.

He pulled his sword and struck off across the strand of white shadowed sand toward the rim edge of the tangle. In there somewhere waited the girl, and the mist-devil, and the promise of life forever, here in this best of all possible worlds, his own Heaven, which he had made from a lifetime of dreams. . . .

Yet the dream seemed relentlessly nightmarish: the jungle resisted him, clawed at him, tempted yet rebuffed him. Griffin found himself hacking at the thick-fleshed twined and interwoven wall of foliage with growing ferocity. His even white teeth, beautifully matched and level, locked in a solid enamel band, and his eyes narrowed with frenzy. The hours melted into a shapeless colloid, and he could not tell whether he was making his way through the dense greenmass, or standing still while the jungle crawled imperceptibly toward him, filling in behind the clots he was hacking away. And darkness, suffocating, in the jungle.

Abruptly, he lunged forward against a singularly rugged matting of interlocked tree branches, and hurled himself through the break, as it fell away, unresisting. He was in the clear. At the top of a rise that fell away below him in softly curved smoothness, toward a rushing stream of gently whispering white water. Around small stones it raced, gathering speed, a timorous moist animal streaking toward a far land.

Griffin found himself loping down the hill, toward the bank of the stream, and as he ran, his body grew more and more his own. The hill grew up behind him, and the stream came toward him with gentleness, and he was there: time was another thing here, not forced, not necessary, a pastel passage, without hard edges.

He followed the stream, skirting banks of thickets and trees that seemed to be windswept in their topmost branches, and the stream became a river, and the river rushed to rapids, and then suddenly there were falls. Not great thundering falls down which men might be swept in fragile canoes, but murmuring ledges and sweeps down which the white water surged sweetly, carrying tinges of color from the banks, carrying vagrant leaves and blades of grass, gently, tenderly, comfortingly. Griffin stood silently, watching the waterfall, sensing more than he saw, understanding more than even his senses could tell him. This was, indeed, the Heaven of his dreams, a place to spend the rest of forever, with the wind and the water and the world another place, another level of sensing, another bad dream conjured many long times before. This was reality, an only reality for a man whose existence had been not quite bad, merely insufficient, tenable but hardly enriching. For a man who had lived a life of not quite enough, this was all there ever could be of goodness and brilliance and light. Griffin moved toward the falls.

The darkness grew darker.

Glowing in the dimensionless whispering dimness, Griffin saw a scene that could only have come from his dreams. The woman, naked white against the ledges and slopes of the falls; water cascading down her back, across her thighs, cool against her belly, her hair streaming back and white water bubbling through the shining black veil of her hair, touching each strand, silkily shining it with moisture; her eyes closed in simple pleasure; that face, the *right* face, the special face, the certain face of the woman he had always looked for without looking, hunted silently for, without acknowledging the search; lusted for, without feeling worthy of the hunger.

It was the woman his finest instincts had needed to make them valid; the woman who not only gave to him, but to whom he could give; the woman of memory, of desire, of youth, of restlessness, of completion. A dream. And here, against the softspeaking bubbling water, a reality. Glowing magically in the night, the woman raised a hand languidly and with joy, simple unspoken joy, and Griffin started toward her as

the mist-devil materialized. Out of the foam spray, out of the night, out of the suddenly rising chill fog and vapor and cloud-slime, out of starshine and evil mists without proper names, the devil that guarded this woman of visions, materialized. Giant, gigantic, massive, rising higher and higher, larger, more intensely defined against the night, the devil spread across the sky in a towering, smooth-edged reality.

Great sad eyes, the white molten centers of ratholes in which whirlwinds lived. A brow: massive leaded furrows drawing down in unctuous pleasure at sight of the woman; creature, this horrendous creature, this gigantic filth, liaison with white flesh? The thought skittered like a poisoned rodent across the floor of Griffin's mind, like a small creature with one leg torn off, pain and blood-red ganglia of conception, then lost itself in the bittersweet crypt beneath thoughts: too repugnant, too monstrous for continued examination. And the mist-devil rose and rose and expanded, and bellows-blew its chest to horizon-filling proportions. Griffin fell back into shadows lest he be seen.

More, greater, still more massive it rose, filling the night sky till it obscured the moon, till nightbirds lived in its face, till molten tremblings—the very stars—served it as exhalations of breath. The mouth of a maniac millions magnified, was its mouth. Terror and fear and whimperings from far underground were the lines of character in a face incalculably old, ancient, decayed with a time that could not be called time by men. And it was one with this woman. It consorted, filthy liaison, subliminal haunted Pleistocene gonadal urgings, it and woman, force incarnate and gentle labial moistures. This: the terrible end-hunger of a million billion eons of forced abstinence.

Forever paramour, the eternity lecher, the consumed-by-desire that rose and rose and blotted the world with its bulk. The mist-devil Warren Glazer Griffin had to kill, before he could live forever in his dreams.

Griffin stood back in shadows, trembling within the golden body he wore. Now, abruptly, he was two men once again. The god with his sword, the mortal with his fear. And he swore to himself that he could not do it, could not—even crying inside that poor glorious shell —and could not, and was terribly afraid. But then, as he watched, the mist-devil imploded, drew in upon itself, shrinking shrinking shrinking down and down and down into a smaller tighter neater less infinitely tinier replica of itself, like a gas-filled balloon suddenly released from the hand of a child, whipping, snapping, spinning through the air growing smaller as it lost its muscled tautness. . . .

Then the mist-devil became the size of a man.

And it went to the woman.

And they made love.

Griffin watched in disgust and loathing as the creature that was age, that was night, that was fear, that was everything save the word *human*, placed hands on white breasts, placed lips on pliant red mouth, placed thighs around belly, and the woman's arms came up and embraced the creature of always, and they locked in twisting union, there in the white bubbling water, with the stars shrieking overhead and the moon a bloated madness careening down a sinkhole of space, as Warren Glazer Griffin watched the woman of all his thoughts take in the manhood of something anything but man. And silently, like a footpad, Griffin crept up behind the devil of mist, consumed in trembling consummation of desire, and locking his wet and sticky hands about the hilt of the weapon, he raised it over his head, spread-legged like an executioner, and drove the blade viciously, but at an angle, downdowndown and with the thickrasping crunch of metal through meat, into and out the other side of the neck of the creature.

It drew in a hideous world-load of air, gasping it up and into torn flesh, a rattling distended neck-straining blowfish mass of air, that ended with a sound so high and pathetic that skin prickled up and down Griffin's cheeks, his neck, his back, and the monstrous creature reached off to nowhere to pull out the insane iron that had destroyed it, and the hand went to another location, and the blade was ripped free by Griffin, as the devil rose off the woman, dripping blood and dripping the fluid of love and dripping life away in every instant, careening into the falls with deadfish stains of all-colored blood in the wake, and turned once, to stare full into Griffin's face with a look that denounced him:

From behind!

*From behind!*

Was gone. Was dead. Was floated down waterfalls to deep Stygian pools of refuse and rubble and rust. To silt bottoms where nothing mattered, but gone.

Leaving Warren Glazer Griffin to stand with blood that had spurted up across his wide golden chest, staring down at the woman of his dreams, whose eyes were cataracted with frenzy and fear. All the dream orgies of his life, all the wild couplings of his adolescent nightmares, all the wants and hungers and needs of his woman sensings, were here.

The girl gave only one shrill howl before he took her. He had thoughts all during the frantic struggle and just at the penetration: womanwhore slutlover trollopmine over and over and over and over and

when he rose from her, the eyes that stared back at him, like leaves in snow, on the first day of winter. Empty winds howled down out of the tundras of his soul. This was the charnel house of his finest fantasies. The burial ground of his forever. The garbage dump, the slain meat, the putrefying reality of his dreams and his Heaven.

Griffin stumbled away from her, hearing the shrieks of men needlessly drowned by his vanity, hearing the voiceless accusation of the devil proclaiming cowardice, hearing the orgasm-condemnation of lust that was never love, of brute desire that was never affection, and realizing at last that these were the real substances of his nature, the true faces of his sins, the marks in the ledger of a life he had never led, yet had worshipped silently at an altar of evil.

All these thoughts, as the guardian of Heaven, the keeper at the gate, the claimer of souls, the weigher of balances, advanced on him through the night.

Griffin looked up and had but a moment to realize he had not succeeded in winning his Heaven . . . as the seventy-eight-foot creature he could have called nothing less than a dragon opened its mouth that was all the world and judgment, and ground him to senseless pulp between rows of triple-fanged teeth.

When they dug the body out of the alley, it made even the hardened construction workers and emergency squad cops ill. Not one bone was left unbroken. The very flesh seemed to have been masticated as if by a nation of cannibal dogs. Even so, the three inured excavators who finally used winding sheets and shovels to bring the shapeless mess up from its five-foot grave agreed that it was incredible, totally past belief, that the head and face were untouched.

And they all agreed that the expression *on* the face was not one of happiness. There were many possible explanations for that expression, but no one would have said terror, for it was not terror. They would not have said helplessness, for it was not that, either. They might have settled on a pathetic sense of loss, had their sensibilities run that deep, but none of them would have felt that the expression said, with great finality: a man may truly live in his dreams, his noblest dreams, but only, *only* if he is worthy of those dreams.

It did not rain that night, anywhere in the known universe.

*Even God needs good rolling stock to get
things done.*

# The Face of Helene Bournouw

These are the sounds in the night: First, the sound of darkness, lapping at the edges of a sea of movement, itself called silence. Then, second, the fingertip-sensed sound of the cyclical movement of the universe as it gnaws its way through the dust-film called Time. And last, the animal sounds of two people making love. The moist sounds of two bodies in concert. Always the same sound, and only set apart from itself by the meters and stop-pauses of generators phasing down, of equipment being hauled into new positions for use.

Weltered, foundering, going down in this downdropping clogature of sound, Helene Bournouw's mouth opened to receive a charcoal-scented passion as brief as the life of a leaf. Wind rushed silently past, deafening as it sucked the breath from both Helene Bournouw and her lover.

In the perfect minds of Gods too perfect even to have been conjured by mortals, there never existed a love as drenched in empathy as the love between Helene Bournouw and the man she accepted gratefully. Under the sun that burned bright and blue-white there was never a passion such as this: straight as steel ties to an indecipherable horizon, gleaming rhodium silver-white in perfection, filled to the top and to its own surface tension with amiability and laughter and random turnings in the dark that signified two merging into one, being taken in completely, warm and forever.

This was the way she made love, Helene Bournouw, the most beautiful woman who had ever seen man through eyes of wonder.

Richard Strike, the only one of the cilia-wafting Broadway columnists with a valid claim to literacy, once referred to her as the most memorable succubus he had ever encountered. The Times Square sharpers, of course, equated the phrase with oral pornography and let it pass; *they* knew what Helene Bournouw was: she was too beautiful.

Yet there was truth in what Strike had said, and the label was a fair one. There was something about Helene Bournouw that drained those who came into her life, within her reach. Of beauty there was no doubt; she *was* almost too beautiful. Abington was the only photographer she would allow to pose her, and together their model-photographer relationship brought forth portraits of Helene Bournouw that became testimonies to her unearthly loveliness, hers alone. (Whether those portraits sold sanitary napkins or compact cars, the viewer saw first Helene Bournouw, and when her image finally released him . . . *then* the product.)

From these two elements—beauty that could not be denied and a nature that left others spent and empty—elements met and altered subtly by the catalyst that was Helene Bournouw, the legend grew. Her private life was her own, something peculiar and rare for a mover in that circle where publicity has monetary value. Other than superficialities concerning what young executive or visiting film star she was dating, little was known of her.

As Abington once remarked to a curious article writer from one of the women's slicks, "When she leaves the studio, I don't know where she goes. She lives on Sutton Place, but she's seldom there; Helene could be making her home in the fog, and we wouldn't know it. All I care about is that she's the loveliest woman I've ever photographed."

And that, from the man who discovered Suzy Parker, who did the first adult portraits of Elizabeth Taylor, who was commissioned to photograph the fifty most beautiful women in the world for *Life*, is perhaps the most telling argument for those who swear there has never been born a more fascinating, gorgeous creature than Helene Bournouw.

Seated early in the day in a corner booth at Lindy's, Helene Bournouw turned a veritable Niagara among smiles on her companion. Her deep gray eyes, subtly changing and compelling, were half drawn closed in a glance both unsettling and intoxicating.

"Jimmy, we're finished," she said with unarguable simplicity.

The clean, strong lines of her companion's face eroded. His glance wavered from hers, and his tongue broke from the cover of his mouth to moisten his lips inarticulately. It had been a week such as he had never known, this James P. Knoll, head of a multi-billion-dollar shipping and cartage chain. A week in which he had known danger, love, excitement, challenge—a range of emotions that had left him spent. He had spent a full week with Helene Bournouw.

Now she had ended it, with three words.

Without preamble, without provocation, after a night so dia-mond-perfect in its wholeness that he had decided to break away to buy the ring, she had shattered it all.

James P. Knoll rose from the booth in Lindy's and knowing without question by the tone she had used, a tone he had thought incapable of coming from her, that they were indeed finished, dropped a hundred-dollar bill on the table to pay for the lunch that had not yet been served, and walked out onto Broadway.

Later that day he would remove the little German .22-caliber short revolver from his wall safe and put a neat, almost bloodless hole in his right temple.

Helene Bournouw ate sparingly of the lunch when it was served. A model with her qualities could not risk overweight.

Later that day, due to the untimely death of its sole driving force, its President, Knoll Transit Incorporated suffered heavily on the mar-ket, causing a stock run that quickly spread like plague to the other rolling cartage firms, causing a major disruption in shipping and trucking throughout the country. All very sudden.

Helene Bournouw moved to her second appointment of the day. . . .

Quentin Dean was not his real name, but whatever unpronounce-able Polish or Latvian origin it had been, it in no way detracted from the quality of his painting. Quentin Dean, though living off day-old bread and canned cream of tomato soup in a Fourteenth Street loft, was perhaps the finest new artist of his generation. He had not yet been discovered by the critics; that might come in a year, perhaps eight months if he could find the right sort of patron, the right sort of interested party who would keep him eating, keep him working, show his efforts around till the break and the recognition came.

The critics had not yet found Quentin Dean, but Helene Bour-nouw had.

She cabbed over from Lindy's and climbed the four flights to Quentin Dean's airy, very clean, very light studio. Though barren—

save for the lumber leaning and stacked against the walls, preparatory to becoming easels and frames; save for the hundreds of paintings resting with their faces against the other walls; save for the huge mattress thrown carelessly into the center of the room—Dean's studio was quite cheery.

Helene Bournouw came into it and the sunlight, so cold and demanding on this too-cold-for-May afternoon, grew warm and golden. She stood behind him, watching him spread the glow of yellow ocher across a city scene.

She laughed lightly. Almost gaily.

Quentin Dean, lost in his work to the exclusion of all sound, spun, brush held like a sword. He smiled as he saw her. "Helene . . . honey, why didn't you call the drug store? . . . They'd have told me you were coming. . . ."

She laughed again, a faint elfin tinkle in the empty studio. "What do you call *that*, Quentin dear?" She pointed one slim white-gloved hand at the painting.

He tried to match her smile with a boyish, uncertain smile of his own, but it would not come. He turned to look at the painting, fearing he might have done something he had not seen, standing so close. But no, it was just the way he wanted to say it, in just the proper tone and with just the right amount of strength. It was his city, the city that had welcomed him, had let him work, that had sent him Helene Bournouw to lift and succor him.

"It's Third Avenue. I've tried to incorporate a dream image— magic realism, actually—of the el, before they tore it down, as it might be seen by someone who had lived under the el's shadow all those years and suddenly began to get the sunlight. You see, it's . . ."

She interrupted, very friendly, very concerned. "It's ludicrous, Quentin, dear. I mean, surely you must be doing it for a lark. You aren't considering it for part of your sequence on Manhattan, are you?"

He could not speak.

Weak as he had found he was, his strength, his sustenance came from his work, and there he was a whole man. No longer the emotional cripple who had fled Chillicothe, Ohio, to find a place for himself, he had grown strong and sure in front of his canvases. But, she was saying . . .

"Quentin, if this is the sort of drivel you're contemplating, I'm afraid I'll have to put my foot down. You can't expect me to take this over to Alexei for exhibit. He would laugh me out of the gallery, darling. Now, I have faith in you . . . even if you've fallen back again . . ."

Helene Bournouw stayed a long while, talking to Quentin Dean. She reassured him, she directed him, she slept with him and gave him the strength he needed to:

Slash most of the paintings with a bread knife.

Ruin the remainder of them with turpentine.

Break his brushes and turn over his easel.

Pack his three shirts in the reinforced cardboard container he had used to mail home dirty laundry from college, and return to Chillicothe, Ohio, where a year later he had submerged himself sufficiently in his family's tile-and-linoleum business to forget any foolishness about art.

Helene Bournouw moved to her third appointment of the day. . . .

When his social secretary told him Miss Bournouw was waiting in the refectory, the Right Reverend Monsignor Della'Buono casually replied he would go in immediately he had signed the papers before him. As the social secretary moved to the door, the Monsignor added, almost as an afterthought, that Miss Bournouw had something of the utmost seriousness to discuss—a personal problem, as he understood it—and they were not to be disturbed in the refectory. The woman nodded her understanding, passing a vagrant thought that the good Monsignor could not much longer support the tremors and terrors of his confidants, that he was certainly due for a rest before his hegira to the Vatican in November.

But when the door had closed behind her, the priest signed the papers without reading them and shoved back his ornate chair so quickly it banged against the wall. He gathered his cassock and went out of his office through the connecting door that led onto a short hallway ending at the refectory. He opened the dining room door and stepped inside.

Helene Bournouw was leaning against the long oak refectory table, her arms rigid behind her, supporting her angled weight. The trench coat was open at the knee, exposing one slim leg, bent slightly and exposed. The priest closed the door tightly, softly, and locked it.

"I told you never to come here again," he said.

His voice belonged to another man than the one who had spoken to the social secretary. *This* man had the voice of helplessness through hopelessness.

"Joseph . . ." she whispered. The barest fluting of moisture gathering in the bell of a flower anxiously awaiting the bagman bee, rasping down out of the sun. "I know what you need. . . ."

He went back against the door, the door he had locked without realizing he was locking it, not to keep others out, but to keep himself in. She unbuckled the belt of the trench coat, threw it wide, and let it slide down off her naked arms.

Helene Bournouw was silk and fulfillment, waiting in her nakedness for his body.

He swallowed nothing and plunged into her, smothering his face between her breasts. She took him to her with an air of Christian charity, and *he* took her, there, openly, on the refectory table. And when his first time was over, and she was readying him for a second, he begged her to put on the little girl clothes he knew she had brought in the wide-mouthed model's handbag. The short pinafore, the white hose, the patent leather buckled shoes, the soft ribbon for the hair, the childish charm bracelet. She promised she would. Helene Bournouw knew what he needed, what was beyond the realities but not the wildest fever-dreams of the Monsignor, who was not allowed to molest small children in the basement of the cathedral. Not even in the Cathedral of his Soul, and certainly not in the Cathedral of his God.

Later that day, he would write his paper, his long-awaited theological treatise. It would serve to sever the jugular of the Judeo-Christian ethic. His God would smirk at him, but not at Helene Bournouw.

Even God does not take lightly a creature of a kind called Helene Bournouw.

But that day was a busy day for Helene Bournouw, for possibly the most beautiful woman in New York, and she moved from appointment to appointment, being the delicious, scented unbelievable Helene Bournouw that she was. A busy day. But hardly over.

She stood before the mirror, admiring herself. It was trite, and she knew it, but the admiration of such a beautiful animal as herself could, by the nature of the narcissistic object, transcend the cliché. She studied her body. It was a beautifully constructed body, tapered that infinitely unnamable bit dividing mere perfection from beauty that burns out the eyes.

It had not quite burned out the eyes of that U.N. delegate from a great Eastern power (who had flashed like a silver fish in still waters when he had seen whom he had been fixed up with by his attaché), but it had unsettled and angered him sufficiently when her favors were not forthcoming so that there would be no mercy or reason in him during the conferences beginning the next day.

Yes, a fine and maddening body.

The apartment on Sutton Place was four-in-the-morning quiet, barely carrying the sound of Helene Bournouw hanging up her evening gown (its work on U.N. delegates done) and showering. The apartment took no notice as Helene Bournouw donned slacks and sweater, flats and trench coat. It made only a small sound as she closed the door.

In the lobby, the doorman created his own mental gossip concerning Helene Bournouw and her need for a cab this late in the day . . . or early in the morning, depending on whether you were a famous model or a night-working doorman.

The cabbie raised an eyebrow when Helene Bournouw gave him their destination. What sort of woman was it who wanted to be let out on a street corner of the Bowery at five in the morning? What sort of woman, indeed, with a face that held him stunned, even in a rear-view mirror.

And when the cab had disappeared into the darkness, its angry red tail light smaller, then gone, Helene Bournouw turned with purpose and direction, and strode off down the Bowery. What sort of woman, indeed.

Her flats made soft, shuffling noises in the still, moist, Manhattan night. She walked four blocks into a section of deserted warehouses, condemned loft buildings and wetbrain saucehounds sleeping halfway to death in their doorways. She turned down a sudden alley, a mouth open where there had been darkness a moment before.

Down the alley and she stopped before the fourth door; door perhaps, more boards and filth and bricked up than door, but door nevertheless.

Her knock was a strangely cadenced thing.

Her wait was a self-contained, restful thing.

When the door opened, she stood silently for a moment, staring at the man. He was perhaps four feet tall, his legs thick and truncated-looking. His body was a shapeless protoplasmic thing, erupting in two corded arms deeply tanned and powerful. His head rested without neck on his shoulders, matched as though with another head by the grotesque and obscene hump on his back. His face was a nightmare fancy. Two eyes, small and beaded and crimson, like those of a white rat, cornered and ferocious. The mouth was a gnome's gash without teeth, without lips. The skin a dark-bock-beer tan, even more wooden across the tight cheekbones and in the pitted hollows under the fanatic eyes.

A mass of black hair, unkempt, filthy, spreading down across the cheekbones like devouring fire ants. A rag of clothing, no shoes, long and black-rimmed fingernails. The magnificent, lovely face of Helene Bournouw stared at this man and found nothing peculiar, found nothing wanting.

Without a word she marched past him across the empty ware-house floor, up the winding staircase high into the deserted building. At the top of the staircase a door stood partially open.

Helene Bournouw pushed it wider and walked into the room. Amid empty packing crates and piles of rubbish, a table with nine chairs dominated the shadowy room. In eight of the nine chairs sat eight dwarfed creatures, uglier by comparison than the one who had opened the door far below.

The door behind Helene Bournouw closed as the grotesquerie who had followed her moved to his vacated seat. The woman stood silently, shifting from foot to foot as the little men talked. She seemed to pay them no heed and, in fact, seemed bored. From time to time she looked around, seeing nothing.

The little men talked:

"You've gone too far!" the one with warts on his eyelids rasped. "Too far! All this involvement. The old ways were good enough, I say. The expenditures, the outlay, and the results . . ."

"The results," interrupted another, with running sores on his cheeks and forehead, "have been fantastic. In a time of public relations, automation, advertising, the only way we can hope to carry on our work is to use the tools of the era."

"But . . ." The warty one tried to interrupt.

Extending a leprous-fleshed finger, a third man cut him off. "We can't afford to be backward. We must deal with matters on their own terms. You've seen how badly we did when we held to the old ways. People just will not accept ideas if they aren't couched in terms they are familiar with. Now, we've gone over this a thousand times; let's get on to planning the directions for the next quarter!"

The warty one subsided angrily, reluctantly.

Helene Bournouw, bored, began to hum. Too loud. The nine faces turned. One of them said snappishly, "Ba'al, turn her off."

The diseased and foul creature who had opened the door for Helene Bournouw rose and, dragging an empty packing crate behind him, stopped very close to her. He climbed up onto it, and his fingers left grease marks across her white flesh as they strayed toward her hairline.

Streaks of dirt on the white, lovely face of Helene Bournouw as the little man reached up under the hair line and massaged a soft spot on the front of the cranium. A sigh escaped Helene Bournouw's lips, and the face that could lead men astray, make them do evil, destroy their purposes, went very blank, very empty, very dead.

The little man climbed down and began to turn. A voice from the table stopped him. "Ba'al, wipe her off; you know we've got to keep the rolling stock in good condition."

As the little man pulled the strip of chamois from his shirt the conversation began anew, with the warty one taking this opportunity to reassert himself: "I still say the old ways are best."

The murmuring rose around the table, and the argument waxed anew while the incarnation of evil itself wiped filth stains off the too, too beautiful face of Helene Bournouw.

Later, when they wearied of formulating their new image, when they sighed with the responsibility of market trends and saturation levels and optimum penetration campaigns, they would suck on their long teeth and use her, all of them, at the same time.

*This is a funny story. Honest to gods.*
*If you don't think so, just consider how*
*Jesus would freak if a Jesus freak handed*
*him one of those dog-eared, fingerprinty*
*handbills on Fifth Avenue.*

# Bleeding Stones

Alchemy high above the crowds.

Over one hundred years of the Industrial Revolution had spewed chemical magic into the air. The aerosols known as smog. Coal and petroleum fractions containing sulfur, their combustion producing sulfur dioxide, oxidized by atmospheric oxygen to form sulfur trioxide, hydrated by water vapor in the air to sulfuric acid. Alchemical magic that weathers limestone. Particles of soot, particles of ash. Unburned hydrocarbons. Oxides of nitrogen. The magic of ultraviolet radiation, photochemical reactions, photochemical smog: it magically cracks rubber. Unsaturated hydrocarbons, ozone, nitrogen dioxide, formaldehyde, acetone. Magic. Carbon monoxide, carcinogenic hydrocarbons, days and nights of thermal inversion in the atmosphere. Carbon particles, metallic dusts, silicates, fluorides, resins, tars, pollen, fungi, solid oxides, aromatics, even the smells of magic. Catalysis. Carriers of electrostatic charges. *To the extent that they are radioactive,* says page 184 of volume 18 of the 1972 *ENCYCLOPAEDIA BRITANNICA, they increase the normal radiation dosage and may be cancer- or mutation-producing factors.*

*Finally,* it goes on, *as plain dust, they soil clothing, buildings, and bodies, and are a general nuisance.*

Alchemical magical nuisance, high above the crowds.

Jammed, thronged, packed, overspilling, flowing and shuddering . . . forty thousand people drawn like iron filings to the magnet of St. Patrick's Cathedral, filling the sidewalks and overflowing into Fifth Avenue . . . the mass bulging outward, human yeast, filling the intersections of 51st Street and Fifth Avenue, 50th and Fifth, 52nd and Fifth . . . rolling to find space along the sidewalks and doorways and garden walks of Rockefeller Center. . . .

Hallelujah! The Jesus People have come to the holy summit of organized religion in the land that is the very apotheosis of the Industrial Revolution. St. Patrick's Cathedral, built between 1858 and 1879, puffed out mightily like the pigeons roosting there for over one hundred years as the magic took its time performing its alchemical wonders, the nuisances of cracking rubber, weathering stone, pitting metal, mutating and inverting thermals. Hallelujah!

They are recognized. The Jesus People. One way, united in the worship of Jesus Christ, the Savior, the Son of God; here, at last, at this greatest repository of the faith in the land of ultraviolet radiation, they have come to spread their potency at the altar of organized power.

While above them, on the spires of the city and the parapets of St. Patrick's, the nuisance bears fruit and the stones begin to bleed.

The Cardinal steps out through the massive front doors. The Archdiocese in person, recognizing them. They raise index fingers, thousands of index fingers raised in homage to the One Way.

The Cardinal lifts his arms slowly, his gorgeous robes resplendent in the sunlight glancing off a thousand automobiles spewing out alchemical magic; his arms lift and he is a human crucifix for a moment before his arms rise up above his head and he lifts his index fingers. The crowd trills and sighs with joy. They are known!

The Cardinal feels moisture on his left hand and looks up at his flesh emerging from his sleeve. There is a drop of blood running down through the fold of skin between his thumb and index finger. A fat, globular drop of blood that glistens in the magic air. It bulges and runs in a line down his palm. He is alarmed for a moment: has he cut himself? Then a second drop falls and he realizes the blood is dropping from above.

He looks up.

On the tallest spires of St. Patrick's Cathedral, there is movement.

For over one hundred years the stones of the Cathedral have been silent, still, solid and unwanting. Now the stones begin to bleed as the gargoyles come to life.

His eyes widen and see only movement. . . .

But above, up here where the winds of the city carry alchemical magic, the stone gargoyles tremble, their rock bodies begin to moisten, and blood stands out in humid beads.

The first of the many shudders and its eyes open slowly. Color comes to its stone flesh. Its taloned hands rise from its knees and flex.

Corded muscles bunched for a hundred years slide and move. Its belly heaves as it draws in life. Its bat wings twitch and suddenly unfurl. It drinks of the sunlight and the air, drinks deep and sucks the carcinogens deep into its bellows lungs; the nuisance mutation is complete. Come to life after a hundred years is the race that will inherit the Earth; hardly meek, the race made to breathe this new air. The gargoyle throws back its head and its stone fangs catch the sunlight and throw it back brighter than the hides of the vehicles below.

The clarion call blasts against the noonday tumult of the Jesus People. And they fall silent. And they look up. And all around them, on a hundred spires of a hundred skyscrapers the inheritors rise from their crouched positions, their shapes black and firm-edged against the gray and deadly sky.

Then, like the fighting kites of Brazil, they dive into the crowd and begin the ritual slaughter.

The first of the many swoops down in a screaming fall that sends the Jesus People scattering. At the final instant the gray death-kite flattens and sails across the crowd, its talons extended, arms dangling. The razor-nails imbed themselves in a skull and rip backward as its flight carries gargoyle and victim forward. It skims skyward again and great muscled arms throw the limp meat against the walls of a building, the body ripped open from occipital ridge to buttocks, entrails bulging, spilling from the sprung carcass. The body slides down the wall leaving a red fluorescent smear.

Another, with a hundred isinglass-thin lids over its lizard eyes, dives straight down at a young girl wearing a halter top and blue jeans with cloth patches of butterflies, flowers and elaborate crosses appliquéd to the fabric. It extends the extraordinarily long and pencil-thin first finger of each four-taloned hand, and drives them deep into her eye-sockets. Then, hooking the fingers, it lifts her, shrieking, into the sky. It drops her from twenty stories.

Two demi-devils with the heads of gryphons and the bodies of hunchbacked dwarves land with simultaneous crashes on the roof of a Fifth Avenue bus, slash it open with their clawed feet and throw themselves inside. Screams fill the air as the bus fills with bloody pulp. A window is smashed as an old man tries to escape and one of the demi-devils saws his neck across the ragged glass, spraying the street outside with a geyser from the carotid artery. The body continues to kick. The windows of the bus smear and darken over with pulped flesh and viscera. The demi-devils wallow like two babies in a bathtub, drinking and splashing.

A gargoyle with a ring of spikes circling its forehead hurtles into a knot of Jesus People on their knees and hysterically singing *Jesus Is a Soul Man*. It rips off the arms of a bearded young man and, flailing about, crushes the skulls of the group. One boy tries to crawl away, his head bleeding, and the gargoyle kicks aside bodies to reach him, grabbing him by the heavy silver chain around his neck. The chain supports a silver crucifix. The gargoyle twists the chain till it sinks into the flesh of the boy's neck. Screaming, the boy tries to struggle erect, clawing at the garrotte with both hands, eyes bulging, face darkening to blue-black as the blood gushes from his ears and mouth. The gargoyle flaps its wings, lifts into the air dangling the struggling boy at the end of the silver chain and, swinging him violently, batters the crowd till the body is dismembered.

A gargoyle has ripped the arms from an old woman and peeled the skin and muscle from the bones, sharpening them with its fangs. It charges up the front steps of St. Patrick's Cathedral and impales the Cardinal through the chest and stomach. The Cardinal, spasming in pain, is carried aloft by two other gargoyles who drop him with titters and giggles onto the topmost spire of the Cathedral. He slides down the spire, the point protruding from his stomach, and the gargoyles spin him like the propeller on a child's wind toy.

A gargoyle crouches on a mound of bodies, eating hearts and livers it has ripped from the not-quite-dead casualties. Another sucks the meat off fingers. Another chews eyeballs, savoring the corneal fluid.

A gargoyle has backed a dozen Jesus People and elegant Avenue shoppers into a doorway and jabs at them with bloody talons, taunting them till they howl with dismay. The gargoyle scrapes its talons across the stones of the building till sparks fly . . . and somehow catch fire as they shower the shrieking victims. The fire washes over them and they run screaming into the fangs and talons of the marauder. They die, smoldering, and pile up in the doorway.

A gargoyle with a belly huge and round flies up and around, crouching and defecating on the hordes as they trample each other, running in all directions to escape the slaughter. The voiding is diarrheic and rains down in a thick green and brown curtain that splashes in heavy spattering pools and begins eating into cement and asphalt. It is acid; where it strikes human flesh it eats its way through to bone leaving burning edges and smoking pits. Hundreds fall and are crushed by stampeding pedestrians with no exit.

A gargoyle alights atop the bronze statue of Atlas holding the world on his shoulders that dominates the entrance to 630 Fifth Avenue, kicks loose the great bronze globe and sends it hammering into the crowd. Dozens are crushed at the impact and the gargoyle, laughing hysterically, boots it again and again. The globe thunders through the street flattening cars and people, leaving in its wake a trail of twisted bodies and a gutter-wash of blood and pulp that clogs drain basins with human refuse.

Three gargoyles have found a nun. Two have lifted her above their heads and wrenching her legs apart like a wishbone they are splitting her in half as the third creature breaks off a bus stop sign and punches the jagged end of the pole up her vagina, shrieking *Regnum dei in vobis est,* the kingdom of God is within you.

The slaughter goes on and on for hours. The screams of the dying rise up to meet the automated chiming of the Cathedral bells. Darkness falls and the hellfire of demon flames and human beings used as torches illuminates the expanse of Fifth Avenue.

All through the night it goes on as the gargoyles range out and around, widening their circles of destruction. Nothing can stop them. The weapons of humankind are useless against them. They are intent upon inheriting the Earth all on the first day and night of their birth.

Finally, nothing moves in the city but the creatures that were once stone, and they fly up, circling the stainless steel and glass towers of industrial magic. They look down with the hungry eyes of those who have slept too long and now, rested, seek exercise.

Then, laughing triumphantly, they flap bat wings and soar upward, flying off toward the east, toward the Vatican.

*This is what happens when a black man worships a white god.*

# At the Mouse Circus

The King of Tibet was having himself a fat white woman. He had
thrown himself down a jelly tunnel, millennia before, and periodically,
as he pumped her, a soft pink-and-white bunny rabbit in weskit and
spats trembled through, scrutinizing a turnip watch at the end of a
heavy gold-link chain. The white woman was soft as suet, with little
black eyes thrust deep under prominent brow ridges. Honkie bitch
groaned in unfulfilled ecstasy, trying desperately and knowing she
never would. For she never had. The King of Tibet had a bellyache.
Oh, to be in another place, doing another thing, alone.

The land outside was shimmering in waves of fear that came
radiating from mountaintops far away. On the mountaintops, grizzled
and wizened old men considered ways and means, considered runes
and portents, considered whys and wherefores . . . ignored them all
. . . and set about sending more fear to farther places. The land rippled
in the night, beginning to quake with terror that was greater than the
fear that had gone before.

"What time is it?" he asked, and received no answer. Thirty-
seven years ago, when the King of Tibet had been a lad, there had been
a man with one leg—who had been his father for a short time—and
a woman with a touch of the tar brush in her, and she had served as
mother.

"You can be anything, Charles," she had said to him. "Anything
you want to be. A man can be anything he can do. Uncle Wiggily,
Jomo Kenyatta, the King of Tibet, if you want to. Light enough or
black, Charles, it don't mean a thing. You just go your way and be
good and *do*. That's all you got to remember."

The King of Tibet had fallen on hard times. Fat white women
and cheap cologne. Doodad, he had lost the horizon. Exquisite, he
had dealt with surfaces and been dealt with similarly. Wasted, he had
done time.

"I got to go," he told her.

"Not yet, just a little more. Please."

So he stayed. Banners unfurled, lying limp in absence of breezes from Camelot, he stayed and suffered. Finally, she turned him loose, and the King of Tibet stood in the shower for forty minutes. Golden skin pelted, drinking, he was never quite clean. Scented, abluted, he still knew the odors of wombats, hallway musk, granaries, futile beakers of noxious fluids. If he was a white mouse, why could he not see his treadmill?

"Listen, baby, I got need of fi'hunnerd dollahs. I know we ain't been together but a while, but I got this *bad* need." She went to snap-purses and returned.

He hated her more for doing than not doing.

And in her past, he knew he was no part of any recognizable future.

"Charlie, when'll I see you again?" Stranger, never!

Borne away in the silver flesh of Cadillac, the great beautiful mother Hog, plunging wheelbased at one hundred and twenty (bought with his semen) inches, Eldorado god-creature of four hundred horsepower, displacing recklessly 440 cubic inches, thundering into forgetting weighing 4550+ pounds, goes . . . went . . . Charlie . . . Charles . . . the King of Tibet. Golden brown, cleaned as best as he could, five hundred reasons and five hundred aways. Driven, driving into the outside.

Forever inside, the King of Tibet, going outside.

Along the road. Manhattan, Jersey City, New Brunswick, Trenton. In Norristown, having had lunch at a fine restaurant, Charlie was stopped on a street corner by a voice that went *pssst* from a mailbox. He opened the slit and a small boy in a pullover sweater and tie thrust his head and shoulders into the night. "You've got to help me," the boy said. "My name is Batson. Billy Batson. I work for radio station WHIZ and if I could only remember the right word, and if I could only *say* it, something wonderful would happen. S is for the wisdom of Solomon, H is for the strength of Hercules, A is for the stamina of Atlas, Z is for the power of Zeus . . . and after that I go blank."

The King of Tibet slowly and steadily thrust the head back into the mailslot and walked away. Reading, Harrisburg, Mt. Union, Altoona, Nanty Glo.

On the road to Pittsburgh there was a four-fingered mouse in red shorts with two big yellow buttons on the front, hitchhiking. Shoes like two big boxing gloves, bright eyes sincere, forlorn and way lost, he stood on the curb with meaty thumb and he waited. Charlie whizzed past. It was not his dream.

Youngstown, Akron, Canton, Columbus, and hungry once more in Dayton.

O.

Oh aitch eye oh. Why did he ever leave. He had never been there before. This was the good place. The river flowed dark and the day passed overhead like some other river. He pulled into a parking space and did not even lock the god-mother Eldorado. It waited patiently, knowing its upholstered belly would be filled with the King of Tibet soon enough.

"Feed you next," he told the sentient vehicle, as he walked away toward the restaurant.

Inside—dim and candled at high noon—he was shown to a heavy wood booth, and there he had laid before him a pure white linen napkin, five pieces of silver, a crystal goblet in which fine water waited, and a promise. From the promise he selected nine-to-five winners, a long shot and the play number for the day.

A flocked velvet witch perched on a bar stool across from him turned, exposed thigh and smiled. He offered her silver, water, a promise, and they struck a bargain.

Charlie stared into her oiled teakwood eyes through the candle flame between them. All moistened saranwrap was her skin. All thistled gleaming were her teeth. All mystery of cupped hollows beneath cheekbones was she. Charlie had bought a television set once, because the redhead in the commercial was part of his dream. He had bought an electric toothbrush because the brunette with her capped teeth had indicated she, too, was part of his dream. And his great Eldorado, of course. *That* was the dream of the King of Tibet.

"What time is it?" But he received no answer and, drying his lips of the last of the *pêche flambée,* he and the flocked velvet witch left the restaurant: he with his dream fraying, and she with no product save one to sell.

There was a party in a house on a hill.

When they drove up the asphalt drive, the blacktop beneath them uncoiled like the sooty tongue of a great primitive snake. "You'll like these people," she said, and took the sensitive face of the King of Tibet between her hands and kissed him deeply. Her fingernails were gun-metal silvered and her palms were faintly moist and plump, with expectations of tactile enrichments.

They walked up to the house. Lit from within, every window held a color facet of light. Sounds swelled as they came toward the house. He fell a step behind her and watched the way her skin flowed. She reached out, touched the house, and they became one.

No door was opened to them, but holding fast to her hair he was drawn behind her, through the flesh of the house.

Within, there were inlaid ivory boxes that, when opened, revealed smaller boxes within. He became fascinated by one such box, sitting high on a pedestal in the center of an om rug. The box was inlaid with teeth of otters and puff adders and lynx. He opened the first box and within was a second box frosted with rime. Within the frost-box was a third, and it was decorated with mirrors that cast back no reflections. And next within was a box whose surface was a mass of intaglios, and they were all fingerprints, and none of Charlie's fit, and only when a passing man smiled and caressed the lid did it open, revealing the next, smaller box. And so it went, till he lost count of the boxes and the journey ended when he could not see the box that fit within the dust-mote-size box that was within all the others. But he knew there were more, and he felt a great sadness that he could not get to them.

"What is it, precisely, you want?" asked an older woman with very good bones. He was leaning against a wall whose only ornamentation was a gigantic wooden crucifix on which a Christ figure hung, head bowed, shoulders twisted as only shoulders can be whose arms have been pulled from sockets; the figure was made of massive pieces of wood, all artfully stained: chunks of doors, bedposts, rowels, splines, pintels, joists, cross-ties, rabbet-joined bits of massive frames.

"I want . . ." he began, then spread his hands in confusion. He knew what he wanted to say, but no one had ever ordered the progression of words properly for him.

"Is it Madelaine?" the older woman asked. She smiled as Aunt Jemima would smile, and targeted a finger across the enormous living room, bullseyed on the flocked velvet witch all the way over there by the fireplace. "She's here."

The King of Tibet felt a bit more relaxed.

"Now," the older woman said, her hand on Charlie's cheek, "what is it you need to know? Tell me. We have all the answers here. Truly."

"I want to know—"

The television screen went silver and cast a pool of light, drawing Charlie's attention. The possibilities were listed on the screen. And what he had wanted to know seemed inconsequential compared to the choices he saw listed.

"That one," he said. "That second one. How did the dinosaurs die."

"Oh, fine!" She looked pleased he had selected that one. "Shefti . . . ?" she called to a tall man with gray hair at the temples. He looked up from speaking to several women and another man, looked up expectantly, and she said, "He's picked the second one. May I?"

"Of course, darling," Shefti said, raising his wine glass to her.

"Do we have time?"

"Oh, I think so," he said.

"Yes . . . what time *is* it?" Charlie asked.

"Over here," the older woman said, leading him firmly by the forearm. They stopped beside another wall. "Look."

The King of Tibet stared at the wall, and it paled, turned to ice, and became translucent. There was something imbedded in the ice. Something huge. Something dark. He stared harder, his eyes straining to make out the shape. Then he was seeing more clearly and it was a great saurian, frozen at the moment of pouncing on some lesser species.

"*Gorgosaurus,*" the older woman said, at his elbow. "It rather resembles *Tyrannosaurus,* you see; but the forelimbs have only two digits. You see?"

Thirty-two feet of tanned gray leather. The killing teeth. The nostriled snout, the amber smoke eyes of the eater of carrion. The smooth, sickening tuber of balancing tail, the crippled forelimbs carried tragically withered and useless. The musculature . . . the pulsing beat of iced blood beneath the tarpaulin hide. The . . . beat . . .

It lived.

Through the ice went the King of Tibet, accompanied by Circe-eyed older woman, as the shellfish-white living room receded back beyond the ice-wall. Ice went, night came.

Ice that melted slowly from the great hulk before him. He stood in wonder. "See," the woman said.

And he saw as the ice dissolved into mist and nightfog, and he saw as the earth trembled, and he saw as the great fury lizard moved in shambling hesitancy, and he saw as the others came to cluster unseen nearby. *Scolosaurus* came. *Trachodon* came. *Stephanosaurus* came. *Protoceratops* came. And all stood, waiting.

The King of Tibet knew there were slaughterhouses where the beef was hung upside-down on hooks, where the throats were slit and the blood ran thick as motor oil. He saw a golden thing hanging, and would not look. Later, he would look.

They waited. Silently, for its coming.

Through the Cretaceous swamp it was coming. Charlie could hear it. Not loud, but coming steadily closer. "Would you light my cigarette, please?" asked the older woman.

It was shining. It bore a pale white nimbus. It was stepping through the swamp, black to its thighs from the decaying matter. It came on, its eyes set back under furred browridges, jaw thrust forward, wide nostrils sniffing at the chill night, arms covered with matted filth and hair. Savior man.

He came to the lizard owners of the land. He walked around them and they stood silently, their time at hand. Then he touched them, one after the other, and the plague took them. Blue fungus spread from the five-pronged marks left on their imperishable hides; blue death radiating from impressions of opposed thumbs, joining, spreading cilia and rotting the flesh of the great gone dinosaurs. The ice re-formed and the King of Tibet moved back through pearly cold to the living room.

He struck a match and lit her cigarette.

She thanked him and walked away.

The flocked velvet witch returned. "Did you have a nice time?" He thought of the boxes-within-boxes.

"Is that how they died? Was he the first?"

She nodded. "And did Nita ask you for anything?"

Charlie had never seen the sea. Oh, there had been the Narrows and the East River and the Hudson, but he had never seen the sea. The real sea, the thunder sea that went black at night like a pane of glass. The sea that could summon and the sea that could kill, that could swallow whole cities and turn them into myth. He wanted to go to California.

He suddenly felt fear that he would never leave this thing called Ohio here.

"I asked you: did Nita ask you for anything?"

He shivered.

"What?"

"Nita. Did she *ask* you for anything?"

"Only a light."

"Did you give it to her?"

"Yes."

Madelaine's face swam in the thin fluid of his sight. Her jaw muscles trembled. She turned and walked across the room. Everyone turned to look at her. She went to Nita, who suddenly took a step backward and threw up her hands. "No, I didn't—"

The flocked velvet witch darted a hand toward the older woman and the hand seemed to pass into her neck. The silver tipped fingers reappeared, clenched around a fine sparkling filament. Then Madelaine snapped it off with a grunt.

There was a terrible minor sound from Nita, then she turned, watery, and stood silently beside the window, looking empty and hopeless.

Madelaine wiped her hand on the back of the sofa and came to Charlie. "We'll go now. The party is over."

He drove in silence back to town.

"Are you coming up?" he asked, when they parked the Eldorado in front of the hotel.

"I'm coming up."

He registered them as Prof. Pierre and Marja Sklodowska Curie and for the first time in his life he was unable to reach a climax. He fell asleep sobbing over never having seen the sea, and came awake hours later with the night still pressing against the walls. She was not there.

He heard sounds from the street, and went to the window.

There was a large crowd in the street, gathered around his car.

As he watched, a man went to his knees before the golden Eldorado and touched it. Charlie knew *this* was his dream. He could not move; he just watched, as they ate his car.

The man put his mouth to the hood and it came away bloody.

A great chunk had been ripped from the gleaming hide of the Cadillac. Golden blood ran down the man's jaws.

Another man draped himself over the top of the car, and even through the window the King of Tibet could hear the terrible sucking, slobbering sounds. Furrows were ripped in the top.

A woman pulled her dress up around her hips and backed, on all fours, to the rear of the car. Her face trembled with soft expectancy, and then it was inside her and she moved on it.

When she came, they all moved in on the car and he watched as his dream went inside them, piece by piece, chewed and eaten as he stood by helpless.

"That's all, Charlie," he heard her say, behind him. He could not turn to look at her, but her reflection was superimposed over his own in the window. Out there in darkness now, they moved away, having eaten.

He looked, and saw the golden thing hanging upside-down in the slaughterhouse, its throat cut, its blood drained away in onyx gutters.

Afoot, in Dayton, Ohio, he was dead of dreams.

"What time is it?" he asked.

*Suggesting that Christ had a homosexual relationship with Prometheus.*

# The Place with No Name

This is how legends are born.

Perhaps it was because Norman had never suffered from an excess of oily, curly hair that he had been unable to make it as a gigolo. Or as Norman had phrased it: "I can't stand patent-leather on my hair or my feet." So he had taken the easy way out: Norman Mogart had become a pimp.

Er, let's make the semantics more palatable. (In an era of garbage collectors who are Sanitation Disposal Engineers, truck drivers who are Transportation Facilitation Executives, and janitors who are Housing Maintenance Overseers, a spade is seldom a spade, Black Panthers please note.) Norman Mogart was an Entertainment Liaison Agent.

Pfui. Norman was a pimp.

Currently marketing a saucy item titled Marlene—a seventeen-year-old Puerto Rican voluptuary with a childlike delight in the carnal act and an insatiable craving for Juicy Fruit gum—Norman was doing nicely. Succinctly put, Norman was doing just whiz-bang. His alpaca coat had a velvet collar; his Porsche had recently been re-bored; his Diners' Club account was up to date; and his $32-a-day habit was nicely in hand.

Norman Mogart was also an Artificial Stimulant Indoctrinaire.

Pfui. Norman was a junkie.

It is not true that cocaine addicts are more sensual than common garden-variety hopheads, vipers, stashhounds, potheads, speed freaks, crystal-spaceouts, pill-droppers, acid-heads or blastbabies. It's just that coke hits like paresis after a while, and when a member of the opposite sex begins to put on (as they used to say around the Brill Building) "the bee," the cocaine sniffer just doesn't have the where-withal to say no.

Consequently, when Marlene—live wire that she was—felt compelled to snuggle up to her entrepreneur, Norman was too weak with happy to resist. It was this inability—nay, rather this *elasticity* of moral fiber—on Norman's part, that brought about his terrible trouble, and the sudden pinching need for the bread to get turned on with. Marlene chose to snuggle up under a bush in Brooklyn's fabled Prospect Park, unfortunately, and it was one of New York's Finest (not to mention chicken-est) who felt honor-bound to bust her, chiefly because he had been called on the carpet only that morning by his Captain for having been caught catnapping (with pillow and alarm clock) in the rear of a police ambulance. The bust left Norman with not only his pants down, but his source of income cut off.

Three weeks and six hundred and seventy-two dollars later, Norman was out of money and out of dust. His connects smelled the nature of his impecunity and magically dried up. Norman was in a sorry way.

There comes a point in the downward slide of the human condition when a man ceases to be a man. He may still walk erect, but it is principally a matter of skeletal arrangement, not ethics. Norman had reached that point . . . and passed it: screaming. Like the Doppler effect of a train whistle as it fades past a fixed point. Norman was going insane. The hunger was no longer even localized; withdrawal was an entity in itself. It clung to him like dark mud, it filled his mouth with rust. In a movie theater where he had fled to catch a few moments of peace and Chaplin's *City Lights,* he smelled the sick-sweet pungency of someone in the darkness tuning in on grass, and he wanted very much to puke. Instead, he lit his eighty-five-dollar GBD, the pipe Elyse had given him for his birthday, the year before she had gone off and married one of her tricks, a canning company executive from Steubenville, Ohio. The aromatic curlicues of tobacco blotted it out a trifle, and Norman was able to continue on his thorny path to furious darkness, unimpeded by the scents of lesser joys.

Inevitably, it came down to finding another hooker—for the ravishing Marlene had been sent to the Women's House of Detention at Sixth and Greenwich Avenues for a big one-twenty, it being her second bust. It came down to finding a new hooker, or boosting a drug store for its till and drug supplies. But: Norman was a Constitutionally Incapacitated Swashbuckler.

Pfui. Norman was a goddam coward.

As for the former solution, it was luck-out there, as well: there were no other girls on the turf worth handling. For in his own way, and in his own pattern, Norman was a dealer in quality goods. Cheap or tawdry merchandise was a stink in his nostrils, inevitably bringing on a loss of reputation. In Norman's line of work, either solution was written in the hieroglyphics of bankruptcy.

Thus, view Norman Mogart, hung between the torture posts of his limitations and his desires. Swinging gently in a breeze of desperation.

The only climate that could have forced Norman to do what he did.

He accosted the woman as she turned to lock her car. It had been the only empty space on Hudson Street, and Norman had known if he lurked for only a few moments in the dark doorway of the Chinese hand laundry, someone coming home late to one of the apartment buildings on Christopher or Bleecker would pull into it. He had been in the doorway no more than five minutes when the woman pulled in, backed and filled, and cut the ignition.

As she emerged, and turned to lock the door, Norman struck. He had a short length of pipe in his topcoat pocket, and he came up on her silently, and jammed it into the small of her back. "A gun, lady."

The woman didn't react as Norman had expected. With one sweeping movement she spun on the toe of her right foot, brought her arm around and directed the muzzle of the "gun" to the side. In two seconds Norman Mogart was grappling with a woman who had taken a course in street self-defense at the West Side YMHA. Norman found himself lifted on a stout hip, slung into the car, and sliding down its side. Then the woman kicked him. It was a very professional kick. It caught Norman directly under the heart and sent slivers of black glass up through his body into his brain. The next part he remembered only dimly: he grabbed her leg, pulled it out from under her and she fell with her skirt up around her hips, and her coat up around her skirt. Then he beat her solidly seven or eight times in the face with the length of pipe.

When the glass had dissolved in his brain and body, he was sitting on the dirty bricks of Hudson Street, half on top of a mound of dead meat.

He was still sitting there, a few minutes later, not quite believing what he had done, when the prowl car's searchlight speared him.

Norman Mogart scrambled to his knees and scuttled around the car. He dropped the pipe—which was now sticky—and crouching low, ran for his life. He ran into a man coming out of a narrow doorway leading up to cold-water flats, and caromed off him. He threw the man away from him and ran up Hudson Street. He kept running, with the squad car behind him, siren shrieking, gumball machine flickering angry red, searchbeam jabbing for him. He ran into Jane Street and kept going till he found a doorway. He ducked into the doorway and ran up a flight of stairs. And another flight. And another. And then he climbed a ladder and came out through a trapdoor on the roof of a Greenwich Village tenement. It was a roof that locked with other roofs, and he fled across the roofs, catching himself in wash hung on poles-and-rope, and screamed because he didn't know what it was.

Then he found a fire escape, and clattered down the iron steps till he came to the drop-ladder, and it squeaked rustily, and he climbed down, dropping into another alley. Then he ran up another street, and onto Seventh Avenue, and across Seventh Avenue, dodging between cars. Then he was on another street, and he walked with head bowed, hands in topcoat pockets, praying he had lost them.

Light pooled on the sidewalk, and he looked up.

The light came from a trip lamp in the window of the store, and the sign it illuminated said:

## ESCAPE INSIDE

Norman Mogart hesitated only a moment. He pulled open the door, and stepped into the shop. It was empty. There was a brown, leathery, wizened little man with pointed ears standing in the exact center of the empty shop.

Yes, the shop was one of those.

"You're early," said the little man.

Norman Mogart was suddenly frightened. There was the unmistakable rattle of lunacy in the little man's voice. He stared for a long moment, feeling his gorge rise. Then he turned and reached out for the doorknob, knowing it was just there, under his questing fingers. There was no door.

"You're almost ninety seconds early," the little man murmured. "We'll have to wait, or throw everything out of phase."

Norman Mogart backed up kept backing up, backed through the

space where the door should have been, the wall should have been, the sidewalk outside the shop should have been, the street should have been. They weren't there. He was still inside the shop, whose dimensions seemed to expand as he moved. "You better let me out of here, crazy old man," Norman quavered.

"Ah. It's time." The little old man hurried toward Norman. Norman turned and ran. Across a faceless, empty plain of existence. He kept running. There were no rises, no dips, no features to the surrounding terrain. It was as though he were in some enormous television studio set of limbo, running and running across an empty plain.

Finally, he slipped, exhausted, to the floor of the shop, and the little old man scampered up to him. "Ah. Fine. Now it's time."

He sat down cross-legged before Norman Mogart. Norman noticed with some alarm that though the little old man was sitting in a lotus position, quite comfortably, there was almost a foot of empty air between his bottom and the floor. The little man was sitting on the air.

Norman shut his eyes tightly. The little old man began talking to Norman as though he had *just* entered the shop, not as though he had been ninety seconds early.

"Welcome, Mr. Mogart. So you want to escape. Well, that's what I sell here. Escape. Inside."

Norman opened his eyes.

"Who are you?"

"A humble shopkeeper."

"No, c'mon now, who *are* you?"

"Well, if you press me . . ."

The little man shimmered, and changed form. Norman shrieked. The form shimmered again, became the little old man. "Will you settle for what I'm showing you?"

Norman bobbled his head eagerly.

"Ah. Well, then, *do* you or do you *not* wish to escape, Mr. Mogart? I can guarantee that if you refuse my offer, the police will apprehend you in a matter of minutes."

Norman hesitated only a second, then nodded.

"Ah. Good. Then we have an arrangement. And, with all my heart, I thank you." Norman had only a moment to consider the peculiar tone in the little old man's voice.

Then he began to dissolve.

He looked down and saw his legs beginning to fade away. Slowly. Without pain. "Wait a second, wait hold it!" Norman implored. "Are you a demon? A devil, some kind of thing like that? Am I going to Hell? Hey, wait a minute, if I'm going to Hell, I shoulda made a bargain . . . what do *I* get? . . . Hey, hold on, I'm fading away. . . . Are you a gnome or an elf, or what? . . . Hey, what are you . . . !?!"

All that was left in the shop were Norman's eyes, his ears, his lower lip and a patch of hair. And even as these faded, the little old man said, "You can call me Simon."

And then, like the Cheshire cat, Norman Mogart faded away completely, hallucinating for an instant that the little old man had added, "Or Peter. It doesn't matter. . . ."

At first, in that painful introductory moment upon returning to consciousness, Norman Mogart knew only that he was looking straight up. He was lying on his back, in a springy bed of some growth, the .30-06 Husqvarna still held at high-port across his chest and one shoulder—but he was flat-out on his back. As that first moment stretched like warm taffy, drawing itself out until it had become one minute or five or ten, strange thoughts faded away: thoughts of another life, of a pain that burned in him, a pain that was now gone, to be replaced by a pain of quite another sort, of a woman, of running, of a little man . . . of an image that faded faded faded away to be replaced by . . . what? His senses crept timorously back to him, each carrying an allotted burden of *new* memories, replacing those old ones, now fading and gone; depositing the new memories in suddenly cleared spaces, and they fit snugly, as though they belonged, settling to rest in his mind.

He was staring straight up, through the interlaced boughs of half a dozen jacarandas, and while he lay there, senses settling carefully back in their niches, he dwelled on flesh that faded and how lovely the blossoms seemed.

Had it been night, in a cold place? Here it was day, and warm. So warm. Had it rained here? Yes.

It *had* been raining. Heavily, he supposed, for the ground on which he lay gave off a moist and repellent squishing when he moved; his clothes were soaked through to the skin; his hair lay matted along his forehead; the stock and barrel of the hunting rifle were beaded with rain that had clashed with cosmoline and encysted itself.

He realized, finally, that the knapsack was still in place on his back, that he must have fallen straight back when he collapsed, and that now it was a painful hump which forced him to lie in a tortured arched condition. He slipped sidewise, and received immediate ease from the pain.

Still he looked up, seeing the huge leafy fronds that had collected their water greedily, and seeing the strange birds that came to slake their thirst at those informal watering-places. One bird he saw . . .

He had never known it, true so true; he had hardly lent credence to the native stories: he had heard it was so, that there were jungle birds of brilliant plumage whose colors ran in the rain, but he had snickered at the thought. Very often, too often (and if *once* too often, then he was a fool on a fool's errand!), the natives were like children, much rather believing their fancy-made-up tales than the truth. Yet here it was, above him, nonchalant, and here—in this wonderland that was certainly no Wonderland—it was true. So who were the children, after all?

He stared up at the wild-eyed huge-billed creature and saw its colors, like a Madras print, running, flowing, melding one into another, red and yellow and green. And he marveled.

Beside him, in the rain-swollen pool, the jacaranda blossoms clotted like sour flesh, sucking at the flow of clear water. *Cocaine? What did that mean? Not him, perhaps some other.*

Now he felt rested, and with the thought, as punctuation, the mad-eyed bird leaped howling into the slate sky. He rose awkwardly, steadying himself on this root, that bole, stiffly, shifting the rick-rack between his shoulderblades. He seemed to rise up and up, a scarecrow, an exceptionally thin man, until he stood unsteadily, staring at the world. Then he looked down, and his reflection, jigsawed by bright blossoms, looked back. He did not recognize himself for a long moment. The body seemed all wrong. He remembered *another* body, in a cold place, and fear, and the hurt that lived in that other body . . . then he recognized himself.

He did not know how long he had lain there, the fever rising higher in him, then abating, then rising once more, a volcanic heat that rose and fell to no discernible rhythm . . . but the burns and sores were better this day. He felt he could go on alone without balming himself with herbs. (He had begun to suspect, in any case, that one of the herbs, he did not know which, was poisoning him further.) (There, *that* was a thought that belonged to this body, not the other.) (Yet the rifle had gotten no lighter: rueful thought.) (Cocaine?)

Before him, the jungle presented its unknown face, many-eyed, uncaring, but ready for him to take that first step away from this clearing, that rain-pool; it would sense the intrusion of this Norman Mogart who was nothing to that ageless green. (My name is Harry Timmons, Jr. My name is) Norman Mogart sighed.

And then, if he persisted, as the White Man always persists, unable to distinguish between folly and futility, the jungle would come for him with claw and tendril and the inhaled hacking cough of the swamp.

He was frightened by strangeness, both within him and around him. (God himself, he felt, would be frightened here!) But he knew that somewhere beyond the gray-green rotting carcass of this jungle, somewhere back where neither the *peons* nor the *Indios* would go, where they all feared a place, a Place with No Name, a place outside thought or memory, he would find the one he sought. He would find the fabled bringer of fire, the one still known as Prometheus, chained to his rock, his liver eaten out and rejuvenated. And that ... *that* was enough to drive him on against fears a thousandfold more potent than this merely terrifying jungle. Or the strangeness within him.

He struck off, by the compass still south by southwest, machete and thick-soled boots beating a way for his long, wiry frame. In the chittering depths of that green denseness he seemed too slight, too terrified to find anything as great as that which he sought. His small blue eyes behind the wire-framed lenses of his glasses seemed so watery, so fragile, so astigmatic, they could never recognize grandeur, even if it were to present itself. But he was here, and he was moving, and somewhere behind these dew-cupping fronds, he would come to the legend-that-lived. He had to believe that, *keep* believing it.

It had not been an easy thing, this trek through the rain forest; the feverish drifting upon the waters of the mesa lake where the plane had crashed, killing the others instantly, spitting itself upon the drogued *fuienta*, plunging with a near-living gasp into the eroded bottom. He remembered with the delirium of heat and pain and the nausea of water fever, finding the *piragua* floating on the edge of the lake. Half-drowned, he had plunged his body into the lean, fire-blackened slit and descended into the darkness of nonthinking. The water, lapping against the seamed side of the dugout, had lulled his muted consciousness. He had sought and found a euphoric state of nonfeeling like that proffered by the peyote of the *serpentes* who see the secret colors of God upon the wind and the night, melting into the chiaroscuro of the jungle night.

(But if he could remember all that, even through the delirium, why did his thoughts continue to scatter and fall past alien memories that he was this other, this small man on a brick street in the cold?)

He kept moving.

And what was it the *Indios* said about him? About Harry Tim—Norman Mogart? He had heard the story from them in a dozen accounts. That he was mad to go to the Place with No Name. And what was it those superstitious wise ones said about . . . *him?* About the legend.

The first time it was among the *Cholos,* when he could barely find the breath to pursue such an impossible tale. Who else but Norman Mogart would have seen in the semblance of the snake totem the identity of the legends that found their way through the *Rig-Veda,* the *Osai nai Komata?* Who else? Why, even the twenty references in the *Heiji Monogatari,* that warrior epic of half a world away . . . all these fitted piece-by-piece to the final pattern.

Now, fevered, moving, skin mottled by the three varieties of diploid fungus so common to the tableland, he knew that his eyes would become the color of llama milk, and his ears become muffled to the sounds of the insinuating fronds in a matter of days; but in that time he might see the thing he had come to see, if it existed.

The *Cholos* had promised him—with fear—as had the *Zenos*—with ridicule—and the *Huilichachas*—with disbelief—that he would find Him. If he went where the colors of the *Yoatl* ran like paint, if he went seven times seven meters, there . . . trapped in the cleft of the living rock . . . He rested, eyes filled with the black tears of fever and pain.

It was not a vulture that assailed Him, of course. No vulture that tore at his vitals. This they told him. That was the Western version; the distorted version of the legend of the fire-bringer. Only He, Huipoclapiol, was the bringer not of fire, but of lies; not the searing brand of truth, but the greater revelation of falsehood, and for this his spleen was ripped from his quivering viscera by the mad-eyed *Yoatl,* whose plumage colors ran like rainbow blood over His brown, immortal body.

And now he had found the bleeding color-bird, and so he knew the rest of it must be true.

Sunk within his own madness (how far into fire-dreams am I gone, he wondered, knowing only one out of six images was of the real world, all others products of the fever, the pain, even this other life I seem to have led, yet know I never led) he faintly heard the sound . . . a mad sound from beyond the green. . . .

Eyes burning bright, he hacked through a cat's cradle of vines, found himself abruptly on a ridge, and looked down to see the sound and what made it. The dull, droning, faraway mad sound of living death. There went the wide brown swath, like an ocean breaker, a ribbon road of desolation and roiling, hungering tumult. The *marabunta!* The warrior ants, the hell-that-moves, the mouth that never knows filling, the army ants that sweep all before them until they inexplicably vanish back into the jungle to wait their time once more.

He stared down at them, far off, feeling a cold return to sanity. No man could look on the face of such total destruction and not burn away the fever of madness; so much death at once cannot be escaped, even by doorways that lead to delusion. For a very long time he stared down into the valley, watching the moving, always moving billion-legged worm that devoured the world as it went. Then, shivering with the knowing of how small he was, how easily this jungle could take him and kill him, he turned away, and sought again the safety of the jungle. The *marabunta* were moving in a line with him, away from him, but they were far off, they were no immediate threat. Merely a reminder (that indescribable sound still drifting back to him) that he was only alone, only a man, and there were greater gods awake in the land.

Had he not been hallucinating in blue and yellow, he would never have found the entrance to the Place with No Name.

The fever had gotten worse, the fungi that now matted his arms and legs seemed in a race with him, to establish sovereignty of his body before he found what he sought. His most paralyzing fear was of the fungus covering his eyes.

And then he began hallucinating, circles of light emanating from each leaf, from every mote of dust, from the sun, from each outcropping of rock. Million circles, pulsing in blue and yellow, filling his world with empty bubble shapes, through which he slogged, half-conscious. Then he came to a ring of low hills, there in the jungle, high atop the mesa. He started around the foothills, hoping for a break that would carry him through, in blue and yellow.

The passage was overgrown with foliage, and he would never have seen it, had it *not* been radiating circles of light. It was, in fact, the only point in his vision that was clear. Almost like a pathway through his delirium. He cleared the vegetation with his machete, and pried away several jagged chunks of rock that had fallen to block the passage. It was quite dark inside.

Norman Mogart took a step inside, then another. Stood waiting. Heard silence. Drew breath. Stepped again. Walked forward with fear. With hope. Saw nothing. Hung his machete on his belt. Slung his rifle. Extended his hands. Felt the walls of the passage. Narrower. Wider. Moving forward. Deeper and deeper into the mountain. Farther. Saw light far ahead. Hurried toward it. Marveled that the circles of light had left him. Came to the mouth of the passage. Stepped out. Saw Him.

Mogart was on a wide ledge that circled almost completely around the inside of the mountain. Below him, far below him, he could make out what had surely been the throat of what-was-now-obviously not a mountain but a dormant volcano. And all the way across the volcano, on the wide ledge directly across from him, Prometheus was chained to the rock.

Norman Mogart started around the ledge, keeping his eyes alternately on his destination, that incredible figure bent backwards over the rock outcrop, and where his feet were placing themselves.

As he neared the figure, he began to realize that if it was a man, it was a man such as had never existed on this Earth. Prometheus was very brown, almost a walnut shade. His eyes, which were closed, were vertical slits. Around the mouth, which was little more than a horizontal gash running completely across the lower face, were tiny fleshy tendrils. They reminded Mogart of the spiny whiskers of a catfish. The tendrils moved in slight, quivering random patterns.

Prometheus was bent backwards over a rock, arms spread and webbed-fingered hands (with more tendrils on the knuckles) pulled down on either side. Huge faceted bolts of a blue metal had been driven through the wrists, into the rock. A chain of the same metal circled the nipped-in waist and was itself bolted to the rock. Bolts had been driven through the flipper-like feet.

Even as he neared, a scream from the sky brought his eyes up, and he saw the *Yoatl* dive straight down, and with mad-eyed purpose it landed on the chest of the creature. (Mogart realized, suddenly, that this—man?—had altogether too many ribs in the huge chest.) The bird arched its neck and drove its beak into the walnut flesh. It came away red with blood, and Mogart could now make out the scar tissue that covered the body of the chained creature.

He yelled, then. As loud as he could. The bird gave him a quizzical stare, then flapped away into the sky. At the sound of Mogart's voice, Prometheus raised his head and looked across the ledge.

He saw Mogart, moving toward him hurriedly.

Then he began to cry.

Mogart came to his side rapidly. He tried to speak, but he had no idea what to say.

Then the chained figure spoke. In a tongue Mogart could not understand.

"I don't know . . . what you're saying. . . ."

The figure closed his eyes a moment, then mumbled something to himself, as though running through a litany of some sort, and finally said, "Your words. This is right."

"Yes. Yes, now I can understand. . . . Are you . . . ?"

The man's face broke into a smile. A tortured, painful smile of relief and passion. "So the Justice finally sent you. My time is done. I'm very grateful to you."

Norman Mogart did not know what he meant.

"A moment," the figure said, and closed its eyes in concentration. "Now. Touch me."

Mogart hesitated. The mute appeal in the eyes of the walnut man urged him, and he reached out and touched the flesh of the chained man.

There was an instant of disorientation, and when he could focus again, he found himself alone on the ledge, now chained where the walnut figure had been. And he was alone. Quite alone. Chained in the place of Prometheus; himself having become the fire-bringer.

That night, after the *Yoatl* had come again and again to him, he had his first dream. A dream that lived in fire. And this was the dream:

They had been lovers. And from their love had come compassion. For the creatures of that primitive world. They had brought the fire of knowledge; against all the rules of the Justices they had interfered with the normal progress of another world. And so they had been sentenced. The one to a fate chained to a rock in a place no man would ever visit. The other to a public death.

They were immortal, so they would live forever and suffer forever. They radiated in a strange way, so the *Yoatl* came to feed, and to run like paint as a result.

But now their sentences were at an end.

So the Justice had selected two. One was even now exchanging places with the other, and Norman Mogart had taken the place of the one men had come to call Prometheus. Of the other . . . he had been an alien, even as Prometheus had been. He had brought the next step in wisdom for the savages of this world. At the same time, though for the savages they were millions of years apart: for time had no meaning to these aliens.

Now, the lovers were freed. They would return and start again, for they had paid their penances.

Norman Mogart lay out on the rock, eyes closed, thinking of the two men who had loved each other, and him, and all the creatures of this world. He thought of them as they returned to *another* Place with No Name.

He thought of himself, and was in pain, and could not be entirely unhappy. How long it would last, he had no idea, but it was not a completely unsatisfactory way to mark out eternity.

And he thought of the man the Justice had found to take the place of that other, and he knew that when April came around again, he would be given his crown of thorns.

For that was how legends came to be born in the minds of savages, even in the Place with No Name.

*If God is good, why does He send us pain and misery?*

# Paingod

Tears were impossible, yet tears were his heritage. Sorrow was beyond him, yet sorrow was his birthright. Anguish was denied him; even so, anguish was his stock in trade. For Trente, there was no unhappiness; nor was there joy, concern, discomfort, age, time, feeling.

And this was as the Ethos had planned it.

For Trente had been appointed by the Ethos—the race of somewhere/somewhen beings who morally and ethically ruled the universes—as their Paingod. To Trente, who knew neither the tug of time nor the crippling demands of the emotions, fell the forever task of dispensing pain and sorrow to the myriad multitudes of creatures that inhabited the universe. Whether sentient or barely capable of the feeblest unicellular reaction-formation, Trente passed along from his faceted cubicle invisible against the backdrop of the changing stars, unhappiness and misery in proportions too complexly arrived at to be verbalized.

He was Paingod for the universes, the one who dealt out the tears and the anguish and the soul-wrenching terrors that blighted life from its first moment to its last. Beyond age, beyond death, beyond feeling —lonely and alone in his cubicle—Trente went about his business without concern or pause.

Trente was not the first Paingod; there had been others. They had come before, not too many of them, but a few, and why they no longer held their post was a question Trente had never asked. He was the chosen one from a race that lived almost indefinitely, and his job was to pass along the calibrated and measured dollops of melancholy as prescribed by the Ethos. It involved no feeling and no concern, only attention to duty. It was his position, and it was his obligation. How peculiar it was that he felt concern, after all this time.

It had begun so long before—and of time he had no conception —that the only marking date with validity was that in the great ocean soon to become the Gobi Desert, paramecia had become more prevalent than amoebae. It had grown in him through the centimetered centuries as layers and layers of forever settled down like mist to form the strata of the past.

Now, it was now.

Despite the strange ache in his nerve-gland, his *central* nerve-gland; despite the progressive dulling of his eye globes; despite the mad thoughts that spat and stuttered through his triple-domed cerebrum, thoughts of which he knew he was incapable, Trente performed his now functions as he was required:

He dispensed unbearable anguish to the residents of a third-power planet in the Snail Cluster, supportable agony to a farm colony that had sprung up on Jacopettii U, incredible suffering to a parentless spider-child on Hiydyg IX, and relentless torment to a blameless race of mute aborigines on a nameless, arid planet circling a dying sun of the 707 System.

And through it all, Trente suffered for his charges.

What could not be, was. What could not come to pass, had. The soulless, emotionless, regimented creature that the Ethos had named Paingod had contracted a sickness. Concern. At last, after centuries too filed away to unearth and codify, Trente had reached a Now in which he could no longer support his acts. He cared.

The physical manifestations of his mental upheaval were numerous. His oblong head throbbed and his eye globes were dulling, a little more each decade; the interlinked duodenal ulcers so necessary to his endocrinal system's normal function had begun to misfire like faulty plugs in an old car; the *thwack!* of his salamander tail had grown weaker, indicating his motor responses to nerve endings were feebler. Trente—who had always been considered rather a handsome example of his race—had slowly come to look forlorn, weary, even a touch pathetic.

And he sent down woe to an armored, flying creature with a mite-sized brain on a dark planet at the edge of the Coalsack; he dispatched fear and trembling to a smoke-like wraith that was the only visible remains of a great race that had learned to dispense with its bodies centuries before, in the sun known as Vertel; he conscientiously winged terror and unhappiness and misery and sadness to a group of murdering pirates, a clique of shrewd politicians and a brothelful of unregenerate whores—all on a fifth-power planet of the White Horse Constellation.

Stopped alone there, in the night of space, his mind spiraling now for the first time down a strange and disquieting chamber of thought, Trente twisted within himself. *I was selected because I lacked the certain difficulties I now manifest. What is this torment? What is this unpleasant, unhappy, unrelenting feeling that gnaws at me, tears at me, corrupts my thoughts, colors darkly my every desire? Am I going mad? Madness is beyond my race; it is a something we have never known. Have I been at this post too long, have I failed in my duties? If there was a God stronger than the God that I am, or a God stronger than the Ethos Gods, then I would appeal to that God. But there is only silence and the night and the stars, and I'm alone, so alone, so God all alone here, doing what I must, doing my best.*

And then, finally: *I must know. I must know!*

. . . while he spun a fiber of melancholy down to a double-thoraxed insect-creature on Io, speared with dread a blob of barely sentient mud on Acaras III, pain-goaded into suicide an electrical wave-being capable of producing exquisite fifteen-toned harmonics on Syndon Beta V, reduced by half the pleasures of a pitiable slug thing in the methane caves of Kkklll IV, enshrouded in bitterness and misery a man named Colin Marshack on an insignificant planet called Sol III, Earth, Terra, the world . . .

And then, finally: *I will know. I will know!*

Trente removed the scale model of Earth from the display crate, and stared at it. Such a tiny thing, such a helpless thing, to support the nightwalk of a Paingod.

He selected the most recent recipient of his attentions, through no more involved method than that, and used the means of travel his race had long since perfected to leave his encased cubicle hanging translucent against the stars. Trente, Paingod of the universes, for the first time in all the centuries he had lived that life of giving, never receiving, left his place, and left his Now, and went to find out. To find out . . . what? He had no way of knowing.

For the Paingod, it was the first nightwalk.

Pieter Koslek had been born in a dwarf province of a minuscule Central European country long since swallowed up by a tiny power now a member of the Common Market. He had left Europe early in the 1920s, had shipped aboard a freighter to Bolivia and, after working his way as common deckhand and laborer through half a dozen banana republics, had been washed up on an inland shore of the United States in 1934. He had promptly gone to earth, gone to seed, and gone to fat. A short stint in a CCC camp, a shorter stint as a bouncer in a Kansas City speak, a term in the Illinois State Workhouse, a long run on the Pontiac assembly line making an obscure part for an obscure segment of a B-17's innards, a brief fling as owner of a raspberry farm, and an extended period as a skid row-frequenting wino summed up his life. Now, as *now* would be reckoned by any sane man's ephemeris, Pieter Koslek was a wetbrain—an alcoholic so sunk in the fumes and vapors of his own liquor need that he was barely recognizable as a human being. Lying soddenly, but quietly, in an alley two blocks up from the Greyhound bus station in downtown Los Angeles, Pieter Koslek, age fifty-nine, weight 210, hair filth gray, eyes red and moist and closed, unceremoniously died. That simply, that unconcernedly, that uneventfully for all the young-old men in overlong GI surplus overcoats who passed by that alley mouth unseeing, uncaring—Pieter Koslek died. His brain gave out, his lungs ceased to bellow, his heart refused to pump, his blood slid to a halt in his veins, and breath no longer passed his lips. He died. End of story, beginning of story. As he lay there, half-propped against the brick wall with its shredded reminder of a lightweight boxing match between two stumblebums long since passed into obscurity and the files of *Ring Magazine,* a thin tepid vapor of pale green came to the useless body of Pieter Koslek; touched it; felt of it; entered it; Trente was on the planet Earth, Sol III.

If it had been possible to mount an epitaph on bronze for the wetbrain, there on the wall of the alley perhaps, the most fitting would have been: HERE LAY PIETER KOSLEK. NOTHING IN HIS LIFE BECAME HIM SO MUCH AS THE LEAVING OF IT.

The thick-bodied orator on the empty packing crate had gathered a sizable crowd. His license was encased in plastic, and it had been pinned to a broom handle sharpened and driven into the ground. An American flag hung limply from a pole on the other side of the makeshift podium. The flag had only forty-eight stars; it had been purchased long before Hawaii or Alaska had joined the union, but new flags cost money, and—

"Scum! Like sewer water poured into your bloodstream! Look at them, do they *look* like you, do they *smell* like you—those smells, those, those *stinks* that walk like men! That's what they are, *stinks* with voting privileges, all of them, the niggers, the kike-jews who own the land and the apartments you live in, what they think they're big deals! The spicks, the Puerto Rican filth that takes over your streets and rapes your women and puts its lousy hands on your white young daughters, that scum . . ."

Colin Marshack stood in the crowd, staring up at the thick-bodied orator, his shaking hands thrust deep into his sport jacket pockets, his head throbbing, the unlit cigarette hanging unnoticed from his lips. Every word.

". . . Commies in public office, is what we have got to be content with. Nigger lovers and pawns of the kike bastards who own the corporations. They wanta kill all of you, all of us, every one of us. They want us to say, 'Hey! C'mon, make love to my sister, to my wife, do all the dirty things that'll pollute my pure race!' That's what the Commies in public office, misusing *our* public trust, say to us. And what do we say in return, back to them, we say, 'No dice, dirty spicks, lousy kikes, Puerto bastards, black men that want to steal our pure heritage!' We say, go to hell to them, go straight to hell, you dirty rotten sonsuh—"

At which point the policemen moved quietly through the crowd, fascinated and silent like cobras at a mongoose convention, and arrested the thick-bodied orator.

As they took him away, Colin Marshack turned and moved out of the milling group. Why is such hideousness allowed to exist, he thought bitterly, fearfully. He walked down the path and out of Pershing Square ("Pershing Square is where they have a fence up so the fruits can't pick the people.") and did not even realize the rheumy-eyed old man was following him till he was six blocks away.

Then he turned, and the old man almost ran into him. "Something I can do for you?" Colin Marshack asked.

The old man grinned feebly, his pale gums exposing themselves above gap-toothed ruin. "Nosir, nuh-nosir, I've just, uh, I was just follerin' along to see maybe I could tap yah for a couple cents 'tuh get some chick'n noodle soup. It's kinda cold . . . 'n I thought, maybe . . ."

Colin Marshack's wide, somehow humorous face settled into

understanding lines. "You're right, old man, it's cold, and it's windy, and it's miserable, and I think you're entitled to some goddam chicken noodle soup. God knows *someone's* entitled." He paused a beat, added, "Maybe me."

He took the old man by the arm, seemingly unaware of the rancid, rotting condition of the cloth. They walked along the street outside the park, and turned into one of the many side routes littered with one-arm beaneries and 40¢-a-night flophouses.

"And possibly a hot roast beef sandwich with gravy all over the French fries," Colin added, steering the wine-smelling old derelict into a restaurant.

Over coffee and a bear claw, Colin Marshack stared at the old man. "Hey, what's your name?"

"Pieter Koslek," the old man murmured, hot vapors from the thick white coffee mug rising up before his watery eyes. "I've, uh, been kinda sick, y'know. . . ."

"Too much sauce, old man," said Colin Marshack. "Too much sauce does it for a lot of us. My father and mother both. Nice folk, loved each other, they went to the old alky's home hand in hand. It was touching."

"You're kinda feelin' sorry for y'self, ain'tcha?" said Pieter Koslek. And looked down at his coffee hurriedly.

Colin stared across angrily. Had he sunk that low, that quickly, that even the seediest cockroach-ridden bum in the gutter could snipe at him, talk up to him, see his sad and sorry state? He tried to lift his coffee cup, and the cream-laced liquid sloshed over the rim, over his wrist. He yipped and set the cup down quickly.

"Your hands shake worse'n mine, mister," Pieter Koslek noted. It was a curious tone, somehow devoid of feeling or concern—more a statement of observation.

"Yeah, my hands shake, Mr. Koslek, *sir*. They shake because I make my living cutting things out of stone, and for the past two years I've been unable to get anything from stone but tidy piles of rock dust."

Koslek spoke around a mouthful of cruller. "You, uh, you're one'a them statue makers, what I mean a sculpt'r."

"That is precisely what I am, Mr. Koslek, sir. I am a capturer of exquisite beauty in rock and plaster and quartz and marble. The only trouble is, I'm no damned good, and I was never *ever* really very good, but at least I made a decent living selling a piece here and there, and conning myself into thinking I was great and building a career, and Canaday in the *Times* said a few nice things about me. But even *that's* turned to rust now. I can't make a chisel do what I want it to do, I can't sand and I can't chip and I can't carve dirty words on sidewalks if I try."

Pieter Koslek stared across at Colin Marshack, and there was a banked fire down in those rheumy, sad old eyes. He watched and looked and saw the hands shaking uncontrollably, saw them wring one against another like mad things, and even when interlocked, they still trembled hideously.

And . . .

*Trente, locked within an alien shell, comprehended a small something. This creature of puny carbon atoms and other substances that could not exist for an instant in the rigorous arena of space, was dying. Inside, it was ending its life cycle, because of the misery Trente had sent down. Trente had been responsible for the quivering pain that sent Colin Marshack's hand into spasms. It had been done two years before—by Colin Marshack's time—but only a few moments earlier as Trente knew it. And now it had changed this creature's life totally. Trente watched the strange human being, a product of little introverted needs and desires. And he knew he must go further, must experiment further with his problem. The green and transparent vapor that was Trente seeped out of the eyes of Pieter Koslek, and slid carefully inside Colin Marshack. It left itself wide open, flung itself wide open, to what tremors governed the man. And Trente felt the full impact of the pain he so lightly dispensed to all the living things in the universes. It was potent hot all! And it was a further knowing, a greater knowledge, a simple act that the sickness had compelled him to undertake. By the fear and the memory of all the fears that had gone before, Trente knew, and knowing, had to go further. For he was Paingod, not a transient tourist in the country of pain. He drew forth the mind of Marshack, of that weak and trembling Colin Marshack, and fled with it. Out. Out there. Further. Much further. Till time came to a slithering halt and space was no longer of any consequence. And he whirled Colin Marshack through the universes. Through the infinite allness of the space and time and motion and meaning that was the crevice into which Life had sunk itself. He saw the blobs of mud and the whirling winged things and the tall humanoids and the cleat-treaded half-men/half-machines*

*that ruled one and another sector of open space. He showed it all to
Colin Marshack, drenched him in wonder, filled him like the most vital
goblet the Ethos had ever created, poured him full of love and life and
the staggering beauty of the cosmos. And having done that, he whirled
the soul and spirit of Colin Marshack down down and down to the
fibrous shell that was his body, and poured that soul back inside. Then
he walked the shell to the home of Colin Marshack . . . and turned it
loose. And . . .*

When the sculptor awoke, lying face down amidst the marble
chips and powder-fine dust of the statue, he saw the base first; and not
having recalled even buying a chunk of stone that large, raised himself
on his hands, and his knees, and his haunches, and sat there, and his
eyes went up toward the summit, and seemed to go on forever, and
when he finally saw what it was he had created—this thing of such
incredible loveliness and meaning and wisdom—he began to sob.
Softly, never very loud, but deeply, as though each whimper was
drawn from the very core of him.

He had done it this once, but as he saw his hands still trembling,
still murmuring to themselves in spasms, he knew it was the one time
he would ever do it. There was no memory of how, or why, or even
of when . . . but it was *his* work, of that he was certain. The pain in
his wrists told him it was.

The moment of truth stood high above him, resplendent in marble, but there would be no other moments.

This was Colin Marshack's life, in its totality, now.

The sound of sobbing was only broken periodically, as he began
to drink.

Waiting. The Ethos waited. Trente had known they would. It
was inevitable. Foolish for him to conceive of a situation of which they
would not have an awareness.

*Away. From your post, away.*

"I had to know. It has been growing in me, a live thing in me.
I had to know. It was the only way. I went to a planet, and lived within
what they call 'men' and knew. I think I understand now."

*Know. What is it you know?*

"I know that pain is the most important thing in the universes.
Greater than survival, greater than love, greater even than the beauty

it brings about. For without pain there can be no pleasure. Without sadness there can be no happiness. Without misery, there can be no beauty. And without these, life is endless, hopeless, doomed and damned."

*Adult. You have become adult.*

"I know . . . this is what became of the other Paingods before me. They grew into concern, into knowing, and then . . ."

*Lost. They were lost to us.*

"They could not take the step; they could not go to one of the ones to whom they had sent pain, and learn. So they were no use as Paingod. I understand. Now I know, and I am returned."

*Do. What will you do?*

"I will send more pain than ever before. More and greater."

*More? You will send more?*

"Much more. Because now I understand. It is a gray and a lonely place in which we live, all of us, swinging between desperation and emptiness, and all that makes it worthwhile is caring, is beauty. But if there were no opposite for beauty, or for pleasure, it would all turn to dust."

*Being. Now you know who you are.*

"I am most blessed of the Ethos, and most humble. You have given me the highest, kindest position in the universes. For I am the God to all men, and to all creatures small and large, whether they call me by name or not. I am Paingod, and it is my life, however long it stretches, to treat them to the finest they will ever know. To give them pain, that they may know pleasure. Thank you."

And the Ethos went away, secure that at last, after all the eons of Paingods who had broken under the strain, who had lacked the courage to take that nightwalk, they had found one who would last truly forever. Trente had come of age.

While back in the cubicle, hanging star-bright and translucent in space, high above it all, yet very much part of it all, the creature who would never die, the creature who had lived within the rotting body of Pieter Koslek and for a few moments in the soul and talent of Colin Marshack, that creature called Paingod, learned one more thing, as he stared at the tiny model of the planet Earth he had known.

Trente knew the feel of a tear formed in a duct and turned free from an eye globe—cool on his face.

Trente knew happiness.

*About forty-five per cent of this is a true story. Eat your heart out figuring which is real and which is phony. Or simply repeat to yourself, "For I am a jealous people," and remember not to screw around with the supplicants, baby.*

# Ernest and the Machine God

Gods in their Heaven, all's right with the world.

Selena: fighting desperately to keep her eyes open.

The road: North Carolina, like a snake, rock mountain wall to the left, sheer drop into nowhere on the right.

The night: black, dead and staring, like the eyes of a man lying on a kitchenette floor in a motel in Washington, D.C. Somewhere back there behind Selena.

The fear: that they could trace her, through his department, or through the woman who had rented them the motel room. And catch her. And put her in prison. And then kill her, for killing *him*.

The car: a 1951 Packard, sea-green, huge as a Tyrannosaurus, bought late the day before, for thirty-two dollars, all she had had in her purse (all she had been able to take off his body) from a street-corner used-car lot in the filthy Negro section of Fredericksburg, Virginia.

The destination: Florida. Getaway. Hideaway.

Her eyes slid quickly guillotine closed. The uneven ratcheting of gravel under the front tires brought her sharply awake again. She pulled the car back onto the road. Over the edge, out through the right-side windows, she knew there was a sheer drop into the valley below. It was too deep and too black even to estimate the fall. Enough to kill a car, and its driver.

The road twisted back and around, heading up and up, always up and up. Fog slithered toothlessly across the road at every minor dip, and the center line had been dimmed to headlights many years before by wheels and weather. The lanes were one each way, and too narrow for a compact, much less the behemoth she spun through the turns. It smelled of vomit in the back seat. Thirty-two dollars. A dead man lying face-up on a linoleum floor, a corkscrew still in his hand.

There was no guard railing or built-up shoulder over there on her right. It ended with frost-chipped road edge, thin rut of dirt, and the drop into the abyss. Her eyes closed slowly, flickering, drooping lids over dull film of sleep . . .

. . . and woke suddenly as the right front tire left the road, skimmed across the dirt, and rode in empty air . . .

. . . her eyes snapped open, and instinctively she wrenched the wheel back hard left. The right front tire spun against the edge, still clawing emptiness, but the Packard lurched left and forward as she hit the accelerator, and the tire chewed its way through loose topsoil and regained the road, the car now plunging hard left, suddenly rushing up the short incline at the base of the rock wall, tilting, and running along the side of the wall almost horizontally.

The car struck an outcropping with a monstrous clang, and Selena was thrown against the steering wheel, crushing her breasts against the ungiving circle. Sudden gray washed over her and she fell back, feet flopping off the pedals, arms limp at her sides. The car rebounded, suddenly stalled, and in the North Carolina night there was only silence . . .

. . . and the sound of a storm, far off in the mountains . . .

Nowhere is North Carolina. Nowhere is the land of fear. Nowhere is flight without destination, only a looming *back there,* where all flights begin.

Selena, in fog gray, lived it again. . . .

Three years at Duke University had taught Selena all she needed to know: that college was a dead end for her. The degree of cunning that she brought to her academic life was more than she needed to get a steady 3.2 average. It was tantamount to hunting a flea with an elephant gun. She had been fascinated briefly by some of the experimental studies done by Rhine and others in the parapsychology labs, but even that had palled quickly; they were fools, tinkering with improbabilities. Selena doted on reality.

Reality for Selena took essential form in one word: *manipulation.*

Hidden deep in the entrails of that word was *its* power-source, the word: *power.*

There was an electrical fascination for her in getting people to do what she wanted them to do. Often it was to their advantage, occasionally not. But they were gambited, and that was the essence of the relationship. After which, Selena vanished in mist and memory.

She had been the most beautiful girl in Minneapolis. From high school on, she had always had her way. It became a constant, an accepted thing—she would date the most eligible boys, she would win the queenship of the senior prom, she would take first-place honors on the debating team. And it became a way of life—they came to her to find out what the theme of the annual school fair should be, they came to her to find out if the new girl should be asked into the sorority, they came to her to be maneuvered, to have their decisions made for them—and it finally passed into the realm of an unnoticed seventh sense. Selena could see and hear and smell and touch and taste and remember and . . .

Order people to her will. Almost unconsciously after her teens. She no longer had to work at it. They came to her and gave her what she wanted, and Selena took it as her due. And when she had left Minneapolis far behind her; when she had left Chicago behind her; when she had left New York behind her; then she no longer needed to ask people to do what she wanted them to do, to enter the regimented little ranks of her life, and march to the intricate route-step she had set for them.

College, and two brief marriages, and a modeling career, and boredom. Oh God, deadly boredom. The end result of getting whomever and whatever she wanted. Boredom . . . scintillant, murk-deep boredom, that drove her to Washington, D.C. Where there were men who ordered entire nations to their will. In that city, she would find the ones who could compete with her on her own level.

But it had been the same for Selena. The same as it had been in Minneapolis, when she had challenged Teddy to climb through the old, broken culvert pipe, and he had done it, though shivering with fear; and a rusted nail protruding from a block of scrap wood had torn his thigh, and he had gotten lockjaw. But had done it. For her. The same as it had been at Duke, when she had seduced the assistant professor of psychology, to get the final term mark that would continue her scholarship, and he had done it, though cursing himself for his weakness; and he had been sacked the following year, when it had come to light, but that didn't matter to Selena for by then she had moved on. But he had done it. For her. The same as it had been in Chicago when she had befuddled the poor homosexual art director of a men's magazine, and gotten him to choose her for their centerfold, thereby making three thousand dollars for her. What had happened to him had been unpleasant, but Selena never heard about it; she had moved on. It had been the same in New York. And in Washington, D.C. The same. Always the same. Selena always got her way, shivered with delight at making these movers-&-shakers move and shake to her designs.

Until she had met the man from the government department.

He had been stronger than she had expected. And he had not thought of it as a game. What Selena had not realized in time was that *he* was a male counterpart of *her*. He was used to winning.

The contention had been a sheaf of papers, light blue in color, that had come from a sealed file in his department. What each of them had wanted to do with those papers became unimportant the moment he stole them. Became *less* than unimportant in the motel, when the showdown came, and each planned on winning. Selena had used all of her standard gambits—those that had worked on the best, and the worst. None of the gambits had any effect. But then, neither had his . . . on her. They had jousted with one another for an hour, in all the subtle, mysterious ways of the manipulators, and in the end he had come for her with the vicious corkscrew in his hand. The corkscrew he had used less than an hour before to open the magnum of champagne.

She had struggled with him, and he had slipped on a spear of melted ice on the linoleum floor, and flailed backward, and smashed his head on the edge of the sink. At that particularly vulnerable juncture of neck and cranium; she had heard the ugly crack, like rotten wood, and he had slid sidewise, onto his back, his eyes wide open and staring, the corkscrew in his hand. And she had rifled his body, taken all the money on him, and fled. . . .

The veil of gray tore away like mist before a storm, and Selena felt her arms hanging straight down on either side of the steering wheel, terribly heavy. She tried to move, to lever herself back into an upright position, but her upper body was without muscular control, lying against the wheel. Her long auburn hair was over her face, and she could not open her eyes.

The sound of the storm was not in her head.

Outside the Packard the mountain night had opened; black rain, thick as lava, thundered down over the silent car. Her window was open. Rain was pattering off the sill, onto her left cheek. She tried to lurch farther to the left, and succeeded in getting her head to loll back and to the side.

Blessed cool wetness cascaded over her hot face, and she opened her eyes. Stringy moist strands of auburn hair hung across her face, and she moved her head idly, shaking them back with difficulty. Then she tried using her arms. They were limp from having been in that bloodless position for so long. But agonizingly . . . she drew her left hand up onto her lap. Her dress was soaked through, on the left side. The Pucci cocktail dress she had worn to aid her manipulation of the man from the government department. It was cold and flat against her side and her left breast. She wore no underwear.

Selena rolled her body back against the seat, and a surf-crash of sickness broke over her. She pulled the door handle and barely managed to swing the door out and up, realizing the car was tilted. The door was incredibly heavy. But she threw her weight against it, and fell from the car. The slamming door barely missed her legs.

The rain helped.

In a few moments she was able to stand, leaning against the side of the car. Her knees were filthy with road mud. The storm beat against her. Lightning exploded all around the mountains, chain-reacting like lunacy in a cyclotron. Thunder boomed *inside* the stones of the hills. Bursting outward on waves of muscularity that promised the ground beneath her would shatter in a moment.

Selena looked up into the rain, and it washed over her, plastering the thin silk cocktail dress to the lines of her body. In a short time, a time without duration, she was able to climb into the Packard again and start the engine. She backed it off the incline, and turned on the lights. They cast fitful light across the desolate Carolina nowhere. Rain slanted through the shafts.

She let the clutch out slowly and the car moved forward, as though testing itself: a wounded creature waiting to feel the sting of pain in one of its appendages.

She drove blindly, pain in her chest and the shivering chill of wet clothes against her flesh keeping her alert. The road went up and around, doubling back on itself as it threaded its way through softly lit passages in the rain-choked darkness.

Somewhere along the way, she took a wrong turn.

In that night, any turn would have been a wrong turn.

It didn't matter until the Packard began chewing itself to pieces.

At first the sound was a soft *ting!* as of a paper clip hitting a revolving fan. She did not realize she was hearing it for some time, until the irregularity of its occurrence struck her. Selena's brow drew down, and she bit her lip. As if the machine had been waiting for this reaction from her, the *ting!*ing sharply changed to a harsh metallic clank that came again and again, then ceased for fifteen minutes till she was lulled that it had cured itself . . . and then clanked again.

By the time she reached the crest of the mountain, and saw the dim lights below, the noise had changed again: it was now the sound of metal chewing on metal, the sickly diseased sound of a creature eating itself alive.

She started down the twisting nightmare with the rain suddenly slackening its beat and then ceasing entirely as she threaded her way around fallen boulders lying in the oncoming lane.

Forty minutes later she passed the blurred and weatherbeaten sign that said PETRIE, pop. 650. It was decorated with Kiwanis and Moose emblems.

She drove down the last of the mountain slopes, and grinding hideously, pulled onto the main street of Petrie, North Carolina.

Five stores. Three on the left, two on the right. And beyond them, thirty feet beyond, a gas station.

She rolled into the station. It was a brand of gasoline she did not know. There were three men lounging on straight-backed chairs, tilted up against the wall of the slatboard station, under a protective overhang. She pulled past the pumps, the Packard ratcheting and grinding, and stopped directly in front of them. She turned off the engine and stared out at them. They stared back, unmoving.

Selena got out of the car.

They still hung there, feet off the ground, chairs back against the wall, three men of indeterminate age, tanned and lined by life in the mountains. They were alive, she could ascertain that much, for two of them were chewing gum, and the third smoked a battered meerschaum, from which a curling filigree of silver-gray smoke regularly climbed into the suspiciously gentle night breeze. She was able to tell they were alive, additionally, by the looks of malicious lechery that invaded their faces. (In the mountains, far back in the hills of nowhere, the term "cool" had been invented, without having ever been named. These people were cool: they would not acknowledge their own unsettled reactions . . . to anything. Like mummies they would sit, until the world around them turned to ash, and the sky dripped fire, and then they would slowly turn to one another and nod. Coolly. But Selena, dress plastered to her ripe body, could draw reaction from a lizard, from a stone, from a gallon of sea water. They registered, and their eyes brightened. But cool. They did not speak.)

"I'm having some trouble with my car," Selena said.

An unspoken chain of command was established, and the youngest of the three men—perhaps thirty-five—nudged himself forward, and the chair legs hit the wooden platform. "What seems to be the trouble?" he asked, bored.

"Something's broken inside," she said.

Slowly, almost languorously, the man slid out of the chair. Selena thought he might just settle in a pool of tired flesh, but he came toward her, hands thrust into the back pockets of his limp coveralls. "Like what?"

Selena's hands went to her hips, and her jaw thrust out. "Friend, if *I* knew 'like what,' I wouldn't be asking *you* to look at it, now would I?"

"You ain't from 'round here," he said, moving toward the car, chewing his gum furiously.

"No, I'm not."

"Where y'from?"

"Are you going to take a look at this damned car or aren't you?"

The gum chewer seemed startled by her language. He stopped, looked dull. On the front porch of the station, the second man—fortyish, nearly bald, wearing a filthy coverall with the gas station emblem on the breast pocket—hit the boards with his feet. The scene had been turned over to him: the young one had come up against something he couldn't handle.

"Well, I c'n take a look at 'er," he said, and got up. The gum moved sluggishly in his mouth, and he matched pace with it toward Selena and the car.

He stood in front of the Packard for a moment, as if trying to decide which end contained the engine. Then he fumbled around the hood, looking for the latch. With exasperation, Selena moved beside him, reaching in through the front grille. "It opens from underneath."

The older man attained a tone of cool disdain that completely repudiated his obvious unfamiliarity with the business end of an automobile: "Why, thank you, ma'am." It was a brand of sarcasm honed to perfection by four hundred years of misdirecting the outsiders.

She opened the hood, and the man leaned over the front bumper, carefully not touching the mud-spattered metal with his already-filthy coverall. He stared down into the guts of the machine for long minutes.

Finally, without looking at Selena, he said, "Why don't y'all start 'er up."

Selena felt a rising tide of frustration and fury. She got in and turned the ignition key. The engine coughed to life. The sound of metal grinding and tearing came up solidly. Superimposed as the latest symptom of a disease that had been built in sixteen years before when the car had been new. It was a strange kind of testimony to the excellence of the Packard manufacturers that the car was even able to *start* sixteen years later; a feat far beyond the capabilities of contemporary Detroit Iron.

The gum-chewing went on apace, the staring into the innards did not change phase, the observers said nothing, the sound of thunder caromed through the mountains.

Selena leaned out through the open door. "Can you *do* anything . . . ?"

The man slowly looked up at her. His expression was one of mixed lechery and disgust. He did not have to say *Lady, shut yore damned face, you're in* awuh *part of the woods now, with yore damned long legs and all yore damned pretty skin a-showin' through that skimpy li'l dress, an' whut* we *want to do is whut we gonna do, so sit back an' don't be harangin' us whilst we playin' with puttin' you in yore place;* he didn't have to say it. There it was, arrogant and infuriating for Selena, in his expression.

The youngest of the three ambled up beside the gum chewer, and they stared down at the machine together.

Nowhere is North Carolina. Nowhere is the land of the Gods. All the Gods. Not only the ancient Gods who have gone to sleep, and the recent Gods who are still worshipped, but the God of Rain, and the God of Lightning, and the God of the Hunt, who have taken on new attributes and new faces. And the newest, youngest, strongest Gods: the God of Neon, the God of Smog, the God of Luck, and the Machine God. People come to worship at strange altars. They place their oblations at the feet of graven images without knowing these are truly

Gods they have found. The War God grows fatter each year, gorged on blood. The Love God fornicates with himself, weakening his genes, rebirthing as a thalidomide monstrosity. Paingod does his work and doles out his anguish, paying no attention to the cries of those crushed beneath his millstones. But the Machine God . . .

The sound had grown more violent. It was an ugly sound. In final frustration, Selena shut the car down, and got out. The tableau was still the same. The little porch on the slat-walled gas station; the old man still tilted against the front wall, smoking his pipe; the two observers still looking down into the engine as though studying a slide under a microscope; the mountains looming huge and dark around the town; the sound of the storm gathering strength to hurl itself against them once more.

"All *right!*" Selena snapped. "Enough is enough."

The two looked at her. Then as one, they looked at the old man in the chair. And Selena realized all at once, that neither of these two fools could have done anything, had they *wanted* to: the old man was the mechanic. The other two were camouflage, the sportsmen who had been given Selena to toy with for a few minutes. It was the old man she should have approached.

He did not move an inch from his comfortable position as he informed her in a doughy, wheezing voice, "Can't he'p you, ma'am. Trouble you got's too big. Have t'take it on in to Shelby, or someplace, where they's 'quipped to make them kinda repairs."

"But you didn't even *look* at it!" Selena yelled.

"Too much. Can't fix 'er," the old man said, and closed his eyes. Smoke rose from the meerschaum once more, lazily.

The two fools stood where they were, staring once again down into the engine, as if hoping the show might resume. Selena shoved them aside and slammed the hood closed. She was speechless with fury. She strode back to the front door and started to get in. And realized . . . she could not go *anywhere*.

She needed this car in working order.

If they were tracking her, she could not afford to be without transportation.

But these fools would not—or could not—repair the engine.

She was hamstrung.

A wave of such helplessness possessed her that she almost sank down on the car seat.

The old man, without opening his eyes, said, "I s'pose you could call old Ernest. . . ."

And the two fools fell down laughing. The youngest one rolled around on the muddy ground as though possessed by St. Vitus's Dance. The middle-aged one barked a kind of laughter Selena had not heard since she had been at the Bronx Zoo. The old man was smiling, smugly.

"Who the hell is Ernest? And what's so funny?"

The old man opened his eyes, and looked at the middle-aged one. His laughter came under control with difficulty, but when he could speak without gasping, he wiped the tears from his eyes and said, with difficulty, "Ernest? Oh, he, uh, he r'pairs things, sometimes . . ."

And they fell down laughing again.

Selena watched them with incredulity. *Something* was funny, unquestionably. But *what* that something was she could not even begin to fathom. The two grown men tumbled back and forth at her feet like an unmatched set of children's toys, loose-jointed, rubber-armed, totally without control of themselves as the *enormity* of the joke paralyzed them. Their laughter drowned out the thunder that whipped overhead.

She had to repeat herself three times before they could hear her: "Well, all right then, why don't you just run and *get* 'old Ernest'!"

The youngest one sat up, suddenly. There on the ground. He looked at her. She was serious. *Why the hell* shouldn't *I be serious?* Selena thought, interpreting his look in an instant. The young one looked over at the old one. The old one nodded with a barely perceptible movement of his head. The young one leaped to his feet and, cackling uproariously, dashed off through the town and was gone in an instant. Selena stood beside the Packard, tapping her foot. Every few seconds, the middle-aged one, now back in his chair on the porch, beside the old man, would chuckle deep in his throat, and build it till he was roaring with laughter. *Fuck you!* thought Selena.

. . . Ah, He is a special God. He loves his gears and his pumps, his springs and his transistors, his printed circuits and his boilers. He is not a jealous God, like some, but he is an attentive God. He tends to business, and keeps his world of machines functioning. But every now and then, every once in a while, every few centuries in a mind that is Machine and not Man, the Machine God finds one He can care about more than the others. A special machine, or a special man, and they become the beloved of the Machine God. Saint Joan had the power of moving masses of men to religious fervor. Ahmad, who was Mohammed, was able to die of his own volition when he was presented with the keys of eternal life on earth, and those of Paradise. Gandhi saw the sheep being led to the slaughter and worship of Kali, and rejected her tenets, turning to the wisdom of the Gautama Buddha, drawing unto himself the powers of peace. Christ was able to heal the lepers, to walk on water. Samson brought down the temple, and David slew Goliath, and Jonah lived in the belly of the whale. And for the Machine God, the beloved child was . . .

Loping down the street, the gum-chewing fool leaped high in the air, like a lovesick schoolboy who has grabbed his first thigh in the schoolyard at recess. He came tumbling, gibbering, capering, laughing up to the station, and pointed back in the direction he had come. He broke up completely, slumping down against the porch-post. The other two men laughed with him. Selena looked in the direction their laughter was fleeing.

He was perhaps six feet tall, incredibly thin, with arms that might have been figs. 87 & 88 in a medical text on rickets. He was the compleat Ichabod Crane. His hands hung six inches below the cuffs of his no-color jacket, his knobbed ankles were exposed between the tattered legs of his pants and his highly-polished cordovan shoes. He moved in a long, disjointed manner, more like some whisper-articulated insect, a mantis or a spider, than a man. His hair was lank and as colorless as his clothing: the color of sand, the color of bricks, the color of rain, the color of teak, but none of these: all of them, with the highlights leached out. Mudpie hair. His face was all angles and planes, eyes big and a little vacant. Mouth as wide as a dog's. He stumbled and stepped, a coordinated spastic, a colt learning its legs.

Selena stared at the apparition, and realized what the joke was. Ernest was the joke. His totality . . . his look, his manner, his walk, his *presence* . . . was a joke. The three men on the porch had extended the scope of their sport. They had brought her a halfwit to repair the car. The viciousness of it did not escape her.

Ernest came to her, and stopped.

She looked up into his eyes.

He was by no means a halfwit.

There was something living behind those eyes, and from silt-deep in her memory came a quote from Gerald Kersh that fit precisely: *. . . there are men whom one hates until a certain moment when one sees, through a chink in their armour, the writhing of something nailed down and in torment.*

He stared at her, and she was beautiful. More beautiful than she had ever been before. For the first time in her life, Selena was uncomplicated. Light bathed her. She felt her flow and her pulse. The boy stared at her. He was no more than sixteen years old, possibly seventeen, but he saw her as she was, reduced to her essentials.

"Can you fix my car?"

He did not reply.

"There's something wrong with it. Can you repair it?"

Shyly, he nodded yes. And the three fools fell down laughing at him.

Then, oh so strange. . . .

Ernest started at the rear of the Packard. His long, delicate, pale fingers barely touched the metal. They grazed the green rusted hide of the ailing creature, and traced four thin lines from the rear fender forward, as he walked to the front of the machine. The light touch of *someone getting to know someone.* He stood in front of the car for a minute (while the fools roared and beat each other on the back), head cocked to one side, the hair hanging down over his right eye; listening. Then he touched the grille.

When Selena had angrily opened the hood for the gum-chewer, it had sprung up just as angrily on its counterbalanced springs, clanging fully open and quivering.

The grille opened smoothly now. Smoothly, slowly, as though exposing its interior to the gentle ministrations of a physician with the power of mist and cool.

Then Ernest laid his hands on the engine.

He touched it.

He touched it all over.

He pressed it. Sensuously. Charmingly.

As they watched, his hands caressed the engine.

Lightly.

He leaned in, and listened to the machine silently.

*He talked to the machine.* Silently.

Then he reached far up under the engine, where there was only darkness, and he moved his fingers delicately.

Selena watched, amazed. It was lunacy, of course, but the way he moved, the sureness and coordination in his hands. It was the joy of watching a good shoemaker at his last, the pleasure of watching a skilled cabinetmaker rabbet-joining two perfectly planed surfaces, the exquisite wonder of a sculptor forming grandeur from base rock; *he talked to the machine.*

After a while, he brought his hands back up into sight, and they held a twisted twig of metal, brightly-smeared down one side where its surface had been scored and abraded.

"Fell down into the engine," he said.

His voice was a small child's voice; the voice of a boy not yet a man, who seldom spoke.

"Can you repair it?" Selena demanded . . . gently.

He nodded.

The three fools were giggling now, holding their sides from the pain. Ernest went past them into the gas station. In a moment he came out with a plain black wire coat hanger. He took a pair of wire snips from a heavily laden workbench just inside the door of the garage and snipped off a straight piece nine inches long. He laid the wire snips where he had found them, returned the useless coat hanger to the station, and came back to the car.

He took the nine-inch piece of coat hanger in his left hand, and with his right he began to bend it.

He should not have been able to bend it so intricately, over such a short span, but Selena watched with growing wonder as he did precisely that. The final shape was something unlike a helix, and something unlike a moebius, and something unlike a buttonhook. It was something else.

Then he reached down, back into nowhere, where he had been, and he did things *inside* the engine. When his hands emerged, the metal had been left inside. There was no grease on his hands, and none on his jacket.

"Well?" Selena demanded. Gently.

Ernest nodded toward the car, and she knew he wanted her to start it up. She got in, turned the key, and listened to the instant surge of thrumming power that coursed through the Packard. It sounded strong, potent, impressive. The sound not even a new car makes.

She turned it off, and got out. She had two dollars in change in her purse. She offered it to him, but he shyly smiled, a childlike grin of embarrassment, and thanked her no ma'am thank you very much.

Then he bobbled back down the street, and was gone.

Selena stood there with the silver in her hand; she wore an empty, startled expression of *what happened*.

The three fools were now prostrate, clutching one another for support even on the ground.

"All right, you three incompetents!" she snapped.

They stopped laughing instantly.

"Ernest fix y'up real good, ma'am?" the youngest asked, snickering.

"He did a hell of a lot more than any of you idiots!"

The old one stared at her smoothly. He wasn't laughing now. "Guess you'll be movin' on now, that right?"

Selena was not moving on.

"Where can I stay overnight in this cemetery? There's a storm brewing and I'm not going on till I find someone in this idiot town who can give me a straight answer how to get back on the main road. If I take directions from any one of you, I'm liable to wind up in Nome, Alaska."

The old one looked at her.

The other two looked at each other.

One of them bit his lip.

One of them coughed into his sleeve.

One of them licked his lips, hoping.

She went to the boardinghouse. Her room was on the first floor, in the rear. It was cold, and it smelled of mildew. She undressed in the dark and used the bath down the hall. Then she came back and started to get into bed. As she pulled back the thin blanket, she felt him staring at her. She turned toward the window, and for a moment she thought it might be the youngest of the three fools, and she made an instinctive movement to cover herself with the blanket. But the feeling passed, and she knew it was him: Ernest.

Dark in the night, wrapped in rain, silent staring, tensed and trembling, molded into shadow, as the storm broke in fragments of sound and light that formed a pattern of violence only hinted-at by the earlier holocaust. Jagged scythes of lightning ripped away the darkness and blasted the earth, a tongue of flame from a thunder dragon crushed, seared and vaporized a tree stump. In the darkness he did not move. Flame lived beside him as the stump returned to its component parts. Rain made a second face on him, filling his eyes and draining down through his hair into his waiting mouth. Wide-eyed and wondrous, he saw her there in the window, only faintly seen through the deepest shadow.

Selena lived to manipulate.

Nowhere is the desolate countryside of the amoralist soul. The twisted, blasted, blackened wreckage littering a landscape of lava pits and brine holes and quicklime pools. Selena, naked, pulse throbbing in her wrist, muscle quivering on the fleshy inner surface of her thigh, smelling sweetly of sudden woman sweat, found her great gambit.

*Out there,* she thought. *This child who has never been with a woman, who has never sunk himself hard into the body of a woman like me. Whatever he is, magician, maniac, wild psi talent, elf gnome troll leprechaun, whatever he is, there's one thing he's not. Yet. Gambit. Point counterpoint. What would it be like to do it with someone like him? I thought at first he was an idiot, a retarded thing. But he isn't. He has a power. And I have a power. Let him feed me that power through the soft place.*

In the darkness, Ernest watched her come to the window, her white flesh shining out at him, as she opened the window, raising it, cutting off the vision at the breasts. Then she stepped over the sill, into the thundering rain, and down in the running Carolina mud, and she came to him, standing beside the smoking burning stump that had been blasted by a God.

He could not move. He held animal still as she moved up to him and the rain washed her body with streaks of line blue and yellow ocher. Her body, a naked woman's body, a miracle in brightness. His belly heaved as he fought for air. Electricity surged and pulsed in the night.

Then she undressed him, carefully, slowly, with subterfuge and stealth, and laid his naked white smooth body down in the mud, and she became more a woman as he became a man for the first time.

She led him the way, guiding him, her own special way, the way only special certain women have that way; it was not the way he could have found with a local town girl; but then, like everyone in the town, they laughed at him.

She did not laugh at him.

Not at first.

No God is sane. How could it be? To be a Man is so much less taxing, and most men are mad. Consider the God. How much more deranged the Gods must be, merely to exist. There can be no doubt: consider the Universe and the patterns without reason upon which it is run. God is mad. The God of Music is mad. The Timegod is punctual, but *he* is mad. And the Machine God is mad. He has made the bomb and the pill and the missile and the acid and the electric chair and the laser and the embalming fluid and the thalidomide baby in his own image. For the lunatic Gods there are minuscule pleasures. The beloved of the Gods are the best, the most highly treasured, the most zealously guarded. God is brutal, God is mad, God is vengeful. But all Gods revere innocence. The lamb, the child, the song. To steal these is to steal from the mad Gods. . . .

Daylight came like a drunk climbing down off a week's binge. Colorless, nervous, tremblingly, wan and wasted.

In front of the gas station, the old one sat silently, flaking out the grime from beneath his fingernails with the plastic edge of a gas credit card someone had driven off and left behind.

Water ran in gullies through the center of Petrie, North Carolina, and returned somewhere to the land to rise and wait to fall again another time.

When the old man saw Ernest walking through town, he sat forward on his chair, his mouth a little open, and he could not believe. The boy walked like you or me. Gone was the loose-jointedness at which everyone laughed.

Gone was the slack mouth at which everyone laughed.

Gone was the wild look in the eye at which everyone laughed.

Gone was the adolescent silliness at which everyone laughed.

Gone was the power.

Later that day, when she did not answer the furious pounding on the door of the boardinghouse, they sent the youngest of the three who hung out at the gas station around by the window. He found it open.

He stared inside, and started to run back inside to tell them, but he licked his lips, knowing he had lost his chance, and climbed up into the room, and touched her body for a few moments before unbolting the door.

Dried Carolina mud covered her body, as though she had been rolling sensuously in it when it had been soft and wet. There was blood on the inside of her thighs, but that wasn't what had killed her.

They could not tell what had killed her.

She did not look peaceful, as if she had died in her sleep; Selena had died reluctantly, fighting every squeeze of the way. She did not look peaceful.

There was not a mark on her.

But one of the crowd lounging in and out of the room said it; he didn't know he'd said it, but he did: he said, "Looks like somethin' stopped her pump."

The Packard ran so well, so beautifully, they could not bear to junk it. So they kept it, and for years thereafter it ran without the slightest difficulty. It ran and ran, and gave generous gas mileage.

*And some gods are so tenacious even Tishman*
*or Zeckendorf can't de-fang them.*

# Rock God

Moist shadow men sang there. A strange song of dark colors. "*Ahwegh thogha!*" Two pure white bulls were brought, and ritual purification was achieved by cutting their throats. Then the white goat, whose blood was sipped from its severed, dripping heart. Then the immense man-like figures of tree limbs and branches were set on fire, the bound human sacrifices in their depths shrieking as they burned. Then the moist shadow men, whom history would call the last Bronze Age people, the Wessex People, drew their animal-hide cloaks about them, cloaks of an animal that existed in dreams only, and they moved within the circle of standing cyclopean posts and lintels. Moved within the dark circle of Stonehenge, and swayed back and forth, murmuring their prayers.

Naked, cold so cold in the winter wind, the great priest stood on the altar stone, and hung down his arms, and let his head droop forward, and invoked the loftiest, the lowliest prayer. To Dis.

On the slaughter stone, the head of the virgin was turned toward the altar, and her shadowed eyes seemed suddenly afire with love of something unnamable. The lesser priests held their ritual knives ready.

Away on the altar stone the great priest called Dis. Begged *him* to come. And there was sound in the earth. And there was sound in the stones. In the great stones. And there was sound in the rocks.

And the priests kneeled to the girl who smiled and whose moist mouth silently begged for climax, and they did things to her, and then carried the meat to the altar stone, laying it at the feet of the great priest. While the worshippers swayed and invoked their god.

Darkness flowed as the sounds of great heavings in the rocks grew louder. Then Dis came. Great, dark Dis came.

They stared through the massive archway toward the heel stone. The first faint glimmer of sunrise splashed its polished dome with the unclean water of the blood sea. And the heel stone began to change.

Dis came from the earth that was his flesh. The rock that was his bone. The stone that was his home that was his essence.

The sunrise ceased. Night came again. Washing up out of the earth, darkness flowed and roiled and the world went dark as Dis came from the rock.

The heel stone shifted shape and grew, and rising from the inanimate stone Dis took form. Hairless flesh as solid as mountains. The great corded legs ran like lava, flowing toward the sinister circle of Stonehenge. Flowed, and touched archway, trilothons, sarsen stone, slaughter stone, lintels, bluestone horseshoe . . . and they fed the body of Dis with their substance, and he grew. Massive, enormous, rising into the night that oozed up from the earth, as darkness covered the world. Greater than the stones, taller than the huge branch-figures wherein had burned the human sacrifices. Two hundred, three hundred feet, towering over the awed and supplicating Wessex People.

Dis, rock god, had come again as he had come one hundred years before, and one hundred years before that.

Words brought him. Needs brought him. Fear of *not* bringing him forth from his own body, the earth, had brought him. Belief had brought him. Now, again, as it had brought him once every century, to the low-fallen ones who worshipped him: not because he promised life after death, not because he promised salvation, not because he promised rich harvests and plentiful rain. Dis was not a god of promise. He was called forth because he would come, called or not. Because he was Dis, and his body was the very ground they walked, and they could do no other. Because it was necessary for him to stride the world once every century. There was no human explanation for his need . . . he was Dis . . . it was reason enough.

More. Darkness seeped up into the skies. The world was dark. He rose, greater and greater still. Stonehenge vanished to become his legs, his torso, his arms, the terrifying shape of his head. Stonehenge fed his bulk and he loomed over them.

A cry of hopelessness, low and animal, came from the Wessex People. From the throat of the great priest and his assistants, and from the throat of the acolyte priest whose name was not yet recorded.

The great priest murmured his words, incantations he had been taught would keep Dis from harming those who worshipped him. There was no way for him to know: they had no effect, they were no protection. Dis had never *desired* their destruction, so they had been spared. Yet they believed. Helpless, yet they believed. And . . .

This rising was not like the others that had occurred in the thousand centuries since Dis had first appeared.

The great priest sensed it first; then the acolyte. The others were frozen, uncomprehending, waiting.

The great horned head of Dis turned; the rock god peered through the eternal darkness that flowed upward from the Earth, as if seeing the stars that were now hidden from all but his sight.

Then the face turned down and for the first time Dis *spoke* to men.

**I will sleep.**

They listened. Fear greater than the fear they had always known at Dis's coming gripped them. They had thought in their dim way there was no greater fear, but now Dis *spoke.* The sound of volcanoes. The sound of winds. Caverns. Pain. Vapor exploding through stone.

> **I will sleep and dream.**
> **I will be safe.**
> **I will give you a thing.**
> **Possess it.**
> **The holiest of holies.**
> **I sleep within.**

And Dis reached into his body, thrust his taloned hand as big as the biggest trilothon into his body of a rock that was flesh, and brought forth a mote of burning blackness. He held it up to his flaming eyes. Vistas of the underworld leaped and scintillated in the fire-pits of his eyes. The black light of the mote met the flames of his eyes and the light melted and merged and leaped and the fire entered the mote, and crimson became blackness and blackness became crimson, and then all was within the mote, and it pulsed, pulsed, waned, subsided, lay quiescent.

Then Dis bent and lowered his hand, laying the mote at the feet of the great priest.

> Keep safe my soul.
> I will come again one day.
> Unending pain if my soul is lost.
> This is my command.

The great priest feared to look up, but his words were to his god, to assure him the life of all his people would be spent protecting the holiest of holies.

But suddenly there was a bold sound from the throng of petrified worshippers, and the great priest had a moment's presaging of terror as the young acolyte priest—who could not wait for succession, who lusted after power *now*—broke from the mass of dark praying shapes, raced across the open space and leaped onto the altar stone.

"No!" the great priest moaned.

"Great Dis!" the acolyte priest shouted, looking up into the face that his race's memory would never be able to describe without a shudder. "Great Dis, we have served you for centuries! Now we ask a boon! I, Mag, demand for your faithful ones who pledge to protect your sleeping soul, the boon of—"

None ever knew what token the acolyte might have demanded to raise himself to a position of power. The rock god reached down and darkness flowed from his taloned fingers. Black fire consumed the acolyte in an instant, and the pillar of black fire sparkled upward, thinned, became a lance-line no man could look into. Then Dis hurled the black fire into the ground, where it burned through and could be seen to shimmer. The sound of Mag's soul shriveling was a trembling, terrible thing.

Then Dis flowed back into the Earth, the rocks became rocks once more, Stonehenge solidified, and all that remained was the power stone, the black mote stone, at the feet of the great priest, whose body shivered and spasmed from the nearness of the god's vengeance.

And when Dis was gone, to sleep his sleep of ages, the Wessex Folk saw there was a new rock in the Stonehenge circle. In its surface was imprinted the memory of a face that had belonged to one they'd known, contorted in agony beyond their ability to describe. But they would never forget: Mag, in the stone, striation lines of anguish, .

forever he would live in pain, dead inside the rock, forever blackly burning in agony, with his unvoiced demand.

They took the mote and kept it holiest of holies, and Dis slept.

Dis, most cunning, had separated himself seven times and one more. To let his flesh sleep with his soul was to permit the chance of destruction. His soul slept within the black mote of Stonehenge. But his flesh he cut seven ways, and there were seven risings, all on the same night. From the mystic number seven, from the seven unearthly risings, had come seven stones to match the mote. They came to be known as the Seven Stones of Power. They were known to the world, for Dis knew a god exists only if there are believers; and as he must sleep, for reasons known only to gods, he must leave behind a legacy for legend, by which he would be remembered.

The Seven Stones of Power:

In Ireland, the Blarney Stone.

The Stone of Scone that came from Scotland and now lived beneath the Coronation Chair in Westminster Abbey.

Hajar al-Aswad, The Black Stone, the great religious symbol of Islam; kept sacred and safe in the Ka'bah sanctuary, the Sacred Mosque in Mecca.

The Koh-i-noor diamond, which the Persians called the Mountain of Light.

The lost Stone of Solomon that had vanished from Palestine and which was said to be the most treasured possession of the Dalai Lama in Lhasa.

The Welsh Stone of Change—which some called merely the Plinth, for time and legends shimmer in the memory of the frightened —that had last been known to reside at the vacant seat of Arthur's Round Table, the Siege Perilous, the seat and Stone that could only be claimed by the predestined finder of the Holy Grail.

And the Amida of Diabutsu, the Great Buddha, in the Sacred Temple of Kyobe in Japan-that-was.

These seven. And the soul mote.

Legend and the ways of men kept these potent stones secreted. Yet there were chips, and bits, and from *them* came the Great Seal of Solomon, the silver crescent of the Great Anthrex, the Talisman of Suleiman the Magnificent, and the Circle of Isis.

It was the seven stones, and the soul mote in which the essence of Dis dreamed his sinister dreams (of worlds where great lizards carried on commerce, where living light in the skies ruled creatures of flesh, where the gods drew breath that cleft the earth to its molten core) in which *true* power resided: sleeping.

The soul mote was buried at Stonehenge, and time passed till even the Wessex People were gone, and their having passed that way was forgotten.

This is what happened to the black soul mote.

It was dug up by one who came in the night and was mad. And so, mad, he was not afraid. But his madness did not stay the terrible death that came to him, the flesh stripped from his body and eaten by things only partially human. But he had already traded the mote to one of Minoan Crete. That one passed it for great wealth to a thinker of Mycenaean Greece from whom it was taken in ransom by a priest of Isis. The Egyptian lost it to a Phoenician and he, in turn, lost it in a game of chance that took all he owned, as well as his life. . . .

From hand to hand it traveled, down through the centuries, with death and shapes in the night following its journey.

A thousand hands, a thousand men of cultures shrouded in antiquity. Till it found its way from an ocean floor to the hand of an adventurer who also worked in silver. He cleaned it and polished it and mounted it. Then women owned it.

And each woman became famous. The names are legend. But always they coveted more, and finally reaped their rewards in blood. The soul mote came across another ocean, where it went from the treasure hordes of Osmanski Cossacks to the coffers of Polish noblemen, from the dowries of Parisian *demimondaines* to the chamois gold-sacks of English vicars, from the pockets of cutpurses to the New World.

And there it passed from brooch to pendant, ring to lavaliere . . .

and was lost.

. . . and was found:

by a Croatian workman who had no idea what it was, and threw it, with a spadeful of refuse, into the hollow center of the cornerstone of a great skyscraper.

And the building rose one hundred and fifteen stories over the sleeping soul of the great rock god Dis. Who knew the time was approaching.

Night hung crucified outside the ninety-fifth floor window of Stierman's office. The night and the men in the room seemed as one. They both accused Stierman. His mouth was dry. He knew at least two of these seven were with the Organization. But which two were deathmen of that "business firm" and which were merely angry entrepreneurs, he did not know. But all seven had partnered him in the construction of the Stierman Building. And any one of the seven could ruin him.

"We were all served today," one of them said. He slapped the summons from the District Attorney's office on Stierman's desk.

"You'll pay for this." It was the one with the reptilian eyes. He was frightening. Stierman could not speak.

"How much did you skim off, Stierman? How much?"

That was number three.

The other four spoke all at once. "Do you have any idea what happens if this building falls?" "We're all in this together, but it's *you*, Stierman, it's *you!*" "Swiss account, Stierman? Is that where you put it?" "I oughta kill you, you scum!"

The building in which they sat was sinking. The foundations had been filled with garbage, with substandard materials; the ground itself had been soft. The building was vanishing into the ground. Nothing strange about it, nothing magical, merely inadequate building procedures. Frank Stierman had pocketed almost two million dollars from the construction costs of the building, and it had showed up in the final product.

The second floor was now below street level. Access to the Stierman Building was obtained by entrance through a hastily-cut door in the side of a second-floor office. From the foyer and the basements, one had to take an elevator upstairs to get out at the ground floor. The tenants had all vacated. The corporations and professional men had fled. Stierman's seven partners were on the verge of ruin, and the insurance companies had already laughed in their faces.

"Speak up, you sonofabitch!"

Stierman knew he had to bluff it out.

At least till he could get out of the country. Brazil. Then Switzerland. Then . . . anywhere.

"My God, you men have known me fifteen years—have you ever known me to do a dishonest thing? What the hell's wrong with you?" Charm. Trust. Frank Stierman.

*He's had an amazing career. Came out of nowhere. One of the biggest developers in Manhattan. Zeckendorf looks like a kid making sand castles next to Stierman. Trust him all the way. Helluva guy. Charming.*

Sand in the cement. Quite a lot of sand.

Specifications cut close to the line. Quite close.

A little juice to the surveyors.

A little juice to the building commission.

A little juice to the councilmen.

Oversubsidized. Oversold. Overworked.

Trust and charm. Frank Stierman.

It was working. The wide blue eyes. The strong chin. The cavalry-scout ruggedness. It was working. *Which two are patched into the Organization?* Work, mouth, work this man out of the East River where fish eat garbage.

"Okay, so we've got a situation here. We've got a contingency we never expected. The ground is settling. Okay, we're losing the building. Maybe.

"And . . ."—he paused, significantly—"maybe not!"

They listened. He dredged lies from the silt of his mind. "I had half a dozen structural engineers in here today, land assayers, men who know what to do with this kind of situation. Now, I'm not going to tell you that we're out of the woods . . . Jesus, we've got some rough sledding ahead of us. But we know there was faulty workmanship in the construction, we know the damned contractors who sank the pylons shorted us on the quality of the fill . . . we know we're going to have some losses . . . but we're *friends!* That counts for a lot. We're going to have to—"

Dis stirred.

Frank Stierman, naked save for loincloth, found his back against a rock wall, found a bronze blade in his right hand, found himself staring across what had been the conference room of his office at a creature of scales and fish-gills that writhed on eight legs with a head of vapor and eyes in the vapor that burned into his own.

He screamed and threw the sword at the thing. . . .

Seven men were staring at Frank Stierman. He had no idea what had happened, but he knew he had lost all ground. In the middle of an impassioned plea for reason and patience, he had suddenly fallen back against a wall, screamed like a madman, and lost all tonus in his face. Whatever Frank Stierman had been a moment before, now he was unreliable . . . perhaps insane. Seven men stared back at him, their resolve now solidified not by anger and suspicion but by the realization that they were dealing with a lunatic.

The connecting door to Stierman's private office opened, and a woman entered.

"Frank, can I see you for a moment?"

Stierman was trembling. The creature. That head, made of . . . of some kind of *vapor* . . . what was happening to him? "Not now, Monica. This is very important."

"I agree, Frank. *Important.* I have to speak to you *now.*"

"Monica, I—"

"Frank, don't make me talk here, in front of these men!"

"You'd better go on, Frank. We want to talk about all this in private for a moment, anyhow."

"Yes. Go ahead, Stierman."

"It's all right. Go ahead and talk to her."

*Oh my God, dear God, it's falling apart!*

When the door was closed behind him, Stierman turned to his wife and said, "Why are you doing this to me? You know what's at stake in there."

"I'm getting out, Frank."

"Don't be a bitch!"

"I'm getting *out*. That's the bottom line, Frank. I was served today, by the District Attorney's office. . . ."

"Don't worry about a thing. I had structural engin—"

"Don't lie to me, Frank. I know you too well."

"I'm *not* lying."

"I'm going to help them, Frank. They said I wouldn't be held responsible. They know you got me to sign my name on the contracts as a dodge. I can't go through any more of this with you, Frank. After that southern thing, I thought—"

"My God, Monica, don't do this to me! Look, I'm begging you."

"Stop it, Frank."

"You're pregnant, you're going to have my child, how can you do this to me?"

"That's the reason, Frank. Because I *am* pregnant, because I can't let a child come into the world with you for its father. I'm getting out. Now, Frank. I came down to tell you, so you wouldn't count on me when you talk to those men. Save yourself, Frank."

She turned to go. He reached across the desk and lifted the obsidian bookend and took three steps behind her. She turned just as he raised the weight. Her eyes were cool, waiting.

He slammed the bookend across her forehead.

She stumbled back, head jerking as though struck from three different directions. Her head opened and the white ash of bone was suddenly coated with blood. She flailed back, eyes glazing, and crashed into the dark window. Then the glass bowed, gave, and she was gone, silently, into the night.

Stierman dropped the bookend. His arms came up and his hands groped out before him, shaking violently. He twitched with cold, a sudden cold that came from a place he could not name. Gone, she was gone, he was alone.

The words burned on the teakwood wall.

AH-WEGH THOGHA

He wanted to scream, but the trembling was on him, the insane twitching that he could not stop. His body was helpless in the spastic grip of the seizure. Gone, she was gone, they were in the next room, the building going down down into the earth, those words, what were those words . . .

"Ah-wegh thogha!" His throat had never been shaped to form those words, but it did.

Dis woke.

He hungered for his body.

Time is a plaything for the gods. It only has substance for those who use it. Men fear time and bow to it. Gods cup it and mold it and use it.

Time ceased its movement.

Dis called for his body.

From seven far lands they came with the stones. From deep within the earth two of them were brought, by creatures that did not walk. From Mecca the worshippers defiled their own temple with theft, and brought it. From across the lost snow lands of Tibet they came with yet another. Seven great religions were gutted. Seven sources of power were lost. All in the moment without time.

Came, and brought with them the seven stones of power, the body of Dis.

To the skyscraper in Manhattan.

And Dis took back what had always been his.

Within the cornerstone the black soul mote glowed and pulsed with the undying fire that lived within. The mote grew, and absorbed the cornerstone. It flowed black and strong, mighty and changing, absorbing the skyscraper as it had absorbed the bulk of Stonehenge.

The building shifted, shaped itself, and inside its growing body Frank Stierman knew a moment of madness before he was absorbed into the rock-flesh of Dis. His face, frozen in that moment of undying death, an eternity of broiling insanity through which he would gibber forever. The face of Mag, burned into the stone.

Dis came alive, and replaced his soul.

And rose, and darkness washed up again from the concrete-covered Earth that was his essence.

Above the city the bulk of Dis rose, spraddle-legged, enormous.

All this was rock. All this was flesh of his flesh. All this belonged to Dis, to be absorbed, to permit him to grow as he had never grown before.

To feed Dis.

*Now* men would know why the rock god had gone to sleep.

*Reality has become fantasy; fantasy has become reality. 35 mm constructs have more substance than your senior congressman, but Martha Nelson is real, no matter what you think. And the search for your soul in a soulless world requires special maps.*

# Adrift Just Off the Islets of Langerhans: Latitude 38° 54′ N, Longitude 77° 00′ 13″ W

When Moby Dick awoke one morning from unsettling dreams, he found himself changed in his bed of kelp into a monstrous Ahab.

Crawling in stages from the soggy womb of sheets, he stumbled into the kitchen and ran water into the teapot. There was lye in the corner of each eye. He put his head under the spigot and let the cold water rush around his cheeks.

Dead bottles littered the living room. One hundred and eleven empty bottles that had contained Robitussin and Romilar-CF. He padded through the debris to the front door and opened it a crack. Daylight assaulted him. "Oh, God," he murmered, and closed his eyes to pick up the folded newspaper from the stoop.

Once more in dusk, he opened the paper. The headline read: BOLIVIAN AMBASSADOR FOUND MURDERED, and the feature story heading column one detailed the discovery of the ambassador's body, badly decomposed, in an abandoned refrigerator in an empty lot in Secaucus, New Jersey.

The teapot whistled.

Naked, he padded toward the kitchen; as he passed the aquarium he saw that terrible fish was still alive, and this morning whistling like a bluejay, making tiny streams of bubbles that rose to burst on the scummy surface of the water. He paused beside the tank, turned on the light and looked in through the drifting eddies of stringered algae. The fish simply would not die. It had killed off every other fish in the tank—prettier fish, friendlier fish, livelier fish, even larger and more dangerous fish—had killed them all, one by one, and eaten out the eyes. Now it swam the tank alone, ruler of its worthless domain.

He had tried to let the fish kill itself, trying every form of neglect short of outright murder by not feeding it; but the pale, worm-pink devil even thrived in the dark and filth-laden waters.

Now it sang like a bluejay. He hated the fish with a passion he could barely contain.

He sprinkled flakes from a plastic container, grinding them between thumb and forefinger as experts had advised him to do it, and watched the multi-colored granules of fish meal, roe, milt, brine shrimp, day-fly eggs, oatflour and egg yolk ride on the surface for a moment before the detestable fish-face came snapping to the top to suck them down. He turned away, cursing and hating the fish. It would not die. Like him, it would not die.

In the kitchen, bent over the boiling water, he understood for the first time the true status of his situation. Though he was probably nowhere near the rotting outer edge of sanity, he could smell its foulness on the wind, coming in from the horizon; and like some wild animal rolling its eyes at the scent of carrion and the feeders thereon, he was being driven closer to lunacy every day, just from the smell.

He carried the teapot, a cup and two tea bags to the kitchen table and sat down. Propped open in a plastic stand used for keeping cookbooks handy while mixing ingredients, the Mayan Codex translations remained unread from the evening before. He poured the water, dangled the tea bags in the cup and tried to focus his attention. The references to Itzamna, the chief divinity of the Maya pantheon, and medicine, his chief sphere of influence, blurred. Ixtab, the goddess of suicide, seemed more apropos for this morning, this deadly terrible morning. He tried reading, but the words only went in, nothing happened to them, they didn't sing. He sipped tea and found himself thinking of the chill, full circle of the Moon. He glanced over his shoulder at the kitchen clock. Seven forty-four.

He shoved away from the table, taking the half-full cup of tea, and went into the bedroom. The impression of his body, where it had lain in tortured sleep, still dented the bed. There were clumps of blood-matted hair clinging to the manacles that he had riveted to metal plates in the headboard. He rubbed his wrists where they had been scored raw, slopping a little tea on his left forearm. He wondered if the Bolivian ambassador had been a piece of work he had tended to the month before.

His wristwatch lay on the bureau. He checked it. Seven forty-six. Slightly less than an hour and a quarter to make the meeting with the consultation service. He went into the bathroom, reached inside the shower stall and turned the handle till a fine needle-spray of icy water smashed the tiled wall of the stall. Letting the water run, he turned to the medicine cabinet for his shampoo. Taped to the mirror was an Ouchless Telfa finger bandage on which two lines had been neatly typed, in capitals:

> THE WAY YOU WALK IS THORNY, MY SON,
> THROUGH NO FAULT OF YOUR OWN.

Then, opening the cabinet, removing a plastic bottle of herbal shampoo that smelled like friendly, deep forests, Lawrence Talbot resigned himself to the situation, turned and stepped into the shower, the merciless ice-laden waters of the Arctic pounding against his tortured flesh.

Suite 1544 of the Tishman Airport Center Building was a men's toilet. He stood against the wall opposite the door labeled MEN and drew the envelope from the inner breast pocket of his jacket. The paper was of good quality, the envelope crackled as he thumbed up the flap and withdrew the single-sheet letter inside. It was the correct address, the correct floor, the correct suite. Suite 1544 was a men's toilet, nonetheless. Talbot started to turn away. It was a vicious joke; he found no humor in the situation; not in his present circumstances.

He took one step toward the elevators.

The door to the men's room shimmered, fogged over like a windshield in winter, and re-formed. The legend on the door had changed. It now read:

#### INFORMATION ASSOCIATES

Suite 1544 was the consultation service that had written the invitational letter on paper of good quality in response to Talbot's mail inquiry responding to a noncommittal but judiciously-phrased advertisement in *Forbes*.

He opened the door and stepped inside. The woman behind the teak reception desk smiled at him, and his glance was split between the dimples that formed, and her legs, very nice, smooth legs, crossed and framed by the kneehole of the desk. "Mr. Talbot?"

He nodded. "Lawrence Talbot."

She smiled again. "Mr. Demeter will see you at once, sir. Would you like something to drink? Coffee? A soft drink?"

Talbot found himself touching his jacket where the envelope lay in an inner pocket. "No. Thank you."

She stood up, moving toward an inner office door, as Talbot said, "What do you do when someone tries to flush your desk?" He was not trying to be cute. He was annoyed. She turned and stared at him. There was silence in her appraisal, nothing more.

"Mr. Demeter is right through here, sir."

She opened the door and stood aside. Talbot walked past her, catching a scent of mimosa.

The inner office was furnished like the reading room of an exclusive men's club. Old money. Deep quiet. Dark, heavy woods. A lowered ceiling of acoustical tile on tracks, concealing a crawl space and probably electrical conduits. The pile rug of oranges and burnt umbers swallowed his feet to the ankles. Through a wall-sized window could be seen not the city that lay outside the building but a panoramic view of Hanauma Bay, on the Koko Head side of Oahu. The pure aquamarine waves came in like undulant snakes, rose like cobras, crested out white, tunneled and struck like asps at the blazing yellow beach. It was not a window; there were no windows in the office. It was a photograph. A deep, real photograph that was neither a projection nor a hologram. It was a wall looking out on another place entirely. Talbot knew nothing about exotic flora, but he was certain that the tall, razor-edge-leafed trees growing right down to beach's boundary were identical to those pictured in books depicting the Carboniferous period of the Earth before even the saurians had walked the land. What he was seeing had been gone for a very long time.

"Mr. Talbot. Good of you to come. John Demeter."

He came up from a wingback chair, extended his hand. Talbot took it. The grip was firm and cool. "Won't you sit down," Demeter said. "Something to drink? Coffee, perhaps, or a soft drink?" Talbot shook his head; Demeter nodded dismissal to the receptionist; she closed the door behind her, firmly, smoothly, silently.

Talbot studied Demeter in one long appraisal as he took the chair opposite the wingback. Demeter was in his early fifties, had retained a full and rich mop of hair that fell across his forehead in gray waves that clearly had not been touched up. His eyes were clear and blue, his features regular and jovial, his mouth wide and sincere. He was trim. The dark-brown business suit was hand-tailored and hung well. He sat easily and crossed his legs, revealing black hose that went above the shins. His shoes were highly polished.

"That's a fascinating door, the one to your outer office," Talbot said.

"Do we talk about my door?" Demeter asked.

"Not if you don't want to. That isn't why I came here."

"I don't want to. So let's discuss your particular problem."

"Your advertisement. I was intrigued."

Demeter smiled reassuringly. "Four copywriters worked very diligently at the proper phraseology."

"It brings in business."

"The right kind of business."

"You slanted it toward smart money. Very reserved. Conservative portfolios, few glamours, steady climbers. Wise old owls."

Demeter steepled his fingers and nodded, an understanding uncle. "Directly to the core, Mr. Talbot: wise old owls."

"I need some information. Some special, certain information. How confidential is your service, Mr. Demeter?"

The friendly uncle, the wise old owl, the reassuring businessman understood all the edited spaces behind the question. He nodded several times. Then he smiled and said, "That *is* a clever door I have, isn't it? You're absolutely right, Mr. Talbot."

"A certain understated eloquence."

"One hopes it answers more questions for our clients than it poses."

Talbot sat back in the chair for the first time since he had entered Demeter's office. "I think I can accept that."

"Fine. Then why don't we get to specifics. Mr. Talbot, you're having some difficulty dying. Am I stating the situation succinctly?"

"Gently, Mr. Demeter."

"Always."

"Yes. You're on the target."

"But you have some problems, some rather unusual problems."

"Inner ring."

Demeter stood up and walked around the room, touching an astrolabe on a bookshelf, a cut-glass decanter on a sideboard, a sheaf of the *London Times'* held together by a wooden pole. "We are only information specialists, Mr. Talbot. We can put you on to what you need, but the effectation is your problem."

"If I have the *modus operandi,* I'll have no trouble taking care of getting it done."

"You've put a little aside."

"A little."

"Conservative portfolio? A few glamours, mostly steady climbers?"

"Bull's eye, Mr. Demeter."

Demeter came back and sat down again. "All right, then. If you'll take the time very carefully to write out *precisely* what you want —I know generally, from your letter, but I want this *precise,* for the contract—I think I can undertake to supply the data necessary to solving your problem."

"At what cost?"

"Let's decide what it is you want, first, shall we?"

Talbot nodded. Demeter reached over and pressed a call button on the smoking stand beside the wingback. The door opened. "Susan, would you show Mr. Talbot to the sanctum and provide him with writing materials." She smiled and stood aside, waiting for Talbot to follow her. "And bring Mr. Talbot something to drink if he'd like it . . . some coffee? A soft drink, perhaps?" Talbot did not respond to the offer.

"I might need some time to get the phraseology down just right. I might have to work as diligently as your copywriters. It might take me a while. I'll go home and bring it in tomorrow."

Demeter looked troubled. "That might be inconvenient. That's why we provide a quiet place where you can think."

"You'd prefer I stay and do it now."

"Inner ring, Mr. Talbot."

"You might be a toilet if I came back tomorrow."

"Bull's eye."

"Let's go, Susan. Bring me a glass of orange juice if you have it." He preceded her out the door.

He followed her down the corridor at the far side of the reception room. He had not seen it before. She stopped at a door and opened it for him. There was an escritoire and a comfortable chair inside the small room. He could hear Muzak. "I'll bring you your orange juice," she said.

He went in and sat down. After a long time he wrote seven words on a sheet of paper.

Two months later, long after the series of visitations from silent messengers who brought rough drafts of the contract to be examined, who came again to take them away revised, who came again with counterproposals, who came again to take away further revised versions, who came again—finally—with Demeter-signed finals, and who waited while he examined and initialed and signed the finals—two months later, the map came via the last, mute messenger. He arranged for the final installment of the payment to Information Associates that same day: he had ceased wondering where fifteen boxcars of maize—grown specifically as the Zuñi nation had grown it—was of value.

Two days later, a small item on an inside page of the *New York Times* noted that fifteen boxcars of farm produce had somehow vanished off a railroad spur near Albuquerque. An official investigation had been initiated.

The map was very specific, very detailed; it looked accurate.

He spent several days with Gray's *Anatomy* and, when he was satisfied that Demeter and his organization had been worth the staggering fee, he made a phone call. The long-distance operator turned him over to Inboard and he waited, after giving her the information, for the static-laden connection to be made. He insisted Budapest on the other end let it ring twenty times, twice the number the male operator was permitted per caller. On the twenty-first ring it was picked up. Miraculously, the background noise-level dropped and he heard Victor's voice as though it was across the room.

"Yes! Hello!" Impatient, surly as always.

"Victor . . . Larry Talbot."

"Where are you calling from?"

"The States. How are you?"

"Busy. What do you want?"

"I have a project. I want to hire you and your lab."

"Forget it. I'm coming down to final moments on a project and I can't be bothered now."

The imminence of hangup was in his voice. Talbot cut in quickly. "How long do you anticipate?"

"Till what?"

"Till you're clear."

"Another six months inside, eight to ten if it gets muddy. I said: forget it, Larry. I'm *not* available."

"At least let's talk."

"No."

"Am I wrong, Victor, or do you owe me a little?"

"After all this time you're calling in debts?"

"They only ripen with age."

There was a long silence in which Talbot heard dead space being pirated off their line. At one point he thought the other man had racked the receiver. Then, finally, "Okay, Larry. We'll *talk*. But you'll have to come to me; I'm too involved to be hopping any jets."

"That's fine. I have free time." A slow beat, then he added, "Nothing but free time."

"*After* the full moon, Larry." It was said with great specificity.

"Of course. I'll meet you at the last place we met, at the same time, on the thirtieth of this month. Do you remember?"

"I remember. That'll be fine."

"Thank you, Victor. I appreciate this."

There was no response.

Talbot's voice softened: "How is your father?"

"Goodbye, Larry," he answered, and hung up.

They met on the thirtieth of that month, at moonless midnight, on the corpse barge that plied between Buda and Pesht. It was the correct sort of night: chill fog moved in a pulsing curtain up the Danube from Belgrade.

They shook hands in the lee of a stack of cheap wooden coffins and, after hesitating awkwardly for a moment, they embraced like brothers. Talbot's smile was tight and barely discernible by the withered illumination of the lantern and the barge's running lights as he said, "All right, get it said so I don't have to wait for the other shoe to drop."

Victor grinned and murmured ominously:

> "*Even a man who is pure in heart
> And says his prayers by night,*

> *May become a wolf when the wolfbane blooms*
> *And the Autumn moon shines bright.*"

Talbot made a face. "And other songs from the same album."

"Still saying your prayers at night?"

"I stopped that when I realized the damned thing didn't scan."

"Hey. We aren't here getting pneumonia just to discuss forced rhyme."

The lines of weariness in Talbot's face settled into a joyless pattern. "Victor, I need your help."

"I'll listen, Larry. Further than that it's doubtful."

Talbot weighed the warning and said, "Three months ago I answered an advertisement in *Forbes,* the business magazine. Information Associates. It was a cleverly phrased, very reserved, small box, inconspicuously placed. Except to those who knew how to read it. I won't waste your time on details, but the sequence went like this: I answered the ad, hinting at my problem as circuitously as possible without being completely impenetrable. Vague words about important money. I had hopes. Well, I hit with this one. They sent back a letter calling a meet. Perhaps another false trail, was what I thought. . . . God knows there've been enough of those."

Victor lit a Sobranie Black & Gold and let the pungent scent of the smoke drift away on the fog. "But you went."

"I went. Peculiar outfit, sophisticated security system, I had a strong feeling they came from, well, I'm not sure where . . . or when."

Victor's glance was abruptly kilowatts heavier with interest. "*When,* you say? Temporal travelers?"

"I don't know."

"I've been waiting for something like that, you know. It's inevitable. And they'd certainly make themselves known eventually."

He lapsed into silence, thinking. Talbot brought him back sharply. "I don't know, Victor. I really don't. But that's not my concern at the moment."

"Oh. Right. Sorry, Larry. Go on. You met with them . . ."

"Man named Demeter. I thought there might be some clue there. The name. I didn't think of it at the time. The name Demeter; there was a florist in Cleveland, many years ago. But later, when I looked it up, Demeter, the Earth goddess, Greek mythology . . . no connection. At least, I don't think so.

"We talked. He understood my problem and said he'd undertake the commission. But he wanted it specific, what I required of him, wanted it specific for the contract—God knows how he would have enforced the contract, but I'm sure he could have—he had a *window*, Victor, it looked out on—"

Victor spun the cigarette off his thumb and middle finger, snapping it straight down into the blood-black Danube. "Larry, you're maundering."

Talbot's words caught in his throat. It was true. "I'm counting on you, Victor. I'm afraid it's putting my usual aplomb out of phase."

"All right, take it easy. Let me hear the rest of this and we'll see. Relax."

Talbot nodded and felt grateful. "I wrote out the nature of the commission. It was only seven words." He reached into his topcoat pocket and brought out a folded slip of paper. He handed it to the other man. In the dim lantern light, Victor unfolded the paper and read:

### GEOGRAPHICAL COORDINATES
### FOR LOCATION OF MY SOUL

Victor looked at the two lines of type long after he had absorbed their message. When he handed it back to Talbot, he wore a new, fresher expression. "You'll never give up, will you, Larry?"

"Did your father?"

"No." Great sadness flickered across the face of the man Talbot called Victor. "And," he added, tightly, after a beat, "he's been lying in a catatonia sling for sixteen years *because* he wouldn't give up." He lapsed into silence. Finally, softly, "It never hurts to know when to give up, Larry. Never hurts. Sometimes you've just got to leave it alone."

Talbot snorted softly with bemusement. "Easy enough for you to say, old chum. You're going to die."

"That wasn't fair, Larry."

"Then help me, dammit! I've gone further toward getting myself out of all this than I ever have. Now I need *you*. You've got the expertise."

"Have you sounded out 3M or Rand or even General Dynamics? They've got good people there."

"Damn you."

"Okay. Sorry. Let me think a minute."

The corpse barge cut through the invisible water, silent, fog-shrouded, without Charon, without Styx, merely a public service, a garbage scow of unfinished sentences, uncompleted errands, unrealized dreams. With the exception of these two, talking, the barge's supercargo had left decisions and desertions behind.

Then, Victor said, softly, talking as much to himself as to Talbot, "We could do it with microtelemetry. Either through direct micro-miniaturizing techniques or by shrinking a servomechanism package containing sensing, remote control, and guidance/manipulative/propulsion hardware. Use a saline solution to inject it into the blood-stream. Knock you out with 'Russian sleep' and/or tap into the sensory nerves so you'd perceive or control the device as if you were there . . . conscious transfer of point of view."

Talbot looked at him expectantly.

"No. Forget it," said Victor. "It won't do."

He continued to think. Talbot reached into the other's jacket pocket and brought out the Sobranies. He lit one and stood silently, waiting. It was always thus with Victor. He had to worm his way through the analytical labyrinth.

"Maybe the biotechnic equivalent: a tailored microorganism or slug . . . injected . . . telepathic link established. No. Too many flaws: possible ego/control conflict. Impaired perceptions. Maybe it could be a hive creature injected for multiple p.o.v." A pause, then, "No. No good."

Talbot drew on the cigarette, letting the mysterious Eastern smoke curl through his lungs. "How about . . . say, just for the sake of discussion," Victor said, "say the ego/id exists to some extent in each sperm. It's been ventured. Raise the consciousness in one cell and send it on a mission to . . . forget it, that's metaphysical bullshit. Oh, damn damn damn . . . this will take time and thought, Larry. Go away, let me think on it. I'll get back to you."

Talbot butted the Sobranie on the railing, and exhaled the final stream of smoke. "Okay, Victor. I take it you're interested sufficiently to work at it."

"I'm a scientist, Larry. That means I'm hooked. I'd have to be an idiot not to be. . . . This speaks directly to what . . . to what my father . . ."

"I understand. I'll let you alone. I'll wait."

They rode across in silence, the one thinking of solutions, the other considering problems. When they parted, it was with an embrace.

Talbot flew back the next morning, and waited through the nights of the full moon, knowing better than to pray. It only muddied the waters. And angered the gods.

When the phone rang, and Talbot lifted the receiver, he knew what it would be. He had known *every* time the phone had rung, for over two months. "Mr. Talbot? Western Union. We have a cablegram for you, from Moldava, Czechoslovakia."

"Please read it."

"It's very short, sir. It says, 'Come immediately. The trail has been marked.' It's signed, 'Victor.'"

He departed less than an hour later. The Learjet had been on the ready line since he had returned from Budapest, fuel tanks regularly topped-off and flight-plan logged. His suitcase had been packed for seventy-two days, waiting beside the door, visas and passport current, and handily stored in an inner pocket. When he departed, the apartment continued to tremble for some time with the echoes of his leaving.

The flight seemed endless, interminable, he *knew* it was taking longer than necessary.

Customs, even with high government clearances (all masterpieces of forgery) and bribes, seemed to be drawn out sadistically by the mustachioed trio of petty officials; secure, and reveling in their momentary power.

The overland facilities could not merely be called slow. They were reminiscent of the Molasses Man who cannot run till he's warmed-up and who, when he's warmed-up, grows too soft to run.

Expectedly, like the most suspenseful chapter of a cheap gothic novel, a fierce electrical storm suddenly erupted out of the mountains when the ancient touring car was within a few miles of Talbot's destination. It rose up through the steep mountain pass, hurtling out of the sky, black as a grave, and swept across the road obscuring everything.

The driver, a taciturn man whose accent had marked him as a Serbian, held the big saloon to the center of the road with the tenacity of a rodeo rider, hands at ten till and ten after midnight on the wheel.

"Mister Talbot."

"Yes?"

"It grows worse. Will I turn back?"

"How much farther?"

"Perhaps seven kilometer."

Headlights caught the moment of uprootment as a small tree by the roadside toppled toward them. The driver spun the wheel and accelerated. They rushed past as naked branches scraped across the boot of the touring car with the sound of fingernails on a blackboard. Talbot found he had been holding his breath. Death was beyond him, but the menace of the moment denied the knowledge.

"I have to get there."

"Then I go on. Be at ease."

Talbot settled back. He could see the Serb smiling in the rearview mirror. Secure, he stared out the window. Branches of lightning shattered the darkness, causing the surrounding landscape to assume ominous, unsettling shapes.

Finally, he arrived.

The laboratory, an incongruous modernistic cube—bone white against the—again—ominous basalt of the looming prominences—sat high above the rutted road. They had been climbing steadily for hours and now, like carnivores waiting for the most opportune moment, the Carpathians loomed all around them.

The driver negotiated the final mile and a half up the access road to the laboratory with difficulty: tides of dark, topsoil-and-twig-laden water rushed past them.

Victor was waiting for him. Without extended greetings he had an associate take the suitcase, and he hurried Talbot to the sub-ground-floor theater where a half dozen technicians moved quickly at their tasks, plying between enormous banks of controls and a huge glass plate hanging suspended from guy-wires beneath the track-laden ceiling.

The mood was one of highly charged expectancy; Talbot could feel it in the sharp, short glances the technicians threw him, in the way Victor steered him by the arm, in the uncanny racehorse readiness of the peculiar-looking machines around which the men and women swarmed. And he sensed in Victor's manner that something new and wonderful was about to be born in this laboratory. That perhaps

. . . at last . . . after so terribly, lightlessly long . . . peace waited for him in this white-tiled room. Victor was fairly bursting to talk.

"Final adjustments," he said, indicating two female technicians working at a pair of similar machines mounted opposite each other on the walls facing the glass plate. To Talbot, they looked like laser projectors of a highly complex design. The women were tracking them slowly left and right on their gimbals, accompanied by soft electrical humming. Victor let Talbot study them for a long moment, then said, "Not lasers. *Grasers.* Gamma Ray Amplification by Stimulated Emission of Radiation. Pay attention to them, they're at least half the heart of the answer to your problem."

The technicians took sightings across the room, through the glass, and nodded at one another. Then the older of the two, a woman in her fifties, called to Victor.

"On line, Doctor."

Victor waved acknowledgment, and turned back to Talbot. "We'd have been ready sooner, but this damned storm. It's been going on for a week. It wouldn't have hampered us but we had a freak lightning strike on our main transformer. The power supply was on emergency for several days and it's taken a while to get everything up to peak strength again."

A door opened in the wall of the gallery to Talbot's right. It opened slowly, as though it was heavy and the strength needed to force it was lacking. The yellow baked enamel plate on the door said, in heavy black letters, in French, PERSONNEL MONITORING DEVICES ARE REQUIRED BEYOND THIS ENTRANCE. The door swung fully open, at last, and Talbot saw the warning plate on the other side:

## CAUTION
## RADIATION
## AREA

There was a three-armed, triangular-shaped design beneath the words. He thought of the Father, the Son, and the Holy Ghost. For no rational reason.

Then he saw the sign beneath, and had his rational reason: OPENING THIS DOOR FOR MORE THAN 30 SECONDS WILL REQUIRE A SEARCH AND SECURE.

Talbot's attention was divided between the doorway and what Victor had said. "You seem worried about the storm."

"Not worried," Victor said, "just cautious. There's no conceivable way it could interfere with the experiment, unless we had another direct hit, which I doubt—we've taken special precautions—but I wouldn't want to risk the power going out in the middle of the shot."

"The shot?"

"I'll explain all that. In fact, I *have* to explain it, so your mite will have the knowledge." Victor smiled at Talbot's confusion. "Don't worry about it." An old woman in a lab smock had come through the door and now stood just behind and to the right of Talbot, waiting, clearly, for their conversation to end so she could speak to Victor.

Victor turned his eyes to her. "Yes, Nadja?"

Talbot looked at her. An acid rain began falling in his stomach.

"Yesterday considerable effort was directed toward finding the cause of a high field horizontal instability," she said, speaking softly, tonelessly, a page of some specific status report. "The attendant beam blowup prevented efficient extraction." Eighty, if a day. Gray eyes sunk deep in folds of crinkled flesh the color of liver paste. "During the afternoon the accelerator was shut down to effect several repairs." Withered, weary, bent, too many bones for the sack. "The super pinger at C48 was replaced with a section of vacuum chamber; it had a vacuum leak." Talbot was in extreme pain. Memories came at him in ravening hordes, a dark wave of ant bodies gnawing at everything soft and folded and vulnerable in his brain. "Two hours of beam time were lost during the owl shift because a solenoid failed on a new vacuum valve in the transfer hall."

"Mother . . . ?" Talbot said, whispering hoarsely.

The old woman started violently, her head coming around and her eyes of settled ashes widening. "Victor," she said, terror in the word.

Talbot barely moved, but Victor took him by the arm and held him. "Thank you, Nadja; go down to target station B and log the secondary beams. Go right now."

She moved past them, hobbling, and quickly vanished through another door in the far wall, held open for her by one of the younger women.

Talbot watched her go, tears in his eyes.

"Oh my God, Victor. It was . . ."

"No, Larry, it wasn't."

"It was. So help me God it *was!* But *how,* Victor, tell me *how?*"

Victor turned him and lifted his chin with his free hand. "Look at me, Larry. *Damn it,* I said *look at me:* it wasn't. You're wrong."

The last time Lawrence Talbot had cried had been the morning he had awakened from sleep, lying under hydrangea shrubs in the botanical garden next to the Minneapolis Museum of Art, lying beside something bloody and still. Under his fingernails had been caked flesh and dirt and blood. That had been the time he learned about manacles and releasing oneself from them when in one state of consciousness, but not in another. Now, he felt like crying. Again. With cause.

"Wait here a moment," Victor said. "Larry? Will you wait right here for me? I'll be back in a moment."

He nodded, averting his face, and Victor went away. While he stood there, waves of painful memory thundering through him, a door slid open into the wall at the far side of the chamber, and another white-smocked technician stuck his head into the room. Through the opening, Talbot could see massive machinery in an enormous chamber beyond. Titanium electrodes. Stainless steel cones. He thought he recognized it: a Cookroft-Walton preaccelerator.

Victor came back with a glass of milky liquid. He handed it to Talbot.

"Victor—" the technician called from the far doorway.

"Drink it," Victor said to Talbot, then turned to the technician.

"Ready to run."

Victor waved to him. "Give me about ten minutes, Karl, then take it up to the first phase shift and signal us." The technician nodded understanding and vanished through the doorway; the door slid out of the wall and closed, hiding the imposing chamberful of equipment. "And that was part of the other half of the mystical, magical solution of your problem," the physicist said, smiling now like a proud father.

"What was that I drank?"

"Something to stabilize you. I can't have you hallucinating."

"I wasn't hallucinating. What was her name?"

"Nadja. You're wrong; you've never seen her before in your life. Have I ever lied to you? How far back do we know each other? I need your trust if this is going to go all the way."

"I'll be all right." The milky liquid had already begun to work. Talbot's face lost its flush, his hands ceased trembling.

Victor was very stern suddenly, a scientist without the time for sidetracks; there was information to be imparted. "Good. For a moment I thought I'd spent a great deal of time preparing . . . well," and he smiled again, quickly, "let me put it this way: I thought for a moment no one was coming to my party."

Talbot gave a strained, tiny chuckle, and followed Victor to a bank of television monitors set into rolling frame-stacks in a corner. "Okay. Let's get you briefed." He turned on sets, one after another, till all twelve were glowing, each one holding a scene of dull-finished and massive installations.

Monitor #1 showed an endlessly long underground tunnel painted eggshell white. Talbot had spent much of his two-month wait reading; he recognized the tunnel as a view down the "straightaway" of the main ring. Gigantic bending magnets in their shock-proof concrete cradles glowed faintly in the dim light of the tunnel.

Monitor #2 showed the linac tunnel.

Monitor #3 showed the rectifier stack of the Cockroft-Walton preaccelerator.

Monitor #4 was a view of the booster. Monitor #5 showed the interior of the transfer hall. Monitors #6 through #9 revealed three experimental target areas and, smaller in scope and size, an internal target area supporting the meson, neutrino and proton areas.

The remaining three monitors showed research areas in the underground lab complex, the final one of which was the main hall itself, where Talbot stood looking into twelve monitors, in the twelfth screen of which could be seen Talbot standing looking into twelve . . .

Victor turned off the sets.

"What did you see?"

All Talbot could think of was the old woman called Nadja. It *couldn't* be. "Larry! What did you see?"

"From what I could see," Talbot said, "that looked to be a particle accelerator. And it looked as big as CERN's proton synchrotron in Geneva."

Victor was impressed. "You've been doing some reading."

"It behooved me."

"Well, well. Let's see if I can impress *you*. CERN's accelerator reaches energies up to 33 BeV; the ring underneath this room reaches energies of 15 GeV."

"Giga meaning trillion."

"You *have* been reading up, haven't you! Fifteen *trillion* electron volts. There's simply no keeping secrets from you, is there, Larry?"

"Only one."

Victor waited expectantly.

"Can you do it?"

"Yes. Meteorology says the eye is almost passing over us. We'll have better than an hour, more than enough time for the dangerous parts of the experiment."

"But you *can* do it."

"Yes, Larry. I don't like having to say it twice." There was no hesitancy in his voice, none of the "yes but" equivocations he'd always heard before. Victor had found the trail.

"I'm sorry, Victor. Anxiety. But if we're ready, why do I have to go through an indoctrination?"

Victor grinned wryly and began reciting, "As your Wizard, I am about to embark on a hazardous and technically unexplainable journey to the upper stratosphere. To confer, converse, and otherwise hobnob with my fellow wizards."

Talbot threw up his hands. "No more."

"Okay, then. Pay attention. If I didn't have to, I wouldn't; believe me, nothing is more boring than listening to the sound of my own lectures. But your mite has to have all the data *you* have. So listen. Now comes the boring—but incredibly informative—explanation."

Western Europe's CERN—*Conseil Européen pour la Recherche Nucléaire*—had settled on Geneva as the site for their Big Machine. Holland lost out on the rich plum because it was common knowledge the food was lousy in the Lowlands. A small matter, but a significant one.

The Eastern Bloc's CEERN—*Conseil de l'Europe de l'Est pour la Recherche Nucléaire*—had been forced into selecting this isolated location high in the White Carpathians (over such likelier and more hospitable sites as Cluj in Rumania, Budapest in Hungary and Gdańsk in Poland) because Talbot's friend Victor had selected this site. CERN had had Dahl and Wideroë and Goward and Adams and Reich; CEERN had Victor. It balanced. He could call the tune.

So the laboratory had been painstakingly built to his specifications, and the particle accelerator dwarfed the CERN Machine. It dwarfed the four-mile ring at the Fermi National Accelerator Lab in

Batavia, Illinois. It was, in fact, the world's largest, most advanced "synchrophasotron."

Only seventy per cent of the experiments conducted in the underground laboratory were devoted to projects sponsored by CEERN. One hundred per cent of the staff of Victor's complex were personally committed to him, not to CEERN, not to the Eastern Bloc, not to philosophies or dogmas . . . to the man. So thirty per cent of the experiments run on the sixteen-mile-diameter accelerator ring were Victor's own. If CEERN knew—and it would have been difficult for them to find out—it said nothing. Seventy per cent of the fruits of genius was better than no per cent.

Had Talbot known earlier that Victor's research was thrust in the direction of actualizing advanced theoretical breakthroughs in the nature of the structure of fundamental particles, he would never have wasted his time with the pseudos and dead-enders who had spent years on his problem, who had promised everything and delivered nothing but dust. But then, until Information Associates had marked the trail—a trail he had previously followed in every direction but the unexpected one that merged shadow with substance, reality with fantasy—until then, he had no need for Victor's exotic talents.

While CEERN basked in the warmth of secure knowledge that their resident genius was keeping them in front in the Super Accelerator Sweepstakes, Victor was briefing his oldest friend on the manner in which he would gift him with the peace of death; the manner in which Lawrence Talbot would find his soul; the manner in which he would precisely and exactly go inside his own body.

"The answer to your problem is in two parts. First, we have to create a perfect simulacrum of you, a hundred thousand or a million times smaller than you, the original. Then, second, we have to *actualize* it, turn an image into something corporeal, material, something that exists. A miniature *you* with all the reality you possess, all the memories, all the knowledge."

Talbot felt very mellow. The milky liquid had smoothed out the churning waters of his memory. He smiled. "I'm glad it wasn't a difficult problem."

Victor looked rueful. "Next week I invent the steam engine. Get serious, Larry."

"It's that Lethe cocktail you fed me."

Victor's mouth tightened and Talbot knew he had to get hold of himself. "Go on, I'm sorry."

Victor hesitated a moment, securing his position of seriousness with a touch of free-floating guilt, then went on, "The first part of the problem is solved by using the grasers we've developed. We'll shoot a hologram of you, using a wave generated not from the electrons of the atom, but from the nucleus . . . a wave a million times shorter, greater in resolution than that from a laser." He walked toward the large glass plate hanging in the middle of the lab, grasers trained on its center. "Come here."

Talbot followed him.

"Is this the holographic plate," he said, "it's just a sheet of photographic glass, isn't it?"

"Not this," Victor said, touching the ten-foot square plate, "*this!*" He put his finger on a spot in the center of the glass and Talbot leaned in to look. He saw nothing at first, then detected a faint ripple; and when he put his face as close as possible to the imperfection he perceived a light *moiré* pattern, like the surface of a fine silk scarf. He looked back at Victor.

"Microholographic plate," Victor said. "Smaller than an integrated chip. That's where we capture your spirit, white-eyes, a million times reduced. About the size of a single cell, maybe a red corpuscle."

Talbot giggled.

"Come on," Victor said wearily. "You've had too much to drink, and it's my fault. Let's get this show on the road. You'll be straight by the time we're ready . . . I just hope to God your mite isn't cockeyed."

Naked, they stood him in front of the ground photographic plate. The older of the female technicians aimed the graser at him, there was a soft sound Talbot took to be some mechanism locking into position, and then Victor said, "All right, Larry, that's it."

He stared at them, expecting more.

"That's it?"

The technicians seemed very pleased, and amused at his reaction. "All done," said Victor. It had been that quick. He hadn't even seen the graser wave hit and lock in his image. "That's *it?*" he said again. Victor began to laugh. It spread through the lab. The technicians were clinging to their equipment; tears rolled down Victor's cheeks; everyone gasped for breath; and Talbot stood in front of the minute imperfection in the glass and felt like a retard.

"That's it?" he said again, helplessly.

After a long time, they dried their eyes and Victor moved him away from the huge plate of glass. "All done, Larry, and ready to go. Are you cold?"

Talbot's naked flesh was evenly polka-dotted with goosebumps. One of the technicians brought him a smock to wear. He stood and watched. Clearly, he was no longer the center of attention.

Now the alternate graser and the holographic plate ripple in the glass were the focuses of attention. Now the mood of released tension was past and the lines of serious attention were back in the faces of the lab staff. Now Victor was wearing an intercom headset, and Talbot heard him say, "All right, Karl. Bring it up to full power."

Almost instantly the lab was filled with the sound of generators phasing up. It became painful and Talbot felt his teeth begin to ache. It went up and up, a whine that climbed till it was beyond his hearing.

Victor made a hand signal to the younger female technician at the graser behind the glass plate. She bent to the projector's sighting mechanism once, quickly, then cut it in. Talbot saw no light beam, but there was the same locking sound he had heard earlier, and then a soft humming, and a life-size hologram of himself, standing naked as he had been a few moments before, trembled in the air where he had stood. He looked at Victor questioningly. Victor nodded, and Talbot walked to the phantasm, passed his hand through it, stood close and looked into the clear brown eyes, noted the wide pore patterns in the nose, studied himself more closely than he had ever been able to do in a mirror. He felt: as if someone had walked over his grave.

Victor was talking to three male technicians, and a moment later they came to examine the hologram. They moved in with light meters and sensitive instruments that apparently were capable of gauging the sophistication and clarity of the ghost image. Talbot watched, fascinated and terrified. It seemed he was about to embark on the great journey of his life; a journey with a much desired destination: surcease.

One of the technicians signaled Victor.

"It's pure," he said to Talbot. Then, to the younger female technician on the second graser projector, "All right, Jana, move it out of there." She started up an engine and the entire projector apparatus turned on heavy rubber wheels and rolled out of the way. The image of Talbot, naked and vulnerable, a little sad to Talbot as he watched it fade and vanish like morning mist, had disappeared when the technician turned off the projector.

"All right, Karl," Victor was saying, "we're moving the pedestal in now. Narrow the aperture, and wait for my signal." Then, to Talbot, "Here comes your mite, old friend."

Talbot felt a sense of resurrection.

The older female technician rolled a four-foot-high stainless steel pedestal to the center of the lab, positioned it so the tiny, highly-polished spindle atop the pedestal touched the very bottom of the faint ripple in the glass. It looked like, and was, an actualizing stage for the real test. The full-sized hologram had been a gross test to ensure the image's perfection. Now came the creation of a living entity, a Lawrence Talbot, naked and the size of a single cell, possessing a consciousness and intelligence and memories and desires identical to Talbot's own.

"Ready, Karl?" Victor was saying.

Talbot heard no reply, but Victor nodded his head as if listening. Then he said, "All right, extract the beam!"

It happened so fast, Talbot missed most of it.

The micropion beam was composed of particles a million times smaller than the proton, smaller than the quark, smaller than the muon or the pion. Victor had termed them micropions. The slit opened in the wall, the beam was diverted, passed through the holographic ripple and was cut off as the slit closed again.

It had all taken a billionth of a second.

"Done," Victor said.

"I don't see anything," Talbot said, and realized how silly he must sound to these people. Of *course* he didn't see anything. There was nothing to see . . . with the naked eye. "Is he . . . is it there?"

"You're there," Victor said. He waved to one of the male technicians standing at a wall hutch of instruments in protective bays, and the man hurried over with the slim, reflective barrel of a microscope. He clipped it onto the tiny needle-pointed stand atop the pedestal in a fashion Talbot could not quite follow. Then he stepped away, and

Victor said, "Part two of your problem solved, Larry. Go look and see yourself."

Lawrence Talbot went to the microscope, adjusted the knob till he could see the reflective surface of the spindle, and saw himself in infinitely reduced perfection

staring up at himself. He recognized himself, though all he could see was a cyclopean brown eye staring down from the smooth glass satellite that dominated his sky.

He waved. The eye blinked.

*Now it begins,* he thought.

Lawrence Talbot stood at the lip of the huge crater that formed Lawrence Talbot's navel. He looked down in the bottomless pit with its atrophied remnants of umbilicus forming loops and protuberances, smooth and undulant and vanishing into utter darkness. He stood poised to descend and smelled the smells of his own body. First, sweat. Then the smells that wafted up from within. The smell of penicillin like biting down on tin foil with a bad tooth. The smell of aspirin, chalky and tickling the hairs of his nose like cleaning blackboard erasers by banging them together. The smells of rotted food, digested and turning to waste. All the odors rising up out of himself like a wild symphony of dark colors.

He sat down on the rounded rim of the navel and let himself slip forward.

He slid down, rode over an outcropping, dropped a few feet and slid again, tobogganing into darkness. He fell for only a short time, then brought up against the soft and yielding, faintly springy tissue plane where the umbilicus had been ligated. The darkness at the bottom of the hole suddenly shattered as blinding light filled the navel. Shielding his eyes, Talbot looked up the shaft toward the sky. A sun glowed there, brighter than a thousand novae. Victor had moved a surgical lamp over the hole to assist him. For as long as he could.

Talbot saw the umbra of something large moving behind the light, and he strained to discern what it was: it seemed important to know what it was. And for an instant, before his eyes closed against the glare, he thought he knew what it had been. Someone watching him, staring down past the surgical lamp that hung above the naked, anesthetized body of Lawrence Talbot, asleep on an operating table.

It had been the old woman, Nadja.

He stood unmoving for a long time, thinking of her.

Then he went to his knees and felt the tissue plane that formed the floor of the navel shaft.

He thought he could see something moving beneath the surface, like water flowing under a film of ice. He went down onto his stomach and cupped his hands around his eyes, putting his face against the dead flesh. It was like looking through a pane of isinglass. A trembling membrane through which he could see the collapsed lumen of the atretic umbilical vein. There was no opening. He pressed his palms against the rubbery surface and it gave, but only slightly. Before he could find the treasure, he had to follow the route of Demeter's map—now firmly and forever consigned to memory—and before he could set foot upon that route, he had to gain access to his own body.

But he had nothing with which to force that entrance.

Excluded, standing at the portal to his own body, Lawrence Talbot felt anger rising within him. His life had been anguish and guilt and horror, had been the wasted result of events over which he had had no control. Pentagrams and full moons and blood and never putting on even an ounce of fat because of a diet high in protein, blood steroids healthier than any normal adult male's, triglycerol and cholesterol levels balanced and humming. And death forever a stranger. Anger flooded through him. He heard an inarticulate little moan of pain, and fell forward, began tearing at the atrophied cord with teeth that had been used for just such activity many times before. Through a blood haze he knew he was savaging his own body, and it seemed exactly the appropriate act of self-flagellation.

An outsider; he had been an outsider all his adult life, and fury would permit him to be shut out no longer. With demonic purpose he ripped away at the clumps of flesh until the membrane gave, at last, and a gap was torn through opening him to himself. . . .

And he was blinded by the explosion of light, by the rush of wind, by the passage of something that had been just beneath the surface writhing to be set free, and in the instant before he plummeted into unconsciousness, he knew Castañeda's Don Juan had told the truth: a thick bundle of white cobwebby filaments, tinged with gold, fibers of light, shot free from the collapsed vein, rose up through the shaft and trembled toward the antiseptic sky.

A metaphysical, otherwise invisible beanstalk that trailed away above him, rising up and up and up as his eyes closed and he sank away into oblivion.

He was on his stomach, crawling through the collapsed lumen, the center, of the path the veins had taken back from the amniotic sac to the fetus. Propelling himself forward the way an infantry scout would through dangerous terrain, using elbows and knees, frog-crawling, he opened the flattened tunnel with his head just enough to get through. It was quite light, the interior of the world called Lawrence Talbot suffused with a golden luminescence.

The map had routed him out of this pressed tunnel through the inferior vena cava to the right atrium and thence through the right ventricle, the pulmonary arteries, through the valves, to the lungs, the pulmonary veins, crossover to the left side of the heart (left atrium, left ventricle), the aorta—bypassing the three coronary arteries above the aortic valves—and down over the arch of the aorta—bypassing the carotid and other arteries—to the celiac trunk, where the arteries split in a confusing array: the gastroduodenal to the stomach, the hepatic to the liver, the splenic to the spleen. And there, dorsal to the body of the diaphragm, he would drop down past the greater pancreatic duct to the pancreas itself. And there, among the islets of langerhans, he would find, at the coordinates Information Associates had given him, he would find that which had been stolen from him one full-mooned night of horror so very long ago. And having found it, having assured himself of eternal sleep, not merely physical death from a silver bullet, he would stop his heart—how, he did not know, but he would—and it would all be ended for Lawrence Talbot, who had become what he had beheld. There, in the tail of the pancreas, supplied with blood by the splenic artery, lay the greatest treasure of all. More than doubloons, more than spices and silks, more than oil lamps used as djinn prisons by Solomon, lay final and sweet eternal peace, a release from monsterdom.

He pushed the final few feet of dead vein apart, and his head emerged into open space. He was hanging upside-down in a cave of deep orange rock.

Talbot wriggled his arms loose, braced them against what was clearly the ceiling of the cave, and wrenched his body out of the tunnel. He fell heavily, trying to twist at the last moment to catch the impact on his shoulders, and received a nasty blow on the side of the neck for his trouble.

He lay there for a moment, clearing his head. Then he stood and walked forward. The cave opened onto a ledge, and he walked out and stared at the landscape before him. The skeleton of something only faintly human lay tortuously crumpled against the wall of the cliff. He was afraid to look at it very closely.

He stared off across the world of dead orange rock, folded and rippled like a topographical view across the frontal lobe of a brain removed from its cranial casing.

The sky was a light yellow, bright and pleasant.

The grand canyon of his body was a seemingly horizonless tumble of atrophied rock, dead for millennia. He sought out and found a descent from the ledge, and began the trek.

There was water, and it kept him alive. Apparently, it rained more frequently here in this parched and stunned wasteland than appearance indicated. There was no keeping track of days or months, for there was no night and no day—always the same even, wonderful golden luminescence—but Talbot felt his passage down the central spine of orange mountains had taken him almost six months. And in that time it had rained forty-eight times, or roughly twice a week. Baptismal fonts of water were filled at every downpour, and he found if he kept the soles of his naked feet moist, he could walk without his energy flagging. If he ate, he did not remember how often, or what form the food had taken.

He saw no other signs of life.

Save an occasional skeleton lying against a shadowed wall of orange rock. Often, they had no skulls.

He found a pass through the mountains, finally, and crossed. He went up through foothills into lower, gentle slopes, and then up again, into cruel and narrow passages that wound higher and higher toward the heat of the sky. When he reached the summit, he found the path down the opposite side was straight and wide and easy. He descended quickly; only a matter of days, it seemed.

Descending into the valley, he heard the song of a bird. He followed the sound. It led him to a crater of igneous rock, quite large, set low among the grassy swells of the valley. He came upon it without warning, and trudged up its short incline, to stand at the volcanic lip looking down.

The crater had become a lake. The smell rose up to assault him. Vile, and somehow terribly sad. The song of the bird continued; he could see no bird anywhere in the golden sky. The smell of the lake made him ill.

Then as he sat on the edge of the crater, staring down, he realized the lake was filled with dead things, floating bellyup; purple and blue as a strangled baby, rotting white, turning slowly in the faintly rippled gray water; without features or limbs. He went down to the lowest outthrust of volcanic rock and stared at the dead things.

Something swam toward him. He moved back. It came on faster, and as it neared the wall of the crater, it surfaced, singing its bluejay song, swerved to rip a chunk of rotting flesh from the corpse of a floating dead thing, and paused only a moment as if to remind him that this was not his, Talbot's, domain, but his own.

Like Talbot, the fish would not die.

Talbot sat at the lip of the crater for a long time, looking down into the bowl that held the lake, and he watched the corpses of dead dreams as they bobbed and revolved like maggoty pork in a gray soup.

After a time, he rose, walked back down from the mouth of the crater, and resumed his journey. He was crying.

When at last he reached the shore of the pancreatic sea, he found a great many things he had lost or given away when he was a child. He found a wooden machine gun on a tripod, painted olive drab, that made a rat-tat-tatting sound when a wooden handle was cranked. He found a set of toy soldiers, two companies, one Prussian and the other French, with a miniature Napoleon Bonaparte among them. He found a microscope kit with slides and petri dishes and racks of chemicals in nice little bottles, all of which bore uniform labels. He found a milk bottle filled with Indian-head pennies. He found a hand puppet with the head of a monkey and the name *Rosco* painted on the fabric glove with nail polish. He found a pedometer. He found a beautiful painting of a jungle bird that had been done with real feathers. He found a corncob pipe. He found a box of radio premiums: a cardboard detective kit with fingerprint dusting powder, invisible ink and a list of police-band call codes; a ring with what seemed to be a plastic bomb attached, and when he pulled the red finned rear off the bomb, and cupped his hands around it in the palms, he could see little scintillas of light, deep inside the payload section; a china mug with a little girl and a dog running across one side; a decoding badge with a burning glass in the center of the red plastic dial.

But there was something missing.

He could not remember what it was, but he knew it was important. As he had known it was important to recognize the shadowy figure who had moved past the surgical lamp at the top of the navel shaft, he knew whatever item was missing from this cache . . . was very important.

He took the boat anchored beside the pancreatic sea, and put all the items from the cache in the bottom of a watertight box under one of the seats. He kept out the large, cathedral-shaped radio, and put it on the bench seat in front of the oarlocks.

Then he unbeached the boat and ran it out into the crimson water, staining his ankles and calves and thighs, and climbed aboard, and started rowing across toward the islets. Whatever was missing was very important.

The wind died when the islets were barely in sight on the horizon. Looking out across the blood-red sea, Talbot sat becalmed at latitude 38° 54' N, longitude 77° 00' 13" W.

He drank from the sea and was nauseated. He played with the toys in the watertight box. And he listened to the radio.

He listened to a program about a very fat man who solved murders, to an adaptation of *The Woman in the Window* with Edward G. Robinson and Joan Bennett, to a story that began in a great railroad station, to a mystery about a wealthy man who could make himself invisible by clouding the minds of others so they could not see him, and he enjoyed a suspense drama narrated by a man named Ernest Chapell in which a group of people descended in a bathyscaphe through the bottom of a mine shaft where, five miles down, they were attacked by pterodactyls. Then he listened to the news, broadcast by Graham MacNamee. Among the human interest items at the close of the program, Talbot heard the unforgettable MacNamee voice say:

"Datelined Columbus, Ohio; September 24th, 1973. Martha Nelson had been in an institution for the mentally retarded for 98 years. She is 102 years old and was first sent to Orient State Institute near

Orient, Ohio, on June 25th, 1875. Her records were destroyed in a fire in the institution some time in 1883, and no one knows for certain why she is at the institute. At the time she was committed, it was known as the Columbus State Institute for the Feeble-Minded. 'She never had a chance,' said Dr. A. Z. Soforenko, appointed two months ago as superintendent of the institution. He said she was probably a victim of 'eugenic alarm,' which he said was common in the late 1800s. At that time some felt that because humans were made 'in God's image' the retarded must be evil or children of the devil, because they were not whole human beings. 'During that time,' Dr. Soforenko said, 'it was believed if you moved feeble-minded people out of a community and into an institution, the taint would never return to the community.' He went on to add, 'She was apparently trapped in that system of thought. No one can ever be sure if she actually *was* feeble-minded; it is a wasted life. She is quite coherent for her age. She has no known relatives and has had no contact with anybody but Institution staff for the last 78 or 80 years.' "

Talbot sat silently in the small boat, the sail hanging like a forlorn ornament from its single centerpole.

"I've cried more since I got inside you, Talbot, than I have in my whole life," he said, but could not stop. Thoughts of Martha Nelson, a woman of whom he had never before heard, of whom he would *never* have heard had it not been by chance by chance by chance he had heard by chance, by chance thoughts of her skirled through his mind like cold winds.

And the cold winds rose, and the sail filled, and he was no longer adrift, but was driven straight for the shore of the nearest islet. By chance.

He stood over the spot where Demeter's map had indicated he would find his soul. For a wild moment he chuckled, at the realization he had been expecting an enormous Maltese Cross or Captain Kidd's "X" to mark the location. But it was only soft green sands, gentle as talc, blowing in dust-devils toward the blood-red pancreatic sea. The spot was midway between the low-tide line and the enormous Bedlam-like structure that dominated the islet.

He looked once more, uneasily, at the fortress rising in the center of the tiny blemish of land. It was built square, seemingly carved from a single monstrous black rock . . . perhaps from a cliff that had been thrust up during some natural disaster. It had no windows, no opening he could see, though two sides of its bulk were exposed to his view. It troubled him. It was a dark god presiding over an empty kingdom. He thought of the fish that would not die, and remembered Nietzsche's contention that gods died when they lost their supplicants.

He dropped to his knees and, recalling the moment months before when he had dropped to his knees to tear at the flesh of his atrophied umbilical cord, he began digging in the green and powdery sand.

The more he dug, the faster the sand ran back into the shallow bowl. He stepped into the middle of the depression and began slinging dirt back between his legs with both hands, a human dog excavating for a bone.

When his fingertips encountered the edge of the box, he yelped with pain as his nails broke.

He dug around the outline of the box, and then forced his bleeding fingers down through the sand to gain purchase under the buried shape. He wrenched at it, and it came loose. Heaving with tensed muscles, he freed it, and it came up.

He took it to the edge of the beach and sat down.

It was just a box. A plain wooden box, very much like an old cigar box, but larger. He turned it over and over and was not at all surprised to find it bore no arcane hieroglyphics or occult symbols. It wasn't that kind of treasure. Then he turned it right side up and pried open the lid. His soul was inside. It was not what he had expected to find, not at all. But it *was* what had been missing from the cache.

Holding it tightly in his fist, he walked up past the fast-filling hole in the green sand, toward the bastion on the high ground.

> We shall not cease from exploration
> And the end of all our exploring
> Will be to arrive where we started
> And know the place for the first time.

> —T. S. Eliot

Once inside the brooding darkness of the fortress—and finding the entrance had been disturbingly easier than he had expected—there was no way to go but down. The wet, black stones of the switchback stairways led inexorably downward into the bowels of the structure, clearly far beneath the level of the pancreatic sea. The stairs were steep, and each step had been worn into smooth curves by the pressure of feet that had descended this way since the dawn of memory. It was dark, but not so dark that Talbot could not see his way. There was no light, however. He did not care to think about how that could be.

When he came to the deepest part of the structure, having passed no rooms or chambers or openings along the way, he saw a doorway across an enormous hall, set into the far wall. He stepped off the last of the stairs, and walked to the door. It was built of crossed iron bars, as black and moist as the stones of the bastion. Through the interstices he saw something pale and still in a far corner of what could have been a cell.

There was no lock on the door.

It swung open at his touch.

Whoever lived in this cell had never tried to open the door; or had tried and decided not to leave.

He moved into deeper darkness.

A long time of silence passed, and finally he stooped to help her to her feet. It was like lifting a sack of dead flowers, brittle and surrounded by dead air incapable of holding even the memory of fragrance.

He took her in his arms and carried her.

"Close your eyes against the light, Martha," he said, and started back up the long stairway to the golden sky.

Lawrence Talbot sat up on the operating table. He opened his eyes and looked at Victor. He smiled a peculiarly gentle smile. For the first time since they had been friends, Victor saw all torment cleansed from Talbot's face.

"It went well," he said. Talbot nodded.

They grinned at each other.

"How're your cryonic facilities?" Talbot asked. Victor's brows drew down in bemusement. "You want me to freeze you? I thought you'd want something more permanent . . . say, in silver."

"Not necessary."

Talbot looked around. He saw her standing against the far wall by one of the grasers. She looked back at him with open fear. He slid off the table, wrapping the sheet upon which he had rested around himself, a makeshift toga. It gave him a patrician look.

He went to her and looked down into her ancient face. "Nadja," he said, softly. After a long moment she looked up at him. He smiled and for an instant she was a girl again. She averted her gaze. He took her hand, and she came with him, to the table, to Victor.

"I'd be deeply grateful for a running account, Larry," the physicist said. So Talbot told him; all of it.

"My mother, Nadja, Martha Nelson, they're all the same," Talbot said, when he came to the end, "all wasted lives."

"And what was in the box?" Victor said.

"How well do you do with symbolism and cosmic irony, old friend?"

"Thus far I'm doing well enough with Jung and Freud," Victor said. He could not help but smile.

Talbot held tightly to the old technician's hand as he said, "It was an old, rusted Howdy Doody button."

Victor turned around.

When he turned back, Talbot was grinning. "That's not cosmic irony, Larry . . . it's slapstick," Victor said. He was angry. It showed clearly.

Talbot said nothing, simply let him work it out.

Finally Victor said, "What the hell's *that* supposed to signify, innocence?"

Talbot shrugged. "I suppose if I'd known, I wouldn't have lost it in the first place. That's what it was, and that's what it is. A little metal pinback about an inch and a half in diameter, with that cockeyed face on it, the orange hair, the toothy grin, the pug nose, the freckles, all of it, just the way he always was." He fell silent, then after a moment added, "It seems right."

"And now that you have it back, you don't *want* to die?"

"I don't *need* to die."

"And you want me to freeze you."

"Both of us."

Victor stared at him with disbelief. "For God's sake, Larry!"

Nadja stood quietly, as if she could not hear them.

"Victor, listen: Martha Nelson is in there. A wasted life. Nadja is out here. I don't know why or how or what did it . . . but . . . a wasted life. Another wasted life. I want you to create her mite, the same way you created mine, and send her inside. He's waiting for her, and he can make it right, Victor. All right, at last. He can be with her as she regains the years that were stolen from her. He can be—*I* can be—her father when she's a baby, her playmate when she's a child, her buddy when she's maturing, her boy friend when she's a young girl, her suitor when she's a young woman, her lover, her husband, her companion as she grows old. Let her be all the women she was never permitted to be, Victor. Don't steal from her a second time. And when it's over, it will start again. . . ."

"*How,* for Christ sake, how the hell *how?* Talk sense, Larry! What is all this metaphysical crap?"

"I don't *know* how; it just is! I've been there, Victor, I was there for months, maybe years, and I never changed, never went to the wolf; there's no Moon there . . . no night and no day, just golden light and warmth, and I can try to make restitution. I can give back two lives. *Please,* Victor!"

The physicist looked at him without speaking. Then he looked at the old woman. She smiled up at him, and then, with arthritic fingers, removed her clothing.

When she came through the collapsed lumen, Talbot was waiting for her. She looked very tired, and he knew she would have to rest before they attempted to cross the orange mountains. He helped her down from the ceiling of the cave, and laid her down on soft, pale yellow moss he had carried back from the islets of Langerhans during the long trek with Martha Nelson. Side-by-side, the two old women lay on the moss, and Nadja fell asleep almost immediately. He stood over them, looking at their faces.

They were identical.

Then he went out on the ledge and stood looking toward the spine of the orange mountains. The skeleton held no fear for him now. He felt a sudden sharp chill in the air and knew Victor had begun the cryonic preservation.

He stood that way for a long time, the little metal button with the sly, innocent face of a mythical creature painted on its surface in four brilliant colors held tightly in his left hand.

And after a while, he heard the crying of a baby, just one baby, from inside the cave, and turned to return for the start of the easiest journey he had ever made.

Somewhere, a terrible devil-fish suddenly flattened its gills, turned slowly bellyup, and sank into darkness.

*And for a farewell shot, a rewritten Genesis, advancing the theory that the snake was the good guy and, since God wrote the PR release, Old Snake simply got a lot of bad press.*

# The Deathbird

## 1

This is a test. Take notes. This will count as ¾ of your final grade. Hints: remember, in chess, kings cancel each other out and cannot occupy adjacent squares, are therefore all-powerful and totally powerless, cannot affect one another, produce stalemate. Hinduism is a polytheistic religion; the sect of Atman worships the divine spark of life within Man; in effect saying, "Thou art God." Provisos of equal time are not served by one viewpoint having media access to two hundred million people in prime time while opposing viewpoints are provided with a soapbox on the corner. Not everyone tells the truth. Operational note: these sections may be taken out of numerical sequence: rearrange to suit yourself for optimum clarity. Turn over your test papers and begin.

## 2

Uncounted layers of rock pressed down on the magma pool. White-hot with the bubbling ferocity of the molten nickel-iron core, the pool spat and shuddered, yet did not pit or char or smoke or damage in the slightest, the smooth and reflective surfaces of the strange crypt.

Nathan Stack lay in the crypt—silent, sleeping.

A shadow passed through rock. Through shale, through coal, through marble, through mica schist, through quartzite; through miles-thick deposits of phosphates, through diatomaceous earth, through feldspars, through diorite; through faults and folds, through anticlines and monoclines, through dips and synclines; through hellfire; and came to the ceiling of the great cavern and passed through; and saw the magma pool and dropped down; and came to the crypt. The shadow.

A triangular face with a single eye peered into the crypt, saw Stack; four-fingered hands were placed on the crypt's cool surface. Nathan Stack woke at the touch, and the crypt became transparent; he woke though the touch had not been upon his body. His soul felt the shadowy pressure and he opened his eyes to see the leaping brilliance of the worldcore around him, to see the shadow with its single eye staring in at him.

The serpentine shadow enfolded the crypt; its darkness flowed upward again, through the Earth's mantle, toward the crust, toward the surface of the cinder, the broken toy that was the Earth.

When they reached the surface, the shadow bore the crypt to a place where the poison winds did not reach, and caused it to open.

Nathan Stack tried to move, and moved only with difficulty. Memories rushed through his head of other lives, many other lives, as many other men; then the memories slowed and melted into a background tone that could be ignored.

The shadow thing reached down a hand and touched Stack's naked flesh. Gently, but firmly, the thing helped him to stand, and gave him garments, and a neck-pouch that contained a short knife and a warming-stone and other things. He offered his hand, and Stack took it, and after two hundred and fifty thousand years sleeping in the crypt, Nathan Stack stepped out on the face of the sick planet Earth.

Then the thing bent low against the poison winds and began walking away. Nathan Stack, having no other choice, bent forward and followed the shadow creature.

### 3

A messenger had been sent for Dira and he had come as quickly as the meditations would permit. When he reached the Summit, he found the fathers waiting, and they took him gently into their cove, where they immersed themselves and began to speak.

"We've lost the arbitration," the coil-father said. "It will be necessary for us to go and leave it to him."

Dira could not believe it. "But didn't they listen to our arguments, to our logic?"

The fang-father shook his head sadly and touched Dira's shoulder. "There were . . . accommodations to be made. It was their time. So we must leave."

The coil-father said, "We've decided you will remain. One was permitted, in caretakership. Will you accept our commission?"

It was a very great honor, but Dira began to feel the loneliness even as they told him they would leave. Yet he accepted. Wondering why they had selected *him*, of all their people. There were reasons, there were always reasons, but he could not ask. And so he accepted the honor, with all its attendant sadness, and remained behind when they left.

The limits of his caretakership were harsh, for they ensured he could not defend himself against whatever slurs or legends would be spread, nor could he take action unless it became clear the trust was being breached by the other—who now held possession. And he had no threat save the Deathbird. A final threat that could be used only when final measures were needed: and therefore too late.

But he was patient. Perhaps the most patient of all his people.

Thousands of years later, when he saw how it was destined to go, when there was no doubt left how it would end, he understood *that* was the reason he had been chosen to stay behind.

But it did not help the loneliness.

Nor could it save the Earth. Only Stack could do that.

### 4

*1 Now the serpent was more subtil than any beast of the field which the* LORD *God had made. And he said unto the woman, Yea, hath God said, Ye shall not eat of every tree of the garden?*

*2 And the woman said unto the serpent, We may eat of the fruit of the trees of the garden:*

*3 But of the fruit of the tree which is in the midst of the garden, God hath said, Ye shall not eat of it, neither shall ye touch it, lest ye die.*

*4 And the serpent said unto the woman, Ye shall not surely die:*

*5 (Omitted)*

*6 And when the woman saw that the tree was good for food, and that it was pleasant to the eyes, and a tree to be desired to make one wise, she took of the fruit thereof, and did eat, and gave also unto her husband with her; and he did eat.*

*7 (Omitted)*

*8 (Omitted)*

*9 And the* LORD *God called unto Adam, and said unto him, Where* art *thou?*

*10 (Omitted)*

*11 And he said, Who told thee that thou* wast *naked? Hast thou eaten of the tree, whereof I commanded thee that thou shouldst not eat?*

*12 And the man said, The woman whom thou gavest* to be *with me, she gave me of the tree, and I did eat.*

*13 And the* LORD *God said unto the woman, What* is *this that thou has done? And the woman said, The serpent beguiled me, and I did eat.*

*14 And the* LORD *God said unto the serpent, Because thou hast done this, thou* art *cursed above all cattle, and above every beast of the field; upon thy belly shalt thou go, and dust shalt thou eat all the days of thy life:*

*15 And I will put enmity between thee and the woman, and between thy seed and her seed; it shall bruise thy head, and thou shalt bruise his heel.*

*—Genesis 3:1–15*

## TOPICS FOR DISCUSSION
(Give 5 points per right answer.)

1. Melville's *Moby Dick* begins, "Call me Ishmael." We say it is told in the *first* person. In what person is Genesis told? From whose viewpoint?

2. Who is the "good guy" in this story? Who is the "bad guy"? Can you make a strong case for reversal of the roles?

3. Traditionally, the apple is considered to be the fruit the serpent offered to Eve. But apples are not endemic to the Near East. Select one of the following, more logical substitutes, and discuss how myths come into being and are corrupted over long periods of time: olive, fig, date, pomegranate.

4. Why is the word LORD always in capitals and the name God

always capitalized? Shouldn't the serpent's name be capitalized, as well? If no, why?

5. If God created everything (see Genesis, Chap. I), why did he create problems for himself by creating a serpent who would lead his creations astray? Why did God create a tree he did not want Adam and Eve to know about, and then go out of his way to warn them against it?

6. Compare and contrast Michelangelo's Sistine Chapel ceiling panel of the *Expulsion from Paradise* with Bosch's *Garden of Earthly Delights*.

7. Was Adam being a gentleman when he placed blame on Eve? Who was Quisling? Discuss "narking" as a character flaw.

8. God grew angry when he found out he had been defied. If God is omnipotent and omniscient, didn't he know? Why couldn't he find Adam and Eve when they hid?

9. If God had not wanted Adam and Eve to taste the fruit of the forbidden tree, why didn't he warn the serpent? Could God have prevented the serpent from tempting Adam and Eve? If yes, why didn't he? If no, discuss the possibility the serpent was as powerful as God.

10. Using examples from two different media journals, demonstrate the concept of "slanted news."

## 5

The poison winds howled and tore at the powder covering the land. Nothing lived there. The winds, green and deadly, dived out of the sky and raked the carcass of the Earth, seeking, seeking: anything moving, anything still living. But there was nothing. Powder. Talc. Pumice.

And the onyx spire of the mountain toward which Nathan Stack and the shadow thing had moved, all that first day. When night fell they dug a pit in the tundra and the shadow thing coated it with a substance thick as glue that had been in Stack's neck-pouch. Stack had slept the night fitfully, clutching the warming-stone to his chest and breathing through a filter tube from the pouch.

Once he had awakened, at the sound of great batlike creatures flying overhead; he had seen them swooping low, coming in flat trajectories across the wasteland toward his pit in the earth. But they seemed unaware that he—and the shadow thing—lay in the hole. They excreted thin, phosphorescent strings that fell glowing through the night and were lost on the plains; then the creatures swooped upward and were whirled away on the winds. Stack resumed sleeping with difficulty.

In the morning, frosted with an icy light that gave everything a blue tinge, the shadow thing scrabbled its way out of the choking powder and crawled along the ground, then lay flat, fingers clawing for purchase in the whiskaway surface. Behind it, from the powder, Stack bore toward the surface, reached up a hand and trembled for help.

The shadow creature slid across the ground, fighting the winds that had grown stronger in the night, back to the soft place that had been their pit, to the hand thrust up through the powder. It grasped the hand, and Stack's fingers tightened convulsively. Then the crawling shadow exerted pressure and pulled the man from the treacherous pumice.

Together they lay against the earth, fighting to see, fighting to draw breath without filling their lungs with suffocating death.

"Why is it like this . . . what *happened?*" Stack screamed against the wind. The shadow creature did not answer, but it looked at Stack for a long moment and then, with very careful movements, raised its hand, held it up before Stack's eyes and slowly, making claws of the fingers, closed the four fingers into a cage, into a fist, into a painfully tight ball that said more eloquently than words: *destruction.*

Then they began to crawl toward the mountain.


# 6


The onyx spire of the mountain rose out of hell and struggled toward the shredded sky. It was monstrous arrogance. Nothing should have tried that climb out of desolation. But the black mountain had tried, and succeeded.

It was like an old man. Seamed, ancient, dirt caked in striated lines, autumnal, lonely; black and desolate, piled strength upon strength. It would *not* give in to gravity and pressure and death. It struggled for the sky. Ferociously alone, it was the only feature that broke the desolate line of the horizon.

In another twenty-five million years the mountain might be worn as smooth and featureless as a tiny onyx offering to the deity night. But though the powder plains swirled and the poison winds drove the pumice against the flanks of the pinnacle, thus far their scouring had only served to soften the edges of the mountain's profile, as though divine intervention had protected the spire.

Lights moved near the summit.

## 7

Stack learned the nature of the phosphorescent strings excreted onto the plain the night before by the batlike creatures. They were spores that became, in the wan light of day, strange bleeder plants.

All around them as they crawled through the dawn, the little live things sensed their warmth and began thrusting shoots up through the talc. As the fading red ember of the dying sun climbed painfully into the sky, the bleeding plants were already reaching maturity.

Stack cried out as one of the vine tentacles fastened around his ankle, holding him. A second looped itself around his neck.

Thin films of berry-black blood coated the vines, leaving rings on Stack's flesh. The rings burned terribly.

The shadow creature slid on its belly and pulled itself back to the man. Its triangular head came close to Stack's neck, and it bit into the vine. Thick black blood spurted as the vine parted, and the shadow creature rasped its razor-edged teeth back and forth till Stack was able to breathe again. With a violent movement Stack folded himself down and around, pulling the short knife from the neck-pouch. He sawed through the vine tightening inexorably around his ankle. It screamed as it was severed, in the same voice Stack had heard from the skies the night before. The severed vine writhed away, withdrawing into the talc.

Stack and the shadow thing crawled forward once again, low, flat, holding onto the dying earth: toward the mountain.

High in the bloody sky, the Deathbird circled.

## 8

On their own world, they had lived in luminous, oily-walled caverns for millions of years, evolving and spreading their race through the universe. When they had had enough of empire building, they turned inward, and much of their time was spent in the intricate construction of songs of wisdom, and the designing of fine worlds for many races.

There were other races that designed, however. And when there was a conflict over jurisdiction, an arbitration was called, adjudicated by a race whose *raison d'être* was impartiality and cleverness in unraveling knotted threads of claim and counterclaim. Their racial honor, in fact, depended on the flawless application of these qualities. Through the centuries they had refined their talents in more and more sophisticated arenas of arbitration until the time came when they were the final authority. The litigants were compelled to abide by the judgments, not merely because the decisions were always wise and creatively fair, but because the judges' race would, if its decisions were questioned as suspect, destroy itself. In the holiest place on their world they had erected a religious machine. It could be activated to emit a tone that would shatter their crystal carapaces. They were a race of exquisite cricket-like creatures, no larger than the thumb of a man. They were treasured throughout the civilized worlds, and their loss would have been catastrophic. Their honor and their value was never questioned. All races abided by their decisions.

So Dira's people gave over jurisdiction to that certain world, and went away, leaving Dira with only the Deathbird, a special caretakership the adjudicators had creatively woven into their judgment.

There is recorded one last meeting between Dira and those who had given him his commission. There were readings that could not be ignored—had, in fact, been urgently brought to the attention of the fathers of Dira's race by the adjudicators—and the Great Coiled One came to Dira at the last possible moment to tell him of the mad thing into whose hands this world had been given, to tell Dira of what the mad thing would do.

The Great Coiled One—whose rings were loops of wisdom acquired through centuries of gentleness and perception and immersed meditations that had brought forth lovely designs for many worlds—he who was the holiest of Dira's race, honored Dira by coming to *him*, rather than commanding Dira to appear.

*We have only one gift to leave them,* he said. *Wisdom. This mad one will come, and he will lie to them, and he will tell them: created he them. And we will be gone, and there will be nothing between them* and the mad one but you. *Only you can give them the wisdom to defeat him in their own good time.* Then the Great Coiled One stroked the skin of Dira with ritual affection, and Dira was deeply moved and could not reply. Then he was left alone.

The mad one came, and interposed himself, and Dira gave them wisdom, and time passed. His name became other than Dira, it became Snake, and the new name was despised: but Dira could see the Great Coiled One had been correct in his readings. So Dira made his selection. A man, one of them, and gifted him with the spark.

All of this is recorded somewhere. It is history.

## 9

The man was not Jesus of Nazareth. He may have been Simon. Not Genghis Khan, but perhaps a foot soldier in his horde. Not Aristotle, but possibly one who sat and listened to Socrates in the agora. Neither the shambler who discovered the wheel nor the link who first ceased painting himself blue and applied the colors to the walls of the cave. But one near them, somewhere near at hand. The man was not Richard *Coeur-de-Lion,* Rembrandt, Richelieu, Rasputin, Robert Fulton or the Mahdi. Just a man. With the spark.

## 10

Once, Dira came to the man. Very early on. The spark was there, but the light needed to be converted to energy. So Dira came to the man, and did what had to be done before the mad one knew of it, and when he discovered that Dira, the Snake, had made contact, he quickly made explanations.

This legend has come down to us as the fable of *Faust.*

TRUE or FALSE?

## 11

Light converted to energy, thus:

In the fortieth year of his five hundredth incarnation, all-unknowing of the eons of which he had been part, the man found himself wandering in a terrible dry place under a thin, flat burning disc of sun. He was a Berber tribesman who had never considered shadows save to relish them when they provided shade. The shadow came to him, sweeping down across the sands like the *khamsin* of Egypt, the *simoom* of Asia Minor, the *harmattan*, all of which he had known in his various lives, none of which he remembered. The shadow came over him like the *sirocco*.

The shadow stole the breath from his lungs and the man's eyes rolled up in his head. He fell to the ground and the shadow took him down and down, through the sands, into the Earth.

Mother Earth.

She lived, this world of trees and rivers and rocks with deep stone thoughts. She breathed, had feelings, dreamed dreams, gave birth, laughed, and grew contemplative for millennia. This great creature swimming in the sea of space.

*What a wonder,* thought the man, for he had never understood that the Earth was his mother, before this. He had never understood, before this, that the Earth had a life of its own, at once a part of mankind and quite separate from mankind. A mother with a life of her own.

Dira, Snake, shadow . . . took the man down and let the spark of light change itself to energy as the man became one with the Earth. His flesh melted and became quiet, cool soil. His eyes glowed with the light that shines in the darkest centers of the planet and he saw the way the mother cared for her young: the worms, the roots of plants, the rivers that cascaded for miles over great cliffs in enormous caverns, the bark of trees. He was taken once more to the bosom of that great Earth mother, and understood the joy of her life.

*Remember this,* Dira said to the man.

*What a wonder,* the man thought . . .

. . . and was returned to the sands of the desert, with no remembrance of having slept with, loved, enjoyed the body of his natural mother.

## 12

They camped at the base of the mountain, in a green-glass cave; not deep but angled sharply so the blown pumice could not reach them. They put Nathan Stack's stone in a fault in the cave's floor, and the heat spread quickly, warming them. The shadow thing with its triangular head sank back in shadow and closed its eye and sent its hunting instinct out for food. A shriek came back on the wind.

Much later, when Nathan Stack had eaten, when he was reasonably content and well fed, he stared into the shadows and spoke to the creature sitting there.

"How long was I down there . . . how long was the sleep?"

The shadow thing spoke in whispers. *A quarter of a million years.*

Stack did not reply. The figure was beyond belief. The shadow creature seemed to understand.

*In the life of a world no time at all.*

Nathan Stack was a man who could make accommodations. He smiled quickly and said, "I must have been tired."

The shadow did not respond.

"I don't understand very much of this. It's pretty damned frightening. To die, then to wake up . . . here. Like this."

*You did not die. You were taken, put down there. By the end you will understand everything, I promise you.*

"Who put me down there?"

*I did. I came and found you when the time was right, and I put you down there.*

"Am I still Nathan Stack?"

*If you wish.*

"But *am* I Nathan Stack?"

*You always were. You had many other names, many other bodies, but the spark was always yours.* Stack seemed about to speak, and the shadow creature added, *You were always on your way to being who you are.*

"But what *am* I? Am I still Nathan Stack, dammit?"

*If you wish.*

"Listen: you don't seem too sure about that. You came and got me, I mean I woke up and there you were. Now who should know better than you what my name is?"

*You have had many names in many times. Nathan Stack is merely the one you remember. You had a very different name long ago, at the start, when I first came to you.*

Stack was afraid of the answer, but he asked, "What was my name then?"

*Ish-lilith. Husband of Lilith. Do you remember her?*

Stack thought, tried to open himself to the past, but it was as unfathomable as the quarter of a million years through which he had slept in the crypt.

"No. But there were other women, in other times."

*Many. There was one who replaced Lilith.*

"I don't remember."

*Her name . . . does not matter. But when the mad one took Lilith from you and replaced her with the other . . . then I knew it would end like this. The Deathbird.*

"I don't mean to be stupid, but I haven't the faintest idea what you're talking about."

*Before it ends, you will understand everything.*

"You said that before." Stack paused, stared at the shadow creature for a long time only moments long, then, "What was your name?"

*Before I met you my name was Dira.*

He said it in his native tongue. Stack could not pronounce it.

"Before you met me. What is it now?"

*Snake.*

Something slithered past the mouth of the cave. It did not stop, but it called out with voice of moist mud sucking down into a quagmire.

"Why did you put *me* down there? Why did you come to me in the first place? What spark? Why can't I remember these other lives or who I was? What do you want from me?"

*You should sleep. It will be a long climb. And cold.*

"I slept for two hundred and fifty thousand years, I'm hardly tired," Stack said. "Why did you pick me?"

*Later. Now sleep. Sleep has other uses.*

Darkness deepened around Snake, seeped out around the cave, and Nathan Stack lay down near the warming-stone, and the darkness took him.

## 13

### SUPPLEMENTARY READING

This is an essay by a writer. It is clearly an appeal to the emotions. As you read it, ask yourself how it applies to the subject under discussion.

What is the writer trying to say? Does he succeed in making his point? Does this essay cast light on the point of the subject under discussion? After you have read this essay, using the reverse side of your test paper, write your own essay (500 words or less) on the loss of a loved one. If you have never lost a loved one, fake it.


## AHBHU

Yesterday my dog died. For eleven years Ahbhu was my closest friend. He was responsible for my writing a story about a boy and his dog that many people have read. The story was made into a successful movie. The dog in the movie looked a lot like Ahbhu. He was not a pet, he was a person. It was impossible to anthropomorphize him, he wouldn't stand for it. But he was so much his own kind of creature, he had such a strongly formed personality, he was so determined to share his life with only those *he* chose, that it was also impossible to think of him as simply a dog. Apart from those canine characteristics into which he was locked by his genes, he comported himself like one of a kind.

We met when I came to him at the West Los Angeles Animal Shelter. I'd wanted a dog because I was lonely and I'd remembered when I was a little boy how my dog had been a friend when I had no other friends. One summer I went away to camp and when I returned I found a rotten old neighbor lady from up the street had had my dog picked up and gassed while my father was at work. I crept into the woman's backyard that night and found a rug hanging on the clothesline. The rug beater was hanging from a post. I stole it and buried it.

At the Animal Shelter there was a man in line ahead of me. He had brought in a puppy only a week or so old. A Puli, a Hungarian sheep dog; it was a sad-looking little thing. He had too many in the litter and had brought in this one either to be taken by someone else or to be put to sleep. They took the dog inside and the man behind the counter called my turn. I told him I wanted a dog and he took me back inside to walk down the line of cages.

In one of the cages the little Puli that had just been brought in was being assaulted by three larger dogs that had been earlier tenants. He was a little thing, and he was on the bottom, getting the stuffing knocked out of him. But he was struggling mightily.

"Get him out of there!" I yelled. "I'll take him, I'll take him, get him out of there!"

He cost two dollars. It was the best two bucks I ever spent.

Driving home with him, he was lying on the other side of the front seat, staring at me. I had had a vague idea what I'd name a pet, but as I stared at him, and he stared back at me, I suddenly was put in mind of the scene in Alexander Korda's 1939 film *The Thief of Bagdad,* where the evil vizier, played by Conrad Veidt, had changed Ahbhu, the little thief, played by Sabu, into a dog. The film had superimposed the human over the canine face for a moment so there was an extraordinary look of intelligence in the face of the dog. The little Puli was looking at me with that same expression. "Ahbhu," I said.

He didn't react to the name, but then he couldn't have cared less. But that was his name, from that time on.

No one who ever came into my house was unaffected by him. When he sensed someone with good vibrations, he was right there, lying at their feet. He loved to be scratched, and despite years of admonitions he refused to stop begging for scraps at table, because he had found most of the people who came to dinner at my house were patsies unable to escape his woebegone Jackie-Coogan-as-the-Kid look.

But he was a certain barometer of bums, as well. On any number of occasions when I found someone I liked, and Ahbhu would have nothing to do with him or her, it always turned out the person was a wrongo. I took to nothing his attitude toward newcomers, and I must admit it influenced my own reactions. I was always wary of someone Ahbhu shunned.

Women with whom I had had unsatisfactory affairs would nonetheless return to the house from time to time—to visit the dog. He had an intimate circle of friends, many of whom had nothing to do with me, and numbering among their company some of the most beautiful actresses in Hollywood. One exquisite lady used to send her driver to pick him up for Sunday afternoon romps at the beach.

I never asked him what happened on those occasions. He didn't talk.

Last year he started going downhill, though I didn't realize it because he maintained the manner of a puppy almost to the end. But he began sleeping too much, and he couldn't hold down his food—not even the Hungarian meals prepared for him by the Magyars who lived up the street. And it became apparent to me something was wrong with him when he got scared during the big Los Angeles earthquake last year. Ahbhu wasn't afraid of anything. He attacked the Pacific Ocean and walked tall around vicious cats. But the quake terrified him and he jumped up in my bed and threw his forelegs around my neck. I was very nearly the only victim of the earthquake to die from animal strangulation.

He was in and out of the veterinarian's shop all through the early part of this year, and the idiot always said it was his diet.

Then one Sunday when he was out in the backyard, I found him lying at the foot of the stairs, covered with mud, vomiting so heavily all he could bring up was bile. He was matted with his own refuse and he was trying desperately to dig his nose into the earth for coolness. He was barely breathing. I took him to a different vet.

At first they thought it was just old age . . . that they could pull him through. But finally they took X-rays and saw the cancer had taken hold in his stomach and liver.

I put off the day as much as I could. Somehow I just couldn't conceive of a world that didn't have him in it. But yesterday I went to the vet's office and signed the euthanasia papers.

"I'd like to spend a little time with him, before," I said.

They brought him in and put him on the stainless steel examination table. He had grown so thin. He'd always had a pot-belly and it was gone. The muscles in his hind legs were weak, flaccid. He came to me and put his head into the hollow of my armpit. He was trembling violently. I lifted his head and he looked at me with that comic face I'd always thought made him look like Lawrence Talbot, the Wolf Man. He knew. Sharp as hell right up to the end, hey old friend? He knew, and he was scared. He trembled all the way down to his spiderweb legs. This bouncing ball of hair that, when lying on a dark carpet, could be taken for a sheepskin rug, with no way to tell at which end head and which end tail. So thin. Shaking, knowing what was going to happen to him. But still a puppy.

I cried and my eyes closed as my nose swelled with the crying, and he buried his head in my arms because we hadn't done much crying at one another. I was ashamed of myself not to be taking it as well as he was.

"I *got* to, pup, because you're in pain and you can't eat. I *got* to." But he didn't want to know that.

The vet came in, then. He was a nice guy and he asked me if I wanted to go away and just let it be done.

Then Ahbhu came up out of there and *looked* at me.

There is a scene in Kazan's *Viva Zapata* where a close friend of Zapata's, Brando's, has been condemned for conspiring with the *federales*. A friend that had been with Zapata since the mountains, since the *revolución* had begun. And they come to the hut to take him to the firing squad, and Brando starts out, and his friend stops him with a hand on his arm, and he says to him with great friendship, "Emiliano, do it yourself."

Ahbhu looked at me and I know he was just a dog, but if he could have spoken with human tongue he could not have said more eloquently than he did with a look, *don't leave me with strangers.*

So I held him as they laid him down and the vet slipped the lanyard up around his right foreleg and drew it tight to bulge the vein, and I held his head and he turned it away from me as the needle went in. It was impossible to tell the moment he passed over from life to death. He simply laid his head on my hand, his eyes fluttered shut and he was gone.

I wrapped him in a sheet with the help of the vet and I drove home with Ahbhu on the seat beside me, just the way we had come home eleven years before. I took him out in the backyard and began digging his grave. I dug for hours, crying and mumbling to myself, talking to him in the sheet. It was a very neat, rectangular grave with smooth sides and all the loose dirt scooped out by hand.

I laid him down in the hole and he was so tiny in there for a dog who had seemed to be so big in life, so furry, so funny. And I covered him over and when the hole was packed full of dirt I replaced the neat divot of grass I'd scalped off at the start. And that was all.

But I couldn't send him to strangers.

### THE END

### QUESTIONS FOR DISCUSSION

1. Is there any significance to the reversal of the word *god* being *dog*? If so, what?
2. Does the writer try to impart human qualities to a nonhuman creature? Why? Discuss anthropomorphism in the light of the phrase, "Thou art God."
3. Discuss the love the writer shows in this essay. Compare and contrast it with other forms of love: the love of a man for a woman, a mother for a child, a son for a mother, a botanist for plants, an ecologist for the Earth.

### 14

In his sleep, Nathan Stack talked.
"Why did you pick me? Why me . . .?"

## 15

Like the Earth, the Mother was in pain.

The great house was very quiet. The doctor had left, and the relatives had gone into town for dinner. He sat by the side of her bed and stared down at her. She looked gray and old and crumpled; her skin was a powdery, ashy hue of moth-dust. He was crying softly.

He felt her hand on his knee, and looked up to see her staring at him. "You weren't supposed to catch me," he said.

"I'd be disappointed if I hadn't," she said. Her voice was very thin, very smooth.

"How is it?"

"It hurts. Ben didn't dope me too well."

He bit his lower lip. The doctor had used massive doses, but the pain was more massive. She gave little starts as tremors of sudden agony hit her. Impacts. He watched the life leaking out of her eyes.

"How is your sister taking it?"

He shrugged. "You know Charlene. She's sorry, but it's all pretty intellectual to her."

His mother let a tiny ripple of a smile move her lips. "It's a terrible thing to say, Nathan, but your sister isn't the most likable woman in the world. I'm glad you're here." She paused, thinking, then added, "It's just possible your father and I missed something from the gene pool. Charlene isn't whole."

"Can I get you something? A drink of water?"

"No. I'm fine."

He looked at the ampoule of narcotic painkiller. The syringe lay mechanical and still on the clean towel beside it. He felt her eyes on him. She knew what he was thinking. He looked away.

"I would kill for a cigarette," she said.

He laughed. At sixty-five, both legs gone, what remained of her left side paralyzed, the cancer spreading like deadly jelly toward her heart, she was still the matriarch. "You can't have a cigarette, so forget it."

"Then why don't you use that hypo and let me out of here."

"Shut up, Mother."

"Oh, for Christ's sake, Nathan. It's hours if I'm lucky. Months if I'm not. We've had this conversation before. You know I always win."

"Did I ever tell you you were a bitchy old lady?"

"Many times, but I love you anyhow."

He got up and walked to the wall. He could not walk through it, so he went around the inside of the room.

"You can't get away from it."

"Mother, Jesus! Please!"

"All right. Let's talk about the business."

"I couldn't care less about the business right now."

"Then what should we talk about? The lofty uses to which an old lady can put her last moments?"

"You know, you're really ghoulish. I think you're *enjoying* this in some sick way."

"What other way is there to enjoy it."

"An adventure."

"The biggest. A pity your father never had the chance to savor it."

"I hardly think he'd have savored the feeling of being stamped to death in a hydraulic press."

Then he thought about it, because that little smile was on her lips again. "Okay, he probably would have. The two of you were so unreal, you'd have sat there and discussed it and analyzed the pulp."

"And you're our son."

He was, and he was. And he could not deny it, nor had he ever. He was hard and gentle and wild just like them, and he remembered the days in the jungle beyond Brasilia, and the hunt in the Cayman Trench, and the other days working in the mills alongside his father, and he knew when his moment came he would savor death as she did.

"Tell me something. I've always wanted to know. *Did* Dad kill Tom Golden?"

"Use the needle and I'll tell you."

"I'm a Stack. I don't bribe."

"*I'm* a Stack, and I know what a killing curiosity you've got. Use the needle and I'll tell you."

He walked widdershins around the room. She watched him, eyes bright as the mill vats.

"You old bitch."

"Shame, Nathan. You know you're not the son of a bitch.

Which is more than your sister can say. Did I ever tell you she wasn't your father's child?"

"No, but I knew."

"You'd have liked her father. He was Swedish. *Your* father liked him."

"Is that why Dad broke both his arms?"

"Probably. But I never heard the Swede complain. One night in bed with me in those days was worth a couple of broken arms. Use the needle."

Finally, while the family was between the entree and the dessert, he filled the syringe and injected her. Her eyes widened as the stuff smacked her heart, and just before she died she rallied all her strength and said, "A deal's a deal. Your father didn't kill Tom Golden, I did. You're a hell of a man, Nathan, and you fought us the way we wanted, and we both loved you more than you could know. Except, dammit, you cunning s.o.b., you *do* know, don't you?"

"I know," he said, and she died; and he cried; and that was the extent of the poetry in it.

## 16

*He knows we are coming.*

They were climbing the northern face of the onyx mountain. Snake had coated Nathan Stack's feet with the thick glue and, though it was hardly a country walk, he was able to keep a foothold and pull himself up. Now they had paused to rest on a spiral ledge, and Snake had spoken for the first time of what waited for them where they were going.

"He?"

Snake did not answer. Stack slumped against the wall of the ledge. At the lower slopes of the mountain they had encountered sluglike creatures that had tried to attach themselves to Stack's flesh, but when Snake had driven them off they had returned to sucking the rocks. They had not come near the shadow creature. Farther up, Stack could see the lights that flickered at the summit; he had felt fear that crawled up from his stomach. A short time before they had come to this ledge they had stumbled past a cave in the mountain where the bat creatures slept. They had gone mad at the presence of the man and the Snake, and the sounds they had made sent waves of nausea through Stack. Snake had helped him and they had gotten past. Now they had stopped and Snake would not answer Stack's questions.

*We must keep climbing.*

"Because he knows we're here." There was a sarcastic rise in Stack's voice.

Snake started moving. Stack closed his eyes. Snake stopped and came back to him. Stack looked up at the one-eyed shadow.

"Not another step."

*There is no reason why you should not know.*

"Except, friend, I have the feeling you aren't going to tell me anything."

*It is not yet time for you to know.*

"Look: just because I haven't asked, doesn't mean I don't want to know. You've told me things I shouldn't be able to handle . . . all kinds of crazy things . . . I'm as old as, as . . . I don't know *how* old, but I get the feeling you've been trying to tell me I'm Adam. . . ."

*That is so.*

". . . uh." He stopped rattling and stared back at the shadow creature. Then, very softly, accepting even more than he had thought possible, he said, "Snake." He was silent again. After a time he asked, "Give me another dream and let me know the rest of it?"

*You must be patient. The one who lives at the top knows we are coming but I have been able to keep him from perceiving your danger to him only because you do not know yourself.*

"Tell me this, then: does he *want* us to come up . . . the one on the top?"

*He allows it. Because he doesn't know.*

Stack nodded, resigned to following Snake's lead. He got to his feet and performed an elaborate butler's motion: after you, Snake.

And Snake turned, his flat hands sticking to the wall of the ledge, and they climbed higher, spiraling upward toward the summit.

The Deathbird swooped, then rose toward the Moon. There was still time.

## 17

Dira came to Nathan Stack near sunset, appearing in the board room of the industrial consortium Stack had built from the empire left by his family.

Stack sat in the pneumatic chair that dominated the conversation pit where top-level decisions were made. He was alone. The others had left hours before and the room was dim with only the barest glow of light from hidden banks that shone through the soft walls.

The shadow creature passed through the walls—and at his passage they became rose quartz, then returned to what they had been. He stood staring at Nathan Stack, and for long moments the man was unaware of any other presence in the room.

*You have to go now,* Snake said.

Stack looked up, his eyes widened in horror, and through his mind flitted the unmistakable image of Satan, fanged mouth smiling, horns gleaming with scintillas of light as though seen through crosstar filters, rope tail with its spade-shaped appendage thrashing, cloven hoofs leaving burning imprints in the carpet, eyes as deep as pools of oil, the pitchfork, the satin-lined cape, the hairy legs of a goat, talons. He tried to scream but the sound dammed up in his throat.

*No,* Snake said, *that is not so. Come with me, and you will understand.*

There was a tone of sadness in the voice. As though Satan had been sorely wronged. Stack shook his head violently.

There was no time for argument. The moment had come, and Dira could not hesitate. He gestured and Nathan Stack rose from the pneumatic chair, leaving behind something that looked like Nathan Stack asleep, and he walked to Dira and Snake took him by the hand and they passed through rose quartz and went away from there.

Down and down Snake took him.

The Mother was in pain. She had been sick for eons, but it had reached the point where Snake knew it would be terminal, and the Mother knew it, too. But she would hide her child, she would intercede in her own behalf and hide him away deep in her bosom where no one, not even the mad one, could find him.

Dira took Stack to Hell.

It was a fine place.

Warm and safe and far from the probing of mad ones.

And the sickness raged on unchecked. Nations crumbled, the oceans boiled and then grew cold and filmed over with scum, the air became thick with dust and killing vapors, flesh ran like oil, the skies grew dark, the sun blurred and became dull. The Earth moaned.

The plants suffered and consumed themselves, beasts became crippled and went mad, trees burst into flame and from their ashes rose glass shapes that shattered in the wind. The Earth was dying; a long, slow, painful death.

In the center of the Earth, in the fine place, Nathan Stack slept. *Don't leave me with strangers.*

Overhead, far away against the stars, the Deathbird circled and circled, waiting for the word.

## 18

When they reached the highest peak, Nathan Stack looked across through the terrible burning cold and the ferocious grittiness of the demon wind and saw the sanctuary of always, the cathedral of forever, the pillar of remembrance, the haven of perfection, the pyramid of blessings, the toyshop of creation, the vault of deliverance, the monument of longing, the receptacle of thoughts, the maze of wonder, the catafalque of despair, the podium of pronouncements and the kiln of last attempts.

On a slope that rose to a star pinnacle, he saw the home of the one who dwelled here—lights flashing and flickering, lights that could be seen far off across the deserted face of the planet—and he began to suspect the name of the resident.

Suddenly everything went red for Nathan Stack. As though a filter had been dropped over his eyes, the black sky, the flickering lights, the rocks that formed the great plateau on which they stood, even Snake became red, and with the color came pain. Terrible pain that burned through every channel of Stack's body, as though his blood had been set afire. He screamed and fell to his knees, the pain crackling through his brain, following every nerve and blood vessel and ganglion and neural track. His skull flamed.

*Fight him,* Snake said. *Fight him!*

I can't, screamed silently through Stack's mind, the pain too great even to speak. Fire licked and leaped and he felt the delicate tissue of thought shriveling. He tried to focus his thoughts on ice. He clutched for salvation at ice, chunks of ice, mountains of ice, swimming icebergs of ice half-buried in frozen water, even as his soul smoked and smoldered. *Ice!* He thought of millions of particles of hail rushing, falling, thundering against the firestorm eating his mind, and there was a spit of steam, a flame that went out, a corner that grew cool . . . and he took his stand in that corner, thinking ice, thinking blocks and chunks and monuments of ice, edging them out to widen the circle of coolness and safety. Then the flames began to retreat, to slide back down the channels, and he sent ice after them, snuffing them, burying them in ice and chill waters that raced after the flames and drove them out.

When he opened his eyes, he was still on his knees, but he could think again, and the red surfaces had become normal again.

*He will try again. You must be ready.*

"Tell me *everything!* I can't go through this without knowing, I need help! Tell me, Snake, tell me now!"

*You can help yourself. You have the strength. I gave you the spark.*

. . . and the second derangement struck!

The air turned shaverasse and he held dripping chunks of unclean rova in his jowls, the taste making him weak with nausea. His pods withered and drew up into his shell and as the bones cracked he howled with strings of pain that came so fast they were almost one. He tried to scuttle away, but his eyes magnified the shatter of light that beat against him. Facets of his eyes cracked and the juice began to bubble out. The pain was unbelievable.

*Fight him!*

Stack rolled onto his back, sending out cilia to touch the earth, and for an instant he realized he was seeing through the eyes of another creature, another form of life he could not even describe. But he was under an open sky and that produced fear; he was surrounded by air that had become deadly and *that* produced fear; he was going blind and *that* produced fear; he was . . . he was a *man* . . . fought back against the feeling of being some other thing . . . he was a *man* and he would not feel fear, he would stand.

He rolled over, withdrew his cilia, and struggled to lower his pods. Broken bones grated and pain thundered through his body. He forced himself to ignore it, and finally the pods were down and he was breathing and he felt his head reeling. . . .

And when he opened his eyes he was Nathan Stack again.

. . . and the third derangement struck:

Hopelessness.

Out of unending misery he came back to be Stack.

. . . and the fourth derangement struck:

Madness.

Out of raging lunacy he fought his way to be Stack.

. . . and the fifth derangement, and the sixth, and the seventh, and the plagues, and the whirlwinds, and the pools of evil, and the reduction in size and accompanying fall forever through submicroscopic hells, and the things that fed on him from inside, and the twentieth, and the fortieth, and the sound of his voice screaming for release, and the voice of Snake always beside him, whispering *Fight him!*

Finally it stopped.

*Quickly, now.*

Snake took Stack by the hand and, half-dragging him, raced to the great palace of light and glass on the slope, shining brightly under the star pinnacle, and they passed under an arch of shining metal into the ascension hall. The portal sealed behind them.

There were tremors in the walls. The inlaid floors of jewels began to rumble and tremble. Bits of high and faraway ceilings began to drop. Quaking, the palace gave one hideous shudder and collapsed around them.

*Now,* Snake said. *Now you will know everything!*

And everything forgot to fall. Frozen in midair, the wreckage of the palace hung suspended above them. Even the air ceased to swirl. Time stood still. The movement of the Earth was halted. Everything held utterly immobile as Nathan Stack was permitted to understand all.

## 19

### MULTIPLE CHOICE
(Counts for ½ your final grade.)

1. God is:
    A. An invisible spirit with a long beard.
    B. A small dog dead in a hole.
    C. Everyman.
    D. The Wizard of Oz.
2. Nietzsche wrote "God is dead." By this did he mean:
    A. Life is pointless.
    B. Belief in supreme deities has waned.
    C. There never was a God to begin with.
    D. Thou art God.
3. Ecology is another name for:
    A. Mother love.
    B. Enlightened self-interest.
    C. A good health salad with granola.
    D. God.
4. Which of these phrases most typifies the profoundest love:
    A. Don't leave me with strangers.
    B. I love you.
    C. God is love.
    D. Use the needle.
5. Which of these powers do we usually associate with God:
    A. Power.
    B. Love.
    C. Humanity.
    D. Docility.

## 20

None of the above.

Starlight shone in the eyes of the Deathbird and its passage through the night cast a shadow on the Moon.

# 21

Nathan Stack raised his hands and around them the air was still, as the palace fell crashing. They were untouched. *Now you know all there is to know,* Snake said, sinking to one knee as though worshipping. There was no one there to worship but Nathan Stack.

"Was he always mad?"

*From the first.*

"Then those who gave our world to him were mad, and your race was mad to allow it."

Snake had no answer.

"Perhaps it was supposed to be like this," Stack said.

He reached down and lifted Snake to his feet, and he touched the shadow creature's sleek triangular head. "Friend," he said.

Snake's race was incapable of tears. He said, *I have waited longer than you can know for that word.*

"I'm sorry it comes at the end."

*Perhaps it was supposed to be like this.*

Then there was a swirling of air, a scintillation in the ruined palace, and the owner of the mountain, the owner of the ruined Earth came to them in a burning bush.

AGAIN, SNAKE? AGAIN YOU ANNOY ME?

*The time for toys is ended.*

NATHAN STACK YOU BRING TO STOP ME? I SAY WHEN THE TIME IS ENDED. I SAY, AS I'VE ALWAYS SAID.

Then, to Nathan Stack:

GO AWAY. FIND A PLACE TO HIDE UNTIL I COME FOR YOU.

Stack ignored the burning bush. He waved his hand, and the cone of safety in which they stood vanished. "Let's find him, first, then I know what to do."

The Deathbird sharpened its talons on the night wind and sailed down through emptiness toward the cinder of the Earth.

## 22

Nathan Stack had once contracted pneumonia. He had lain on the operating table as the surgeon made the small incision in the chest wall. Had he not been stubborn, had he not continued working around the clock while the pneumonic infection developed into empyema, he would never have had to go under the knife, even for an operation as safe as a thoracotomy. But he was a Stack, and so he lay on the operating table as the rubber tube was inserted into the chest cavity to drain off the pus in the pleural cavity, and he heard someone speak his name.

NATHAN STACK.

He heard it, from far off, across an Arctic vastness; heard it echoing over and over, down an endless corridor; as the knife sliced.

NATHAN STACK.

He remembered Lilith, with hair the color of dark wine. He remembered taking hours to die beneath a rock slide as his hunting companions in the pack ripped apart the remains of the bear and ignored his grunted moans for help. He remembered the impact of the crossbow bolt as it ripped through his hauberk and split his chest and he died at Agincourt. He remembered the icy water of the Ohio as it closed over his head and the flatboat disappearing without his mates' noticing his loss. He remembered the mustard gas that ate his lungs as he tried to crawl toward a farmhouse near Verdun. He remembered looking directly into the flash of the bomb and feeling the flesh of his face melt away. He remembered Snake coming to him in the board room and husking him like corn from his body. He remembered sleeping in the molten core of the Earth for a quarter of a million years.

Across the dead centuries he heard his mother pleading with him to set her free, to end her pain. *Use the needle.* Her voice mingled with the voice of the Earth crying out in endless pain at her flesh that had been ripped away, at her rivers turned to arteries of dust, at her rolling hills and green fields slagged to greenglass and ashes. The voices of his mother and the mother that was Earth became one, and mingled to become Snake's voice telling him he was the one man in the world

—the last man in the world—who could end the terminal case the Earth had become.

Use the needle. Put the suffering Earth out of its misery. *It belongs to you now.*

Nathan Stack was secure in the power he contained. A power that far outstripped that of gods or Snakes or mad creators who stuck pins in their creations, who broke their toys.

YOU CAN'T. I WON'T LET YOU.

Nathan Stack walked around the burning bush as it crackled impotently in rage. He looked at it almost pityingly, remembering the Wizard of Oz with his great and ominous disembodied head floating in mist and lightning, and the poor little man behind the curtain turning the dials to create the effects. Stack walked around the effect, knowing he had more power than this sad, poor thing that had held his race in thrall since before Lilith had been taken from him.

He went in search of the mad one who capitalized his name.

## 23

Zarathustra descended alone from the mountains, encountering no one. But when he came into the forest, all at once there stood before him an old man who had left his holy cottage to look for roots in the woods. And thus spoke the old man to Zarathustra:

"No stranger to me is this wanderer: many years ago he passed this way. Zarathustra he was called, but he has changed. At that time you carried your ashes to the mountains; would you now carry your fire into the valleys? Do you not fear to be punished as an arsonist?

"Zarathustra has changed, Zarathustra has become a child, Zarathustra is an awakened one; what do you now want among the sleepers? You lived in your solitude as in the sea, and the sea carried you. Alas, would you now climb ashore? Alas, would you again drag your own body?"

Zarathustra answered: "I love man."

"Why," asked the saint, "did I go into the forest and the desert? Was it not because I loved man all too much? Now I loved God; man I love not. Man is for me too imperfect a thing. Love of man would kill me."

"And what is the saint doing in the forest?" asked Zarathustra.

The saint answered: "I make songs and sing them; and when I make songs, I laugh, cry, and hum: thus I praise God. With singing, crying, laughing, and humming, I praise the god who is my god. But what do you bring us as a gift?"

When Zarathustra had heard these words he bade the saint farewell and said: "What could I have to give you? But let me go quickly lest I take something from you!" And thus they separated, the old one and the man, laughing as two boys laugh.

But when Zarathustra was alone he spoke thus to this heart: "Could it be possible? This old saint in the forest has not yet heard anything of this, that *God is dead!*"

## 24

Stack found the mad one wandering in the forest of final moments. He was an old, tired man, and Stack knew with a wave of his hand he could end it for this god in a moment. But what was the reason for it? It was even too late for revenge. It had been too late from the start. So he let the old one go his way, wandering in the forest, mumbling to himself, I WON'T LET YOU DO IT, in the voice of a cranky child; mumbling pathetically, OH, PLEASE, I DON'T WANT TO GO TO BED YET. I'M NOT YET DONE PLAYING.

And Stack came back to Snake, who had served his function and protected Stack until Stack had learned that he was more powerful than the god he'd worshipped all through the history of Men. He came back to Snake and their hands touched and the bond of friendship was sealed at last, at the end.

Then they worked together and Nathan Stack used the needle with a wave of his hands, and the Earth could not sigh with relief as its endless pain was ended . . . but it did sigh, and it settled in upon itself, and the molten core went out, and the winds died, and from high above them Stack heard the fulfillment of Snake's final act; he heard the descent of the Deathbird.

"What was your name?" Stack asked his friend.

*Dira.*

And the Deathbird settled down across the tired shape of the Earth, and it spread its wings wide, and brought them over and down, and enfolded the Earth as a mother enfolds her weary child. Dira settled down on the amethyst floor of the dark-shrouded palace, and closed his single eye with gratitude. To sleep at last, at the end.

All this, as Nathan Stack stood watching. He was the last, at the end, and because he had come to own—if even for a few moments—that which could have been his from the start, had he but known, he did not sleep but stood and watched. Knowing at last, at the end, that he had loved and done no wrong.

## 25

The Deathbird closed its wings over the Earth until at last, at the end, there was only the great bird crouched over the dead cinder. Then the Deathbird raised its head to the star-filled sky and repeated the sigh of loss the Earth had felt at the end. Then its eyes closed, it tucked its head carefully under its wing, and all was night.

Far away, the stars waited for the cry of the Deathbird to reach them so final moments could be observed at last, at the end, for the race of Men.

## 26

## THIS IS FOR MARK TWAIN

"Impiety: your irreverence toward my deity."
—Ambrose Bierce

## GRATIA GRATIAM PARIT

It took ten years to complete this cycle of stories. I never suffered from a lack of support from those around me, who were unstinting with their enthusiasm and encouragement. These are some of the people who had the right words and smiles when I needed them: Holly Bower, Ben Bova, R. Glenn Wright, Leonard Isaacs, Edward Ferman, Ralph Weinstock, Bentley Morriss, James Sallis, Thomas Disch, Dona Sadock, Dr. Richard Carrigan, Mildred Downey Broxon, Terry Carr, Robert Silverberg, Martin Shapiro, Max Katz, Karen Friedrich Katz, James Tiptree, Jr., Norman Spinrad, Ed Bryant, David Calkins, Rosalind Harvey, Huck and Carol Barkin, Louise Farr, Damon Knight, Kate Wilhelm, the students of the Clarion Writers' Workshops, 1971 and 1972, Jane Rotrosen; and most specially, with utmost patience and a concern for this book that went far beyond mere publishing courtesy, my original editor, Ms. Victoria Schochet, without whose pushing and shoving and ramrodding and affection, this book might never have been completed. For Vicky, and to the memory of my friend and agent during those years, the late, and very dear, Robert Mills, there are no words rich enough to convey my continuing thanks.